These powerful milli... get revenge...inc...

Australian Millionaires

Three exciting and passionate stories from favourite Desire™ author Maxine Sullivan

Australian Millionaires

MAXINE SULLIVAN

MILLS & BOON

All the characters in this book have no existence outside the imagination of the author, and have no relation whatsoever to anyone bearing the same name or names. They are not even distantly inspired by any individual known or unknown to the author, and all the incidents are pure invention.

All Rights Reserved including the right of reproduction in whole or in part in any form. This edition is published by arrangement with Harlequin Enterprises II B.V./S.à.r.l. The text of this publication or any part thereof may not be reproduced or transmitted in any form or by any means, electronic or mechanical, including photocopying, recording, storage in an information retrieval system, or otherwise, without the written permission of the publisher.

This book is sold subject to the condition that it shall not, by way of trade or otherwise, be lent, resold, hired out or otherwise circulated without the prior consent of the publisher in any form of binding or cover other than that in which it is published and without a similar condition including this condition being imposed on the subsequent purchaser.

® and ™ are trademarks owned and used by the trademark owner and/or its licensee. Trademarks marked with ® are registered with the United Kingdom Patent Office and/or the Office for Harmonisation in the Internal Market and in other countries.

First published in Great Britain 2012
by Mills & Boon, an imprint of Harlequin (UK) Limited,
Eton House, 18-24 Paradise Road, Richmond, Surrey TW9 1SR

AUSTRALIAN MILLIONAIRES
© by Harlequin Enterprises II B.V./S.à.r.l 2012

The Millionaire's Seductive Revenge, The Tycoon's Blackmailed Mistress and *The Executive's Vengeful Seduction* were first published in Great Britain by Harlequin (UK) Limited.

The Millionaire's Seductive Revenge © Maxine Sullivan 2007
The Tycoon's Blackmailed Mistress © Maxine Sullivan 2007
The Executive's Vengeful Seduction © Maxine Sullivan 2007

ISBN: 978 0 263 89698 5
ebook ISBN: 978 1 408 97063 8

05-0812

Printed and bound in Spain
by Blackprint CPI, Barcelona

THE MILLIONAIRE'S SEDUCTIVE REVENGE

BY
MAXINE SULLIVAN

Dear Reader,

I'm thoroughly delighted to say that this is my first book, and, like any firstborn, it's very special to me. It's an unbelievable feeling holding my "baby" in my hands and knowing it will be read by romance readers around the world. There's nothing more thrilling to me than being able to share this very first book with others who will appreciate it.

My story is set in Darwin, in the tropical north of Australia, where I lived for many years. Writing the book allowed me to revisit a city that holds treasured memories for me and my family, so it was only natural I chose such an exotic place for my characters to fall in love. No handsome hero will be able to resist a beautiful heroine once those mesmerizing sunsets start to work their magic.

With such a perfect setting for love, is it any wonder I used Darwin as the setting for a further two books?

Happy reading!

Maxine

Maxine Sullivan credits her mother for her lifelong love of romance novels, so it was a natural extension to want to write her own romances that she and others could enjoy. She's very excited about seeing her work in print, and she's thrilled to be the second Australian to write for the Desire line.

Maxine lives in Melbourne, Australia, but over the years has travelled to New Zealand, the UK and the US. In her own backyard, her husband's job ensured they saw the diversity of the countryside, including spending many years in Darwin in the tropical north where some of her books are set. She is married to Geoff, who has proven his hero status many times over the years. They have two handsome sons and an assortment of much-loved previously abandoned animals.

Maxine would love to hear from you, and she can be contacted through her website at www.maxinesullivan.com

For Andrea Johnston, Suzanne Barrett and
Nolene Jenkinson, Critique Partners,
Mentors and Friends

One

Every man in the room was staring at Kia Benton. And Brant Matthews was one of them. He'd seen many beautiful women in his life but none who affected him like the woman who'd entered the ballroom of Darwin's Shangri-La Hotel. Australia's most northerly city may possess a tropical lifestyle that was the envy of the rest of the country, but it still didn't hold a candle to this woman's beauty.

Dressed for an evening that promised glitz and glamour, Kia looked stunning tonight, with her ash-blond hair pulled back in a stylish chignon, her perfectly made-up features accentuated by the black liner circling her eyes.

The eyes of a seductress, Brant mused, his gaze

sliding down over bare shoulders to the shimmery silver dress that hugged her breasts, then slid over slim hips and long legs.

But it wasn't just her looks that coiled sexual hunger in the pit of his stomach. She had something that called to him on another level. A quality he'd never found in another woman, not even in his ex-fiancée, Julia. Hell, definitely not Julia. Julia had only been about one thing.

His mouth tightened. He had to remember that Kia was no different. Both women wanted the same thing.

Money.

He'd been suspicious of Kia from the moment he'd stepped onto the plane on his way back from Europe and caught sight of a photograph of her and his partner Phillip in the society section of a Darwin magazine. It was being read by the man next to him, and the picture had shown her arm in arm with Phillip at a cocktail party, looking very pleased with herself. The last he heard, Phillip still had his secretary from years back. This Kia was a total shock.

The caption had read, "Has one of Australia's richest bachelors finally been hooked by his new personal assistant? Miss Kia Benton obviously knows a thing or two about getting 'personal.'"

Yes, this woman knew how to get her hooks into someone all right. But what she didn't know was that he'd heard her on the telephone when he'd gone into the office the next day.

Of course I'm working on getting myself a rich man, she'd been saying when he'd passed by Phillip's office and seen her leaning against the desk, looking for all the world as if she owned the place. Then she'd laughed and said, *It's as easy to love a rich man as a poor one, right?*

This was the reason she'd made herself indispensable to his business partner so quickly. Within two months she'd had Phillip eating out of her hand. Oh, yes, she was a gold digger, this one. A beautiful, deceitful gold digger.

"Oh, don't they make a lovely couple?" one of the executive wives tossed into the conversation going on around him, pulling Brant from his thoughts and dropping him back into the Christmas festivities that were a necessary evil at this time of year.

"Yes, they're perfect together," one of the others agreed after all heads turned toward Kia and Phillip standing beneath the Merry Christmas sign in the doorway.

Then the head of the Legal Department's wife put her hand on her husband's arm. "Hon, I don't know what they're putting in the water at your office, but she's beautiful."

Simon puffed up with an odd sort of fatherly pride. "That's Kia. She's got brains as well as beauty."

Brains as well as beauty.

And she had no qualms about using those assets, Brant thought, hating the pull of her attraction but unable to do anything about it.

Dammit. If only he'd met her first. But two months ago, as senior partner, he'd gone to Paris to establish their new office and get everything up and running. Phillip hadn't wanted to go because he'd been heavily involved with his then girlfriend, Lynette. Yet when he'd returned a month later, Phillip's secretary had resigned due to ill health and Kia had been firmly ensconced as Phillip's personal assistant during work hours.

And his constant companion out of hours.

Like now.

Of course, if he'd seen her first, they would have been lovers straight away. No doubt about it. He'd known it from the moment he'd gazed into her sparkling aquamarine eyes.

Why?

Because she knew what she did to him, that's why. She knew the attraction he felt for her. This deep, pulsing need to make her his own. She merely had to glance his way and sizzling heat coursed through his veins. Even now he could feel himself burning to be inside her, feeling her close around him as he moved ever so slowly in and out, watching her eyelids flutter against her cheeks, hearing his name a murmur on the parted bow of her lips.

"She's got a brand new car, too," someone interrupted his thoughts, making him stiffen in disbelief. "A Porsche. It's fantastic."

"Lucky girl," one of the guys said. "Did Phil buy it for her?"

Simon darted a look at Brant, as if he knew this wasn't a subject they should be discussing in front of the boss. "Er...I'm not sure," the other man said awkwardly.

"It's understandable," Simon's wife added in a sympathetic tone. "He probably doesn't want her to have a similar accident to the one he had."

Pretending to ignore the conversation, Brant leaned back in his chair and took a sip of his whiskey. Late one night, Phil's car had broken down after he'd gone out on a date with Kia. When he'd stepped out to check the problem, a passing vehicle had clipped his leg, busting up his knee and breaking his ankle, leaving him with what would eventually be a permanent limp.

And Kia…God bless her, Brant mused cynically… had been quite happy ever since, going back and forth between the hospital and the office, assisting Phil with his workload. Through it all she must have been manipulating him to get the car. And a Porsche, to boot. Bloody hell. His friend and business partner deserved better than someone who was only using him for his bank account.

He was tempted to show Phil what sort of woman he was involved with. Kia would be easy enough to get into bed if he really put his mind to it. Only he couldn't. Not for *her* sake but for Phillip's. He knew how it felt for someone close to steal your woman.

And he'd be damned if he'd put the business at risk. He may've had to correct some of Phillip's poor decisions since they'd started buying up other businesses three years ago, but the last thing Brant wanted was instability within the company that was now riding the wave of phenomenal success.

Yet all of it could be jeopardized because of a woman who was out to get everything she could, he reminded himself as he watched the pair moving through the tables toward him, Kia pushing Phil's wheelchair but stopping to talk to people on the way. Oh, she was good at what she did. She knew how to work her audience.

Sickened that such beauty hid a heart of stone, Brant stood up. "Back in a minute," he muttered to no one in particular and headed for the exit behind him. His date had vanished into the nether regions of the ladies' room a while back, so he was unconcerned she would miss him until his return.

He needed to get outside and let the ocean air fill his lungs and clear away the smell of deception. Then maybe his body wouldn't ache so much for a woman who deserved nothing more than his contempt.

After finally reaching their table, Kia sat back with a glass of champagne and tried to relax. Brant seemed to have disappeared for a while, though she knew he'd be back. And he always affected her in some crazy way, no matter how hard she tried not to let him.

Tonight, for instance, it had started as soon as she entered the ballroom. She'd felt his eyes upon her, scrutinizing her, undressing her. This wasn't the only time she'd sensed his desire. Far from it. From the moment she'd met him she'd known he'd wanted her, despite himself. In his bed and out of it. Anywhere and anytime.

And as much as she had fought it, his want always bonded with a need deep inside her. That knowledge had pulsed through her veins tonight, making her breathless, wanting more, wanting him.

"Everything all right, Kia?"

She took a breath and fixed a smile on her lips for Phillip, fully aware of the attention from the other tables guests. "Everything's fine."

His gaze slid to her throat and a glint of humor appeared in his eyes. "I'm glad you like your present."

Her hand went to the sparkling diamond necklace he'd asked her to wear. He'd wanted her to keep it, but she'd refused, so they'd compromised and she'd said she'd wear it only for the night. "It's fabulous."

"A fabulous gift for a fabulous lady."

She shifted in her seat. Did he have to lay it on quite so thick? Just because he wanted to give the impression they were a couple didn't mean they should act like characters in a thirties melodrama. It made her uncomfortable.

Suddenly the hairs on the back of her neck began to rise. There Brant was, dancing with a woman at the far end of the dance floor. Her breath caught at the sight of him, desire shooting to every region in her body.

He was certainly something to look at. Handsome, wealthy, extremely sexy in a black suit that matched the color of his gleaming dark hair and fitted his lean body to perfection. He exuded an attraction she found difficult to deny.

"Who's that dancing with Brant?" a visitor to the table asked the question on Kia's mind.

"That's his date," someone replied.

Kia hid her surprise. Brant usually only dated blondes. Beautiful blondes with gorgeous figures and impeccable style, if the photographs in the newspaper were anything to go by. Certainly the women who frequented his office were blond and beautiful. And according to Evelyn, his personal assistant, so were the women who called him constantly on the phone.

This brunette was definitely not in his league. The woman wasn't beautiful, though she wasn't unattractive either. She just lacked the confidence of those other women, and that red-and-white floral dress looked totally wrong on her. It seemed to swallow her up. Just as Brant's presence seemed to be doing.

And didn't she know how *that* felt, she scoffed to herself as the other woman smiled shyly up at him and Brant returned the smile with a devastating one of his own. The woman stumbled, and who could blame her? Brant Matthews, Womanizer Extraordinaire, had struck again. Maybe she could suggest he have that printed on his business cards.

All at once she realized Phillip had spoken. "Sorry, Phillip. What did you say?"

"I said she's my new physiotherapist."

Ah, so this was Serena. They'd spoken on the telephone. But why had *Brant* chosen her as his date? It didn't make sense.

Then it hit her.

"Phillip, you didn't," she said for his ears only.

"Didn't what?"

"Fix them up together."

He frowned. "Why not? I thought it would do Serena good to be asked out by someone like Brant. He didn't mind."

Oh, that poor girl. Why were men so insensitive at times?

"That's exactly why he's wrong for her."

His brows drew closer together. "What do you mean?"

"She'll know people will be wondering what Brant sees in her and that'll make her feel even worse."

"I was only trying to help," he said a touch defensively.

Kia's heart softened. "I know you were. It's just that…" How to explain the mind of a shy, insecure woman? It wasn't easy delving into her own past and reliving her inadequacies.

"Merry Christmas, Kia."

Without warning, Brant was beside her, his lips brushing against her cheek in a gesture that meant nothing yet everything. Kia's pulse almost fell over itself as his warm hand touched her bare shoulder and she caught a whiff of his masculine scent. Her throat went dry.

Then he moved away and held the chair out for his date. "Serena, this is Kia, Phillip's personal assistant."

"We've spoken on the telephone," Kia said with a smile as the woman sat down opposite her.

"Oh, yes." The other woman gave a wavering smile in return, and empathy stirred within Kia, helping her recover from the shock of Brant's greeting.

"Serena's a lovely name," Kia said, wanting to put her at ease.

Serena smiled tentatively. "You think so?"

"It suits you," Brant said before Kia could respond.

Serena blushed, looking quite pretty. "Thank you."

He sat down and handed her a glass of champagne.

"Not too many women are as restful as you to be around, Serena."

Kia saw his eyes flick toward her. Was he saying *she* wasn't restful to be around? What a cheek. It wasn't her fault he wanted her but couldn't.

"Some men aren't restful to be around either," Kia pointed out, not willing to let him get the upper hand.

He eased back in his chair, confident but with a dark look in his deep blue eyes that sent shivers down her spine. "Are you saying that some men disturb you, Kia?"

Was he asking if *he* disturbed her?

"People only disturb you if you let them. I don't ever intend to let any man disturb me."

"Really?" His eyes slid across to Phillip at her side, then back to her again. They hardened, reminding her that from the day he'd met up with her outside the hospital room after he'd returned from his trip, this man had grown more and more hostile toward her. He hid it well, but she knew it was there. She could only assume that because Phillip had been going home after a date with her, Brant blamed her for the accident.

And that was totally unfair, but she wasn't about to challenge him over it or he might start delving into her and Phillip's relationship and discover the truth. How it had all started when Phillip had begged her to be his partner at a business dinner with people who knew his ex, Lynette. Things had snowballed after that and now they were out of control. Totally out of control.

Glancing at Brant, she saw a muscle pulsating in his lean cheek. Then, as if he'd had enough of her, he turned away to talk to one of the others.

She felt a spurt of anger at his dismissal. Was this the way he treated women when he had enough of them? Did he use them to amuse himself, then get rid of them once they'd passed their use-by dates? Of course he did. So why did she feel surprised? Did she think she was any different just because she shared in this intense physical attraction?

Schooling her features, Kia sipped at her champagne and watched the couples dancing out on the floor. She could hear Phillip talking about going home to Queensland to be with his family for Christmas. It reminded her of her own plans to fly south to Adelaide to spend Christmas with her mother and stepfather. She was looking forward to having some downtime with her family. She badly needed time away from the office—and the men who ran it.

All at once, Phillip leaned forward and said loudly across the table, "Hey, Brant. How would you like to dance with Kia for me?"

"Wh-what?" Kia said before she could stop herself. She didn't want to be in Brant's arms. Close to him. Touching him.

Brant's eyes narrowed slightly, but was she the only one to see the flash of hunger in them? "Maybe Kia doesn't want to dance," he said, giving her an out, telling her that as much as he wanted her in his arms, another part of him didn't.

She managed a short laugh. "Phillip, don't be silly. I don't need to dance."

"I saw your foot tapping to the music," he said, surprising her because she hadn't been aware she'd been doing that.

She opened her mouth to say she really didn't feel like dancing but then noticed all eyes upon her. Making a fuss would only make them wonder why she objected to dancing with Brant. And if that happened…

"Okay, Phillip. Anything for *you*," she emphasized, making sure Brant knew it wasn't for *him*.

And then, like a gentleman, Brant stood beside her, helping her out of her chair. She tried to smile, but already his closeness affected her. Every nerve in her body suddenly started to tingle as he led her out onto the dance floor and straight into his arms. Knowing she was in danger of melting against him, she stiffened and pulled back.

"We're only dancing," he mocked, knowing full well the effect he had on her.

On any woman.

On women in general.

"Mr. Matthews—"

His mouth thinned. "I've told you before. Call me Brant."

"You're my employer. I prefer to keep it formal."

"Why?"

"I was brought up to respect my elders."

His laughter was low and throaty, his lips showing

the tip of perfect white teeth. *All the better to eat you with, my dear,* she thought.

He moved his hand more comfortably against the small of her back. "Thanks for putting me in my place."

"I try." She moved to dislodge his fingers. They were an inch too low for her liking.

"I know you do." He tilted his head. "It makes me wonder why."

She looked somewhere past his shoulder. "Because you're the boss."

His hand moved imperceptibly lower, snatching her breath away, drawing her eyes back to him. "If I'm the boss, then you should do what I say," he murmured, making the simple statement sound very, very personal.

Recovering, she squared her shoulders and lifted her chin. She was beginning to feel as if she were some sort of puppet to be manipulated. "I never *was* good at doing what I was told."

"Shame." His eyes hardened. "But I bet you know how to get your own way now."

"Doesn't everyone?" she quipped, not sure where this was heading.

"Every *woman,* you mean."

Ah, so the womanizer had a low opinion of women. Color her surprised.

"Actually, I meant every *person*. Man. Woman. Child. Even animals—"

"I hear you've got a new car," he cut across her. "A Porsche."

Her mind reeled in confusion, not only at what he'd said but at the hint of accusation in his tone, though what she was being accused of she had no idea.

"Yes, I do have a new car."

His lips twisted with a touch of cynicism. "We must be paying you well."

His animosity was growing in leaps and bounds. "You get what you pay for," she pointed out coolly.

"I'm sure we do." He leaned closer so that his lips were practically pressed to her ear. "Or should I say *Phil* gets what he paid for."

She stiffly drew back. "What do you mean by that?"

The corners of his mouth curved in a smooth smile that didn't match the piercing glint in his eyes. "Merely that you're a top-notch PA. I'm sure Phil believes he's lucky to have you."

"That sounds like a backhanded compliment."

"Does it?" He pulled her slightly closer again, making her feel his heat.

Well, if he could be hot, she would be cold. Let him think she couldn't care less about his little games.

"Serena seems nice," she said, pasting on a cool smile.

He appeared casually amused by the change in subject. "I'm enjoying her company."

"Naturally," she said somewhat sourly. No one was safe from a womanizer like Brant.

The amusement left his face and he scowled. "What does that mean?"

"What do you think it means?" Two could play at this.

"Are you going to answer all my questions with a question?" he said, the scowl still in place.

"Is that what I'm doing?"

His glance sharpened. "You thought I'd ignore her, didn't you?"

The thought had briefly crossed her mind, but she knew he would never miss an opportunity to charm a woman, whether young or old, beautiful or plain.

But she had to admit she was still annoyed with Phillip. "Actually, I know Phillip meant well, but I wish he hadn't put her in this predicament. Believe me, I know what it's like being an ugly duckling."

His head went back in shock. "You? Never!"

"It's true. I was always very plain-looking."

"You're kidding, right?"

"I'm not. Ask my father. He was very good at telling me how plain I was." She smiled grimly, remembering all the hurt. How many times had she looked into the mirror and wished she was beautiful? "Naturally he was delighted when I suddenly started to blossom into something resembling a female."

Brant's eyes probed far too deeply. "Shouldn't a father's love be unconditional?"

"Not my father," she said, on some level surprised she was telling him so much. "He only likes being with women who are beautiful."

"Women?"

She pretended not to care. "My parents are divorced. Luckily my mother settled down to a life of bliss with a man who truly loves her. Dad's on his third marriage, to a model half his age."

"How do you feel about that?"

"I'm thrilled my mother found happiness."

"And your father?"

She'd suddenly had enough. Already she'd told him more than she should have about herself.

She glanced back at the table to where the others were talking. "We were talking about Serena."

His eyes said she wasn't fooling him but he'd accept the change in subject anyway. "Serena's a nice kid."

"She wouldn't appreciate being called a kid. She's not much younger than me."

"But you're so much more—"

"Cynical?"

He broke into a sexy half smile. "I was going to say mature."

Before she could stop it, she found herself smiling back at him.

"You should smile at me more often, Kia."

As Serena had, she stumbled—just a little—then recovered. "But if I smile, you might think I like you," she said with false sweetness.

As if he realized he'd let down his guard, the smile froze on his lips. "We wouldn't want that to happen, now would we?" he said, but his voice sounded flat and he'd withdrawn into himself.

Thankfully the song ended. She cleared her throat and went to move away. "Thank you for the dance, Brant."

But he surprised her by holding on to her arm. "Say it again, Kia."

She blinked. "What?"

"Say my name again."

In a way, she was grateful the womanizer was back. "Brant Matthews," she said defiantly.

Looking satisfied, he dropped her arm the way he'd drop her heart if she dared let him near it.

Not that she would, she told herself on the way back to the table, then forced her face to maintain a calm expression when Phillip gave her an odd look. Phillip didn't know it, but he'd taken on the role of a buffer between her and the man who was her principal employer.

She spent the next hour listening to a couple of speeches, then talking to the other guests at the table and to the staff who stopped by to pay their respects to the top table.

"Hello, Phillip."

Kia blinked as a wave of apprehension swept over her. She'd seen a picture of this woman hidden in Phillip's desk. Lynette Kelly. Phillip's ex-girlfriend.

Phillip smiled coldly. "Lynette. What brings you here?"

The other woman straightened her shoulders. "I'm here with Matthew Wright," she said quietly, looking beautiful in a silky black evening gown, her dark hair framing a lovely oval face with high cheekbones and a dainty nose.

"So you've finally found your Mr. Right, have you?" Phillip said rather nastily, and Kia turned to look at him in dismay. He and Lynette had been deeply in love until her career as a flight attendant had come between them.

Lynette's chin lifted with an odd dignity. "Yes, Phillip. I believe I have."

Kia was sure she was the only one who heard Phillip suck in a sharp breath. Thankfully the others at the table didn't appear to realize what was going on.

Except Brant, she noted.

"What a coincidence," Phillip said, recovering quickly as he picked up Kia's hand and eyed Lynette with cold triumph. "I've found the right one this time, too. Kia's agreed to marry me."

Two

"Ma-marry?" Lynette stuttered just as there was a lull in conversation at the table. Then all hell seemed to break loose.

"Marry? Who's getting married?"

"You and Kia are getting married?"

"Oh, I just *knew* something serious was going on between you two."

Kia was frozen in her seat. It wasn't often she was lost for words, but this time she was, shock causing any protest to wedge in her throat. Had Phillip just said what she thought he'd said? In front of everyone?

He looked at Kia, brought her hand to his lips and kissed it. "I know we were going to wait until after Christmas, darling, but I think now's as good a time as any." He smiled, but his eyes implored her not to make a scene. "Forgive me for telling everyone our little secret?"

She was going to kill him. Doing a favor for her boss was one thing, but this was going too far. But what could she do? Make him look a fool in front of everyone? In front of Lynette? The other woman had been the reason for all this pretence in the first place.

A faint thread of hysteria rose in her throat. "I—"

"Details," someone cut across her, which was probably best because she had no idea what she'd been about to say.

"Yes, give us details. We want to know everything."

"Yeah, like where's your engagement ring?"

Phillip laughed. "We don't have any details yet. I only proposed tonight." He smiled lovingly at her. "We'll pick out a ring after Christmas, won't we, darling?"

Still in shock, Kia was trying to think what to say. "Um…"

"How romantic," one of the women said on a sigh.

"Yes, isn't it," Brant said, a penetrating look in his eyes that made Kia feel as if he knew everything about them and didn't like what he saw.

Yet Phillip had been insistent when they'd started this charade that no one know about it but themselves. Not even Brant. *Especially* not Brant, Phillip had said, worried his business partner might think he was being irresponsible. Apparently Brant still hadn't forgiven Phillip for some silly error he'd made with one of their clients. It hadn't been that important, Phillip had told her, but Brant had been watching him like a hawk ever since.

And she'd gone along with the secret for her own reasons. It had afforded her some degree of protection against the desire she saw in Brant's eyes. Always he was around…watching…waiting…as if ready to pounce on her the minute Phillip was out of sight, both physically and mentally.

"You're a lucky woman, Kia," Lynette suddenly said in a quiet voice, her face pale as she took a shaky breath. An awkward silence fell. "Well, I must get back to my table." She looked at Phillip, her bleak eyes riveted on his face. "Congratulations, Phillip. Goodbye."

His very breath seemed to leave him, then he appeared to gather his resolve. "Goodbye, Lynette," he said brusquely.

She walked away with stiff dignity that made Kia inwardly flinch. God, she felt bad about her involvement in all this, having met the woman now. It had started out so innocently…so uncomplicated. No one should have gotten hurt.

But Lynette was hurting badly right now. And so was Phillip. He couldn't have known she'd be here. Couldn't have prepared himself for—

Suddenly something fell into place and Kia realized that Phillip *had* known Lynette was going to be here tonight. It was the reason he'd been distant after lunch. The reason he'd given her the diamond necklace to wear. And the reason he'd asked Brant to dance with her, making sure she was on the dance floor and on show for the other woman.

To *hurt* Lynette.

The thought tore at Kia's insides. She'd never deliberately hurt someone in her life and didn't appreciate being a part of this now. She'd tell Phillip on the way home and make him promise to set things right after this once and for all.

It was as well the DJ announced he would take a break while they served the meal, and everything became a flurry of people returning to their tables.

All at once she realized Brant was watching her with narrowed intensity. Every instinct inside her told her not to let him figure out the truth just yet. He was the senior partner—the boss—and he would take no hostages.

She felt uneasy as Brant continued to watch them while they worked their way through each course. By the time dessert was served she felt as though her relationship with her new fiancé had been scrutinized.

Suddenly Phillip pushed his wheelchair back from the table and gave a weak smile to the other guests. "You'll have to excuse me, but I think I'll call it a night. My leg is really starting to give me hell." He looked at Kia apologetically. "Darling, you stay and enjoy yourself."

She'd been concentrating so hard on Brant that his announcement took her completely by surprise. Come to think of it, Phillip hadn't eaten much and he'd been very quiet throughout the meal.

Probably from guilt, she decided, anger building at him even *thinking* about leaving her here and throwing her to the wolves. Or should that be *wolf*?

As in, Brant Matthews.

"I'll come with you," she said, reaching for her purse, determined to get away from all prying eyes.

He gave her a tired smile that was offset by the wary gleam in his eyes. "There's no need, darling. I'll be going straight to bed."

Kia wasn't about to let Phillip get away with this. They needed to talk. *Tonight.*

She pushed her chair back farther. "Still, I think I'll go home, too."

Phillip put up a hand. "Please stay, darling. I don't want to spoil your fun."

What fun? She didn't call Brant's company fun, not with him watching her, waiting. And if Phillip called her "darling" one more time, she was going to scream. She was no man's "darling," not when her father liked to call her his "darling girl."

She turned back to Phillip, ready to insist on going with him. Only the look in his eyes stopped her dead. Seeing Lynette again had upset him.

Compassion stirred within her, diminishing her anger to a degree. "Okay, Phillip. I understand. You just get plenty of rest so that we can go to the art exhibition tomorrow." Her eyes said she intended talking to him then about all this.

His eyes darted away uneasily. "I'll call you in the morning."

"I'll make sure she gets home safely," Brant said out of the blue.

Kia's heart lurched. She couldn't imagine being in

the confines of a car with Brant. Why, even the ballroom wasn't enough to stop his silent seduction.

"No, that's okay," she said quickly. "I'll take a taxi."

"Not in that, you won't," Brant said arrogantly, giving her breasts a raking glance in the clinging silver dress. "There was a woman attacked just last week after she left one of the hotels by herself."

"Yes, and they caught the guy, remember?" she pointed out, resisting the urge to tug at her bodice and cover her cleavage. "It was an old boyfriend." She turned to Phillip. "I'll be fine."

But Phillip was frowning. "No, Brant's right. You're too attractive to be out on your own late at night."

Okay, this was getting crazy.

"Phillip, don't be ridiculous. I'm a grown woman. I know how to take care of myself."

Phillip opened his mouth, but it was Brant who spoke. "I don't think it's ridiculous that your…" He paused. "…*fiancé* is concerned for your safety."

She grimaced inwardly. What could she say to that? "Fine. You can drive me home then."

God help her.

Satisfied with that, Phillip fobbed off someone's suggestion that they announce the engagement over the microphone before he left. She shuddered at the suggestion, knowing it would be public knowledge soon enough. Oh, heavens, and wasn't that idiotic journalist who'd written the comment about her getting her hooks into Phillip going to just love all this?

Thankfully Phillip's male nurse, Rick, was in the

hotel and was ready and waiting by the time Kia pushed the wheelchair through the ballroom doors. She tried to speak to Phillip, but all she got was a quick apology and a promise to talk later.

Then Rick wheeled him away. Suddenly the hardest thing to do was turn around and walk back into that room. Brant would be there with his arrogance and his hostility, and if he said so much as one word out of place, she would pour his drink over his head.

She smiled to herself. As a matter of fact, she hoped he did, she mused as she pushed open the doors and immediately felt those hard eyes eating her up from across the room. They scorched her with a look that bordered on physical intensity.

Unable to stop herself, she glanced at Brant. Through the sea of people and smoke-filled air, her knees weakened as sexual heat enveloped her, even as he pretended to be listening to something Simon said to him.

And it *was* a pretence. Every feminine instinct told her that he'd like nothing more than to sweep her into his arms and lose himself in her body. *Her body.* She had to remember that's all he wanted.

"Hey, babe. Wanna dance?"

Startled, she turned and looked into the face of Danny Tripp, the teenage son of one of the executives who worked a few days a week in the accounts department, and who turned beetroot-red whenever she came into the room. She'd never been able to get him to say more than two words at a time.

But not tonight, it seemed. Tonight tall, young,

clean-cut Danny Tripp, fortified by alcohol, had a silly grin on his face and was game for anything, especially with a group of his mates egging him on.

Great. Now she had *two* men lusting after her. Well, one was really only a boy in a man's body. And the other? Yes, Brant Matthews was all man. And more. Much more.

She glanced across the room and saw the alert look in his eyes that told her he sensed another male moving in on his territory. *His* territory. How ridiculous to think that way. Yet she couldn't shake the feeling.

Dragging her gaze away, she gave Danny a friendly smile so that he wouldn't feel embarrassed in front of his friends. "I'd love to dance with you, Danny."

"You would?" For a moment he appeared stunned. Then he grabbed her hand and dragged her out onto the dance floor.

She stumbled into his arms when he spun around to face her, and before she knew it, he'd slid his hands onto her hips, pulled her close to his lanky body and buried his face in her hair. There was none of the finesse Brant had exhibited earlier when he'd taken her in his arms. This was pure adolescent male, hungry for sex, and all the better with a woman he fancied.

Slightly alarmed—and hearing his pals' whistles over the slow music—she put her hands against his chest and forced some distance between them. "Danny, I—"

"Don't talk, babe." He went to pull her back into position.

She held firm against him. "Dan-ny…" The tone of her voice must have gotten through to him, because the hold on her hips slackened. She breathed a sigh of relief and looked up at him, pleased to see some of the alcoholic glaze disappear from his eyes.

He gave her a self-conscious grin. "Sorry, Kia. I guess you went to my head."

She relaxed with a smile, finding his boyishness easier to handle. "I think the drink had more to do with it than me."

He shrugged wryly. "Yeah, well, I'm not used to drinking rum."

Kia suspected he wasn't used to drinking at all. "I once got drunk on brandy and was sick for a full week."

"*You* got drunk? No foolin'?"

"I was young once, too, you know," she joked, even while her heart cramped with pain at the reason she'd been drinking. It had been the day her father had married his second wife. He hadn't wanted his "plain-looking" daughter at the wedding—or that's what he'd been telling her mother when Kia had accidentally picked up the telephone to make a call.

She'd been crushed by his rejection, though at fifteen she should have been used to his insensitivity. Afterward she'd feigned ignorance when her mother had gently explained about her father's remarriage. She had then gone out and gotten rotten drunk at a friend's party, learning the hard way that drinking didn't solve a thing.

"I hope you won't spread that around?" she said now, pushing aside her painful memories to smile up at Danny.

"Er…" His eyes darted to his friends at the table behind them, then back to her. "Sorry. What did you say?"

Someone yelled out, "Yea, Danny," but she pretended not to notice. They were only having fun. "I said I hope you won't tell anyone that I once got drunk. I have a reputation to uphold," she teased.

His gaze went beyond her again, seemed to hesitate. Then, taking a deep breath, he pulled her up close once more. "I won't say anything," he said as if whispering sweet nothings in her ear. "I promise, babe."

He was obviously more concerned with his own reputation than hers, so it was silly to feel a flutter of apprehension just because he wanted to show off for his friends. He was really just a kid who'd had too much to drink.

Should she wait until the music stopped, then go back to her table? Or go now? The room was full of people. Surely nothing would happen to her in the middle of the dance floor....

She jumped when he began to nuzzle her neck. Okay, no way could she let this go any further. "Danny, I—"

"Let the lady go," a deep male voice said beside them, startling them both, the warning in Brant's voice clearly evident.

Danny shoved himself away from Kia, a slightly belligerent look on his face until he caught sight of who'd spoken. His cheeks began to turn red as he looked at Brant's thunderous expression. "I'm sorry, Mr. Matthews," he said quickly. "I wasn't doing anything wrong."

"I know exactly what you were doing, Daniel." Brant jerked his head at the table behind them. "I suggest you go back to your table before I decide to tell Mr. Reid what you were trying to do with his PA."

Danny looked horrified. "I was just fooling around, Mr. Matthews—promise," he said, then scurried away, obviously terrified he would lose his job.

Kia couldn't help but feel sorry for the young man. Brant could be a formidable figure when he chose to be, though why he chose to throw his weight around now was anybody's guess.

She winced inwardly. That wasn't quite true. She knew *exactly* why he wanted Danny away from her. But before she could think further, Brant swept her into his arms and began to lead her around the dance floor. His touch was impersonal enough, so why did she feel acutely aware of him and his sexual power over her?

Angry with herself for her reaction, she shot him a look that would make a lesser man stumble. "You didn't need to frighten him like that."

"Yes, I did."

And she saw that deep down he did. It fit his dangerous persona. The predator who never gave up his prey without a fight. All very subliminal, yet it was there, hidden beneath his civilized exterior. God, was she the only one who saw it? Who felt it? She must be.

She swallowed a lump of apprehension. "You had no right to interfere."

His grip tightened. "I had every right. Philip would expect me to protect his…fiancée."

She ignored another insulting pause. "Danny's just a boy. He was having some fun, that's all."

A cynical smile immediately twisted his lips. "He's a young man who was almost having his way with you right there on the floor." He shrugged. "But, hey, if that's how you get your kicks, then maybe—"

"Shut up, Brant."

For a moment it was hard to tell who was the more surprised, but then a satisfied light came into his blue eyes. "Hurrah! She said my name."

Kia found herself exchanging a subtle look of amusement with him. Okay, so he'd won that small victory. She could allow him that, seeing he really had saved her from a possibly unpleasant situation.

"If it'll make you feel any better, I'll talk to Danny on Monday," he said. "For now, it'll do him good to stew over the weekend. He needs to learn a lesson about not making a move on the boss's woman."

Which boss? she wanted to ask, a tingle running down her spine at the thought of being Brant's woman. She grimaced. *One* of Brant's women. "Thank you."

There was a moment's pause, then, "So congratulations are in order," he said in a harsh voice that suddenly matched his eyes.

Unable to bring herself to say yes, she merely nodded.

"I'm surprised," he continued. "Most women couldn't have kept it a secret."

"I'm not most women."

"True." But it didn't sound like a compliment. His burning gaze slid down the column of her throat, to the necklace, and rested there for a moment. "Diamonds look good on you," he said almost as if he disliked her for it. "Another expensive gift from Phillip?"

"Another?"

"As well as the Porsche."

Good grief. Did he think Phillip had bought the car for her? She felt her cheeks redden. "Phillip did *not* give me the Porsche."

His eyes flickered with surprise. "But he gave you the necklace, right?" His expression darkened, grew stormy. "He's generous to a fault."

The way he said it was as if Phillip was generous and *she* was at fault. For a moment she wondered what she'd ever done to this man—apart from *not* hopping into bed with him.

As for the necklace, how could she tell him she was giving it back to Phillip? He'd have to ask why. So let him think what he liked. He did anyway.

After that, he seemed to sense her withdrawal, because he remained quiet while they danced around the floor. Kia fought hard to concentrate on being angry with him, but the music was growing insistent, bringing his body against her own, each step sensuously rubbing leg against leg.

His hand rested on her hip, every movement making his palm slide a little up, a little down.

Up. Down.

Hot. Cool.

In. Out.

Oh, God.

"Are you all right?"

His husky words snapped Kia's head back and she gazed into eyes that smoldered with awareness. Her heart lurched sideways, his magnetism so potent, so compelling that she could imagine him taking her right here and now in a raw act of possession that had everything to do with pure sex and erotic pleasure and nothing to do with reason. And he knew. Oh, yes, he knew, because that feeling was rushing through him, too. She could see it in his eyes. In every beat of his heart.

"It's—" she moistened her lips "—a bit hot in here, that's all," she said, pretending it was the crowd of people on the dance floor affecting her, and not him. "Too many people wanting to let their hair down, I guess."

His gaze dropped to her mouth, and the blue of his eyes darkened. Then he glanced up at the blond hair she'd put up for tonight. "Do *you* ever let your hair down, Kia?" he murmured.

What was he really asking? Whether she'd dare go to bed with him? Somehow, somewhere, she had to find the strength to pull herself out of this. If Phillip were here…

Of course!

Stronger now, she planted a cool smile on her lips. "Phillip's really the only one I let my hair down for now."

He tensed, a muscle ticking at his jaw. "Phillip didn't seem himself tonight."

She knew what he was implying. That Lynette's presence had upset him. "He's been doing too much this week."

"Nothing else?"

Kia remembered the deciphering way Brant had

looked at her and Phillip after Lynette had left and she felt a flutter of panic. "Maybe being the center of attention tonight was too much for him."

"Perhaps."

Everything had been crazy since the accident, and with Phillip having been told he'd have a permanent limp, she knew Brant couldn't be sure that *hadn't* been the problem tonight. She was banking on that to save her from further interrogation.

The music ended, and her heart skipped with relief when he let her slip from his arms without another word. He escorted her back to the table, fortunately without touching her, but she still resisted the urge to fan herself as she took her seat. One more dance with him and she'd have gone up in smoke.

"Are you enjoying yourself?" Serena asked.

Kia smiled at the other woman and tried not to show how her pulse was bubbling like the fresh glass of champagne in her hand. What a question. How could she enjoy herself when every look sent her way told her that this woman's date wanted her with a passion.

"I'm having a great time," she lied, watching Brant sit down on the opposite side of Serena. "I just wish Phillip hadn't left so early." That, at least, was the truth.

Serena's eyes turned sympathetic. "He needs time to adjust."

Kia felt her throat close up. She didn't deserve Serena's sympathy. Or anyone else's, for that matter. She was such a fraud. "I know," was all she could manage.

After that, talk around the table turned to other

things. Her heart took the chance to settle back to its regular beat as she listened to the discussions going on around her. They were all such nice people.

She glanced at Brant, his dark head tilted toward Serena while she spoke to him. Well, *nearly* all of them were nice. She couldn't exactly call Brant Matthews "nice."

It didn't apply to a man with probing eyes and an inscrutable expression, a man whose body coiled with barely controlled sensuality but bordered on an unfriendliness that belonged to an archenemy.

Thankfully the music started up again, this time playing rock and roll, and Simon asked her to dance. Desperate to forget thoughts of Brant, who was now asking Serena to dance with him, she willingly went with the older man to the dance floor, where he showed her that being middle-aged still made him capable of some daring moves.

"He'll be paying for that tomorrow," his wife teased to Kia when she returned to the table with Simon after only one song.

Kia smiled, but before she could catch her breath, Bill Stewart grabbed her hand and insisted on a dance, too. She figured out then that they were making sure she was having a good time even without her fiancé.

When she eventually got to sit down, she saw Simon about to get to his feet again. "No more," she gasped, reaching for the jug of ice water. They were killing her with kindness.

"Oh, but—" Simon began.

"No more," Brant said firmly across the table, the look in his eyes reminding them all who was boss. "Kia looks tired."

Kia didn't want to agree with him, but she didn't want to dance again either. "I am a little," she smilingly apologized to Simon.

"That's okay," the older man said with obvious relief. "I wasn't sure I had another one in me anyway."

After that, the music got even louder, until it became more impossible to talk. It wasn't long before the older couples decided to call it a night.

"Would you ladies like to go home soon?" Brant said, encompassing both her and Serena with his question. "It's nearly midnight."

Rather than going home with Brant, Kia would have sat here all night if she knew she hadn't been inconveniencing Serena. "That's up to both of you."

"I'm ready when you are," Serena agreed, giving a delicate yawn followed by a self-conscious laugh. "I have an early appointment in the morning anyway."

"No sleep-in for you then," Kia teased.

Brant quickly finished off his drink. "Right. Let's go," he rasped, getting to his feet.

Startled by his tone, Kia got to her feet, too, followed by Serena, who didn't seem to notice and continued to talk while they made their way through the tables to the exit.

Kia listened even while she wondered why Brant's face looked like thunder. Had it been her mention of sleeping in tomorrow morning? Did it remind him of being in bed? Of making love? She must have reminded him that he *wasn't* about to get any sex tonight. Not from Serena. And certainly not from *her*.

Of course, he would still have plenty of other woman friends who would willingly sacrifice themselves for his pleasure. He only had to make a phone call and it would be his.

But she soon forgot all that when they reached the front of the hotel and were discussing where they lived while waiting for Brant's car to be brought around. It appeared Serena lived closest.

"Then we'll drop you off first, if you don't mind," Brant said as the gray Mercedes glided to a stop in front of them.

Serena smiled shyly. "Of course I don't mind," she said, and before Kia could do a thing about it, Brant was holding the back door open for Serena and she had slid onto the backseat.

Kia was tempted to slide in right next to her, but as if he knew, Brant took her by the elbow and walked her to the front passenger door.

His touch made her shiver in the balmy night air. Soon she'd be alone with a man who had no need to touch to get his way. A man who had perfected foreplay with just a look. Perhaps it was as well she was an "engaged" woman now.

Three

Kia consoled herself on the way home that at least her presence wouldn't give Brant the opportunity to seduce the innocent Serena. Not that she really thought he would now, not after the brotherly way he'd been treating the younger woman all night.

Then she remembered her father and all the young women who'd passed through his life and she knew that some men just couldn't help themselves.

Five minutes later, she watched from the car while Brant walked Serena to the front door of her house. The security light had come on at their approach and Kia saw everything clearly. She breathed a sigh of relief when Brant gave Serena a smile and a quick peck on the cheek, then strode back to the car.

"Was that chaste enough for you?" he mocked as he started the engine.

Chaste? A kiss from this man could never be considered chaste. Not for her, anyway.

She forced a cool smile. "I didn't think you knew what the word meant."

He smiled grimly as he pulled out from the curb. "I could say the same about you."

"Me?"

He glanced sideways, his eyes boldly raking over her. "Sweetheart, you *ooze* sex appeal. Why do you think young Danny was falling over himself?" Obviously seeing her surprise, his eyes narrowed. "Surely Phillip's told you how sexy you are?"

Sexy? No, Phillip had never told her that.

"Yes, of course," she lied.

"You don't sound too sure."

She stiffened. "Of course I'm sure. It's just that…" *Think.* "Well, since the accident we've been concentrating on him rather than me."

He appeared to consider that. "He's going through a tough time right now." Once more his gaze slid over her, almost contemptuously this time. "But if any woman can make him think like a man again, it's you."

She didn't appreciate the comment. "You've missed your calling. You should be doing talk shows."

This time he laughed. A deep, rich sound that made her catch her breath and confirmed why women of all kinds wanted him. She didn't even *like* him and *this* was her reaction.

Luckily for her, they came to some night roadwork and Brant had to slow the car and concentrate for the next kilometer. After that, except for her directing him, they both remained quiet until they reached her street.

"It's the house at the end," she said as they came around the corner into the leafy cul-de-sac.

A few moments later he pulled into the driveway and cut the engine. "You live here by yourself?" he asked, his eyes going over the ground-level house nestled amongst the lush garden. It was obviously too big for one person.

"I live by myself, yes, but the house has been divided into two. The owner lives in one apartment and I live in the other."

It was a bonus that June didn't drive, so Kia got to use the garage at the far end of the driveway. But why, oh, why hadn't she driven herself tonight? If she'd known Phillip would leave early and she'd be stranded with Brant, she would have insisted on taking her Porsche.

The Porsche Brant thought Phillip had bought for her.

He opened his door, letting in the late-night sounds of a tropical summer. "I'll walk you inside."

She'd known he would. Her front door was actually around the back of the house, so it wouldn't be possible to dismiss him easily. The minute he saw her walking down the driveway alongside the house he'd be out of the car and following her anyway.

"It's around the back." She moved to get out of the car, but her long dress proved difficult, and before she knew it he stood beside her, offering her his hand. For a moment she hesitated. Already her pulse was skittering all over the place. What would his touch do to her?

Having no option but to appear unruffled, she held her breath and put her hand on his. Her skin immediately tingled from the contact, but surprisingly his fingers didn't close around hers. His hand remained open, palm up, allowing her to grip him as she chose.

Is this how he lets a woman make love to him? At her own pace?

That thought spread the tingle through her body as her fingers closed around his hand and she pressed her palm against his, using his strength to bring her to her feet.

He stepped back before their bodies could touch further, making her grateful for small mercies.

"It's this way," she said huskily and hurried forward, the path illuminated by small garden lights mingling through the palm trees, the clicking of her high heels in competition with a chorus of green tree frogs.

But when she came up to the door, it was standing open. She began to frown, then gave a soft gasp as realization hit. Someone had broken in.

"Oh, my God," she whispered in disbelief.

"Stay there." Brant strode the few feet to the door, swearing softly when he tread on some broken glass. He reached inside for the nearest switch, flooding the kitchen with light.

Kia came up behind him and they both stood there looking around. At first it appeared as if nothing had happened but the glass on the floor showed that someone had smashed one of the panels on the door.

"Careful," Brant warned, stepping over the mess, then helping her while she lifted the skirt of her long dress with one hand and gingerly stepped over the glass.

Kia's heart was almost jumping out of her chest. "Do you think he's still here?" she whispered.

Brant peered toward the darkened hallway, his expression hard. "If he is…" He pulled his cell phone out of his jacket pocket. "He's going to regret it."

Kia shivered as he dialed the police and spoke quietly for a moment. She almost felt sorry for the robber if he was still here. He'd be in for a shock if Brant got hold of him.

He swore as he ended the call. "They've had a busy night. They could be a while."

Kia's stomach churned with anxiety. She'd hate to think what would happen if she were here alone. For the first time, she was glad of Brant's presence. "What now?"

He reached over to grab a knife from the block on the sink. "I guess I'm going to play the bloody hero," he muttered, stepping toward the hallway, but he stopped when he saw her face. "What's the matter?"

"You're not going to use that, are you?"

He grimaced. "It's only for protection. Come on. Stick with me."

Kia needed no second bidding. She stuck like wallpaper while they went from room to room, switching on each light, her knees knocking with relief when no one jumped out at them.

In the loungeroom they discovered her laptop and DVD player missing, plus a small antique clock, along with other knickknacks. Her bedroom appeared untouched, thank God. She'd hate to think of some stranger handling her personal things. Perhaps fondling her silky bra and panties...

She shuddered, and Brant put his hand on her forearm and turned her to face him. "Are you all right?"

"Yes," she murmured, though she knew she wasn't. She couldn't seem to stop shaking.

"Shhh," he said, starting to massage her arm in a comforting gesture that made her drop her gaze to his hand on her, suddenly wanting to lean into him and let his strength wrap around her.

She looked up and all at once he was staring into her eyes.

"Kia?" he growled, and she opened her lips slightly despite a silken thread of warning in his voice. He was going to kiss her…. She wanted him to, dear God, she did.

Just then the sound of crunching glass came from the kitchen and a male voice called out, "This is the police. Everything all right in there?"

Brant immediately stepped back. "About bloody time," he rasped without looking at her and left her side to stride down the hallway. "We're here, Constable," he said more loudly. "We were just seeing if there was any damage."

Kia stood there for a moment, fighting intense disappointment. Brant obviously hadn't suffered from the same frustration—or if he had, he hadn't shown it. He'd turned away from her so fast she'd almost got whiplash watching him.

Which only reminded her that's exactly what he'd

do if he ever got her into bed. He'd use her, then he'd walk away without a second glance.

Kia took a deep breath and straightened her shoulders. Now she felt strong again. She'd resisted him this far and would continue to do so. She'd been weakened by the shock of the robbery, that's all.

For the next ten minutes she sat at the kitchen table and answered questions for the two very nice policemen who'd responded to the call, while Brant leaned back against the sink and watched the proceedings like a judge in a courtroom. He certainly made the younger policeman uneasy, by the looks of things, though the older one didn't bat an eyelid.

"Probably an addict," the older policeman said now, giving a world-weary shrug. "Got to get their fix somehow. Just as well you were wearing that necklace, Miss Benton, and didn't leave it at home."

Kia gave a soft gasp as her hand went to the diamonds circling her neck. Then she saw Brant's jaw clench and the way his eyes burned her and she couldn't help but think he was somehow angry over Phillip giving her the necklace.

The policeman interrupted her thoughts by going on to suggest ways of tightening her security, including putting a bolt on the door and getting a dog.

"Oh, but we do have a dog. I mean, the lady in the apartment next door has a dog." Something occurred to her. "Oh, no. I wonder if he broke into June's place, as well? The house has been divided in two, you see." She swallowed. "Do you think you could check? She's not home this weekend, thank goodness. She went to visit her sister and took Ralphie with her."

"I'll go take a look around," the younger policeman said after getting a nod from his boss, then nervously looked at Brant before leaving the room, as if glad to get out from under such a strong presence.

The older policeman glanced at Kia. "Have you got someone to stay with you tonight, Miss Benton? Something like this can shake people up pretty bad."

"*I'll* be staying with her," Brant said before she could open her mouth.

She shot to her feet. She couldn't have Brant stay here. She just couldn't. "I can look after myself. I don't need anyone. I—"

"What if he comes back?" Brant cut across her.

The spew of words froze on her lips. Somehow she managed a short laugh. "He won't. He got what he wanted."

"Did he?"

She shivered and hugged her bare arms. "Stop it. You're scaring me."

"Well, you should be bloody scared," he said, straightening away from the sink. "You've got a door with a broken lock and no one close enough to hear you scream." His jaw tautened, making him look dark and dangerous. "I'm staying."

How silly to feel relief. She should be more scared of Brant and her own attraction for him than of being robbed again. Only if the robber came back he might not only want to rob her. He might want more than that....

"I really think that's a good idea, Miss Benton," the older policeman coaxed, looking at her in a fatherly fashion, reminding her that they weren't alone.

She swallowed deeply. "Yes, of course."

Right then the younger policeman stepped back into the kitchen, interrupting them. "Everything's fine next door." He shot a look at his boss. "Sarge, that call we were expecting just came through."

"Right." The older man straightened and immediately put his notebook in his pocket. "We'll be in touch," he told them quickly, then was gone.

A moment's tense silence stretched between her and Brant, then she cleared her throat, determined to be as businesslike as possible. "I'll get the couch ready for you."

Brant's mouth twisted. "I doubt I'll get much sleep on that two-seater in your loungeroom."

She felt as if her breath cut out. *Was he asking to share her bed?* Over her dead body.

Well, maybe not her *dead* body, she mused, hurrying to the refrigerator to get a cool drink. "Isn't that the point? To stay awake and protect me?" She lifted out the jug of cold water, almost tempted to hold it up to her forehead to cool herself down. "Anyway, it opens out to a sofa bed. You'll have plenty of room."

He began loosening his tie. "Fine. I like being able to spread out."

"That must be a novelty for you," she said before she could stop herself.

The look in his eyes held a spark of eroticism. "You make it sound like there's a woman in my bed every day."

She feigned ignorance. "You mean there isn't?"

"Sweetheart, I'm not married. I only let a woman in my bed when I'm looking for some affection."

"That's what I said. Every day." She placed the jug on the bench and walked toward the hallway door. "I'll get you a blanket," she said before he could respond. She had to get out of that room or she'd strangle him with her bare hands. Either that or smother him with one of the pillows she was about to get him.

The ringing of the telephone next to him woke Brant with a start the next morning. It seemed as if he'd only just fallen asleep, having tossed and turned for most of the night, blaming the sofa but knowing it was because the sexiest woman alive lay in a bed not meters away from him, with only a thin wall between them.

So he didn't appreciate being woken now. "Yes?" he barked into the mouthpiece.

A moment's silence, then a man's shocked voice came down the line. "Brant!"

Brant's eyes flew open. "Phil?"

The other man sucked in a sharp breath. "What the hell? Where's Kia?"

"Look, it's not what you think," Brant growled, shooting to a sitting position and regaining his composure. "Someone broke into her place last night. I slept on the sofa so I could keep an eye on her, that's all."

"Is she okay?" Phil asked, anxious now.

"She was a bit shook up last night, but I'm sure she'll be fine in the light of day."

He looked up and saw Kia standing in the doorway. Her blue eyes were sleepy, her blond hair sexily tousled, not a bit of makeup on her beautiful face as she wrapped the sash of a silky blue creation around her waist. She looked so bloody gorgeous he had to stop himself from throwing the phone down and ravishing her on the spot.

"I'm glad you were there for her," Phil said slowly, dragging Brant's thoughts away from the woman in front of him. Phil still sounded depressed.

"Phil, I'm sure she would rather have had you here," he said, watching her eyes come fully awake at the mention of the other man's name.

"Is that Phillip?" she said, stepping into the room and hurrying toward him. In an instant Brant could feel her female heat coiling around him. Could hear the silky swish of her thighs. The soft gasps of her breath that came closer and closer. If he reached out, he might just be able to caress her.

Instead he held out the phone. "Yeah, it's Phil."

She snatched it to her and immediately turned her back on him. "Phillip? Did Brant explain what happened?" She gave a delicate shudder. "It was awful. I can't believe someone would do this." She listened for a moment, then said, "He broke the glass door. The police think…"

She continued to talk, but Brant had stopped listening. And he'd almost stopped breathing. She didn't know it, but with the morning sun streaming in the room he could see straight through her gossamer robe to the line of her buttocks. God, how he'd love to run his hands over them. They'd be so smooth to his touch.

Giving a silent groan, he leaned his head back against the pillows and closed his eyes. Dammit, he had to stop this. She wasn't worth the looking…the wanting….

"Brant?"

Did she have to say his name in such a husky voice? As if she was his lover, waiting for him to stir. The next thing she'd be reaching out to touch him….

"Yes?" His voice sounded rough, like the night he'd just had.

"Are you awake?"

"No. I always talk in my sleep," he mocked and opened his eyes. Disappointment rippled through him when he saw she'd moved out of the sunlight.

Her mouth tightened. "That's one thing *I'll* never find out."

"No, you won't, will you?" And suddenly it was the biggest regret of his life. His lips twisted. Okay, that and getting involved with Julia all those years ago. She hadn't been too innocent when she'd run off and married his brother.

He threw back the sheet and swung his legs over the side of the sofa bed, his black briefs his only covering. "Tell me. Does Phillip ever talk in his sleep?" he asked, forcing himself to remember who this woman belonged to…and what she was about.

Money.

She gave a light laugh. "Only to murmur sweet nothings in my ear."

An intense jealousy slashed through him. It should have been *him* who whispered in her ear. *Him* who lay beside her. *Him* who made love to her. That's what felt right. Not her and Phillip. Every minute he grew more certain of it.

He reached for his trousers. God, what was going on here? Why didn't he suddenly feel right about those two? There was something he couldn't quite put his finger on. Something important. Yet all he had was a gut feeling he couldn't shake. And a bloody hunger for Kia Benton that wouldn't stop.

"Would you like coffee before you go?"

At the crack in her voice he looked up and caught her appraising his bare chest and taut stomach. Despite being newly engaged, the look in her eye said she wanted *him*.

His muscles immediately tensed as he zipped up and asked the question that hit him from out of nowhere. "How come you didn't call Phillip last night?" All at once he found it interesting that she hadn't gone running to her fiancé after the burglary.

She'd been about to turn away, but now her eyelids flickered, as if the question startled her. "What? Er...I didn't want to worry him."

"If you were my fiancée, I'd *want* you to worry me."

She moistened those oh-so-enticing lips. "You know he was tired and in pain when he left the party."

"I'd still want to know if you were in danger."

Her chin angled. "Phillip's not like you, Brant."

No, he wasn't, was he? Phillip was a one-woman man. And that woman was Lynette Kelly, of that Brant was suddenly certain. Ever since he'd seen Phillip's reaction to his old girlfriend at the Christmas party last night, he'd had this deep nagging feeling. And what about Lynette's reaction to Phillip? They were both still in love with each other, no doubt about it.

Brant looked at Kia and wondered if she knew. Surely she'd noticed something amiss?

"Forget the coffee," he rasped as he quickly slipped on his shirt and made a grab for his jacket. He had to get out of here before he did or said something he'd regret. Phillip may be in love with Lynette, but the other man obviously wasn't prepared to do anything about it. And Kia must be thanking her lucky stars she'd found a man who didn't give a damn that he was being taken to the cleaners.

Ignoring the tight knot forming in his stomach, he sat down again and began putting on his socks and shoes. "I'll call a locksmith and get him to fix the door for you." What he should really do is get someone to lock *her* up. Only then would men be safe from her beauty and self-seeking ways.

"I'm quite capable of picking up a phone."

"I didn't say you weren't, but I can get it fixed faster. I have connections."

"What you mean is you'll offer him more money to fix it today?"

"The company can afford it."

She drew in a sharp breath. "Don't be ridiculous. I won't be letting the company pay for anything."

His mouth clamped into a thin line. Who was she trying to fool? This was a token protest at best.

"So you're going to sleep another night with your

door wide-open?" He stood up, ready to leave. "I could always come back and use your sofa again." It was a foolhardy threat. He'd never be able to handle another night without touching her. And he had better things to do with his time.

"I'll go to a motel."

His teeth clenched. "Fine and dandy. And when you get home, the rest of your stuff will have been stolen." Without waiting for a response, he started toward the door. "Someone will be round within the hour."

"Brant—" she warned, only to have the ring of the telephone interrupt her.

"Answer that," he said and left the house before she could get another word in. What he found interesting was that she hadn't mentioned staying at Phillip's place, when that would be the ideal solution. Perhaps she was holding out for a white wedding, he mused cynically.

Four

Later that day, when Phillip's attendant knocked on her door to pick her up to take her to the art exhibition, Kia had to take a calming breath before answering. She was furious with Brant over the locksmith he'd sent here. All the names she'd been calling him seemed too tame for the thoughts bubbling in her brain right now.

But instead of showing her feelings, she smoothed her hands down the front of her slim-fitting sleeveless dress and reached for the door handle. She wouldn't let Brant spoil her afternoon. She'd rather eat rat poison.

"G'day, Kia."

The breath caught in her throat. The man on the other side of the doorway emitted a sex appeal so potent it cracked through the air like a whip, invisibly wrapping around her body and almost pulling her toward him. Black trousers fitted his lower torso to perfection, a light gray polo shirt molded over his chest. He looked casual and confident. A man any woman would be proud to be seen with.

Anyone but her.

"Aren't you going to invite me in?" Brant said, stepping past her into the house without waiting for an invitation.

She spun around to face him. Of all the arrogant... "How dare you!" she managed to say.

He merely looked amused. "How dare I be in your house? You didn't mind me being here last night."

She glared at him. He made it sound as if they'd been making love all night. "I'm talking about the security alarm."

His forehead creased. "He didn't do a good job?"

"Yes, he did a good job, but that's not the point. He was supposed to fix the lock, not put in an alarm system." She'd thought the man had been merely checking security risks when he'd started going from room to room. By the time she'd realized he was doing the whole thing, he'd climbed on the roof and had half the place wired.

"I thought an alarm system would be better."

"*You* thought? Where do you get off ordering an alarm for *me*?"

"I told you. The company will pay for it."

"It's not the money," she said through gritted teeth.

His eyebrows lifted with cynicism. "Really? Then what's the problem?"

"This is *my* home, Brant. *My* private life. You're interfering in it. You've no right to even be here, let alone tell someone to install an expensive piece of equipment like this. Heck, it's not even technically my house."

His shrug belied the hard gleam in his eyes. "Don't make a big deal out of this, Kia. You're Phillip's fiancée now. He wants you to be safe."

She tried not to wince. "Phillip knows about the alarm?"

"As you're now his fiancée, I suggested it and he agreed. We all know it's quite common for criminals to return to the scene of the crime. You either had to get an alarm or move."

She flashed him a look of disdain. "Oh, really. And where would you like me to live?"

"How about with your fiancé?"

She gulped and quickly spun away to turn off the air-conditioning. Anything not to look at Brant. "Phillip and I haven't discussed that yet."

"That's what Phil said."

Relief rushed through her. "There you are then." She remembered the security alarm and glared at him. "Anyway, you and Phillip have no right to tell me what to do or what to put in my own house. And as soon as he gets here, I'll be making that quite clear."

"Then you're going to have a bit of a wait," he said, his gaze seeming to watch her reaction. "He's not coming. He rang and asked me to take you to the exhibition instead. He said he wasn't feeling up to it today."

Her stomach knotted. She didn't want to go to the exhibition with Brant. Damn Phillip for being selfish enough not to turn up. She was beginning to think taking the easy way out was a weakness he couldn't control.

"Why didn't he phone me himself?"

"He said he'd tried a couple of times but kept getting the busy signal."

She bristled with indignation. "Because the alarm was being connected to the phone line, that's why." She waved a dismissive hand. "Oh, it doesn't matter. I'm not going without Phillip."

His eyes narrowed. "Phil said one of our clients invited him to the exhibition."

"Er…yes…" She licked her lips. "But it just wouldn't be the same without Phillip. I'm sure they'll understand."

"*They* may, but *I* won't. This is a work assignment, Kia. Think of it as payment for the security alarm."

Her mouth tightened. So there *was* a catch to his free and easy statement of "the company will pay for it."

"Perhaps I should go by myself…on behalf of the company, that is. There's no need for you to waste your Saturday afternoon." She didn't want to deprive some poor besotted female of his company either.

"I wouldn't think of it as a waste. I'd like to see the exhibition, too. Early Australian art fascinates me."

It fascinated her, too, but she didn't want to say so. Yet could she spend hours with him and survive the draw of his attraction? She swallowed. It looked as though she wasn't getting a choice. But after she put in an appearance for their client, she'd make sure it was the quickest walk around the gallery on record.

* * *

An hour later she and Brant strolled through the art gallery by themselves after they'd shared an afternoon tea of pineapple scones, finger sandwiches and a delicious tropical fruit platter. Brant had been his charming self with their client and the others. A couple of times she'd even let her guard down and surprised herself by actually laughing at some of his witty remarks.

Of course, being witty and a womanizer was what he was about. That's how men like him got women into bed, and if the looks some of the other women were giving him were anything to go by, he'd have had plenty of offers today if she hadn't been around. Yes, he knew exactly how to charm the panties right off a woman. She stiffened. *Not this woman.*

"I like this painting of the early settlers," he said now, his deep voice bringing her out of her thoughts. "I saw a print of it years ago, but the brushstrokes and paint textures are nothing compared to the original." He turned to look at her. "It's very evocative, don't you agree?"

She fumbled for words when she saw the piece of work he was referring to. "Um…yes."

He arched a brow. "You sound surprised?"

A thrill raced through her, but she managed to shrug as if it were no big deal. "It's my favorite painting."

"And you didn't expect us to have the same tastes, right?" He paused, his blue eyes darkening. "I think we'd have a lot in common if we looked closely."

She moistened suddenly dry lips. "Yes. Phillip, for one thing."

He gave a slightly bitter smile. "Ah, Phillip. We'll always have him in common, won't we?" He turned back to the painting. "Tell me. Why is this your favorite?"

Obviously he wanted to keep things on an even keel, and she was only too happy to oblige. Yet she couldn't help but feel a burst of excitement that he found the imagery of the painting as touching as she did. Perhaps there was more to him than met the eye.

She turned to the painting and let her gaze wander over the picture of their pioneer ancestors, losing herself in its sheer vibrancy and color. "I'd say it's because it personifies the Outback spirit. That it's possible to overcome any obstacle, no matter how big or daunting."

"So you like challenges?" he pounced.

She drew in a shaky breath. Always the predator. He just couldn't help himself. "*Some* challenges," she admitted.

"I like certain challenges, too," he drawled, his eyes intense. "If somebody tells me I can't have something, then that's when I want it."

And he wanted her. He had no need to say it out loud. The wanting poured from him like a familiar scent.

She plastered a smile on her lips. "Then you'd better get used to disappointment," she quipped, knowing her first instincts about him were correct. She hadn't misjudged him. Not in the slightest.

A few hours later the two of them sat at an outdoor café not far from the exhibition, sipping at fruit daiquiris. The pre-Christmas festivities were still continuing, and people were out in force and in holiday mode, enjoying a stroll along the sail-shaded Smith Street Mall, listening to a busker play her guitar, watching a mime artist perform.

Brant couldn't have cared less where they were or who was nearby. His concentration was solely and fully on one person. Kia looked as beautiful as always, with her blond hair pulled back in a French knot, and wearing a lemon-colored dress that displayed the elegant line of her neck and showed off her tanned shoulders and arms.

But something else about her today set his pulse spinning like a top. Watching her talk to the others at the gallery, he'd glimpsed an innocence in her lovely eyes that had been at odds with the knowing look in them, as if she couldn't quite hide the sweet beneath the spice. Yet *sweet* was hardly a word he'd expect to use about Kia Benton.

He swallowed some of his drink, then decided he didn't need any more intoxication right now. Apart from a brief time last night and again this morning, he'd never really been alone with her like this before. It had gone to his head—no, his *body*. His state of constant arousal was killing him.

And she knew it. That's why she wasn't quite facing him as she sat sipping her daiquiri, her body turned slightly toward the crowd.

But she was only fooling herself. There could be a brick wall between them and the attraction would still seep through. Didn't she know there was no stopping it? Not unless they made love and got it out of their systems, and then he had the feeling it would probably only intensify.

"Tell me more about your father," he said, suddenly interested in what made her tick.

She raised a wry eyebrow. "Why?"

He gave a smile. "Are you this suspicious of everyone or is it just me?"

"Just you," she said, her lips curving into a sexy smile that was as unexpected as was her words. God. She was lovely, with her smooth cheekbones, perfect nose, eyes that could dazzle a man with just one look and a deliciously tempting mouth.

She put her glass down, and when she looked up again her face had sobered. "There's nothing much to tell. My father thinks he's one of the beautiful people. He can't stand being around someone who isn't."

Brant frowned. "You're still his daughter."

Her slim shoulders tensed. "The only reason he wants me around is because he thinks it's good for his image."

All at once something occurred to him. "Good Lord. Your father isn't Lloyd Benton, is he?"

If it were possible, she tensed even more. "The one and only."

Now he knew where she was coming from. Lloyd Benton owned the biggest fleet of used-car yards up and down the east coast of Australia. He was constantly in the newspapers with some young thing hanging off his arm—usually his current wife but not always. The man gave *sleaze* an added dimension.

"*He's* your father?"

She raised her chin in the air. "I won't apologize for him."

"I don't expect you to."

No wonder she didn't seem to hold men in high regard. Well, *some* men. He freely admitted that men like himself, who took one look and wanted to take her to bed, would only confirm her low opinion of the male species. Dammit, suddenly he was seeing another side to this woman that he wasn't sure he wanted to see.

"It certainly explains a lot about you and Phillip."

She tensed. "If you mean I want to marry someone who doesn't have to bed every beautiful woman he meets, then you're dead right. Phillip's a nice man." Her gaze dropped to her glass, then up again. "He'll be a wonderful father and a faithful husband."

"You didn't say you loved him." And he found that interesting. *Very* interesting.

"That goes without saying."

"Does it?"

"Yes."

And perhaps it was all an act. Perhaps working on people for sympathy was how she wormed her way into men's beds…and their hearts. Perhaps it was all about paying back her father for being so weak.

"What about you?" she said, catching him off guard. "Are your parents still alive, Brant?"

He had no wish to talk about himself. "No. They died when I was eighteen."

Sympathy flashed in her eyes. "I'm sorry. Any brothers or sisters?"

His jaw tightened. "A brother. And before you ask, he's younger than me by a couple of years." He looked at his watch and stood up. "Come on. Let's go. It's getting late."

For a moment, surprise mixed with hurt appeared in her eyes, then cynicism took over. "Got a date, no doubt."

"No doubt." He didn't tell her he was getting together with his two best mates for dinner, though Flynn and Damien would no doubt find it amusing that they were to be his "date" this evening.

Not that he'd tell them. The three of them had grown up together on the same street in this town—had shared everything from stories of their first kiss to their first million—but Kia Benton was one thing he wasn't about to share with his rich and successful friends.

"Phillip Reid, how could you!" Kia exclaimed the next day as she swept into his study. She'd been phoning him on and off since returning from the art exhibition yesterday. He hadn't answered, but she suspected he'd been at home. He'd been feeling low so she'd given him a reprieve, but now she had a few words to say to him whether he still felt bad or not.

He looked up and winced. "What can I say, Kia? I'm sorry."

She stopped right in front of his desk. "I don't like being used," she said through gritted teeth.

His dark brows drew together. "I wasn't... I didn't mean..."

"Yes, you did." She slapped the box containing the diamond necklace down in front of him. "Don't try and fool me, Phillip. You gave me this because you knew Lynette was going to be at the party. And then you had Brant dance with me so she'd see who you'd brought as your partner. And to top things off, you tell everyone we're engaged and leave me high and dry to field all sorts of questions."

He looked thoroughly shamefaced and embarrassed. "I really *am* sorry. I didn't mean for it to go so far."

She was nowhere near ready to forgive him. Not after what she'd been through. "And yesterday? What happened to coming to the art exhibition with me?"

He swallowed hard as he leaned back in his wheelchair. "I'm sorry. I just wasn't up to going out." Then he looked confused. "Didn't Brant take you? He said he would."

"Yes, but I'd rather have gone by myself," she said sourly, preferring not to think about how much she'd enjoyed herself. She had to remember Brant could charm *any* woman into having a good time.

A speculative look came into Phillip's eyes. "Are you upset because I didn't go? Or because Brant did?"

Kia tensed, then forced herself to relax. "It's awkward spending time with one's boss," she said, avoiding a direct answer.

"You don't mind spending time with me."

She shrugged. "You're different."

"Look, if there's something between you two—"

Somehow she managed to hide her panic. "Don't be an idiot, Phillip. And, by the way, what's the deal about my security alarm? I don't remember giving either of you permission to put one in my place."

Phillip frowned, falling for the diversion. "It was the only thing to do, seeing you're my...er...fiancée. Brant would have been suspicious otherwise."

Her teeth set on edge. "Engaged or not, I am *not* some feeble female who can't take care of myself," she said with more bravado than she'd felt the other night after the robbery. "And if Brant thinks he—"

"So this *is* about Brant?" Phillip said, pushing his wheelchair back from the desk, looking very much the all-knowing male now that the heat had been taken off him.

She realized she'd given too much away. "Phillip, will you stop this. I don't know what's come over you today."

He wheeled his chair around the desk and toward her. "He gets to you, doesn't he?"

She gave a hollow laugh. "Of course not."

"And I've gone and spoiled it for you by telling everyone you're my fiancée." He stopped a few feet in front of her and thumped his hands on the armrests in helpless anger. "Hell. This is all such a bloody mess."

"That's an understatement." She just wished he'd stopped to think things through before making drastic announcements like they were engaged. "The question is, what are we going to do about it?"

He looked up at her, his expression thoroughly wretched. "I'm not sure."

"This can't go on, Phillip."

"I know. God, we were just supposed to be a couple for *one* date."

Sympathy started to soften her. "Phillip, you didn't know Lynette's father was going to be at that dinner."

"Yeah, but I knew he shared the same business circles. Dammit, I shouldn't have asked you to continue with the charade after that. It wasn't fair of me." He looked down at his leg and his lips twisted. "Pity the accident got in the way and ruined everything. But this…" He gestured at the plaster from toe to thigh. "I *know* Lynette. She would've convinced herself that I needed her. And then she would have convinced *me*. I couldn't let that happen." He took a shuddering breath. "She deserves better than a cripple for the rest of her life."

"Oh, Phillip." She crouched down in front of his wheelchair. "Don't say that. A limp does *not* make you a cripple."

He took a deep breath. "Sorry. I'm just full of self-pity today."

"Look," she said, thinking hard. "Let's wait until after Christmas, then we'll make an announcement that things didn't work out after all."

His eyes lit up, then drooped just as quick. "But your name will end up being mud. No one will care about the details, especially not the press. They'll just know you broke off the engagement during a bad time for me." He grimaced. "I'm sorry, Kia. I never meant for any of this to happen."

She squeezed his hand, trying not to think about all this being made public to the people of Darwin. "Let's ride it out, Phillip. In the meantime, we'll carry on for another week until Christmas. I heard you tell Mary that you were going home to Queensland for the holidays anyway. That'll give us some breathing space."

Intense relief surged across his face. "Good idea."

All at once Kia couldn't help but think that Brant would never let anyone else sort out his problems for him the way Phillip was doing here. Brant would have taken charge and done what he had to do. Actually, on second thought, he would never have gotten himself in this situation in the first place. Brant relied on no one except himself. He needed no one.

Just like her.

"Don't let him get to you, Kia."

She feigned ignorance. "Who?"

"Brant."

She pretended to be unconcerned. "I wish you'd stop implying that there's something going on between me and Brant. There isn't. End of story."

Is it? Phillip's eyes asked, but she promptly looked away. She wasn't about to tell him she suspected he was right.

The next week leading up to Christmas proved difficult for Kia. Not only was she extremely busy tidying things up at work so that she could enjoy their two-week closure over the holidays, but Brant seemed to sense something amiss between her and Phillip. She had the funny feeling he was homing in for the kill.

Then, just as she thought she might be able to relax, the airline phoned at the exact moment Brant walked into her office. They were checking to see if there was anything else they could do to assist Phillip on his trip to Queensland tomorrow.

Kia tried to sound as if she were talking to a client. She didn't want Brant to know she wasn't joining Phillip at this stage. "Thank you, but I believe everything's under control."

"What about on arrival in Brisbane?" the woman persisted on the other end of the line. "Can we arrange transport from the airport?"

"That's kind of you, but there will be someone to meet him," she said, then could have kicked herself when the look in Brant's eyes sharpened.

"That's fine then. But please let us know if there's anything we can do."

"Thank you, I will." Kia hung up, swallowed, then planted a polite smile on her face. "Can I help you, Mr. Matthews?"

His mouth thinned. "You can't keep calling me 'mister' for the next twenty years."

She kept a reign on her temper. "Who knows where any of us will be by then?"

"You'll be married to Phillip, of course."

She'd forgotten that was what he'd think. "Yes, of course."

"Who was on the telephone just now?"

Her heart thumped as she quickly began to tidy up some papers. "Oh, no one you should worry about."

A pair of hands flattened on the desk in front of her, stilling her. "That was someone from the airline, wasn't it?"

She drew a shaky breath and looked up into blue eyes that were riveted on her face. The caress of his warm breath on her cheeks stirred her senses. "Yes."

"So you're not on the same flight as Phillip?" he demanded, shooting each word at her with the precision of gunfire.

"No."

"Are you catching another flight?"

"Yes." To Adelaide.

"To Queensland?"

She lifted her chin in the air and decided she'd had enough of this. "I'm not going to Queensland. I'm spending Christmas with my family in Adelaide."

He leaned in that little bit closer. "So you're not spending Christmas with your new fiancé?"

She resisted shrinking back in her chair. "Not this year, no."

"Why?"

"What do you mean why?"

Anger flared in his eyes as he pushed himself back from the desk and straightened. "It's usual for an engaged couple to spend Christmas together."

"We're not a usual couple." She realized what she said too late. "I'd already made other arrangements," she pointed out as she slowly began to breathe again.

An odd glint appeared in his eyes. "I'd have thought you wouldn't want to let him out of your sight."

"I trust Phillip," she said, slightly puzzled by his question. It wasn't as though Phillip would be out nightclubbing every night. Now if it was Brant who was her fiancé...

"But do you trust Lynette Kelly?" he purred.

Shock ran through her. Had he guessed that Lynette still had feelings for Phillip? Did he know things hadn't really been settled between them?

"Lynette and Phillip are no longer an item," she said coolly, and before he could say anything further she handed him a piece of paper. "I believe this belongs to you, Mr. Matthews."

His face hardened. "Kia, I swear if you call me Mr. Matthews one more time..." He trailed off as he opened the slip of paper. His head shot up. "What's this?"

"A check for my security alarm." She'd rung the man who'd come to her home only to find out the bill had already been paid.

Cynicism entered his eyes. "Forget it. You paid for it by coming to the art exhibition, remember?"

Yes, so why did she deserve that mocking look in his eyes? "I'm sorry, I don't see it that way. Not even as Phillip's fiancée."

"My offer was non-negotiable." He ripped it in two.

She got to her feet and walked to a cabinet too close to Brant to get her purse. "Fine. I'll write another one and give it to Phillip."

"No need for drama, Kia. Let it go."

"Mr. Matthews, if you think you can do what you like—"

He captured her arm with his warm hand, sending a slew of shivers racing over her spine. "Listen, if I did what I'd really like—"

"Is everything all right in here?"

Kia drew a ragged breath before she looked up to see Phillip had wheeled to the office door and was looking at them in concern. She stepped sideways and Brant dropped his hand.

Somehow she planted a stiff smile on her lips. "Yes, everything's fine. I was just reminding Mr. Matthews that you're going to Queensland tomorrow."

"The name's Brant," Brant snapped and stormed out of the office.

Phillip raised his brows as he looked at Kia. "Sure you don't want to come with me tomorrow? It might be safer."

Kia shook her head. There was no place on earth safe for her. Not another state. Not another country. No, she'd just have to polish her armor and pray that Brant had better things to do on Christmas Eve than harass her.

And if she believed that, then maybe Santa Claus really did exist.

Five

Kia saw Phillip off at Darwin airport the next morning, then returned to the office to finish up some work before doing some last-minute Christmas shopping. She found Brant in Phillip's office, riffling through some papers on his desk.

He looked up when she appeared in the doorway, and his eyes darkened when he saw her. "You're back," he said as if she'd returned just for him.

And suddenly she knew she had. Despite all the attraction she *didn't* want to feel for this man, she still felt it. Her armor was paper-thin at best.

"Yes," she murmured, willing him to come to her. To pull her into his arms. To make love to her. Long moments crept by, and she saw the struggle on his face to resist doing that very thing.

He cleared his throat. "Phil's plane get off okay?"

Phillip. Her so-called fiancé wasn't gone half an hour and she was ready to fall into bed with Brant. Dear God, why did this man have such a hold over her? She hated it. She would fight against it...with every fiber of her being.

Her gaze dropped to the paperwork in his hands. "Can I help you?" she asked, injecting cool disapproval in her tone.

His face closed up. "I was looking for the Robertson file." He went back to searching through the papers. "Phil was supposed to do some work on it."

"He did. I just have to finish typing some notes, then you can have it. Give me an hour and I'll get it to you."

"Fine." He strode around the desk and came toward her, all business now. "I'll be in my office."

She stepped back and moved to her desk before he could come anywhere near her. He sent her a mocking smile as he passed by. Well, he could mock, she told herself as she sat down and opened up the file. It wouldn't get her into his bed any faster.

Or at all.

An hour later she hurried down the hallway to his office, determined to leave the paperwork with his PA, only Evelyn was nowhere to be seen. He must have heard her in the outer office, because a few seconds later he called out to bring it in to him.

She swallowed hard, not wanting to go into his inner sanctum when no one else seemed to be around.

"Kia?"

She straightened her shoulders and walked forward.

For all its luxury, she may as well have been walking into a prison cell.

"How did you know it was me?" she said.

He gave her a look that told her he always knew when she was around. "Bring it over here," he said, putting down his pen and leaning back in his chair as if she were about to put on a show and he didn't want to miss a second of it.

She hesitated. Her legs felt like jelly. Then she moved forward, and just as she'd known it would, his gaze slid over her blue tailored skirt and white silky blouse. She could see him mentally stripping the clothes from her body, piece by piece.

She was wishing that she hadn't discarded her jacket before coming in here. At least then she wouldn't have the urge to cover up the tight feeling in her nipples, and her arms wouldn't be goose-bumping in reaction.

She put the correspondence on his desk. The hint of sandalwood aftershave filled the air and stirred her senses. "I'll be leaving now. I want to finish some Christmas shopping this afternoon."

"When are you off to Adelaide?"

"Tomorrow morning."

"You'll miss Phil, no doubt?" It was a question, not a statement. Those eyes watched her like a cat stalking a mouse, waiting for her to make one wrong move. Well, she didn't much like cheese.

She pasted on a smile. "Naturally, but I'll be kept pretty busy. My mother loves to put on a bash at Christmas," she chatted on nervously, until all at once she saw a hint of bleakness in his eyes that clutched at her heart. She spoke before she could stop herself. "What about you, Brant? Any plans for Christmas?"

"So you remembered my name, eh?" Then he straightened in his chair. "A friend has invited me around for Christmas dinner, but I'm not sure I'll go yet. I've got too much work."

"What about your brother?" she said, curious to see his reaction again.

"What about him?" he snapped, his eyes turning colder than winter.

She swallowed. "I just thought—".

"Look, I don't want anything to do with my brother and that's the way I like it."

She took a step back. "Oh."

Tension filled the air and hung there for a few seconds before Brant appeared to make himself relax. Then he leaned over and took something out of the drawer in his desk. "I have a Christmas present for you."

Her heart jumped in her throat. "A...a present?"

He held out the small package toward her. "I gave Evelyn one, too. Can't let the best two PAs in town not know they're appreciated."

His tone held something biting, though she knew it was intended for *her*, not Evelyn. But she accepted the gift anyway. Phillip had given Evelyn a present, so what was wrong in Brant giving *her* one?

Then she met his eyes and she knew that everything *was* wrong about this. This wasn't because of her work. It was because he wanted her. This was a man wanting his woman and telling her in the only way he could.

Her hands shook as she undid the wrapping paper and lifted the lid on the small box inscribed with the top jeweler's name in Australia. She gasped when she saw the small medallion nestled on a velvet bed amongst the gold chain.

"It's not a diamond necklace," he said with cutting emphasis, "but it should keep you safe on your journey home."

"It's a St. Christopher medallion," she murmured, pushing his cynicism aside, touched by the charming gift. "Thank you. It's lovely. I'll make sure I put it on before I leave."

"Let me," he rasped.

Her breath hitched. Could she bear to have him touch her, no matter how briefly? Oh, how she wanted this. Was this one little thing too much to ask?

"Thank you," she whispered, her voice shaky.

He came around the desk and took the present out of her hands. "Turn around."

She did, and for a long moment everything in the room went quiet. Her heart skipped a beat. She could feel him standing there looking at her, his warm breath flowing over the nape of her neck, making her light-headed. If she leaned back, his arms would snake around her and then... *Oh, for heaven's sake, Kia, get a grip on yourself,* she scolded inwardly.

The package rustled and then the gold chain came

around her neck. The medallion lovingly touched the base of her throat, cooling her skin.

He placed his hands on her shoulders and slowly turned her around to face him.

"Merry Christmas, Kia," he said hoarsely, moving in to kiss her.

She lifted her lips. She had to. An avalanche could be coming their way and she'd still wait for that kiss.

His lips touched hers briefly. So brief that it should have been a chaste kiss. But every pore of her skin felt him there, acknowledged him, cried out for more.

He moved back and their eyes locked. Her throat seemed to close at the intense desire written in his eyes and the struggle within him not to take her.

He stepped back with a low sound in his throat that seemed to wrench from deep inside him. It broke the spell of the moment.

She drew in a shaky breath. "Merry Christmas to you, too, Brant."

A muscle knotted in his jaw as he walked back around to the other side of the desk. "I hope you get everything you want."

If ever there was a time for *not* getting what she wished for, it was now. When she wanted *him*.

She spun around and hurried toward the door, needing to get out of there.

"Have a good holiday, Kia...even without your fiancé."

Kia stopped to glance at him and saw the look in his eyes was harder than ever. She tensed. They were right back where they'd started. And that was fine with her.

"I intend to," she said coolly and left the room.

Kia normally loved being with her family at Christmas. Neighbors dropped by for a Christmas drink in the morning, and her sister, Melanie, came around for lunch with her husband and young son. The weather usually proved to be hot at this time of year, so a variety of seafood and salads was the order of the day, followed by an English-style trifle that her mother made to perfection. A treat her stepfather loved. All very normal and comforting. Usually.

So why did she feel as though something was missing this year? It was a nagging thought inside her that remained there throughout the day and began again when she woke on Boxing Day. She felt restless. As if she should be some place else but didn't know where.

It wasn't until a barbecue lunch in the backyard, where she was playing peekaboo with her six-month-old nephew, that she looked up and her heart dropped to her feet. The laughter died on her lips. And suddenly she knew what had been missing. *Brant.* He stood near the corner of the house, watching her, his eyes piercing the distance between them. Her family faded from her mind.

"Who's that?" she heard her mother say, and all at once Kia realized he *was* there. He wasn't a figment of her imagination. And here she was dressed in denim jeans and a stretch knit top, far from the businesslike persona she kept for the office and even for Phillip.

She handed Dominic to her sister and jumped up. "It's okay, Mum. It's one of my bosses. I'll be right back."

She raced toward him, her hand going to her throat as something occurred to her. Something must be wrong. Terribly wrong.

"Phillip?" she croaked as she got closer.

Irritation flickered across his face, then disappeared. "Relax. He's okay, as far as I know."

She moistened her lips. "Then what are you doing here?" It had to be something important if he'd flown from the north of the continent to the south, over three thousand kilometers.

"The Anderson project needs redoing. Phillip must have been having a bad day when he met with them, because he got all their instructions wrong. If we don't present them with another option by Thursday morning, we lose the account."

Kia remembered she'd been a bit uneasy about that particular project. She'd even said something to Phillip about it and gotten her head snapped off at the time.

"I've got a ton of work ahead of me and I need a PA."

She frowned. "What about Evelyn?"

He smiled without humor. "Remember that medallion I gave her that was supposed to keep her safe? It didn't work. She came down with a stomach virus yesterday morning. It looks like she'll be out of action for the rest of the week."

She grimaced. "Poor Evelyn." But why did she suspect he was pleased about this? Not about Evelyn being sick but about needing *her* as replacement.

Probably because he was enjoying ruining her holiday like this.

Her eyebrow lifted. "Why not hire a temp?"

"This project is too important, Kia. The company will still survive if we lose them as a client, but I'm not sure about Phil. How do you think he's going to feel if he finds out what's happened? He's pretty down at the moment." He had her with that and they both knew it. "No, I need you to come back to Darwin and help me out. I flew down last night and I've got a jet waiting at the airport now. I'll pay you triple time, of course."

She waved a dismissive hand. "I don't care about the money."

"Then think of it as repayment for the security alarm."

Her shoulders tensed. "You said that was already paid in full," she reminded him, though she still had every intention of paying off the debt herself, and in cash. "Or is this one of those debts that only seem to compound interest?"

A half smile crossed his face. "Perhaps."

"Kia, love," her mother's voice said behind her, and Kia froze. "Why not bring your boss over to meet the family?"

Kia leaned toward Brant. "Please don't mention Phillip," she whispered.

"What?" he muttered.

"They don't know about him." She saw his flash of surprise just before she swung around to face her mother to make the introductions.

But surprised or not, he soon recovered. Kia watched

him turning on the charm, but she knew he'd be asking some hard questions when they were alone.

"I can certainly see where Kia gets her looks," he told her mother with a warm smile that only seemed to be available for other women.

Kia mentally rolled her eyes, but she had to admit her father would never have married her mother if she hadn't been a looker. Her mother had the warmest of natures, too. She hadn't deserved to be treated so badly.

Marlene blushed with pleasure. "Thank you, Mr. Matthews."

He darted a wry glance at Kia that said *like mother, like daughter* for calling him "mister," then turned back to her mother. "Call me Brant."

Marlene nodded. "Well, Brant. Come over and meet the rest of Kia's family." She slipped her arm through his and began walking toward the others. "Have you had lunch yet?"

"Yes, but thanks for the offer."

"Then have a drink. It's Christmas, after all." She gave a warm smile. "Besides, we want to get to know Kia's boss." She leaned slightly closer to Brant. "We worry about her up there in Darwin by herself."

He smiled. "No need to worry. We're keeping a very close eye on her," he said, and Kia's heart lurched at the hidden meaning behind those words. Suddenly her jeans felt too tight and her pink top too skimpy.

"Oh, I'm so pleased to hear that." They reached the others. "Brant, this is my husband, Gerald." The two men sized each other up and shook hands. "And this is Kia's sister, Melanie. And her husband…"

Kia gritted her teeth as she watched the females succumb to Brant's charm like a line of dominoes toppling over. The men weren't so accommodating at first, but before long Brant had them eating out of the palm of his hand, too. Did this man know no bounds?

"So why have you come to see Kia?" her stepfather asked, and Kia saw that maybe Brant hadn't quite charmed the older man as much as she'd thought. She smiled at Gerald, loving him all the more for his protection.

"There's a major problem at the office and I need Kia's help. She's been working on the project with Ph—" He hesitated, then smiled at Kia. "She knows it by heart and I can't do it without her. I have no choice but to beg her to return to the office with me. Believe me, I wouldn't ask her if it wasn't important."

"Of course you wouldn't," her mother said. She glanced at her daughter. "Darling, are you still doing your studies?"

Brant's ears pricked up. "Studies?"

Kia groaned inwardly. "I'm learning Chinese."

"And she's doing very well, too," Marlene said proudly. "She's got quite a knack for languages and is already fluent in French and Italian."

Brant regarded her with a speculative gaze. "You really are a mystery at times, aren't you?" he said, but she could see a slight hardness back in those eyes.

He glanced at his watch. "We'd better be going."

She nodded. "I'll just get my things together." She left him talking to the others, a little regretful that she hadn't had more time to spend with her family. But, on the other hand, helping out in a time of crisis was a small sacrifice to make for the good of the company.

Then she thought of working alone with Brant when they got back to Darwin and she pushed aside a level of excitement that had nothing to do with the challenge of the project and everything to do with the man himself. She swallowed hard. Correction. This wasn't a small sacrifice. This was going to be a *big* one.

Her hands shook as she quickly showered before slipping into a floral-print shirtdress with a short-sleeved jacket that was easy-wearing for travel but stylish enough for the office. Not bothering with stockings, she stepped into high-heeled sandals that complimented her long, tanned legs. A light touch of makeup and a quick deft of her hand to twist her hair up and she was ready. For battle. For Brant.

"Perhaps you can explain something to me," he said once they were seated in the plush jet and were heading back to Darwin.

Warning shivers started going up and down her spine. "Like what?"

"Like why you didn't tell your family about Phillip?"

She tried not to flinch. "Oh. That."

"Yes. *That.*"

Her cheeks reddened. "I just want to be sure, that's all."

He straightened in his seat, on full alert now. "You're not sure?"

"Yes, of course I am," she said quickly. "It's just that it all happened so fast. I don't want my family to worry and I know they would."

A moment's pause, then he said, "Tell me. Do you love Phil?"

If she hesitated, she was lost. "Yes."

His jaw clenched. "When do you plan on telling them?"

"When the time is right. Thank you for not saying anything today. It would have been...awkward."

God, she didn't like lying, but what else could she do? If she told the truth, Brant would go all out to seduce her. She'd be putty in his hands and she had no doubt she'd enjoy it. But that would be just a physical release. It wouldn't be enough. She needed more from a man than a quick roll in the hay.

Besides, this wasn't just about her. She couldn't give the game away yet. How could she tell Brant the truth and dump all this on Phillip's shoulders without giving him any warning? She didn't think she was better than Phillip, but she couldn't do to him what he'd done to her. No, she'd have to wait until he returned to the office in another two weeks. She just hoped she survived until then.

"I'm sure they'd be happy for you," Brant said. "Phillip's a great catch."

"Yes." She ignored the cynical tone to his voice, not quite up to verbally fencing with him right now.

About to look away, something about him grabbed her attention and she was surprised to catch a bleak look in his eyes before his gaze dropped to the papers in his lap. An odd feeling of sympathy caught at her heartstrings. Was his coming to fetch her more than just the problem at work? Had he been feeling lonely, despite a "friend" inviting him for Christmas lunch?

"Did you have a nice Christmas, Brant?"

His gaze shot toward her. "Why?"

"I just wondered."

His smooth look made her wish she'd kept her mouth shut. "Yes, I was kept very...busy."

She winced inwardly. "I see." He was a womanizer, so he'd been with a woman most likely. She understood him only too well. He was just like her father.

Nine o'clock that evening Brant decided to wrap things up for the day. Exhausted, he eased back in his leather chair and flexed his fingers. He could hear the clack of the keyboard in the outer office and knew that no matter how tired he was he would still want Kia Benton.

Even today, when he'd caught her offguard at her mother's place, she'd made his stomach knot with desire. Hell, he could still remember how he'd felt when he'd seen her dressed so casually in those tight jeans that lovingly hugged her body. She'd looked so different. So carefree and friendly.

And when he saw her with that toddler in her arms...it was as if he'd been seeing a glimpse of the future.

His and Kia's future.

For the first time since Julia, he imagined actually being with a woman. Having more than just a physical connection. But not even Julia had roused the same level of yearning that had ripped through him today when he'd seen Kia.

But Kia was only out for one thing.

The woman needed money the way she needed air to breathe. Her assertion that she loved Phillip had sounded hollow to his ears, but even if he were tempted to forget it, he only had to remember that while her beautiful mouth might lie, the camera hadn't. The self-satisfied smirk she'd been wearing in that photograph of her and Phillip had said it all: Kia Benton had caught her man.

He straightened in his chair, disgust tightening his mouth. So how could he even think about Kia on a deeper level? It was all this damn Christmas stuff, that's what it was. It stirred too many memories of when he was growing up.

Not that he could complain about his childhood. His parents had been the best, practically adopting the other kids in the street. Many a time Flynn had taken refuge in Brant's house when his father had been too drunk to care. And Damien's parents hadn't meant to be so distant from their son, leaving the small boy starving for parental affection. Brant knew if it hadn't been for Barbara and Jack Matthews, his two friends may not have turned out as well as they had. It had bonded the three of them together.

Like brothers.

His mouth tightened. Unlike his own flesh and blood, who had stolen his fiancée.

He got to his feet and walked to the doorway, pushing

aside the thought of his younger brother, Royce, as he forced his mind back to the business at hand.

For a minute he stood watching Kia's fingers fly over the keyboard while she continued to type up the reams of paperwork needed to get the project back on track. He didn't know what Phil had been thinking, putting together a package like that. It had been totally wrong, full of errors and not feasible.

"You knew, didn't you?" he said, coming into the room. "That the presentation was all wrong?"

She blinked in surprise, then nodded. "I had an idea. I mentioned it to Phillip, but he thought he was right, so I left it at that." She shrugged. "He's the boss."

"And so am I. You should have come to me."

She arched a brow. "And tell you what exactly? That my boss wasn't thinking straight because he'd lost the use of his leg and now I was telling him he was beginning to lose his mind, too?"

"I admire your loyalty, Kia, but next time save us both some stress and just tell me about it. I won't go running to Phil, but I'll find a way around it. If Phil's not coping, we need to get him some help."

She sighed. "Yes, you're right."

He went to speak, to tell her how Phillip's judgment was sometimes suspect and had caused problems before, but then he remembered whose fiancée she was.

"Right. Let's call it a night. Would you like to get a bite to eat on the way home?" Suddenly he didn't want to go home alone. He had nothing waiting for him there.

And no doubt they'd still have all those sappy Christmas movies on television.

She began stacking papers. "No, thanks. The pizza was more than enough."

"We ate that hours ago."

She looked up with a rueful gleam in her eyes. "I'm still full from Christmas lunch yesterday."

That gleam hit him right in his chest. There was a warmth in her eyes whenever she spoke of her family that just didn't correspond with the cold, callous player he knew her to be.

He stared at her for a minute more, then spun around and went back into his office. He supposed even criminals had their good points.

Six

The next day Kia would have loved to concentrate on the job at hand, but with everyone still on vacation, just being alone with Brant in the executive suite left her scarcely daring to breathe. It was the reason she'd insisted on working from her own office at the other end of the floor. Away from him. Away from temptation. And out of the sexual firing line.

He'd seen right through her, but she'd still held her head high when she told him she felt more comfortable at her own desk. It had been the truth, after all.

"Bring me the next twenty pages when you've finished them," was all he'd said midafternoon, the glint in his eyes telling her that even a crucial project couldn't surpass this attraction between them.

"Aye, aye, sir," she'd snapped, spinning on her heels and leaving the room, but not before she'd seen the arrogance in his eyes. Okay, so he was the boss, but that didn't mean he had to "boss" her about. It only made her madder, and ever since, her fingers had been flying across the keyboard, wanting to finish the twenty pages as soon as possible so she could march into his office and slam them down on the desk.

And that's exactly what she did—in half the time it normally took. But to her amazement, when she got to his office, he was nowhere to be seen. The adrenaline that had given her fingers strength dissipated, leaving her drained and ludicrously disappointed. She sighed. The considerate thing for him to do would have been to tell her he was going out.

She placed the papers in the center of his desk and turned to go back to her office. A figure in the doorway made her jump. For a minute she thought it was Brant. Adjusting her eyes she realized it was Lynette Kelly.

Kia breathed in deeply, her heart not quite settling back into place. "Lynette, what are you doing here?"

Lynette blushed as she took a few steps into the office. "Oh, hello, Kia."

She looked so nervous Kia felt sorry for her. "Can I help you?" she asked gently.

"Er...I need to see Phillip. I called him at home, but there was no answer. I thought he might be here."

"I'm sorry. He's not." Lynette's face fell and Kia spoke before thinking. "He's gone home to Queensland for a couple of weeks."

The other woman's eyes widened. "Without you?"

Kia's gaze darted away then back. "I had to stay here. To work."

"Oh." Her shoulders slumped. She turned away. "I guess I'd better—" She spun back. "Kia, do you really love Phillip? I mean, like a woman should love a man? Please, I need to know."

There was such anguish in her eyes, guilt stabbed Kia in the heart.

"Kia, he needs me. I know he does. I love him with all my heart and I'm swallowing my pride in front of you and begging you to tell me the truth."

Kia couldn't stand Lynette's pain any longer. It just wasn't right to keep the other woman in the dark. She owed it to her—and to Phillip—to help straighten things out.

"No, Lynette. I don't love Phillip. Not in that way."

"Thank God." Lynette swayed, then quickly gathered herself, blinking back tears. When she'd recovered, a crease formed between her eyes and she looked confused. "So why did you get engaged?"

Kia told her the truth and explained how one thing had led to another. "I'm sorry for all the pain we've put you through, Lynette. I was just trying to help Phillip."

"Do you...?" Lynette swallowed. "Do you think he still loves me?"

"I know he does."

Hope filled Lynette's eyes and made them shine. "I have to go to him."

Kia nodded. Behind the other woman's delicate appearance, she sensed a strength of character she suspected would surprise Phillip. "If he gives you a hard time, tell him I said he's a fool."

Lynette quickly hugged her. "I hope you find someone for you soon."

"I'm not sure I want anyone," Kia said with a small smile. The only person who had ever really affected her was Brant. And he…well, there was nothing more to say there.

Lynette left the room, so happy she looked as if she were walking on air. Kia smiled as relief swept through her that she'd told the other woman of Phillip's love. It was in Lynette's hands now.

Just then, the hairs on the back of Kia's neck stood to attention. Even before she turned toward the connecting door she was certain Brant would be standing there.

And he was. He'd been in the small conference room the whole time. A fear such as she'd never known skittered under her skin. Primal fear. Sexual fear. She only had to look at the anger in his eyes to know he had overheard.

"Um…Brant. I didn't know you were there."

For a moment the air hung between them like a sheet of humidity.

"So the gold digger's conscience got the better of her, did it?" he sneered, leaning against the doorjamb, about as laid-back as a crocodile lazing in the sun.

She sucked in a sharp breath. "Gold digger?" *Was he crazy?* "Are you talking about *me?*"

"Too bad, sweetheart. You missed out on marriage

this time, but I'm sure you can find another man to fall for that innocent act."

"Wh-what?" She had no idea what he was talking about.

"Don't deny it. I saw your picture in a magazine. Even the journalist could tell a fortune hunter when he saw one. In fact, he remarked on how you'd hooked one of the Australia's richest bachelors."

Was she really hearing this? "That *journalist*—and I use the word loosely—has got it in for me because I refused to go out with him. He's just trying to make me look bad." She'd felt ill when she'd seen the photograph and the comment he'd made.

"Really?" Brant's eyes said he didn't believe her. "Even if that's the case, I heard you on the telephone. My ears don't deceive me."

She frowned. "Telephone?"

"That's right. When I came back from Paris I heard you bragging to someone on the phone about it being as easy to fall in love with a rich man than a poor one." His top lip curled. "The next thing, you were Phillip's shadow and engaged to him."

She tried to think. Then it hit her. "I was talking to Gerald…my stepfather. It's a joke between us. Good Lord. So this is why you've been a pig to me since I first met you? You thought I was marrying Phillip for his *money?*"

He made a harsh sound. "You were quick to take the diamond necklace from him."

"He asked me to wear it to the Christmas party. I

gave it back the next day. Ask him if you don't believe me."

Something flickered in his eyes. "The Porsche?"

"My father gave it to me. He deals in cars, remember?" Her heart twinged. "He likes his 'Barbie' to come with accessories."

For a moment there was a flash of sympathy, then his face hardened. "If you dislike your father so much, why take the car?"

"He offered and I thought why not? I figure the man owes me for all he's put me through. If he wants to give me a Porsche, I'm taking the Porsche. There's nothing wrong with that." She paused. "Anyway, if I wanted money, I only have to ask him for some…not that I would. He's got enough money to keep me in luxury for the rest of my life. Unfortunately it comes with a price."

A tic beat in his jaw. "Even if all that's true, you're obviously very good at conning people. You've been living a lie."

She winced. "For Phillip's sake."

"And for your own. You used him just as much as he used you."

Her chin lifted. He was so conceited. "Now why would I do that?" she said, then realized it was a challenge.

Suddenly he turned and closed the connecting door behind him. "To keep *us* apart."

Her eyes darted to the doorknob where his hand still rested. "Us? There's nothing between us."

He strode across the room to the main office door.

"Lying again, Kia?" He shut that door too. Then he turned back toward her in the middle of the room.

Her knees began to shake. "Er...what are you doing?"

"What do you think I'm doing?" His voice flowed over her like liquid silk.

Her throat went dry. "You're playing games with me."

"No game, Kia. Far from it."

She straightened her shoulders. "Brant, stop it. This is ridiculous. You're my boss. I'm—"

"About to be kissed," he murmured, stopping right in front of her. He didn't touch her. Didn't reach out. He just stood there, looking at her. And what she saw melted every bone in her body. He was still angry, but oh, God, he wanted her.

She licked her lips. "Brant, I—"

"I'm so angry with you right now I'm either going to swear or kiss you."

She tried to step back.

He grabbed her arm to prevent her from moving, his touch shooting desire to every region of her body. "And then I'm going to take the clothes off that delicious body of yours and taste all of you."

She felt the room twirl around her. "I don't know if this is a good idea."

He pulled her closer, his pupils darkening. "I've waited too long already."

A ripple of anticipation ran through her as she watched his head lower...watched those lips come closer...and when he touched her, she could no longer deny him or herself. Every moment from the minute she'd met him had been rushing headlong toward this kiss. Ever since her first look at him in this very office, nothing else had mattered, nothing but wanting to feel the consuming pressure of his lips on hers, as they were doing now.

At last.

The kiss still took her by surprise. She expected him to plunder and ravish her on the carpet, but he didn't, and she soon forgot all about his anger as the velvet warmth of his mouth stirred every nerve ending on her lips, before he used his tongue to slide inside her.

And there he stayed, exploring the soft, sensitized recesses of her mouth until she thought she might fuse with him. But she wanted him closer. She wrapped her arms around his neck and cupped the back of his head to hold him to her. It felt so good to be like this with him. This was where she belonged. If only for a short while.

Raising his mouth from hers, he gazed deeply into her eyes, so deep that she suddenly worried he might see the real her. Not the outside person but the inside person. The person who didn't know how she was going to handle this man.

"What's the matter?" he said, watching her.

"Um…nothing." Her gaze darted down to his chest, lowering her eyelids, briefly covering her face from him. She wanted to remain like this and not let him see her thoughts. She needed to keep something of herself to herself.

And then he took her arms from around his neck and put them at her sides. He lifted her chin, holding her gaze. "I won't let you hold back from me," he warned softly.

She took a shaky breath. "You won't *let* me?"

"No." He reached out and undid the top button of her dress, and suddenly she didn't have the strength to argue with him. She stood there and let him undress her. She *wanted* him to do it. *Wanted* him to undo all the buttons and feel his touch on her skin. *Wanted* to give all of herself to him.

His hands were sure and never missed a beat as they slid down from one button to the next, opening the material wider, more fully. For him.

She could see the pulse in his neck thumping wildly and she wanted to reach out and run her finger over it. Touching him would be like throwing a match onto kerosene.

He pushed the material off her shoulders and let it slide down her arms, down her body, to the carpet. She heard him groan as she stood there in a lacy bra, bikini panties, no stockings, and high-heeled sandals. For a moment she wished she'd worn them. It may have put up a barrier.

But who was she kidding? Nothing was going to stop this. She didn't want it to stop, God help her.

"I like the color peach on you," he murmured, his eyes flaring with hot desire. "It flatters you."

She moaned and whispered, "Touch me," and he suddenly swung her in his arms, carrying her over to the large mahogany desk. With one hand he swept the papers aside, then planted her in the middle of it. Her stomach somersaulted as he stood looking down at her.

"I've fantasized you like this for weeks," he murmured,

reaching out to twine his fingers in her hair, loosening the blonde strands at the nape of her neck. "And this," he said, lifting her hair up in his hands, then leaning forward and burying his face in her locks, inhaling deeply.

She stilled, breathing in the mingled scent of his body heat and aftershave as it soaked into her pores...until the soft peck of his lips moved to her ear, to her jawline and finally her mouth again.

Eventually he broke off the kiss. "Here, let me," he murmured, his fingers sliding under her bra straps and slowly pushing them off her shoulders.

She trembled when his palms caressed the bare skin there before slipping around to her back to undo the catch. Her bra fell away, and suddenly she was naked from the waist up. She wanted to hide, not from him but from herself. She didn't know if she could let herself go like this.

"Beautiful," he said in a gravelly voice, teasing her breasts with his hands until her breathing quickened even more and she had to close her eyes from sheer pleasure.

His head lowered, his mouth closing over one nipple, and she gasped, her breasts surging at the intimacy of it all.

"Brant!"

He pulled back, his eyes searing a path over her. And then he moved and his lips followed that same path, kissing down the center of her, teasing her belly button with the tip of his tongue before stopping at the top of her thighs.

He inhaled deeply through the thin lace, and she

almost dissolved. She'd never done anything like this before. Never *let* a man do this to her. She'd had one lover in high school and nothing since.

He pushed the material to one side. "I have to taste you," he said, his fingers seeking her, opening her to him. He placed his mouth against her, and she cried out his name as his tongue darted out to taste her, explore her, tracing the shape of her, teasing the small part of her that suddenly felt as if she were about to explode.

"Oh, Brant," she moaned again. She closed her eyes as something powerful inched up inside her with every touch of his tongue. It felt so good…so right…so exquisite.

"Ooh!" She exploded with one more stroke, going up in flames like a bushfire sweeping through her, burning everything in sight, leaving nothing of her unmarked. She would never be the same again, never forget what it was like to have this man touch her like this.

And when she opened her eyes, Brant was leaning back in the chair, watching her with such possessive satisfaction that her breath caught in her throat.

Her heart gave a triple beat. She wanted to look away, only she couldn't. There'd been too much between them all these weeks. Too much longing. Too much wanting each other. They'd earned this moment between them.

Brant spoke first. "Here, let's get you dressed," he said brusquely and gently closed her legs.

"Oh, but…" She could feel her cheeks growing red as he passed her bra. "I mean…um…aren't we going to…?"

"Make love? Not yet." He stood up and helped her off the desk as intense disappointment swept through her. She went to turn away, but he held her still. "My place. Seven o'clock."

She blinked. "To-tonight?"

"Yes." He ran a finger across her lips, his eyes a mixture of need and still-deep anger. "No more waiting. For either of us. And I can't do everything I want to do to you in the office."

She swallowed, suddenly panicked by the magnitude of it all. He overwhelmed her. He made her feel things she didn't want to feel. Made her do things she *wanted* to do.

"No, I can't. I—"

"I've put my stamp on you now, Kia. You can't deny that."

She sucked in a shaky breath, very much aware he was right. "Brant, this was just a…brief interlude."

"It was a prelude," he insisted, putting his hand under her chin. "You were ready for me a minute ago," he reminded her, and she almost dissolved again.

"Yes, well…" She cleared her throat. "That was then. This is now."

His eyes darkened dangerously. "Kia, we should have been lovers weeks ago."

Her shoulders tensed. She could see his anger over Phillip still simmering beneath the surface. "Even if you hadn't thought I was with Phillip, it doesn't mean—"

"Yes, it does," he cut across her. "Have no doubts, Kia. We *would* have been lovers. You're only fooling yourself if you think otherwise."

To prove it, his hands slid around her waist and brought her close. Her body immediately arched against him, her near-naked curves tucking in against his hard contours. Heat rippled under her skin and jolted her mind into the realization that once again he was right. She pushed herself away, and thankfully he let her go, but the smoldering look in his eyes said it all.

Trying to maintain her composure, she hurried around the desk to get the rest of her clothes, feeling exposed in more ways than one. His gaze remained on her, watching her every move, and she silently shuddered as she dressed as fast as she could.

"Kia."

She did up the last button, then looked up at him. The hunger in his eyes sent a tremor through her.

"You owe this to yourself," he growled, challenge in his voice.

Kia made her way back to her office on shaky legs and collapsed onto her chair. She couldn't believe what had just happened. Had she really let herself be taken in such a way? No man had made love to her with his mouth before, though she knew it was an aspect of lovemaking that most couples enjoyed. Dear God, now she could see why.

What she hadn't expected was to come apart in Brant's hands quite the way she had. Where was her control? Her self-respect? She'd known she was a challenge to him. That he only wanted her body. So what had she done? She'd handed herself to him on a platter, that's what.

Or a desk, she corrected, feeling a blush rising up from the tips of her toes. How could she hold her head high now? Suddenly she knew she had to get out of there. She'd earned the right to leave early...in more ways than one.

Jumping to her feet, she grabbed her handbag and headed for the door. If she remained here alone with Brant, he might be tempted to take up where they'd left off and not wait for tonight.

Tonight.

You owe this to yourself, he'd said.

He was right, yet how could she turn up at his place when he thought she was a gold digger? Had thought it from the start. A woman who was mercenary enough to use men for her own advantage. That hurt.

So why did her heart turn over at the thought of *not* making love with Brant?

Brant tossed the pencil on the desk. He needed to get these reports out, but his mind kept dropping back to Kia. Could he accept she wasn't a gold digger? Her answers had made sense, but isn't that what con artists did? They conned you into believing what they wanted you to believe.

And all these weeks she'd been living a lie by pretending to be involved with Phillip. Had even let herself become engaged to him. Just as Julia had lived a lie. Until she'd run off with his own brother.

Hell. He thought he'd been hearing things when Kia had told Lynette she didn't love Phil the way a woman should love a man. She'd lied to *him*, dammit. He'd asked her straight out if she loved her fiancé and she'd said yes.

Why? Because she knew he'd have her in bed in no time, that's why. She wouldn't be able to help herself. She'd wanted to make love with him, too.

Yet how different she'd been to the experienced women he usually bedded. Women who proudly strutted their stuff. Women who took the initiative, the way he liked. Women who hadn't shattered in his arms as Kia had. Her passion, her innocence in this way, convinced him she hadn't been with a man or come alive under a man's mouth in years. That was something in her favor. Surely a gold digger wouldn't hesitate to use her body to get men to fall in love with her? Oh, hell. He just didn't know what to think anymore.

What he *did* know was that she'd been perfect. Had tasted better than perfect. It's the reason he'd held himself in check and not taken her fully as he'd ached to do. He wanted to love her slowly, take his time, make up for all those weeks of aching. Tonight he'd brand her with his body and make her his.

When he opened the door to his penthouse that evening, Brant almost forgot to breathe. The soft blue material of Kia's dress bared her tanned shoulders and arms and fell lovingly over the length of her body to just above her knees, in a simple design that would have looked plain on another woman. Yet on her it looked stunning. She couldn't look unattractive if her life depended on it.

He stepped back to allow her to enter. "Relax. I'm not going to ravish you on the spot," he said, even if the thought was more than tempting.

She moved past him in a cloud of perfume that was endlessly alluring, then stopped in the middle of the room and faced him, the light of battle entering her eyes. "That's a relief," she quipped, a becoming flush staining her cheeks.

He closed the door, knowing he could always count on her to be defiant even in the most difficult of circumstances. And this had to be the most difficult for her ever. But her uncertainty didn't change a thing. They would make love tonight.

"Take a seat while I pour you a drink." He gestured to the black leather sofa. "Gin and tonic, right?"

"Extra large."

"Oh, no, you don't," he drawled. "I don't want you to forget a moment of tonight. *I* certainly don't intend to."

She moistened her lips. "Brant, I think this is a mistake. I shouldn't have come."

"It isn't a mistake. It's called being grown-up. It's about being adults over a situation that we both clearly need to address."

Her chin rose in the air. "I thought it was more childlike when you give in and take what you want."

"Ah, so you admit you want me," he said as he poured the drinks at the bar.

She glared at him. "I think we should leave things as they are. My being here will only complicate matters."

He picked up the glasses of liquid and walked toward

her. "A complication I'll willingly embrace, if you'll pardon the pun."

She ignored that as she accepted her glass. "How do you know I won't be faking it? After all, I faked the engagement and you never knew the difference, for all your extensive experience."

"I suspected something was amiss."

Her mouth set in a stubborn line. "I did it for a reason. To help Phillip."

"And to keep me at arm's length."

"It worked."

"And now it doesn't. Accept it."

Her blue eyes lit with anger. "Look, you said yourself that I'm a gold digger. If you want a woman tonight, why pick on me? Wouldn't any *body* do?"

His amusement deserted him. "No," he said tersely. No other woman in the world would do. It was the reason he hadn't returned any of his women friend's calls. Why he hadn't made love in weeks now. The reason he'd thrown himself into his work even harder. And why he'd been so bloody snappy with everyone lately. It just hadn't been humane that the one woman who turned him on had been involved with his business partner.

He expelled a breath he hadn't realized he'd been holding. Yes, she *had* been involved with Phil. *Had* been untouchable. *Had* been out of reach.

But she was no longer.

He nodded at the sliding glass doors. "Let's go out on the balcony. We can have dinner out there."

Her shoulders stiffened. "I'm not hungry."

"Then perhaps we should give dinner a miss?"

She immediately stepped forward and strode past him to the balcony, her set mouth telling him what she thought of that idea.

"I figured that would change your mind," he murmured, following her over to the railing, where she stood looking out over the spectacular sunset view of Mindil Beach and Darwin Harbor. It was glorious out here at any time of year, but during the beginning of the wet season, like now, he loved watching the incredible lightning displays that lit up the sky most nights.

Yet tonight the only thing he wanted to light up was the woman standing next to him. He turned to look at her. The evening sun reflected on the delicate contours of her face, giving her a special glow, making her look more beautiful.

"Do you have to look at me like that?" she said in a throaty voice, a blush creeping into her cheeks.

"Yes," he said huskily. Right now he didn't think he'd ever get enough of looking at her.

She swallowed hard. "You're not making this any easier for me."

"Nothing worthwhile is ever easy."

She turned to face him, her expression growing resentful. "That's the attraction, isn't it, Brant? You couldn't have me, so you decided you wanted me."

"I admit I like a challenge." His eyes dipped to her parted lips. "But wanting you wasn't a decision I chose to make. I took one look at you and knew the decision had already been made for me."

"How nice," she said with false sweetness.

He smiled. She could fight herself all she liked, but it wouldn't make one speck of difference. She would be in his arms tonight. And in his bed. He was sure of that.

"Shall we eat?" he said and took great pleasure in placing his hand under her elbow to lead her over to the small dining table in the middle of the balcony. Her shiver was from desire, he saw it in her eyes, and it sent a hunger for more than food racing through him. But he could wait. He wanted to savor her first.

They dined on prawn cocktail as an entrée, followed by a grilled lamb with zucchini and tomatoes that his housekeeper had made. Brant watched in amusement over Kia's attempt to go slow as she chewed each mouthful as though it was the last food she'd ever eat.

"This is very good," she said, taking another tiny bite of the lamb. "Did you cook this yourself?"

He shot her a mocking smile. "Do I look like a cook?"

She stiffened. "I don't think there's anything wrong with cooking. Lots of men like to do it."

"And lots of men like to make love," he said, purposefully seductive. "How many men have made love to you, Kia?"

She almost choked, then recovered quickly. "How many have *you* made love to?"

"I don't find men attractive. Now women, that's more my style."

Her eyes filled with derision. "I guess it's more an art form than a technique with you then."

He leaned back in his chair, curious at her remark.

She pressed on. "I'd say you've had plenty of practice having sex."

"True. But I've always practiced safe sex, so you have no worries on that score."

"I'm relieved," she said drily.

"It's important, Kia."

She sighed. "I know."

"So, Kia." He paused and took a sip of wine. "How many lovers have you had?"

"One."

He arched a brow as the muscles at the back of his neck tensed. Could she really be as innocent as all that?

She shot him a defiant look. "Hey, you asked, so don't blame me if you don't like the answer."

His eyes narrowed. "I know your game. You think I'll back off if you tell me you're inexperienced."

She placed her fork on the table. "Actually, I don't care what you think. It's the truth."

His gut clenched. "Tell me about it."

"Why should I?"

"Because I want no more secrets between us, Kia. Not in bed, anyway."

She considered him for a long moment. Then she said, "I lost my virginity at a party when I was fifteen. It was the one and only time I got drunk and I gave it away to the first boy that looked at me because my father had just gotten married and didn't want his 'plain-looking' daughter at his wedding and I needed to feel loved. He didn't even ask me my name."

She said it so matter-of-factly that he believed her. He swore under his breath.

She shrugged. "I hardly remember most of it. I was just so lucky not to have found myself pregnant."

He scowled. "The boy didn't use protection?"

"I was too drunk to notice."

"But surely—" His jaw clenched, then he forced himself to relax. "I'll make a deal with you. We'll make love, but if at any time you want me to stop, I will."

Her throat convulsed. "You'd do that?"

Something softened inside him. "I want a willing female in my bed. I don't get my kicks from forcing a woman." Rising, he held out his hand. "I need you. Need to make love with you, Kia Benton," he said, deliberately saying her name, wanting her to know that he knew exactly who she was, unlike the boy who had stripped her of her virginity. "I promise you this won't be like your first time."

Seven

The evening breeze gently lifted the lace curtains away from the open window as Kia followed Brant into the bedroom. In a way, she felt like those curtains. As if she was lifting a part of herself, unveiling herself for him to see.

Yet it was a risky move to make, and for a moment she hesitated. Did she really want him to leap the boundaries she kept around herself? Today in his office she'd relinquished her body to him. But now, once his body was inside her, once he knew her so physically, what would happen to her emotionally?

Just then, he squeezed her fingers and she looked at him. The sheer depth of desire in his eyes made her shiver with longing. All her doubts disappeared.

"I want you, Brant," she admitted, unable to stop the words from spilling from her. She couldn't deny herself this. No matter what happened afterward, no matter what he thought of her, she would always have this memory. "I want you so much."

Heat flared in his eyes. "Then you've got me," he muttered, pulling her close.

She went willingly into his arms, the palms of her hands pressing against his chest, feeling his warmth and vibrancy through the material of his shirt.

"I have *never* had a more beautiful woman in my arms," he rasped, his warm breath flowing over her.

"You make me *feel* beautiful," she murmured. And he did. As if someone had waved a magic wand over her and turned her into more than she was.

She lifted her face for his kiss, and his mouth swept down and took possession of hers. And from that moment on she was his. Her need had been smoldering inside her for so long now. She needed this release.

His mouth moved against hers, silently telling her how much he wanted her. She reveled in it, opening her lips, letting him take whatever he wanted yet returning the favor. She wanted to be a part of him, so much a part of him that he'd never forget her.

The kiss deepened, lengthened. His hands caressed her spine through her dress, then eased down the zipper to stroke her bare skin, gliding up to the curve of her shoulders and provocatively pushing the material aside like a maestro playing their song.

He broke off the kiss and skimmed his lips along her

jaw. Hypnotized by his touch, she arched her neck, as his mouth continued to her earlobe and then proceeded down the smooth column of her throat. He planted a tantalizing kiss at the hollow of her neck and she gave a soft moan and slid her hands beneath the material of his shirt, not prepared to wait another millisecond to touch him.

Her head spun at the first feel of his warm flesh beneath her tingling palms. "Oh, my God," she whispered, the shock of his taut muscles running through her body even as she luxuriated in feeling the strong beat of his heart against her palms. Strong and fast.

"You're playing with fire," he said, shuddering, then stormed her mouth again in a kiss that sent her up in flames. At the same time he clasped her hips, grounding her against him. She'd felt his arousal once before when they'd danced together. This was different. This was her first full contact of him as a man. It stunned her. Delighted her. It made her ache for him.

He pulled away and in one swift motion tugged at her dress, letting it rush down her body and fall to the floor. But he didn't stop to stare, though she felt his gaze on her. Her bra vanished next. Her panties followed. Then he swept her up in his arms and carried her over to the bed, laying her out on top of the comforter.

And that's when he finally stopped to look down upon her. The intensity in his eyes sang through her veins, making her very much aware of being not only a woman but the woman he wanted.

"Tonight you're mine, Kia."

Her throat went dry. She wanted to deny it, but how could she deny something so intrinsically right?

"Yes," she whispered.

His hands went to his shirt and he quickly began to undress. It hit the carpet, followed by his trousers. It didn't take long before he stood beside her all naked and in full glory.

Her breath caught in her throat. He was absolutely magnificent, with a beautifully proportioned body that shot her pulse right off the chart. His broad shoulders topped a powerful chest that fostered wisps of dark hair and tapered down to lean hips and long, muscular legs. And to a commanding erection that magnified his masculinity tenfold.

He joined her on the bed and she surrendered to the moment, to herself, to him. She gasped when his lips moved to her breast and enclosed a nipple, pleasuring her into a mindless state even as his hand brushed over her hip and dipped to the junction at her thighs. His fingers slid between her feminine folds and ran around the small, sensitive nub in circles. Sanity began to blur as her world shrank to that one caress of his finger, to the sweet tug of his mouth at her breast.

But then, just as she was about to go over the edge, he pulled away, making her cry out in intense disappointment. "Don't stop!"

"Shh. This time we make love together," he murmured, reaching for a foil packet on the bedside table. He sheathed himself and poised at her thighs. She softened beneath him, ready to take him into her. *Needing* him in her.

"Open yourself to me," he said, nudging her legs farther apart, and she did willingly.

He entered her slowly, his eyes never leaving her face as her tightness confirmed what she had told him earlier. No *man* had ever filled her in this way before. Acknowledging this, his eyes bathed her with a tenderness that took her breath away. Then he filled her completely, gently, only stopping when he could fill her no more. His sensitivity made her heart roll over.

For one long moment they stayed still, each studying the other, connected in both body and spirit. It was the most profound moment Kia had ever experienced. She sensed it was the same for him.

As if in silent agreement, he took a deep breath and slowly began to withdraw. Then he moved forward and filled her again. He took another breath and withdrew as far as he could without separating their bodies. He kept repeating the motion, and she lifted her hips to take more of him into her, feeling something building, something so electric she had to close her eyes.

"Look at me," he said hoarsely, and she moaned but she did what he told her, finding it incredibly erotic when he mesmerized her with his eyes and began to move once more. He picked up the pace, and that rush of heat turned into a whipcord of male muscle, stamping her with each thrust of his body, taking everything she had within her. She offered it up to the one man in the world worthy of everything she had to give.

"Brant!" she cried as he rasped out her name in a strangled tone that said he couldn't hold on much longer either.

He kissed her then. A deep, deep kiss that was followed by a final plummet of his body as she arched against him.

They reached their climax together, holding themselves as one, in total sync at this precious moment in time.

Kia spiraled down to a hazy aftermath with a series of lingering kisses before he rolled over and held her in his arms for a few moments.

Then she watched his long, lean length disappear, as he rose and headed toward the bathroom. She lay back and closed her eyes. She had to, otherwise when he came back he would see something that had just hit her.

She had fallen in love with him.

Shock ran through her. She went hot, then cold. *She loved Brant Matthews.* She would love him until the day she died, even knowing she would never be enough for him. Dear God, this couldn't be…yet she knew it was, felt it in her heart.

The bed sank on one side and she scarcely dared to breathe. Brant was sitting beside her, waiting for her to look at him.

"Kia?" he murmured, tenderly pushing some strands of hair from her face.

She had no alternative but to look at him and pray that he didn't see what was so obvious to her now. How had she not seen this coming?

Her eyelids lifted, and her breath hitched in her throat at the look in his eyes. It was all-knowing. All male. Full of sexual satisfaction.

And he had no idea she loved him.

Thank God. She could breathe easier now and enjoy

their time together. That's all she'd let herself ask for. That's all she'd let herself want. It would be over soon enough. And if he ran true to form—as her father did with his women friends—having gotten what he'd wanted from her, she wouldn't be seeing much more of him after this anyway. She shivered. Already that thought cut through her heart.

"Did I hurt you?" he murmured.

"No." But he would. When he dumped her.

His shoulders relaxed, his mouth curving with sheer sensuality. "Woman, that was the best sex I've ever had."

Yes, that's all it came down to with Brant. She tried not to show her hurt. "Me, too."

"For all intents and purposes, you were a virgin." He leaned forward and gave her a long, slow kiss, then looked into her eyes. "I'm honored I was the first *man* to sleep with you." He kissed her again briefly, then leaned back, an odd look in his eyes. "Why?"

Her breath stopped and she realized he saw more than she'd thought. She licked her lips. "Because I…I mean, you…" She shrugged. "Well, what woman wouldn't want to make love with you?"

His mouth twisted. "Flattery will get you everywhere," he mocked, but she had the feeling he wasn't happy with her answer.

But if he expected a declaration of love, he was going to be disappointed. Maybe that's what his other women always provided, but she wasn't about to copy them. She swallowed hard at the thought of all those other women who would come after her. She couldn't bear to think about it. And she wasn't going to wait around for him to throw her away like some piece of garbage that was past its use-by date either.

Panicking, she sat up, almost knocking him out of the way. He put his hands on her shoulders, stilling her.

"What's the matter?" he said with a scowl.

"I'm going home." She tried to push him away, but he kept his body firmly in front of her.

Surprise came and went in his eyes before they flared with anger. "I won't let you run out on me, Kia."

"*You* won't let *me?*" she choked out. Did he think because he'd made her his own she would leave her brains at the door?

"I've already had one woman who mattered run out on me. I'm not going to let you do the same. Not yet, anyway."

She gave a soft gasp. A woman *who mattered* had run out on him? And she was in the same category? But what did he mean by mattered?

"Are you saying that I'm...that we...?" She tried to find the words to say it. "Is there something more between us than I think, Brant?"

He stood up, and she saw he had wrapped a white towel around his lower half. "You bet there's something between us. And we're going to see it through to the end."

The end. She shouldn't be surprised by his choice of words, yet she was. How could she love this devil of a man? Fate had certainly played a sick joke on her.

"Don't tell me what to do, Brant."

"If I told you everything I wanted you to do, you'd run for your life."

She got to her feet, wrapping the sheet around her as she did. "I don't need to run. I'm leaving anyway."

"I don't think so," he warned ominously.

Her heart jumped in her chest. "You can't stop me."

Can't I? his eyes said arrogantly. "Then you have nothing to lose by coming over here and kissing me like you mean it. Do that, and I'll even hold the door open for you on the way out."

She moistened her suddenly dry lips. "And if I don't?"

"Then I'll come over there and kiss you, and we'll see where it leads."

"What a choice," she muttered.

She swallowed. One kiss. Could she kiss him this one time and get away with it? She knew she would melt in his arms again. She knew she would want more. But hadn't she always prided herself on her strength of will?

Without stopping to think further, she pulled the sheet tighter and closed the distance between them. Then she went up on her toes and quickly kissed him on the mouth before turning away.

He grabbed her arm and spun her back toward him, his eyes holding a faint glint of humor. "Like you mean it, I said."

Somehow she'd known he wouldn't let her get away with that chaste peck. "Oh, but I did mean it like that," she mocked, even as a thrill raced through her. This time she'd give him exactly what he wanted and more. Then she'd walk out that door, put everything back on a business level and hope to God she could cope with knowing she'd fallen in love with a man who thought *woman* was a synonym for *sex*.

Her heart beating at full speed, she moved back toward him. In the split second before she put her lips to his, she saw his eyes darken and she realized she'd never once instigated a kiss with him. The other two Christmas kisses had been him coming to her, not the other way around. She felt thrillingly provocative.

She placed her mouth to his and began a kiss that gave him all the love she had inside her. Her stomach quivered even as she let her tongue slide around his mouth, then briefly dip between his slightly parted lips. She heard his groan deep within his throat, so she repeated the action, this time her tongue sliding over the top of his, tasting him, loving him.

The clean male scent of him exuded an attraction she found difficult to deny, and her arms slid up around his neck and cupped the back of his head, holding him to her, deepening the kiss. The sheet slipped down between them, and she felt the muscles of his chest tighten against her bare breasts. She rubbed herself against him, the feel of curly male hair teasing her nipples.

Suddenly he broke off the kiss with a guttural sound that made her think he had almost reached his limit. Then he swung her up in his arms and strode toward the bathroom.

"You're heading the wrong way," she murmured,

not really caring right now that she was supposed to be leaving and not coming back.

"No, I'm not. I know exactly where we're going."

They made leisurely love in the spa surrounded by tropical plants that gave a dreamy quality to the setting. Kia responded to Brant's instructions and sat on his lap facing him, with him inside her. It was an incredible experience. And the most brave. Face-to-face like that, she had to stop herself from crying out she loved him.

Then they made their way back to the bed, and she reveled in taking her time to explore his male body before he growled her name, rolled on top of her and made love to her all over again. Exhausted, they fell into a deep sleep.

The ringing of the telephone next to the bed woke them during the night. Kia groaned and pressed her cheek against Brant's bare chest, wanting to hold on to the euphoria, hoping the noise would go away so she could go back to sleep.

Vaguely she was aware of Brant reaching out an arm to pick it up. She heard the deep rumble of his voice as he answered it. Then, the next thing she knew, he'd jerked into a sitting position, throwing her off him.

"What the hell?" she heard him say as she lay on her back and came fully awake. "My God! Julia?"

There was silence for a moment as the person on the other end of the phone responded. Then Brant's gaze skidded to Kia and darkened. "Yes, I have company," he answered in clipped tones. He listened. "Now?" He looked at Kia again, then away. "Okay. Give me half an hour." He hung up and turned back to her. "I've got to go out for a while. Something's come up."

Yes, and her name is Julia.

"Don't worry, I understand. Totally."

His face hardened as he swung his legs over the side of the bed. "I didn't ask for your understanding."

That hurt. "Aren't you lucky I gave it anyway?" she snapped, throwing back the bedclothes.

"You don't have to leave."

Did he think she would wait for him to go to this woman, then come back to bed and make love to *her?*

"I don't want to stay."

A long moment crept by as she gathered her clothes from the floor.

"Then I'll walk you down to your car."

"Don't bother." She looked up and caught his eyes going hungrily over her naked body. A quiver surged through her veins and she wondered if she could stop him going to this Julia.

Then she realized what she was thinking and her lips tightened. Did she really want to compete with another woman? No, she'd had enough of watching her mother fight for her father's love.

Brant pulled on his trousers. "Nevertheless, I insist. It's late."

Yes, far too late, she thought, glancing at the clock and seeing it was two in the morning. It had been a mistake to make love to him. A beautiful mistake at the time but a mistake nevertheless.

In a damning silence they finished dressing, then he walked down with her to the underground car park.

"Call me as soon as you get home," he ordered, holding the car door open for her. "Use my cell phone number. I want to know you're safe."

She squashed the spark of warmth at his concern. He was only protecting what he thought was temporarily his. "I'll be fine."

"Call me," he warned, his dark gaze holding hers. "If you don't, I'll call you."

She didn't respond as she started the engine and drove out of the car park without looking back. Which is exactly what she'd have to do where he was concerned anyway. Walk away and not look back.

She was halfway home when something occurred to her. Was this Julia the woman who had "mattered"? Without a doubt she knew that she was. And obviously Julia *still* mattered or Brant would still be in bed with *her* right now.

Kia didn't call him when she got home. Worse, he didn't call her, and that made her heart sink more. Obviously she wasn't as important to him as Julia.

Kia got no sleep for the rest of the night and by morning she felt exhausted. Not even her usual shower, followed by a breakfast of sliced mango, nor a cup of coffee, could make her feel the slightest bit better.

If only she didn't love Brant. It would all be so much easier if he was the kind of man she thought might eventually love her in return. Only he wasn't. And he never would be. A leopard didn't change its spots. A womanizer didn't become trustworthy. The word *faithful* wasn't in his dictionary.

Phillip rang as she headed out the door. She'd decided to go to work early and get some of the paperwork typed and on Brant's desk before he came in. He was bound to be late, if he turned up at all.

"What do you think you're doing sending some woman to seduce me?" Phillip joked, his tone so heartbreakingly light that Kia had to smile.

"And did Lynette succeed?"

"Let's just say she surpassed all expectations." There was a slight hesitation. "How can we ever thank you for all you've done, Kia?" he said softly.

"Just be happy. That's all the thanks I want."

"We will. And we want you to come to the wedding in two months time. We would have scheduled it earlier, but I have to see one more doctor, then I'm all hers."

Kia knew she wouldn't want to go to the wedding. How could she bear seeing Brant in a social situation? Worse, with Julia by his side.

"I'll put it in my calendar."

"Speaking of calendars, aren't you supposed to be spending Christmas with your family in Adelaide? Lynette told me you were in the office yesterday."

She tried to think quickly without worrying him. "I did spend Christmas at home, but I got away early." She gave a light laugh. "Too much noise. Too many people. You know how holidays are."

"But you didn't have to go back to work so soon."

He paused. "Or is there a problem at the office I'm not aware of?"

"No, of course not," she assured him quickly. "I just popped in yesterday to pick up something I'd left behind, and Brant was there and needed something typed so I stayed."

A moment's silence, then he said, "Remind me to give you a bonus. Of course, most women think working with Brant would be bonus enough...." He trailed off suggestively.

"No doubt."

"I'll have to tell him, you know. About me and Lynette." He sounded worried. "You'll be open season after that."

She pretended to be unconcerned. "He already knows. He overheard Lynette and I talking yesterday."

"And?"

"And nothing." Time to go. "Phillip, I have an appointment and I'm running late."

"Oh, damn. I've just realized something. Word's bound to get out about you and I breaking up." He swore. "And I can't get back there just yet to help you."

"I'll manage." Phillip's idea of helping would probably make the situation worse anyway.

"But you're going to bear the brunt of it, Kia. Some people might think you dumped me because of my limp," he reminded her.

She pushed aside thoughts of what that journalist would say and knew there was only one answer. "Not if we're honest with them." Holding back the truth from everyone was of little value now anyway. "It's the best way to go."

He drew in a long breath. "Yes, you're right."

"Look, I really must be going."

"Kia?"

She stiffened. "Yes?"

"Are you sure you're okay?"

"Of course I am, Phillip. Thanks for asking. I'll talk to you soon." She quickly hung up so he wouldn't hear the catch in her voice. She couldn't bear that anyone else knew her feelings for Brant. As far as she was concerned, loving Brant was something so private, so personal, she couldn't share it with another soul.

Eight

Kia stepped out of the elevator at ten past eight and was tempted to tiptoe to her office just in case Brant was at his desk. But that would be acting like a coward, she decided, straightening her shoulders and striding down the hallway. The empty offices were quiet.

She reached Brant's door and glanced inside, her throat aching with defeat when she saw the room empty. Had she really thought he'd be at work? Dear God, how could he make love to her last night, then go to another woman? Her heart squeezed in anguish. It was morally wrong. So why was she surprised? Just because she loved him didn't change what he was.

Swallowing hard, she forced herself to continue to her office. She was beginning to have a new appreciation for the turmoil her mother had gone through with her father. She loved her mother dearly, but she'd never really understood how a woman could stay with a man who cared for her so little. She'd even sometimes thought of her mother as weak when it came to her father. Now she knew it had taken a special kind of blind loyalty to stay with him as long as she had.

An hour later Kia stretched, rose from her desk and went to stand at the window. She looked down at the sun-shadowed street below. The world continued to turn, but inside she felt dead, as if her heart had shriveled into a rock. She had to forget Brant, but she couldn't even summon the energy to do that right now. He still hadn't arrived. He was still with—

"Kia?"

She spun toward the sound. The heart she thought dead leaped to life. Brant stood in the doorway, dressed in a fresh set of clothes that made him look clean and vital and so disturbingly handsome that her knees turned weak.

She lifted her gaze to find him watching her with a knowing intensity that made heat surge into her cheeks. His look said she couldn't hide from him. That she was *his*.

Then reality kicked in and her stomach clenched tight. Physical closeness wasn't enough. It would never be enough. Her feelings for him ran too deep.

"I didn't think you'd be here so early," she said coolly, determined to keep her distance.

His eyes narrowed. "Why not?"

"I thought you'd be…preoccupied."

He started to close the gap between them. "Preoccupied with what?" he said silkily. "Or should I say *whom?*"

She managed a shrug. "With Julia, of course."

He stopped right in front of her. "Ah...you mean *in bed* with Julia, don't you?"

Did he have to rub it in? Was he getting some masochistic pleasure from pointing this out?

Her chin lifted. "Look, if you want to sleep with other women, that's fine. Just don't expect me to like it. Or to accept it. I won't share any man." She saw something flare in his eyes. "Julia's welcome to you," she ended in disgust.

There was a lethal calmness in his eyes. "So you're telling me to choose between you and Julia?"

"No, I'm telling you to choose between me and any other women you want to sleep with, *including* Julia."

"I don't take kindly to ultimatums. And I don't explain my actions to anyone." His arrogant gaze slid over her, pausing a moment on the swell of her breasts. "But for you, dear Kia, I'm going to relent on that last one. I did *not* sleep with Julia last night. The only woman I slept with was you, and then we got very little sleep, as I recall."

She wanted to believe him. Oh, how she wanted to. But how could she forget those nights listening to her mother's hushed accusations and her father's denials. Denials that had always proven to be lies.

She met his gaze with steely-eyed determination. "Very clever, Brant, but unlike some women, I don't believe everything I'm told. You say you didn't *sleep* with Julia. But you didn't deny having sex with her."

A shadow of anger swept across his face. "That's because I *didn't* have sex with her."

"I've heard *that* one before," she said, turning away.

He grabbed her by the shoulder and spun her back. "Listen. I am *not* your father."

She sucked in a sharp breath, stunned by his perceptiveness. Was she so transparent? Or did she subconsciously wear her thoughts blazoned across her back?

His hold tightened. "Kia, you once said you wouldn't apologize for him. Well, I'm not going to apologize for him either. Your father is a shallow man without integrity. Do you really think I'm like him?"

Her mind reeled in confusion. She'd never even considered the possibility that he *wasn't* like her father.

His jaw clenched. "You either believe me or you don't. It's your decision."

She stared up at him, trying to assess if he was telling the truth. If he was, then she'd have to reverse her opinion of him. That wasn't an easy thing to do.

She saw the strain in his eyes and etched around his nose and mouth. Suddenly she knew that if she didn't believe him, then it would be the end of them. He would shut her out of his life for good without a single regret.

And it was *that* very thing that made her admit he had a deep sense of personal integrity, unlike her father. She just hadn't let herself see it until now.

"I believe you," she said softly but firmly.

His chest rose and fell, but it was the flash of relief in his eyes that made her heart constrict. It overwhelmed her to know he really cared what she thought of him.

His fingers loosened on her shoulders. "Thank you," he said with a casual sort of dignity that was at odds with the arrogance just beneath the surface.

All at once she knew this was no longer just about her believing Brant.

"And now you've got to believe something about *me*," she said, taking this chance, knowing this was important to her. "I'm telling you truthfully that I'm *not* a gold digger, I've never worked anyone to get either money or marriage out of them and I'm not with *you* for money or marriage." She lifted her chin with clear determination, her heart slamming against her ribs. "You can choose to believe me or not."

He studied her face for more than one heartbeat, his eyes not leaving hers for a second, but she saw the jolt of surprise in them, the assessment of her words, a decision and finally the admiration.

"I believe you," he murmured, pulling her into his arms, holding her close, which was just as well because her knees had given way. The knowledge that he was seeing her as the person she was for the first time made her feel gloriously thankful.

He leaned back. "And for the record, just in case you think you're like your mother because you believe me like she did with your father, you're *not*. So you have no need to feel guilty."

She frowned. "Guilty?"

The sensual spread of his mouth made her heart hammer against her ribs. "For wanting me."

Her frown disappeared as her lips began to twitch. "Who said I wanted you?"

"I seem to remember a few whispered pleas in my ears last night," he murmured, lifting her hands and placing them around his neck. She didn't resist.

"Hey, that was me begging you to let me sleep."

"Oh, really? Perhaps we should repeat it tonight and see." His warm breath caressed her cheeks.

"Not tonight," she teased. "I'm busy."

"You'd better not have a date," he growled.

"I want to wash my hair."

"I'll wash it for you."

"Will you do my ironing, too?"

He chuckled and pulled her closer. "We can come to a compromise. Wear non-crushable clothes. Better yet, wear no clothes at all. It'll make for a very interesting evening."

Just the thought of how interesting it could be made her feel very sexy. "My place or yours?" she asked throatily, amazed at how easily she'd slipped into the role of seductress.

"Mine," he murmured, nuzzling her neck. Then he gave her a quick, hard kiss and let her go. "I've got a meeting in an hour with one of the Anderson executives. We'll continue this tonight. I'll pick you up at seven."

She was melting so fast she had to keep some independence. "I can drive myself."

"Fine, but don't plan on leaving early." He gave her

a smile that sent her pulse spinning. "In fact, I doubt I'll let you leave at all."

At seven-fifteen Kia found herself once again standing in front of Brant's penthouse. It was hard to believe she'd been here twenty-four hours ago, and even then she'd sworn to herself it was a one-off thing. Talk about making the same mistake twice. Talk about being a woman weakened by love.

When he opened the door, it was like opening the door to her heart. Everything inside her reached for him, enveloped him, made him hers. It was the oddest feeling, yet it felt so right.

He didn't say a word. He just stepped back and let her pass, then kicked the door shut with his foot, his hand sliding around her arm and turning her to face him. She had no idea how long they stood gazing at each other.

"Come here," he finally murmured and tugged her toward him. She went willingly, and his lips found hers, and she simply gave herself up to him and his touch. He made her feel whole. As if her world had been split in two until this moment and now the top and bottom half of her heart had been sealed with love. Her love for him.

Overwhelmed with emotion, wanting him, needing to touch him, she broke off the kiss and began undoing the buttons on his shirt, stripping it from his broad torso as he stood and watched her with a look in his eyes that seared through to her soul.

"Too much," she whispered, not just about him standing in front of her but about her feelings for him.

"Yes," he said brusquely, watching her as she placed her hands on his hair-roughened chest. She skimmed her palms over him and heard him groan, loving the feel of him and the scent of him. She inhaled deeply against his skin.

In one smooth motion she reached for his trousers and pulled down the zipper, freeing him. His erection was all male and challenged her to touch him more. He rasped her name as her hand slithered around him and gripped him, moving over his hard flesh, rousing his passion, rousing her own even more.

"Not yet," he muttered, grabbing her hand and moving her back from him. Then he stripped the clothes from her body with a quickness and hunger that astounded her before swinging her up in his arms and carrying her to bed, where he lay her down, then sheathed himself.

In one quick motion he entered her. And just like that she came. No slow crawl toward orgasm. No indulgent inching to reach the pinnacle of pleasure. Just a powerful, all-fulfilling climax that made her shudder and cry out his name.

And when she caught her breath, he was looking down at her with another one of those arrogantly satisfied looks on his face that somehow didn't offend her this time. It made her feel very womanly.

And in a womanly way, she lifted her body slightly, nudging him farther into her.

"Too much," he growled, repeating her words, and he began to move. Slow at first, then faster and faster, the muscles in his neck growing taut with strain. He allowed her to have one more glorious climax before groaning her name and plunging deeper into her, burning them both in a downpour of fiery sensation.

It was a long, long moment before either of them could breathe, let alone move. Brant was the first to stir, and all at once Kia didn't want him to leave her. She wanted to stay right here, like this, forever. She tightened her arms around his back and held him close against her. She heard the rumble of his voice, but her fingers couldn't seem to unlock themselves.

"Kia?" he repeated, giving a low, masculine laugh against her neck. "As much as I love being inside you, you've got to let me go sometime."

His words finally penetrated. Her fingers loosened. He was right. She was making a fool of herself.

He lifted his upper body away from her, his eyes sexily amused yet strangely serious. "What was that all about?"

She forced a slight smile. "Just faint with hunger. I haven't eaten much today," she admitted. She'd been too nervous to eat.

"Then you need food, woman," he teased. He gave her one brief, hard kiss, rolled off her and headed to the bathroom. She hardly had time to think before he was back carrying a white bathrobe.

"Here," he said, tossing the robe toward her, his gaze sweeping over her naked body with male appreciation before he disappeared.

She could get used to this, she decided as she stood

up and wrapped herself in the fluffy material, enjoying its warmth in the air-conditioned apartment, burying herself in its male scent.

Her eyes widened as he came back into the room wearing nothing but a pair of well-pressed jeans. Jeans, for heaven's sake. Brant Matthews in jeans? And black ones at that. Normally he dressed as the consummate businessman. In jeans he looked what he was—the ultimate female fantasy.

He caught her staring and his eyes smoldered back in return. "If you want me on the main menu, you only have to say so."

A delicious shudder heated her body. "Actually, I think I'd like to keep you for dessert."

"That can be arranged."

They ate dinner in the small, intimate dining room. Or perhaps it seemed intimate because of the casual way they were dressed—her in his bathrobe, him in jeans.

Or maybe it was the look in his eyes. She tried to keep her cool, but that knowing look heated her cheeks and made her want to follow him like a lamb back into the bedroom.

Suddenly panicked by her loss of willpower, she said the first thing that came to mind. "Tell me about Julia," she heard herself say, then bit back a groan of dismay, not meaning to bring up the other woman again.

Or had she? Julia still played on her mind. Oh, not because she believed Brant was having an affair with her any longer, but there was something there, something still not quite right.

His eyes hardened as he put his coffee cup down. "She's my sister-in-law."

"Your what! Why didn't you tell me? Why did you let me believe she was—"

"One of my women?" His mouth tightened. "She *was* one of my women. Then she ran off to marry my brother."

"What! Oh, Brant, I'm so sorry."

"Don't be. It ended up for the best."

She frowned, not so sure he really believed that. It obviously wasn't for the best that a woman who had mattered had left him for the one person in the world he should have been able to trust, his brother. He wouldn't be bitter about it otherwise.

"So why is she contacting you now?" she asked, almost afraid to hear the answer. Did the other woman want Brant back? Is this what all this was about?

His piercing blue eyes contrasted sharply with the shrug he gave. "She wants help with Royce. He can't handle the fact that Julia and I were once an item and he's developed a drinking problem over it. Julia asked me to speak to him and make him see sense."

A swell of relief filled her. "Did you?"

"No."

She stared at him in astonishment. "He's your brother, Brant."

"I know."

A shiver skittered under her skin. "Surely that means something?"

"Does it?"

This, more than anything, showed her exactly how

he would treat her when the time came. And come it would. When he tired of her.

Dear God, it stunned her to know how much she'd been fooling herself. Just because she'd admitted Brant had more integrity than her father didn't mean he'd suddenly turned into Mr. Nice Guy. When he wanted her out of his life, he'd take the appropriate measures to do exactly that. No exceptions.

Well, maybe one.

Julia.

"You're a coldhearted bastard," she muttered, her heart twisting painfully inside her.

His eyes turned as unreadable as stone. "Feel free to think what you like."

"Oh, I will," she said, holding his gaze, determined he knew she didn't appreciate this side of his character.

For a moment silence hung angrily in the air.

Then he said, "Tell me one thing, Kia. Do you think if you went to your father right now and told him how you feel about him, it would change the way he thinks?"

She frowned. "What's my father got to do with this?"

"You're asking *me* to go to my brother and change his mind. It's a similar situation. And it won't work."

"But how do you know unless you try?"

His eyes bored into her. "Did you try with your father?"

She blinked in surprise. "Yes, I did."

"And what happened?"

She blanched, remembering. "He wouldn't listen."

"Exactly."

She sighed. Brant had a point.

His eyes softened. "Look, my uncle was an alcoholic. It ruined his family even before he killed himself and my aunt in a car accident while he was driving drunk. So don't you see? I *know* I can talk until I'm blue in the face and it won't change how my brother feels. I *know* I can get his promise that he'll get help, and tomorrow he'll break it. No, he has to want to seek help for himself. Not expect his wife to fix it for him. Or me."

Kia heard the rough edge of emotion in his voice and knew he wasn't as cold as he made out. "You're right."

He stood and pulled her up into his arms, his eyes darkening. "I don't want to argue anymore. I want to make love to you. Let's forget the rest of the world tonight."

"But—"

"Enough," he murmured, undoing her belt to slide his hands inside the robe and over the bare skin of her hips.

Hypnotized by his touch, she tingled under his fingertips. Greedily she gave herself up to him and to whatever he wanted to do to her.

"You need another lesson in some loving, Ms. Benton," he said, nuzzling her neck beneath the collar of her bathrobe.

She gasped with delight as his hands slid up her rib cage and cupped her breasts.

He leaned back. "Good. That's lesson number one completed."

Her breath caught in her throat as he squeezed her nipples, his touch sending shock waves to every nerve center in her body. "Er...number one?"

"Always respond when I touch you."

That was easy. "What's…number two?"

"Always say my name when I'm inside you."

She moaned as his hands slid up to her shoulders. "And if I don't?"

"Then we start over until you do," he murmured, pushing the robe off her shoulders and letting it fall to the carpet.

She licked her lips. "I was always a quick learner."

His eyes devoured her. "That's too bad."

"Why?"

"I was looking forward to teaching you the next lesson," he said huskily.

Her body was heavy with warmth. "Um…next lesson?"

"Lesson number three. How to get a man to kiss you all over."

She shuddered. And suddenly she wanted to know what *he* tasted like. What he would feel like against her tongue. "Do I get to reciprocate?"

His eyes darkened dangerously. "Only if you want to."

"Oh, I do."

"Then that'll be lesson number four," he murmured, rubbing a thumb across her lips.

"When do we start, teacher?"

"Now is as good a time as any," he drawled and pulled her closer.

Her mouth parted the instant his lips met hers and he kissed her with a hunger that shocked her. It was as if it had been years since they'd been together instead of a mere half hour.

He kissed a path down to her breasts, anointing each one with his mouth before going down on his knees and kissing her intimately through the curls at her thighs. His tongue flicked over the hot, moist core of her, and she gasped his name out loud, grasping his head to her as his tongue did marvelous things to her over-sensitized body.

"Come inside me," she implored, her hands pulling at his head to make him stop before she spilled over the edge. "Please, Brant."

He paused briefly. "Soon," he promised and returned to what he was doing, making her legs weaken as she melted around him, shuddering with intensity, suspended in time.

When he swung her up in his arms and carried her into the shower, her brain felt clouded, her body thoroughly seduced. He kissed her back to life and then led her into the bedroom.

"I want to please you like you pleased me, Brant," she murmured, following him down on the bed.

His eyes smoldered. "Are you sure you're ready?"

"Absolutely."

So he told her in explicit terms how a man liked to be made love to. She didn't need much encouragement as she kissed his chest, letting her mouth move all over him, and downward through the arrow of hair on his taut stomach, until she covered the tip of his erection with her lips.

"Kia," he growled her name as she began her own lesson in loving that had nothing to do with experience and everything to do with womanly instinct. She wanted him. *All* of him. And she almost got it.

Until he pulled her head up and away from him with a growl. "No," he muttered tightly, twisting to reach a condom on the bedside table. A few seconds later he rolled her beneath him and plunged inside her in one swift motion, quickly reigniting the fuse of desire inside her, plunging deeper and deeper until both of them shattered together in a sea of sensual pleasure.

Afterward she lay with her cheek resting against his chest. She had to ask, "Why, Brant? I wanted to."

He kissed the top of her head. "I know, but you weren't ready to take such a step, as good as you were."

"But…"

"Sweetheart, let me be the judge of that," he murmured sleepily.

Kia tilted her head back to look at the angular contours of his face. She loved the inherent strength in his features. That firm thrust of his jaw. Those undeniable lips. But she had to wonder exactly *who* wasn't ready for a full sexual commitment. The man who knew the score? Or the woman who supposedly didn't?

Brant waited for Kia's soft breath to tell him she was asleep before he opened his eyes and looked down at her naked body entwined with his. She was so beautiful. So bloody gorgeous.

And she was the only woman he hadn't let "go all the way." He wasn't sure why, but he did know he couldn't let her do what other women had done for him. Maybe because she'd asked first instead of taken. No other woman had ever asked. Not even Julia.

Not that it wouldn't have given him pleasure. It would have. Intense pleasure. But being with Kia wasn't about mere physical pleasure anymore. Deep down he'd known that all along but today when she'd stood her ground, forced him to admit she wasn't the gold digger he thought she was, something inside his chest had shifted. He just hadn't realized how profoundly she touched him. Yet it wasn't love. No, never that. He'd had one kick in the guts from a woman. He'd never let that happen again. Not even if she asked.

Nine

The next morning the telephone rang as soon as Kia stepped inside her house. Thinking it was Brant calling to tease her why she was late for work, she laughed softly and raced to answer it on legs that almost flew across the living room. For the first time she felt almost happy to be in love.

"How's my beautiful girl then?" a booming male voice came down the line.

The animation died on her face. Dear God, why did her father have to call now?

She forced herself to relax. "Hello, Dad."

"You sound disappointed. Not expecting anyone else to call, were you? One of your many boyfriends, no doubt."

"I've never been one for many boyfriends," she said

as calmly as she could. She wasn't like *him*. She didn't need adoration every minute of the day.

"A man friend then. Is it serious?"

"How are things, Dad?" Her feelings for Brant were private.

He chuckled. "That's my darling girl. Don't tie yourself down until you're at least thirty. Until then, have a good time. A really good time, if you know what I mean."

"Oh, I will." Kia's heart ached. Her father had really sunk to a new low.

"Anyway," he continued. "I'm in Darwin for a couple of days on business and I thought we might have brunch together today."

"Brunch?"

"Yeah. I want to see if you're still as charming as ever."

"And if I'm not?" she quipped to hide her hurt.

"Then I'll trade you in," he joked and laughed out loud as if it was the funniest thing in the world.

Moisture filmed her eyes and she squeezed her eyelids shut. Thank heavens he couldn't see her.

"What do you say then, darling girl? Coming to see your old man for an early lunch?"

She blinked rapidly and took a deep breath. He didn't really care if he saw her or not, so she should tell him flat out no. Then it occurred to her—if she went, she could dispel any lingering doubts that Brant was like him. He really wasn't, she knew that, but why not take this opportunity to put it behind her once and for all?

"Will Amber be there?" she asked. It wouldn't be a

pleasant lunch if the other woman attended. Not when her father's third wife was childishly jealous of her. Of course, Amber *was* half her father's age.

"No. I told her to stay in Sydney."

Kia's heart sank. So their marriage was on the rocks already. How sad. "Where and when?"

He named a restaurant in the heart of the city. She would have preferred to lunch at his hotel, but there was no chance of that. Her father liked to be seen when he was in town.

She laid the receiver on the cradle, then picked it up again, intending to call Brant and tell him why she wouldn't be in until later. Hearing his voice would be reassuring.

Then she remembered the invisible barrier he'd put up between them in bed last night and she stirred with sudden uneasiness. Perhaps it was best they both kept some distance.

Brant was just about to reach for the telephone for the tenth time when he heard the soft ping of the elevator door opening onto the executive floor.

Intense relief washed over him. It had to be Kia. Thank God nothing had happened to her. He'd already driven over to her place once this morning, to find out why she hadn't turned up at work after leaving his place earlier, and found no one at home. Her Porsche hadn't been in the driveway either. It had scared him silly, and that's something he didn't like to feel.

Bloody hell, he was going to demand an explanation, he decided, striding to the door, growing angry because she'd put him through this. He couldn't even think of an explanation that would satisfy him right now. Not unless...

His heart stopped, then began to thud like the deafening sound of tropical rain. Could she be seeing someone else? Was it possible so soon? Even Julia hadn't been quite that quick to run off with his brother.

With his gut tied up in knots, he reached the door...only it wasn't Kia coming toward him. It was Flynn Donovan.

Brant swore.

"That's a nice way to greet an old friend," Flynn mocked as he approached.

Brant grimaced. "Sorry, mate. I wasn't swearing at you."

Flynn's dark brows lifted. "Then who?"

"It doesn't matter." He planted a wry smile on his face, trying to appear nonchalant. "This *is* an honor," he said, turning back into his office and going to stand in front of the window. He glanced down at the street below, hoping to see...

"Is it?"

Realizing his friend knew him too well and had astutely picked up on some of his anxiety, Brant spun around. "What are you doing here, Flynn?" he said, gesturing for him to sit on the leather couch.

But the other man remained standing, his finely tailored suit reflecting the successful businessman that he was, the watchful look in his eyes one that no doubt his competitors in the boardroom had seen many times. "I've come to ask why you haven't been returning my calls. I thought we were supposed to get together over Christmas."

Brant gave a short laugh. "That's a bit hard to do when you were in Japan and Damien was in the States."

"I was back for Christmas, and Damien will be here tomorrow. But that's not the point. The fact is you've been avoiding us."

Brant walked to his desk and dropped down on the chair. "I've been busy."

"Haven't we all?"

Brant silently swore to himself, not liking being under the microscope. It was okay when he got together with his friends and they ribbed each other mercilessly about other things, but this was about Kia, and she was no joke.

"Well, I've been extra busy." He decided to throw Flynn a crumb to satisfy him for now. "You remember how Phil had his accident?" Flynn gave a nod. "He almost lost us a major account. I've been working double time just to set things right."

A sharpening look from Flynn said he'd taken the bait. "Anything I can help you with?"

"Thanks, no. I've got it all under control now," he said, relaxing a little, then darted a look at the door when he thought he heard the sound of the elevator.

"You seem kind of jumpy," Flynn said, and Brant realized his friend hadn't been fooled at all.

He shrugged. "I'm just waiting for Phillip's PA to arrive."

"Kia Benton?"

Brant sucked in a lungful of air. "You know Kia?"

"No, but I saw her at a couple of functions with Phil. She's a stunner. I wouldn't mind dating her for a bit. No wonder Phil—"

"Shut it, Flynn!"

For a moment there was silence.

Then Flynn spoke. "What's she mean to you, Brant?"

"Nothing."

Flynn's lips twisted. "Come on, mate. I know when you're lying through your teeth."

"We're lovers."

Another moment's silence. Then Flynn said, "Does Phil know?"

"No, but he wouldn't be too concerned if he did." Brant briefly explained the part about Kia pretending to be Phillip's fiancée. He left out the bit about him thinking she was a gold digger, which was just as well. If she was playing him for a fool, she'd regret it, he vowed, swallowing a hard lump in his throat.

"So this is about you bedding a beautiful woman because you thought she was out of reach and then she wasn't?"

"Yes."

Flynn gave a sardonic laugh. "Pull the other one, mate. I've known you all your life. There's more to you and Kia Benton than you're letting on. Am I right?"

Brant swore, hating being so obvious. "You're a son of a bitch," he said through half-gritted teeth.

"And how does she feel about you?" Flynn said, ignoring the tension coming out of his friend.

"How the hell do I know?"

"Perhaps you'd better do some fast talking or you might just find the lady will be snatched out from under you."

"Is that a threat?" Brant growled.

"Don't be stupid. All I'm saying is that she's a beautiful woman. She'd be a nice trophy for some men."

The thought of Kia being any man's trophy made him feel ill. "She wouldn't be interested."

"Really?" Flynn said in disbelief. "Let's see, a man could offer a woman like her riches beyond her imagination, travel across the globe, luxury like she's never seen before—and you're saying she wouldn't be interested? Get a grip, mate. Most women wouldn't be able to help themselves."

Brant stabbed his friend with his eyes, not appreciating having it spelled out like this. "When did you get to be so cynical?"

Flynn Donovan's eyes took on an odd glitter. "When I made my first million."

A couple of hours later Kia wondered how she'd ever thought Brant was like this man. The only thing the two men had in common was their gender. Brant may have a thing about commitment, but if he ever did fully commit to a woman, she knew it would be forever. And Brant's children would know they were loved for who they were, not for what they looked like. Brant was nothing like Lloyd Benton. Thank God.

It was a relief to get away from her father. Now, more than ever, she appreciated loving Brant. It was a privilege to love him, even if he would soon break her heart.

So she was surprised and delighted to see the gray Mercedes parked out front of her house when she got home just after midday, needing to collect some papers before going into the office. She parked in the driveway, almost falling over herself getting out of the car and into his arms.

Only, after a couple of steps toward him, she realized something was wrong. Her steps faltered. A sick feeling rolled inside her stomach. "Brant?"

"Where have you been?" he said in an ominously low voice.

"Wh-what?"

"I came around two hours ago to look for you."

"You did?" Oh, how she would have preferred being with him.

His eyes hardened. "Where have you been all this time?"

She stiffened, her own anger beginning to mount. If he'd asked nicely, she would have answered nicely. As it was, she didn't like his possessive tone. Or the implication that she belonged to him. She wasn't even sure where this was coming from.

She sent him a glare even as she squashed a queasiness rising inside her. "I didn't realize I had to get your approval to go out."

His eyes impaled her. "If I'm being faithful to you, then you can bloody well be faithful to me."

She gasped. "Faithful? Who said anything about being *un*faithful?"

"If you've got nothing to hide, then why not just say where you've been?"

"It's the principle of the thing, Brant. You don't own me. I'm not your puppet to say and do what you please. You wouldn't like me if I was." Her lips twisted. "I'm a challenge, remember? Or I *was*."

His mouth tautened. "You still haven't told me where you've been."

"None of your damn bus—" All at once, nausea swelled in her throat. She felt clammy. Her head began to swirl. She grabbed hold of him to balance herself.

"Kia?" he said as if from a long way off. "What's the matter?"

"I feel…sick."

"Damn," he muttered, swinging her up in his arms. "Let's get you inside."

She wanted to tell him not to move too fast, but he seemed to sense that. He was surprisingly gentle as he carried her to the door and logged in the security code she managed to tell him before carrying her into the bedroom.

He went to lay her on the bed, but she motioned for him to take her into the bathroom instead. Somehow she found the strength to push him out of the room in case she lost her lunch. Luckily she didn't, and after a short while she began to feel a bit better.

After splashing water on her face, she looked up and jumped when she saw him standing there with a towel in his hand. Gratefully she accepted the cloth and began dabbing it against her cheeks.

His gaze went over her in concern. "Feeling better?"

"A little."

"Let's get you to bed."

She began to shiver. "I'm okay."

"Yeah, I can see that." He gave her a hand into the bedroom.

"You shouldn't have stayed," she mumbled as he helped her lay down on the bed.

"Why not?"

"I can take care of myself."

He covered her with a light blanket, but his look told her what he thought of that comment. "Rest. I'll be back in a minute." He left the room before she could ask where he was going.

A short time later she was back in the bathroom. And this time she *did* disgrace herself but was too sick to feel mortified with Brant's hands on her head, holding back her hair. When she'd finished, she rinsed her mouth, then he carried her back to bed, where she lay against the pillows.

She closed her eyes for a moment, and the next thing she knew was Brant gently shaking her awake. "Kia, wake up. The doctor's here."

She groaned and opened her eyes to find Brant and a strange middle-aged man standing beside her bed.

"How do you feel now, Ms. Benton?" the doctor asked.

She tried to sit up but fell back against the pillows. "Like my stomach's seasick."

"I'd better examine you." He glanced at Brant. "Perhaps you'd like to wait outside?"

"Perhaps not," Brant said, an inflexible look on his face that said he wasn't budging.

The doctor arched a brow at Kia. "Do you mind?"

Her eyes darted to Brant. It wouldn't matter if she did. "No."

"Right. Then let's take a look at you."

He examined her for a few minutes, then put his stethoscope away. "There's a stomach bug going around. I'd like to rule out food poisoning, though. Have you eaten anything today?"

"She had breakfast with me," Brant said before she could speak. "And I feel fine."

The doctor nodded. "That's good. What about lunch? Did you eat together?"

Brant's gaze stabbed her. "No."

Kia wanted to groan. There was no getting around this. "I had something to eat in town," she said and saw Brant's shoulders tense.

The doctor frowned. "Hmm. Did you eat with anyone else? If you did, we'd better contact that other person and see if they're feeling okay. If they're not, we'll have to let the authorities know straightaway."

Kia glanced at Brant, who glared back in waiting silence. It was just as well she *wasn't* having an affair with anyone else. She'd be caught out otherwise. Not that she'd live to tell the tale.

"I had brunch with my father." She named the restaurant. "If you need to contact him, his cell phone number is written down near my phone."

"I'll call him now," Brant said, heading for the door, but not before she caught a glimpse of relief in his eyes. Her heart jolted painfully. He really *had* believed she was capable of an affair.

She was still mulling over that fact when he came back in the room.

"He's fine," he said, the unreadable look on his face telling Kia her father had been his usual irksome self but that Brant wasn't going to say anything about it to her. She swallowed a lump in her throat, suddenly overwhelmed by a strange feeling of relief. Brant truly didn't think any the less of her because of her father. In her heart, she hadn't been sure.

"Good," the doctor said, closing his medical bag with a snap. "I'll leave you something for the nausea."

"Thank you, Doctor," Brant said, then shortly after escorted the older man out of the bedroom.

A few minutes later he came back with a glass of water and a couple of the pills the doctor had given her. He helped her sit up while she took them, then laid her back against the pillows and tenderly pushed some blond strands of hair off her cheek.

Yet, oddly, his gesture brought to mind the time she had chicken pox and her father hadn't been able to hide his distaste at her appearance. Suddenly she felt self-conscious.

"I must look a mess," she said apologetically and tried to pat her hair in place.

He stared at her for a moment, then something flickered in the back of his eyes. "Never," he muttered, swinging away from her. He picked up the glass of water and took it into the bathroom.

Her heart jumped in her throat. She had the feeling he meant what he said. And if that were the case… No, she wouldn't get her hopes up.

He came back in the room, then straightened the light blanket over her. Suddenly he put his hand under her chin, making her look at him. "Why didn't you tell me you met with your father?"

Even feeling sick didn't stop the tingle that shot through her at his touch. "You're relentless, aren't you?"

"When I want something, yes."

She scarcely dared to breath. "And what do you want, Brant?"

"A straight answer."

She noted that's what he wanted from *her*, yet *he* wasn't giving any himself.

"You don't own me," she said quietly, feeling they were walking on dangerous ground. "Is that straight enough for you?"

He dropped his hand from her chin, then moved back from her, his expression inscrutable. "Get some rest. I'll stay and make sure you're okay."

"There's no need."

"Yes, there is." He left the room without further explanation.

***

Kia woke a couple of hours later and the nausea had gone, though she still felt a little headachy.

"I see you're awake," Brant said, lounging against the doorway.

She jumped in fright, then let out a slow breath as her gaze went over him. At least there was nothing wrong with her eyes. She could still appreciate how handsome he was. "You stayed?"

"I had to make sure you didn't collapse again."

"I didn't collapse the first time."

"No, but you would've if I hadn't been here to help you inside the house."

Her mouth tightened. "Perhaps if I hadn't been accosted in the driveway I would have been inside before I felt sick."

He straightened and walked toward her. "Don't hide anything from me, Kia. You'll find it's not worth it in the long run."

Suddenly she felt too weak to argue. Anyway, she couldn't tell him she loved him, no matter what. He wouldn't want to know. Not after his reaction last night when he'd held himself back from her. *That* more than anything proved he wasn't ready for a serious relationship.

As if satisfied that he'd gotten his message across, he walked over to the window and looked out. "I think we should go away for a few days."

She blinked in surprise. "Wh-what? With you?"

He turned to face her. "It had better not be with anyone else," he drawled.

The thought of having Brant to herself sounded wonderful. "Do you have a place in mind?"

"I have a house in the wilderness about an hour's drive south of here. I like to escape there every so often. It has enough luxuries to keep any woman happy."

Her bubble burst. How many other women had he taken to this house of his? "Sounds fine to me," she said stiffly.

His expression softened. "Kia, I've never taken another woman there, I promise. I want to get *away* from people when I go there."

Relief filled her. "When do you plan on going?"

"Tomorrow, if you're up to it. I have a couple of things to finish first, then we'll leave mid-afternoon. You just stay in bed and get yourself better. I'll swing by and pick you up around two."

For once, she would do what she was told. She didn't want anything spoiling these few precious days away with the man she loved. It would be moments like those she would always treasure.

The next morning Kia felt more alive than she'd ever been. All lingering nausea had disappeared during the night, and now she was ready to face the world. In fact, today she would *embrace* it. And for the next couple of days she would revel in her love for Brant. He need never know.

But first she'd drive into the office and leave a note for Evelyn, in case the other woman decided to pop in during the next week to check things over. Knowing

Evelyn and the way she took her job seriously, she would want to make sure there were no problems.

And deep inside, Kia couldn't wait until this afternoon to see Brant. Her heart was full of love for him. So full she was almost bursting.

Her steps light and buoyant, she stepped from the elevator and headed down the hallway to Brant's office. Not only were her steps light but her whole body—as though she could float to Brant's office....

"You've got it all wrong, Royce," Brant's voice warned from inside the office.

A feeling of apprehension shivered down Kia's spine and she stopped dead. Royce? Wasn't that Brant's brother?

"So you deny meeting Julia on numerous occasions?" the other man demanded with all the menace of a tiger about to pounce.

"No, I don't deny it," Brant answered, his tone firm. "But it's not what you think."

Royce gave a harsh laugh. "Yeah, right. I heard her calling you on the phone, telling you she needed you."

"To talk. That's all."

"At a hotel?"

There was a moment's damning silence, and Kia's breath caught sharply in her throat. She prayed there was some sort of mix-up. She waited for Brant to speak, to explain....

"There are other reasons for being at a hotel," he finally said, and Kia's heart sank at his detached tone. What other reasons? *Please, Brant, tell us.*

"I'm not a fool," Royce snapped, obviously unconvinced, too. "I took away your fiancée and now you want her back."

"Don't be so bloody stupid. Julia loves—"

"Stay away from my wife or you'll be sorry. I don't care if you *are* my brother."

Kia felt as though her legs had been cut from under her. Julia had been Brant's *fiancée?* They'd been *engaged?* Had been contemplating *marriage?* And Brant hadn't bothered to tell her.

A lead weight settled in the pit of her stomach. Dear God, it showed how little he thought of her. She was just another one of the harem. Oh, what a fool she was. An absolute idiot. Brant was no different than her father. She had believed Brant because she'd *wanted* to believe him.

She needed to get away. Be alone. She whirled around to leave, but then Brant spoke again. Her heart pounded. His voice sounded closer. He was going to come out of his office and at any moment he'd catch her eavesdropping.

"You're jumping to conclus—" He followed his brother through the doorway, stiffening when he saw her. "Kia!"

She swallowed, her gaze going from Brant to his brother. Somehow seeing Royce Matthews in the flesh made the accusations, the possibility of Brant's affair with Julia, more concrete. The younger man wore a business suit and looked rich and successful, and perhaps it was empathy, but in that split second she could see past the anger to the shadows under his eyes, to the bone-deep misery emanating from every pore of his skin. And she knew how Brant's brother felt.

Betrayed.

"Remember what I said, Brant," Royce warned, then strode past her and toward the elevator.

For a long moment Kia stared at Brant, trying to hold on to her composure. She heard the elevator door open with a whoosh, then close. And she knew this was the end for them. Utterly and totally. Anguish ripped her heart apart. The feeling was far worse than she'd expected.

Yet somehow, dear God, she had to face him with dignity. Experience with her father had taught her how.

She forced her expression to turn cool. "I have to get something from my desk."

Brant watched her in tight-lipped silence for a moment. "You should have phoned. I would have collected it for you."

"Perhaps it's better this way," she said pointedly and saw his gaze narrow.

Finding strength in her legs was difficult, but she managed it. She stepped past him.

He put his hand on her arm, stopping her. "What's the matter?"

She looked down at his arm, afraid to show him her eyes…and the pain that must be there. "Nothing."

"So you're all packed?"

"No." She shrugged off his hand.

"No?" he repeated, his tone hardening. "Why not?"

She looked up, unable to stop herself from spitting fire.

"I'm not going away with you, Brant. I've decided I've got too much self-respect to play second fiddle to Julia."

His jaw tautened. "I presume you heard Royce and I talking just now?"

"Yes."

"And you think Julia and I are having an affair?"

"That pretty well sums it up."

A sudden chill hung in the air. "Really?"

"I know what I heard." She went to spin away.

But he held her back. "What if I said you mean more to me than Julia ever did?"

A lump lodged in her throat. "Then why didn't you tell me about your engagement?"

A muscle flicked at his jaw. "It wasn't important."

"It is to me."

"Look, what Julia and I had—"

"Is none of my business," she finished for him. "Yeah, I get the point. I guess your brother does, too."

His eyes darkened. "Royce isn't thinking straight."

"Gee, I wonder why?" Her lips twisted. "Or maybe it's because of his *drinking* problem," she said with sarcasm.

His gaze stabbed her. "You think I lied about that?"

"How else could you hide your affair from me?"

Cold dignity descended over his face. "I'm only going to say this one more time. Royce *does* have a drinking problem, whether you believe me or not."

Oh, how she wished she could. But the evidence spoke otherwise. "Then why didn't you tell him that was the reason you've been meeting his wife?"

His jaw went rigid. "There's more to it than that."

"More?"

His eyes flicked away from her. "That's all I can say."

Because he was guilty. Guilty of loving his brother's wife. Just thinking about it squeezed pain through Kia's heart.

"None of this matters now anyway, Brant. It won't work between us. It's never going to work. I won't be second best."

Without warning, he grabbed her and kissed her hard. It was like kissing a stranger.

Until he softened it. And for a split second she turned boneless. The moment she did, he broke off the kiss.

"Does that kiss feel like you're second best?" he demanded, still holding her shoulders so she couldn't escape.

"Yes," she whispered. "That kiss was about *you*, not me."

He swore. "Kia, don't be so damn—"

"Let it go, Brant. Let *me* go. There's nothing more to be said." It was over. The end had come sooner than expected.

"Kia, it's not—"

Just then, the elevator doors opened and a female voice cried out Brant's name. Kia heard him take a harsh breath, and her head snapped around to see a slim blonde fly past her and into Brant's arms, her face pale.

"Oh, Brant, he was here, wasn't he?"

Brant's arms wrapped around the other woman even as his gaze flickered to Kia. She saw a flash of despair in his eyes, and a hot ache grew in her throat.

This man loved Julia so much he was willing to fight his brother for her.

Then he pulled back slightly and looked down at the exquisite features surrounded by a golden mist of hair. "Julia," he said softly. "We need to talk."

Tears glistened in Julia's eyes. "Darling, what are we going to do?"

Kia couldn't stand it any longer. These two people belonged together. She had to get out of there. Had to somehow put Brant out of her life. And her heart.

"Kia," he growled just as she was about to twirl on her heels.

She pasted on a false smile. "I won't stay, Mr. Matthews. I can see you've got your hands full."

Then she rushed toward the elevator. The last thing she saw before the doors closed was Brant leading the woman he loved into his office. Kia's knees buckled and she leaned against the elevator wall. She had never felt more devastated in her life.

Ten

Kia went straight home and packed a small bag, then tossed it in the car and drove off. She had to get away from here and she didn't care where.

She'd lost Brant. Lost him to the one woman she could never compete with. The one woman who had "mattered." He'd only wanted *her* body until Julia was free to love him again. He'd never wanted *her* heart.

But she'd given it anyway.

And Julia would soon be free. Brant and Royce would fight over her some more, but in the end Brant would win, of course. Then he and Julia would celebrate with champagne and caviar and they'd make love with so much emotion it would bring tears to Julia's eyes.

Kia swallowed a sob. The pain cut too deep to cry. She

just hoped Julia never found out what sort of man Brant really was. A man who loved one woman but thought nothing of sleeping with others to satisfy his sex drive.

Being at the northern tip of Australia, Darwin wasn't an easy place to leave on the spur of the moment, not with thousands of kilometers of desert between it and the southern major cities.

So for two hours Kia sat on Casuarina Beach and tried to think where she could go to lick her wounds. Eventually an approaching tropical thunderstorm made her look up, and she saw a billboard for one of the large hotels nearby. She made the decision to stay there for a few days instead.

She spent those days sitting on the balcony or walking along the beach, the breeze off the ocean providing a refreshing relief from the high humidity caused by the monsoon rains. In the evening she forced herself to eat in the restaurant and even managed to smile at people as if her heart weren't breaking and the food she was eating didn't taste like plastic. It all meant nothing without Brant.

But eventually she had to pull herself together and get on with her life. Tomorrow she would go home and pick up the pieces. She could do it. She had to.

But first she had to make her weekly phone call to her mother and pretend she was home and nothing out of the ordinary had happened. She was already overdue with the call.

"Darling, where are you?" her mother said the instant Kia spoke. "Are you okay?"

Kia's fingers tightened around the telephone. "I'm fine, Mum. Why?"

"We've been so worried. Brant's been looking for you and—"

She sank to the bed. "B-Brant?"

"Your boss, darling. Remember?"

Oh, she remembered all right. That's all he was to her now. One of her bosses. Soon to be ex-boss.

"He said you'd gone away for a few days but he didn't know where." Her mother paused. "We were really worried about you, sweetie. You never mentioned going away."

"It was a spur-of-the-moment thing, Mum," Kia said, feeling guilty for not calling sooner. Then she thought of Brant and her heart began to thump harder. "Do you know what he wanted?"

"He didn't say. I assumed it was another problem at work he needs your help with. He seemed quite upset about it, whatever it was."

Brant upset? He should be ecstatic now he was back with the woman he loved. She frowned. Or perhaps there really was a problem at work? Yes, that would be more likely.

"Anyway, darling, he asked me to call him the minute I heard from you. Where are you staying? If you give me the telephone number, I'll get him to call you."

"Mum, I'd prefer not to say," Kia said quietly. Brant would charm the information out of her mother if she told her. "I'm having a holiday and—"

"Darling, this isn't like you to just run off. I know

you're a grown woman and all, and some things mothers probably shouldn't know, but I'll always be here for you if you want to talk."

Kia blinked back tears. "Thanks, Mum. I know that. I just needed some time by myself, that's all."

A moment's silence ticked by. Then her mother spoke. "This isn't about work, is it? It's about Brant."

"Yes," Kia murmured. She took a shaky breath. "But please don't say anything to him. I'll call him shortly to see if there really is a problem at work. And I'll be going home tomorrow anyway. I'll call you then. I might even come down to Adelaide for a week after that." Suddenly she needed to go home. It would be for the best. Her mother, more than anyone, would understand her pain.

"Darling, you're always welcome here. You know that. Please call me tomorrow. I'll worry otherwise."

"I promise."

"And call Brant now. It may be important."

"I will." Kia hung up the telephone and stared at the wall. So he was upset, was he? Did he think she'd do something crazy just because he loved another woman? She wasn't that stupid. She was heartbroken, but life would go on.

Taking a deep breath, she picked up the phone again and dialed the number for his office. He answered on the first ring.

Just hearing his voice constricted her heart. Oh, God. How was she ever going to forget him?

"Kia?" he said when she didn't immediately announce herself.

"Yes." She swallowed hard then cleared her throat. "Yes, it's me."

"Thank God!" He paused. "Where the hell have you been?"

"On holiday."

He swore under his breath. "You've had everyone worried about you."

Anger hardened her voice. "They wouldn't have been if you hadn't called my mother."

"I had to see if you were there."

"Why, Brant? It's over."

"Don't be ridiculous. It's far from over. Not by a long shot."

She gasped. "If you think I'm going to carry on an affair with you behind—"

"Look, we can't talk about this over the telephone. Tell me where you are and I'll come to you."

"No," she said with a catch in her voice. In the flesh, he'd seduce her with more than words.

"Kia, I'm beginning to lose patience." He took a deep breath. "Please listen. This is important. I need to see you. I want to feel my arms around you and—"

"My God. Isn't one woman enough for you? Go to Julia, Brant. She'll be waiting for you."

"Dammit, there is no—"

"I'll come to the office tomorrow. Until then, just accept that I'm the one who got away. Goodbye, Brant."

"Kia, don't hang up. I'll—"

She carefully placed the phone in its cradle.

Whatever he'd do to her would have to wait until tomorrow. It still wouldn't change her mind.

At exactly noon Kia stepped out of the elevator and strode toward Brant's office. She'd come straight from the motel, dressed in a mauve knit top, white jeans and sandals. She'd never dressed so casually at the office before. Never even contemplated it. It was kind of freeing.

Just like the letter of resignation in her hand.

Of course, telling herself she should be feeling free was different to actually *feeling* free. That would come with time. Dear God, she hoped so.

For now, she had to face Brant and get it over with. Then she'd put one foot in front of the other and march out that door and out of his life.

She squared her shoulders just before she stepped in the open doorway, but it didn't stop the impact of seeing him sitting at his desk while he studied some paperwork in front of him. He looked so handsome. So...Brant.

For one precious moment she didn't think she had the strength to do this. But she had to. For God's sake—for *her* sake—she had to stay strong.

He looked up and their eyes met. And in that split second her heart cried out for him and all that she'd lost. She had come so close to finding happiness, utter fulfillment, only to lose all chance for both. The grief over that loss cut right to the center, the heart of her. She would never be the same, not even close.

"Kia," he said hoarsely, as if feeling that same pain. But that couldn't be. He would have to love her to suffer the same sense of desolation she felt. Yet she knew he didn't. He loved Julia.

Somehow, from somewhere deep inside her, she found the strength to enter the room. "I'm not staying," she told him in a firm voice.

His shoulders tensed. A mask came down over his face. "Why not?"

"I'm only here for one thing." She saw his eyes flicker over her, and her lips tightened. "No, it's not what you're thinking."

A muscle began to throb in his cheek. "And what would I be thinking?"

"Sex. That's all it ever was with you, Brant."

Those blue eyes bored into hers as he stood up and walked around the desk. "No. That's all you ever let yourself *believe* it was."

She stiffened. "So it's my fault, is it?"

He stopped right in front of her. "Who said anyone was at fault?" he asked quietly.

She gaped at him in disbelief. "Surely you don't think this is how a relationship should be?"

He reached out and cupped her chin, looking deep into her eyes. "Just because two people fall in love doesn't mean everything runs smoothly, sweetheart. But that doesn't mean they should end what they have."

She sucked in a sharp, painful breath and jerked her chin away. Dear God, was he enjoying the wounds he caused by his affair with Julia? "In other words, I should just let things slide along as they are? Boy, you really take the cake."

He seemed to freeze for a long pause. Then he said, "Kia, did you hear what I said?"

"No! I don't want to hear any more. I've come to give you this." She thrust the envelope at him.

Moments crept by as he stared hard at her, and she shifted uneasily. Then his gaze dropped to her hand. "What is it?"

"My resignation."

"You're not resigning," he said softly, taking the envelope and tearing it in half, just as he'd done with the check she'd written out for him over the security alarm.

She pulled out another envelope from her pocket. "I thought you might do that. You can tear this one up, too, but it doesn't matter. I've already sent one to Phillip in this morning's mail."

"You are *not* resigning," he repeated.

She gave a short laugh. "Unless you chain me to my desk, I won't be coming back."

"Chaining you to your desk sounds a bloody good idea right now," he muttered, grabbing her shoulders and lightly shaking her. "Kia, you say you listen, but you don't actually *hear* what I'm saying. I love you, Kia Benton. I'm not going to let you walk out of my life. I can't."

Her heart lurched in her chest. "Please don't do this to me, Brant," she whispered. "I can't be your mistress."

His hands tightened on her shoulders. "I don't want you for my mistress. I want you to be my wife."

Her mind spun in shock. His wife? For just a moment hope blossomed. Oh, yes, she wanted to be married to him so badly she ached with it. But did he love her, truly love her?

Then she remembered Julia, and that hope shriveled. There was only one woman he loved. A woman who belonged to another man at the moment. Kia's heart plummeted even further. Is that why he was asking *her* to marry him now? Had something gone wrong between him and Julia?

Regret and pain at what could have been flowed through her, cutting deep. "I'm sorry, Brant. I can't."

His head reeled back. "Why?" he rasped in a voice low and raw with something that sounded like need.

She blinked back tears. "You want me, but that's not enough. It'll never be enough for me."

"It's more than enough. For both of us."

"You're wrong. I won't be a substitute for Julia. I can't," she cried, spinning away. She had to get out of there before she fell apart. Before she let herself be taken on any terms.

"Stay."

His plea stilled her. Slowly she turned. Their gazes met for a long moment that seemed to last for eternity. She searched to the depth of his soul in those dark eyes, wanting to believe he loved her yet afraid to accept that the pain, the longing in his eyes, was real and not her imagination. She shook her head. No, she was too emotional to trust her judgment right now.

She was about to turn away again, to really go this time, but all at once she saw the anguish in his eyes and her legs refused to move. Brant wasn't a man to show his emotions and certainly not his vulnerability. Yet here he was showing that very thing. Hope and wonder bubbled inside her. Dare she believe? Could she believe in him? In herself? Her judgment?

She needed to stay rational. She needed to find out more about his relationship with the other woman before deciding. "What about Julia?"

The intensity of his gaze remained strong on her face. "She's already a wife. To Royce."

"But...you love her. You said things don't always run smoothly for people in love."

He took a step toward her and slipped his arms around her waist. "I meant *us*. I love *you*."

Yet something held her back, kept her from trusting him. An inner fear that she would still be second best, runner-up to Julia. He may think he loved *her* in a moment of madness, but for how long? Today? Tomorrow? For how many tomorrows would he love her? Would he secretly long for Julia, long to have her in his arms, even as he held *her*?

She just didn't know. She drew in a ragged breath, trying to think rationally, to get some clear focus. The only way she would get any kind of perspective was to have space to think about what had happened. She had to think about Brant's words of love. So much depended on her making the right decision.

"I need to think, Brant." She started to turn away, pain choking her words at the shock on that handsome face she so loved.

He stopped her, his gaze intense on her face. "You've got to believe, Kia. Trust in my love for you."

Something in his words got through to her this time. She didn't move, but suddenly she listened. Really listened.

A smile turned lovingly at the corners of his mouth. "Hear my heart, darling. Hear and learn." He put her hand against his chest. She could feel his heart thudding hard beneath it. And she could actually *hear* it as she looked deep into his eyes.

"You *really* love me, Brant?" she murmured, one inch from believing.

"You and no other," he said, his voice thick and unsteady. "I began to get an inkling when you were sick. You were going on about looking a mess, and I realized then I'd never tire of looking at you. That I would always find you beautiful, inside and out. No matter what."

Her knees wobbled. She felt weak and giddy all over. Finally she did believe.

Relief flooded her that she no longer had to fight her love for him. "Dear God, I've been wanting you so much. I…" She hesitated, still half-afraid to say the words out loud, as if all this would just disappear if she did.

His gaze filled with so much love she wondered how she ever doubted it. "I'm waiting."

She looked up at his strong, vital countenance, that firm mouth, those compelling blue eyes, that dark hair. "Oh, Brant, I love you, too."

He let out a slow, shaky breath that warmed her insides. "I know."

A soft gasp escaped her. "What?"

"Once I let go of the notion you were a gold digger..." His eyes apologized for ever thinking that. "I finally realized you weren't the sort of woman to get involved with a man unless your heart was involved, too. You see, I didn't listen to my heart either."

She moved closer, loving the feel of his hard body against her own. She'd never get enough of him. "Kiss me, darling."

His eyes darkened and he obliged her by doing exactly what she asked. And then some. Their kiss was so slow and deep it spoke more than words ever could.

When they pulled back from each other, she wanted to wallow in her joy. "Oh, Brant, I didn't know I loved you. Not at first. I thought it was just sexual attraction. It wasn't until we made love that it hit me."

His mouth curved into a smile. "You should have said something."

She rolled her eyes. "Oh, right. You would've disappeared off the face of the earth if you'd known I was serious."

He grinned and his love for her shone through. "Loving you isn't *that* bad."

"May I remind you of that in fifty years' time?" she teased, smoothing her fingers along his jaw.

"Definitely." He kissed her with a brief, hard kiss that still managed to touch her soul. "I have some other news. Phil's decided to stay in Queensland with Lynette and become a 'gentleman farmer'. I'm going to buy him out."

She nodded, knowing it was a good idea for all concerned. "It's best this way. As much as I like Phillip, he isn't a good businessman."

"You're right." His gaze held hers. "Now there's something else. About Julia…"

"You don't have to tell me. I trust you completely."

"Thank you, sweetheart, but I can tell you now anyway. I couldn't before because it was Julia's secret, not mine." He brushed a strand of hair off Kia's cheek. "She has a child. With a previous boyfriend. She had him when she was sixteen, and her parents forced her into adopting him out."

Her heart squeezed. To never see one's child…the pain of it. "Oh, poor Julia."

"I never knew and neither did Royce. It was only recently when the adoptive parents died in a boating accident that Julia found out where her son was. She came to me because Royce had started drinking and she didn't know what to do."

"Has she told Royce?"

"Yes, and he wants the boy. He's vowed to stop drinking. I know he'll do it, too. The first step is admitting he's got a problem. That was something my uncle would never do."

His brother's willingness to get his drinking under control was one good thing, at least. "How does Royce feel about you and Julia now? You'll always have a past together."

"Let's just say I convinced him I have other interests," he said, pulling her hips closer so she could feel his arousal.

Her breath hitched in her throat. "Uh...other interests?"

His gaze dropped to her mauve knit top. In one swift motion he stepped back, took hold of the hem and lifted it over her head, leaving her in her black bra and white jeans.

"Are you seducing me, Mr. Matthews?" she said huskily.

He ran a finger along the tops of her breasts. "Do you *want* to be seduced, Ms. Benton?"

"Hmm...no, I don't think so." Quickly she moved away and hurried to lock the door. Then she pocketed the key and turned to face him with a wicked smile. "This time I want to be the *seducer.*"

His eyes filled with a slow, sexy gleam that would always stir her senses. And her heart. "You realize this is an office, young lady."

"Oh, so that's what that big wooden desk is for. And that leather chair." She strolled toward him and slipped her hand in his. "Come and sit down, Mr. Matthews, and let me take note."

* * * * *

THE TYCOON'S BLACKMAILED MISTRESS

BY
MAXINE SULLIVAN

Dear Reader,

This is my second book for Desire and I'm just as excited and thrilled about it as my first one. Writing for the Desire line is such a dream come true for me.

And just like my first book, this one is also set in Darwin in the tropical north of Australia, where I lived for many years with my family. It's a special setting that deserves a unique story for my characters. I loved writing about a rich, arrogant hero who falls for a beautiful woman pregnant with another man's child. It takes a special couple to make something like that work. Of course, all those balmy sun-filled days and long summer nights might have helped Flynn and Danielle fall in love just a little.

Happy reading!

Maxine

For Serena Tatti
Terrific Writer and Caring Friend
"One of the Best"

One

"We meet at last, Mrs. Ford," Flynn Donovan drawled, looking into a pair of heart-stopping, exquisitely arresting blue eyes. In that instant, *he wanted her.* With a passion as absurd as it was unexpected.

For a moment the woman appeared startled, then whatever she saw made her delicate chin rise and her delicious mouth tighten. "I'm sorry to disturb you…" she said coolly.

Disturb him? Hell, despite her poise, Danielle Ford radiated a sex appeal that reached out and grabbed him by the…throat.

"Mr. Donovan, you sent a letter demanding repayment of a loan my husband and I—"

Suddenly he was angry with her for being so damn gorgeous on the outside and so damn dishonest within.

He knew her type. Robert Ford had said his wife was superb at acting and that her "innocent" look could hook a man until she got all she could out of him. He wasn't fool enough to believe everything Robert Ford had said, but any woman married to that liar and cheat must be tarred with the same brush.

"Don't you mean your *late* husband?" he snapped, flicking his pen on the desk.

Her slim shoulders tensed, even as her eyes reflected surprise at his tone. "My *late* husband, then." She took a breath. "About the letter. It says I owe you two hundred thousand dollars but I have no idea what this is about."

"Come now, Mrs. Ford," he mocked. "What you actually thought was that you'd try and con your way out of repaying back the loan you took out from my company."

She gasped, her thick lashes blinking in confusion. "But I don't know anything about a loan. And certainly not for such an amount. There must be some mistake."

And he was supposed to believe that?

"Don't play dumb."

A blush stained her cheeks, making her appear oddly vulnerable.

Or guilty, but then, a person could only feel guilty if they had a conscience. He doubted this woman had one.

"I assure you I'm not playing dumb, Mr. Donovan."

His jaw clenched. "Is this the same assurance your husband gave us when he borrowed the money from one of my loan officers?" He pushed some papers across his desk toward her. "Isn't that your signature alongside your husband's?"

Her eyes clouded with apprehension as she took a few steps closer, before looking down at the paperwork.

Then she paled and sank onto a chair. "It *looks* like my signature but..." Her voice trailed away to nothing.

Oh, so that's how she was going to play it. Robert had been right about her. She wasn't about to admit to anything, not even when the evidence of her guilt was right in front of her.

"It *is* your signature, Mrs. Ford," he said, ignoring her "helpless female" act. "And now you owe me two hundred thousand dollars."

Her head snapped up, her eyes wide and panicked. "But I don't have that kind of money."

He knew that already. After some investigating he'd learned she had exactly five thousand dollars in the bank here in Darwin. The rest she'd flittered all away, as evidenced by a variety of empty accounts around the rest of Australia. He was beginning to feel sorry for that poor guy who'd married her. She'd turn any man's head.

God, she was beautiful.

And that body...

His gaze slid down her simple pink dress and matching jacket that made a soft statement of style, to the slender legs revealed by the hem of her dress.

Nice.

Very nice.

They'd look really sexy in a tub full of fluffy white bubbles, one shapely calf raised as she smoothed soap over its silky length, the water's edge just stopping short of covering her breasts. The image aroused him without any effort at all, sending the blood pounding through his veins, telling him he needed a woman.

This woman.

"Then perhaps we can come to a compromise?" he said, leaning back in his leather executive chair to watch her more closely.

Her eyelids gave the slightest flutter, before she angled her chin, as if daring him to take another look. For a moment he was tempted.

She pulled herself up straighter. "Maybe I can pay you back a little each week. It'll take a long time but—"

"Not good enough." There was only one payment he wanted now.

Her lips parted in surprise, their perfect bow shape too damn appealing. "Wh-what?"

"You'll have to do better than that, I'm afraid."

She hesitated, as if trying to understand. "I'm not sure—"

"You're a very beautiful woman, Mrs. Ford."

Her eyes held his for a heartbeat, then a pulse began to leap crazily in a tiny vein in her neck. "I've been widowed for two months, Mr. Donovan. Have you no sensibility?"

"Apparently not." He wanted to place his lips on that neck and feel her heart beating against him.

She let out a sigh. "Then you must tell me how I can repay you. I can certainly do with some money at the moment."

Ah, yes. Money is what it came down to with this woman. His gut knotted at the reminder of how mercenary she was.

"Sorry, sweetheart. You don't get another cent from me until you pay back the loan. In full."

Her cheekbones instantly reddened. "Oh, but I didn't mean—"

"Yes, you did."

She looked taken aback for just a moment, then quickly recovered. "Oh, yes, of course I did," she said with sarcasm. "I'll take as much money as I can get out of you. I'm good at that, you know."

As a bluff, it didn't work. He knew what she was trying to do. "Yes, you're very good at that."

She threw him a glare. "I'm glad you can read my mind. I hope you can read what I'm thinking right now?"

He felt a ripple of amusement. "A lady shouldn't know such words."

"A lady shouldn't have to sit here and listen to you blackmail her, either."

"*Blackmail* is an ugly word, Danielle." He rolled the name over in his mind the way he wanted to roll her over in bed. "I merely want what is mine."

And she was one of them.

Her lips pressed together briefly before she answered, "No, you want revenge. I'm sorry, but I can't be blamed for my husband's mistakes."

Flynn stared hard. "What about *your* mistakes, Danielle? You signed for the loan, didn't you? Therefore you are just as liable to pay me back."

"With my money or with my body?" she scoffed.

He arched a brow. "I wonder how many hot tropical nights two hundred thousand dollars is worth?" He thought for a moment, then answered his own question. "Hmm. About three months, I'd say." Expensive, yes, but he knew he'd pay that for just *one* night with this woman.

Her blue eyes turned disbelieving, as if only now realizing he was serious. "Three months! You expect me to *sleep* with you for *three* months?"

His gaze lingered on her mouth. So perfect. "I didn't say anything about sleeping with me, though I guarantee it wouldn't be a hardship," he said, as her surprisingly sensual fragrance wafted across the desk and slid into him, stirring his blood. "No, I have a lot of engagements coming up and I could do with a…mistress to accompany me."

Awareness flickered in the back of her eyes, then was quickly blanked out.

She got to her feet. "Mr. Donovan, you're dreaming if you think I'll give my time…or my body…to a man like you. Let me suggest you wake yourself up and find a woman who would actually welcome your company." With those words, she spun on her heels and left the office.

In cynical amusement, Flynn watched her go, then got to his feet and stood looking out the huge window of Donovan Towers to the sparkling expanse of harbor spread before him. He rather liked her response. It was a far cry from some of the females he'd been out with lately, who'd left him cold with their easy acquiescence to anything remotely connected to bedroom games.

And then he remembered.

Danielle Ford was more sinner than saint. Her token resistance was only a game, one she'd already played with her late husband. From what Robert Ford had said, she'd taken him on a wild ride during their marriage, though he doubted Robert had needed any encouragement. They had obviously deserved each other. No, he wouldn't forget she had belonged to Robert Ford and that the two of them had reneged on a loan. A pair well-matched.

He muttered a swearword and turned back to his desk, knowing he had a morning of video conferences with personnel in Sydney and Tokyo ahead of him, yet for once the thought of work didn't appeal. Not even the promise of a particularly satisfying takeover tomorrow.

He preferred instead another sort of takeover, with a woman who had gorgeous blue eyes and golden-blond hair and a willowy body.

Despite her protestations, he would make her his mistress. No doubt she would sell her soul for a chance to rub shoulders with him and his billions.

After catching a taxi home, Danielle still trembled from her encounter as she let herself into her air-conditioned apartment. She'd come to love living in this tropical paradise…this vibrant capital city at the top of Australia's Northern Territory…but now there was a serpent in paradise by the name of Flynn Donovan. God, he had to be deranged if he thought she would pay off her debts with her body.

Her debts.

She swallowed hard and sank down on the gray leather sofa, her knees suddenly weak. What had Robert been thinking when he'd forged her signature on that document? Because it *was* a forgery, that was certain. She even remembered when he'd tried to get her to sign some paperwork. He'd said it was a business deal and he needed her signature as a witness. Only she'd felt uncomfortable and *accidentally* misplaced it. She heard nothing more about it from Robert. Pity she hadn't read it before she'd thrown it away.

Two hundred thousand dollars! For what? It made her wonder what else he had done. Had she known her husband at all?

Not that Flynn Donovan would have believed her if she'd told him the truth. He clearly thought she was as guilty as her husband and any further attempt to refute that would have been met with suspicion.

She blinked back tears. This was supposed to be a new beginning for her. After three years of being smothered by Robert and his mother, she'd finally broken free after his death and moved into this luxury apartment. Living with her mother-in-law had been hard enough during her unhappy marriage, but since Robert's death, Monica had been trying to manipulate her, just as she had her "Robbie." And feeling sorry for the other woman's loss, she had given in too many times to count.

But eventually she'd had enough. A Realtor who'd been an acquaintance of Robert's had offered Danielle this penthouse at minimal rent. Signing the lease had lifted a lead weight from her shoulders. The place was beautiful and made her happy. She loved the spacious living room and open-plan kitchen, and the glass doors leading to the balcony looked over a wide expanse of ocean. Being surrounded by such beauty made her feel as if she could breathe again. It had been exactly what she'd needed, and better yet, it was all *hers*. For a year, anyway.

And now *this*.

Now she owed Donovan Enterprises a large sum of money and had no idea how she was going to pay it back. And pay it back she would. She just wouldn't feel right about it if she didn't. Robert had taken the money and she was Robert's wife and, as much as she wanted to walk away from it all and say it wasn't her problem, she couldn't. It *was* her problem.

But the five thousand dollars she'd managed to save from her part-time job was woefully inadequate. Besides, she wouldn't give that up. *Couldn't* give it up. It was her security blanket, held in an account Robert had known nothing about. Thank God. He hadn't wanted her to be independent, and she'd fought hard to hold on to her job during her marriage—against both Robert's and Monica's wishes. If she'd given it up to become a lady of leisure the way they'd wanted, then somehow she may as well have given up on herself.

No, she'd just have to find another way to pay the money back. And not through sleeping with Flynn, either, even though she couldn't deny her heart had skipped a beat over him.

The tycoon had definitely been at the front of the line when they were handing out good looks, with the sort of handsome features that stole a woman's breath and curled her toes.

Strong, silent and sexy. With broad shoulders more than enough for one woman to caress, not to mention the kind of thick dark hair that invited a woman's hands.

She could imagine feeling its shining silkiness beneath her fingertips.

Perhaps some would call her crazy for refusing to go to bed with a man with such remarkable dark eyes and a sensually molded mouth. She called it survival.

He was one of those men who expected everyone to do his bidding. She'd spent three years being smothered by a man who'd fought to control her and she wasn't about to step back into another relationship like that—no matter how much money Flynn Donovan said she owed.

Two

The next day Danielle had just bent to pick up some broken glass when the doorbell rang, making her cut herself on one of the pieces. Sucking in a sharp breath, she quickly drew back her hand, relieved to see the cut was only small. She already had a lump on her head where the heavy gold picture frame had toppled onto her as she'd been adjusting it.

But all that was forgotten when she opened the door and found the stunningly virile Flynn Donovan standing there, dressed in a dark business suit that fit his body as if it were a labor of love.

"I heard breaking glass," he said without preamble, his gaze taking in her orange-burst silk tunic over white pants, down to her white sandals, as if looking for injury. There was more in that look than necessary and she fought not to react. But her skin quivered anyway. That look was too seductive…too physical….

And then she remembered who this man was and what he wanted from her. At the very least he wanted money.

At the worst…

She forced aside her apprehension and shot him a cold look. "How did you get in the building? We have a security code, you know. It's supposed to keep out unwanted guests."

"I have my ways," he said, dismissively, with all the arrogance of someone rich enough to get anything he wanted. "The broken glass?" he reminded her.

She raised one slim shoulder. "A picture frame fell off the wall."

His eyes sharpened with a concern that was at odds with the forbidding set of his jaw. "Are you hurt?"

For a moment she was tempted to lie. "A small cut, that's all." Nonchalantly she lifted her finger to show him, but when she saw how much blood covered the tissue, she gasped.

He swore. "Danielle, that is no small cut," he muttered, reaching for her hand, his touch scorching her. She tried to pull back…tried not to welcome the feel of his skin against hers…but he held firm.

To counteract the effect, she glared at him. "I wouldn't have cut it at all if you hadn't rang the doorbell just as I was picking up the glass."

"Next time I'll leave you to bleed to death," he said brusquely, undoing the tissue to reveal the injured finger. He scowled as he examined it. "There's a lot of blood, but I think you'll get away without stitches." He raised his head, his dark eyes stabbing her. "Any other injuries I should know about?"

Tell him no.

But the truth slipped out. "Only a bump on the head."

"Show me."

She winced where she felt the lump. "It's nothing, really. It's—"

"Bleeding," he growled, moving in closer, touching her head.

She swallowed convulsively. "I'll be fine."

"Where's your first-aid kit?"

"In the kitchen, but—"

"Right." He cupped her elbow and started her forward with him. "Let's take a proper look at it."

Her skin continued to scorch where he touched. "Mr. Donovan, I'm sure you've got better things to do than play doctor with me," she said as they sidestepped the broken glass.

He shot her a masculine look that coiled tension inside her. His thoughts didn't need to be said out loud to fill the silence between them.

As soon as she reached the kitchen, she quickly moved away from him and took the small box out of a cupboard to place on the bench. He followed her, then began searching through the contents. Taking advantage of the moment, she stepped back, grateful the kitchen was large and airy and far less intimate than two people standing in a doorway.

"Move that stool over there and sit under the light," he ordered. "I'll be able to see better."

That was what she was afraid of. But, her heart thudding against her ribs, she did what he said anyway. Better to get it over and done with so he'd leave sooner rather than later.

He came toward her, the ball of cotton in his hand contrasting with the tan of his skin. And then he stood behind her, bringing a very male scent with him. She'd noticed it when he'd walked in but now the scent intensified like a potent wine, ready to lull her into blissful surrender.

She jumped when he brushed a lock of her blond hair aside and began dabbing at the cut. His touch was gentle yet probing, the way a man's touch should be. Would he be the same in bed? Oh, yes, he'd know how to turn a woman on.

"Mr. Donovan—"

"Flynn," he suddenly said in a rough voice.

She ignored that. "Mr. Donovan, I think—"

"How long will it take you to pack?"

That pulled her thoughts up short. "Pack?"

"For Tahiti. I have to go there for business. My jet's on standby. We can leave within the hour."

"Tahiti?" She spun to face him, barely wincing as his fingers brushed her scalp. Dear God, what was he saying?

His dark eyes watched her with a knowing look in them. "I have a house there. Our privacy will be assured."

It fell into place then. He expected her to go away with him as payment for the loan. God, did he really think she would do such a thing?

"I don't need any privacy," she choked, strangely hurt. "I don't intend to go away with you." A burst of anger hit her. "Anyway, just who do you think you are? You snap your fingers and I'm to drop everything?

Sorry. Your women friends may do that but I have a mind of my own."

His eyes hardened. "Oh, come now, Danielle. Who are you trying to fool?"

She straightened her shoulders. "The only fool around here is *you*."

His face tightened, making her aware of the firm thrust of his jaw and the broad plane of his forehead. "Don't underestimate me."

A frisson of fear slipped down her spine. This man had wealth, power and the right connections and he believed she'd done him an injustice. As much as she wanted to deny he could make life uncomfortable for her, she knew he would do it if pushed. She couldn't afford that. There wasn't only herself to think about now.

She moistened her mouth and tried to be conciliatory. "Mr. Donovan, please... I don't sleep with men I barely know."

"That isn't what your late husband told me."

She felt the blood drain from her face.

"I see you don't like being caught out," he mocked, seeming to watch her more closely.

Pain squeezed her heart. Robert...her husband...the man she'd been married to for three years...had told Flynn Donovan such lies about her? Why?

"Um..." She cleared her throat. "What exactly did Robert say?"

"That you married him for his money. And that you slept around and spent it all," he said bluntly.

It was just as well she was sitting on the stool or she may well have fallen. How *could* Robert have said those things about her? She'd thought she'd loved Robert when she married him. And she never, ever slept around and she'd never wasted his money. *Never.*

Then she looked at Flynn Donovan. At that moment she hated Robert for his lies, but she hated Flynn more for his lack of compunction over her feelings. "I see. You obviously believed him."

His lips twisted. "When he explained the reason for defaulting on the loan, I wasn't actually concerned with character references."

"Yet you lent the money to us based on character," she said, her voice remarkably calm considering the turmoil inside her.

His eyes narrowed. "No, we based it on the fact that he was coming into money and would pay us back as soon as he received it. He seemed a good risk at the time. We didn't take into account that you had the money spent before he could even get to it."

Danielle remembered Robert mentioning something about coming into an inheritance from one of his aunts, but she hadn't realized it was a large enough amount to serve as collateral for a loan. For him to have then spent that amount plus the two hundred thousand he'd borrowed from Flynn Donovan spoke of sheer irresponsibility.

And Monica? Had she known? Danielle didn't think so. Her mother-in-law was well-off in her own right but had never discussed money and, in any case, she knew Monica had never suspected her son had a problem with money.

She certainly hadn't suspected any problems, Danielle mused as she realized Flynn had walked over to the first-aid kit and was rummaging around in it. One thing was clear. No one would believe her if she chose to refute Robert's claims.

"Why deny it?" Flynn said coldly over his shoulder, confirming her fears. "Your car alone cost fifty thousand dollars, not to mention your frequent European holidays and shopping sprees. Your credit cards were maxed to the limit, too."

Credit cards? European holidays? Shopping sprees? She fought to take it all in. Had someone stolen her identity? It certainly hadn't been *her* doing all those things. Robert had been the one to…

Oh, God. Is that what Robert had been doing on his frequent business trips? The ones where he'd wanted her to stay home as company for his mother?

As for the car, she'd had no idea of its cost. Robert had always seemed to have plenty of money and as far as she'd known, the car had been in his name only. He definitely hadn't insured it. Or himself. If only he had, she could at least have paid back some of the money now.

And then something occurred to her. The holidays, the shopping, didn't sound like something one did alone. Had Robert been unfaithful to her? Looking back, she knew he was selfish enough to want his cake and eat it, too. What sort of double life had he been living? And why didn't that thought hurt as much as it should?

Suddenly she realized Flynn was in front of her, bringing her into the present with a rush. In that moment they were right back to one man, one woman.

Her heart gave a sudden lurch when he picked up her

finger and covered it with the antiseptic cream before placing a plaster around it. The gentleness of his touch confused her. How could he be tender in one aspect and so hardhearted in another?

But she wasn't about to show him her uncertainty. He would take advantage of it. "Mr. Donovan, you think I want you for your money, yet you're willing to take me away with you? That doesn't make sense."

"It makes perfect sense," he murmured, his throaty tone faint but potent. "We were meant to spend time together."

"Of all the…" She almost jumped to her feet but that would have brought her closer to him and at the last millisecond she stopped herself. His eyes darkened at how close she'd come to being in his arms.

She leveled him a look. "Don't let me keep you," she said, but cursed her husky voice and refused to allow the tip of her tongue to moisten her suddenly dry lips.

He cupped her chin with his warm fingers, holding her head still, as if he wanted to wet her lips for her. "You won't," he said huskily, his eyes intent on her mouth.

His head began to lower. She lifted her face up to him…ready…ready to become *his*.

And then he moved imperceptibly closer, and the movement broke through the fog of desire that seemed to swirl around them.

His? Dear God, what was she thinking? She never wanted to belong to another man again.

And definitely not Flynn Donovan.

She pulled her head back. "There is no way I'm going away with you," she murmured, shaken at how close she'd come to kissing him.

Something flickered far back in those dark eyes before they flashed a now-familiar display of arrogance. "Is that so?" To prove his point, he lifted some strands of her hair from her cheek and tugged her toward him.

She held her head still, refusing to wince at the slight pain, unwilling to let him force her into submission. She wasn't going to become his plaything. She couldn't, despite the desire coursing through her.

"Do you think you could leave now?" she said coolly, determined not to let him see his effect on her. "I'm expecting a…" She paused deliberately. "Friend."

He let her strands of hair drop back into place and drawled mockingly, "You have no…friend."

"You don't know that."

"Perhaps I've been checking up on you?" He smiled in satisfaction when she jumped. "But that's not how I know. A man just knows these things. You tremble when I touch you…." He touched her cheek. "See."

She jerked her head away. "With revulsion."

He gave a hard laugh. "That's a new one. No woman has ever told me that before."

"Then you'd better get used to it."

"Why? Do you expect I'll touch you a lot?" he mocked but his voice had a raw edge. His eyes raked over her. "No, *you* had better get used to the trembling. I intend to make you…tremble…often."

She inwardly trembled now. "Stop playing games."

"Oh, but the games have only just begun," he said silkily. "You owe me money and I *will* collect."

"Wh-what? *Now?*"

He seemed to take inventory of each feature on her face. "No. I'd rather wait and savor you in my own time, at my own pace."

She felt as if her breath was cut off. "I'm not a delicacy to be enjoyed."

"Really? I think you'd be very good in small bites."

She snorted. "I would give you food poisoning."

"Aah, but I'd enjoy myself first." A sardonic gleam of amusement entered his eyes. "Just like you. Spend now, pay later. That's your motto, isn't it?" Without warning, one brow lifted with cynicism. "I wonder how many other people you've tried to cheat?"

She went rigid. She'd never tried to cheat anyone in her life. She'd always considered herself dependable and loyal. Even with Robert, she'd stayed with him because she'd believed in her marriage vows.

Of course, she hadn't known Robert had taken his vows less than seriously in return.

"Nothing to say?"

These allegations had gone on long enough. She had to make him see sense. Yesterday she'd been shocked by his accusations and hadn't really believed he intended to make her his lover.

But now…today…with him coming here…with his jet ready for Tahiti…she couldn't let this sham go on.

Yet, dare she tell him? Would it make him even angrier with her when he knew he couldn't have her? *Why* he couldn't have her? Would he get spiteful, the way Robert used to when he didn't get his own way?

She drew herself up without actually getting off the stool. "Mr. Donovan—"

"Flynn."

"Flynn," she said, conceding just this once. "I'm sorry, but there is no way I can share your bed."

"You can't, eh? And why would that be?" Thankfully he moved back to lean against the sink, but the sheer insolence in his stance made her heart dip. It was obvious he thought she was just being difficult for the sake of it.

Still, she had to try. She slipped off the stool, automatically arching her spine, her silky top a river of orange as it flowed into place over her white slacks. Her back was aching a little lower down but she hoped that was to be expected.

Then she heard him suck in a breath. "My God! Are you pregnant?"

Danielle straightened, shocked that he'd guessed the truth even though she wasn't showing. And suddenly she was aware that her actions had spoken louder than words. Perhaps that wasn't a bad thing. Hopefully for him to see that she was going to be a mother would be more effective than all the words in the world.

He raised his eyes to her face and there was a terrible pain in them that tugged at her heartstrings. She wasn't sure why, but her hands went to her stomach, protectively. "Um…that's what I wanted to tell you."

He stood there for a long moment. Staring… And then he pushed himself upright and away from the sink, his body rigid, his mouth curling with contempt. "*Now* I see what this is all about," he rasped. "No wonder you wouldn't fall into bed with me. You wanted more, just like your husband said you did with him."

She blinked. "More?"

"A marriage license to be exact."

Shock ran through her. "You're crazy," she managed to say, if a little unsteadily. She wouldn't be thinking about marriage again. Not for a long time.

"You've gone through one husband's money—" the words hit her like bullets "—and now you're trying to tie yourself to another. What better way to get sympathy than to play the grieving but pregnant widow without a penny to her name? Poor, beautiful Danielle," he sniped at her in a harsh voice. "Most men would give up their freedom to possess you, and being pregnant makes you even more attractive to some. There's something dignified about having a wife with child." His angry gaze swept over her. "Is it even your husband's baby?"

She felt sick with the horror of it all. "I resent you asking, but, yes, it's my husband's baby." His mocking words echoed in her mind. "Or should I say my *late* husband's baby."

"Did he know?"

It wasn't any of Flynn's business but she inclined her head anyway. Robert had been ecstatic, for which she was grateful, no matter what she was finding out about him now. She hadn't wanted a child until things had improved between them, but somehow she must have missed taking her contraceptive pill one time and she'd fallen pregnant.

Naturally she'd been fearful at first, not because the child would go unloved, but because Monica and Robert loved in a smothering way. But she knew she was strong enough to keep that in check and she had even begun to welcome her pregnancy. Her baby would bring some happiness back into their lives.

And it still would, she told herself, feeling Flynn's eyes burning into her.

Ignoring the pain of insult, she raised her chin. "Mr. Donovan, let me make one thing clear to you. I have no intention of looking for a surrogate father for my baby." She paused for effect. "And even if I was, I'd never pick someone like you. My baby deserves more than someone with a checkbook for a heart."

He walked toward her, his dark eyes without a glimmer of kindness. "Don't presume to know me, lady. If that was my child growing in your belly you wouldn't have a choice." With those words, he stormed past her and out of the apartment.

Eyes misting over, Danielle just stood there as the door slammed behind him, a terrible ache in her breast, her thoughts in turmoil. Never in a million years would she have believed all this could be happening to her.

Yesterday morning she hadn't even met Flynn Donovan. She'd assumed his letter about the money was a mistake. Now she'd been accused not only of cheating on her husband and abusing his money, but of being a calculating schemer who wanted nothing but a rich man to play father to her child. It was clear he had far from a high opinion of her.

Well, she didn't have one of him, either. He may

be one of the richest men in Australia but as far as she was concerned he could keep his money and his private jet and...and...

She swiped at her tears. What did it matter now, anyway? The way Flynn had stormed out of here left her in no doubt he wouldn't be back. No, he'd be putting the debt collectors onto her now. They'd be hounding her like a pack of dogs after a bone.

She took a shaky breath. He needn't bother. She'd find a way to pay the money back. How could she enjoy her independence knowing that her late husband had "stolen" the money, not just from Flynn but from Donovan Enterprises, as well?

And she had too much to lose if she didn't.

Oh, God. Suddenly it hit her that the debt collectors would go talk to Monica. And if the older woman became aware of the loan, she would use it to get custody of the baby. Oh, dear God, she would. Danielle was never more certain of anything in her life. Her mother-in-law wanted...no, *needed* someone to replace her son...and who better than Robert's unborn child?

And if Flynn Donovan believed she'd defaulted on the money, then Monica would, too, and could make a case for Danielle being an unfit mother, and probably with Flynn's help. After all, how did she prove that it *hadn't* been her signature? Her mother-in-law only needed a sympathetic judge...or a corrupt one.

Danielle's heart squeezed so tightly with pain it felt as if it had wedged under her rib cage. She couldn't take the risk of losing her child, no matter how slender.

Three

Life rarely took Flynn by surprise anymore, but when it did, he didn't like it one bit. Danielle Ford was pregnant. Hell! He didn't want to get involved with a pregnant woman. Anything could happen to a woman when she was pregnant.

It had happened to his mother.

He could still remember his mother's voice calling to him where he'd been playing in the backyard under the mango tree with his friends Brant and Damien.... The same mango tree that still stood a few suburbs away from here. He'd come inside the house and found her on the floor, covered in blood.

"The baby's coming," she'd said, her face screwed up in pain. "Go get Auntie Rose."

More terrified than he'd ever been in his five-year-old life, he'd run next door with his friends as fast as his little legs had allowed. After that it had been a whirl of people running and sirens screaming. And all the while, he'd stood in the background, watching his mother's life slipping away…away from him.

He hated thinking about it, and as always he shut his mind off and pushed aside the past. He had to concentrate on the here and now, and that no longer included Danielle Ford. She could forget about the money she owed him. Forget about it and go find some other poor sucker to con with those "come-to-bed" eyes and that "give-me-your-money" mouth. As far as he was concerned, Danielle Ford no longer existed.

It was just a pity that spending the following weekend in Sydney at his apartment overlooking the million-dollar view of the Harbor Bridge and Opera House wouldn't be enjoyable. Something was missing.

Or someone.

Dammit, he'd never let a woman get under his skin before. Not like this. He'd had women friends who'd tried every trick in the book to get him to marry them, but Danielle Ford had chosen a different way of getting his attention. Unfortunately for her it had the opposite effect to what she'd wanted. The one thing he wouldn't let himself do was get involved with a pregnant woman.

Not that pregnant women weren't beautiful. He'd seen some stunners in his time and thankfully none had been his responsibility, but he'd decided years ago he'd never put any woman's life at risk with a pregnancy.

So why couldn't he get this one woman out of his mind, especially since he *hadn't* taken her to his bed?

Or perhaps it was because of that?

Yet she was only one woman. There were plenty of others to choose from. But those women would only have been a poor substitute for a sexy sorceress…a witch…but a cheat, he reminded himself.

He had to stop thinking about a certain long-legged, blue-eyed blonde stripped naked and in bed….

His bed…

He wasn't surprised the following week after returning from a business lunch with the Lord Mayor when his personal assistant followed him into his office, an angry look on her middle-aged face. Connie rarely lost her cool. It was one of the things he appreciated about her. She kept calm under the most trying of circumstances.

Usually.

"This was delivered downstairs at reception," she said tightly, slapping an envelope down on the desk in front of him. "It's for *you*."

He leaned back in his chair, his eyes narrowing, not sure what it was about. "And?"

A disapproving motherly look puckered her lips. "It's from Mrs. Ford."

"Danielle?" he said, tensing, and caught the suddenly watchful look in his assistant's eyes at his slip of the tongue.

"Yes."

He wondered what Danielle was up to now, even as mild surprise at Connie's reaction filled him. "You didn't like her?"

A soft look filled her eyes. "Of course I liked her, Flynn. She's lovely. So well-mannered." Then her expression tightened again as she shot him daggers. "You had better read the letter, that's all I'm saying."

Hiding his wariness, he merely inclined his head. "Thank you, Connie. Just leave it there."

She looked as if she was going to say more, but then obviously knowing how far *not* to push him, she left the room, closing the door behind her.

For a moment Flynn just sat there, marshaling his thoughts. He stared at the open white envelope. His name had been written on it in a soft style that bespoke of femininity and charm. The uppercase initials of *F* and *D* fashioned with little curls tugged on something inside him, as if it were an echo of her voice wanting him.

God, he could still hear the throaty sound of her voice back in her kitchen when he'd been administering to her injuries.

Didn't this woman know when to give up?

Never one to shirk anything unpleasant, he seized the envelope and pulled out the folded piece of paper inside. He began to read.

Dear Mr. Donovan,
Please find enclosed a check for one hundred dollars as first payment on the outstanding loan of two hundred thousand dollars that my late husband and I owe your company. I apologize if this is unacceptable, however due to my pregnancy I am unable to take a second job at this stage. Please

take this as official notice that I will repay the loan as soon as I can.
Yours sincerely,
Danielle Ford.

Flynn threw the letter on his desk, his lips twisting at the word *sincerely*. No wonder Connie had been upset with him. Danielle's words might have been businesslike in tone but it made him sound like an ogre who was insisting on his money, come hell or high water.

Obviously this was the way she worked. And now the pregnancy angle had added a whole new avenue to her manipulation skills. She'd certainly hit the jackpot with that one.

As for her "supposed" job, it was probably some sort of volunteer work she did once a month at the hospital. Something that made her look respectable without getting her pretty little hands dirty, he decided, tearing up the check and dropping the pieces in the wastepaper basket.

No doubt once he ignored this, they wouldn't be hearing from her again. Her little ploy for sympathy would soon die a natural death once she realized he wasn't about to come running with a magic wand in one hand and an unlimited checkbook in the other.

Then the same thing happened the following week. A check arrived, but without a letter this time.

"Another check," Connie said tightly, slapping the envelope down in front of him, as if everything were *his* fault. She smacked another piece of paper on top of it and blurted, "And here's my resignation."

His head snapped up. "Your *what?*" He didn't wait for her to answer. "What the— Why?"

She straightened her slim shoulders, color coming into her cheeks. "I'm afraid I can't work for you anymore, Flynn. Not like this."

He exhaled an impatient sigh and leaned back in his chair. *This* was Danielle Ford's fault. Damn her. And damn Danielle's flashing blue eyes, those enticing lips above the intimate underside of a chin that more often than not was raised in the air at him.

"So you're going to throw away five years of working for me because some..." he hesitated to say *lady* "...woman owes me money?"

"Yes."

From his experience he knew females were often unpredictable, but he'd never actually thought of Connie that way. She'd been his right-hand man, always on top of things, never one to pull these kinds of tricks.

"She's not worth it, you know."

Connie met his gaze levelly. "I think she is. She's a real lady, Flynn. Classy. She deserves better than this."

No, Danielle was just good at fooling people, though he had to admit that not many people fooled Connie. And that just went to prove that his assistant wasn't infallible.

"She owes me a great deal of money," he pointed out.

Connie continued to stand her ground. "I'm sure she had her reasons."

His mouth thinned with derision. "That means she *spent* a great deal of money, or hadn't you thought of that?"

"I don't care. A pregnant woman shouldn't have to worry about getting a second job to pay the bills."

"Then maybe she shouldn't have borrowed the money in the first place."

Her expression was resolute. "That may be so, but she's genuinely trying to pay the money back now." A wave of concern crossed her face. "Look, her husband is dead, she's pregnant and she has a debt that is obviously weighing heavily on her. It could affect her health."

"No," he growled. He wasn't going to have *that* on his shoulders.

Connie hesitated for a second, then a determined look filled her eyes. "Flynn, I never told you this before but I was pregnant once."

His brows met in a frown. They'd never discussed her private life. She worked long hours at times and had never complained, so he assumed she lived alone.

"You never mentioned being married."

"I wasn't." Her eyes didn't waver from his. "I hope that doesn't change how you think of me."

"That's a fool thing to say," he said brusquely. "Of course it doesn't make a bloody difference."

Her features relaxed with slight relief. "Thank you," she murmured, but there was inner pain flickering at the back of her eyes. "Let me tell you a little about my baby. I lost him before he was born. You see, I'd been in poor health for some years, I had no family and the man I loved had left town before he even knew I was pregnant. I thought I was too proud to accept charity, but when you lose your baby…" her voice grew slightly shaky "…when that baby no longer warms your womb and you have nothing in your arms to hold…" She took another breath. "Accepting charity suddenly looks the better option."

The world briefly shifted out of focus as memories of his mother rose to the surface again.

Then he looked at his PA. To think Connie had gone through a similar thing…

His mouth firmed with purpose. "Put your resignation away, Connie. I'll go see her."

Of course, he couldn't just drop everything right there and then, but a few hours later after moving a mountain of paperwork, he eventually left to go see Danielle, the loan contract tucked inside his jacket. He knew he was playing right into her hands by coming to see her, but how to tell his PA that? The first check and accompanying letter had been a brilliant idea, but the second check was sheer stubbornness. It was obvious Danielle was determined to get his attention.

And he was equally determined not to give it. Not in the way she wanted, anyway.

Still, she wouldn't be complaining too loudly once he'd finished talking. He was about to officially cancel the loan, thereby letting her walk away with two hundred thousand of his dollars. Not a bad day's work for some.

However the first thing he saw when he turned his sports Mercedes into her street was the reckless idiot in a red sedan who cut across the road and slammed on his brakes in front of her building.

Flynn swore as he pulled up behind the car and turned off the engine.

Bloody hell! Danielle was in that car. In the passenger seat. He'd recognize her profile anywhere.

And then he saw the young thug in the driver's seat next to her, his tattooed arm leaning out the window. Fear for her safety chilled his blood. The young man looked as if he'd just got out of prison, and the vehicle as if it had been driven by one too many drunks. The trunk of the car had a huge scratch down the middle and the back left-hand side had a dent in it the size of Kakadu National Park. There was a For Sale sign on its back window.

He swore again. Why on earth would she get into a car with such a man? She didn't belong there. It made his skin crawl just to see her sitting inside it.

And why buy that piece of garbage? She lived in a lavish penthouse apartment for God's sake, with a mesmerizing view of the marina and the vast Timor Sea beyond that. A view that even the most jaded would appreciate.

And then he figured out what she was *really* up to. She'd known he'd come here this afternoon and had somehow planned this, waiting in the afternoon heat and humidity, wanting him to feel sorry for her over the car and her condition. She'd probably counted on charming her way into his life. His nostrils flared with fury. She had about as much chance of that as of it snowing here in Darwin.

He was about to start the engine and go back to the office when he remembered his promise to Connie. If he went back now without speaking to Danielle, the older woman would hand in her notice. And then it would take too much time and trouble to find anyone half as efficient, let alone that he'd darn well miss her around the office.

Just then Danielle opened the car door and started to get out of the vehicle. Against his will, his pulse shifted upward when he glimpsed a pair of slim ankles encased in pretty white sandals more suited to getting out of a Mercedes than a run-down wreck. But it was the other car door being flung open and the jerky way the driver got out of the car that suddenly drew his attention.

Something was going on here.

Something not right.

Instinct told him this wasn't part of Danielle's plan.

Danielle had just been for the ride of her life. Not only was her stomach still trying to catch up from where "Turbo" had left it back there on a lonely stretch of the Stuart Highway, but her heart was still in her mouth. Living up to his name, he'd scared her half to death by crossing the other side of the road then coming to a screaming stop in front of her building.

Holding on to her stomach, she took a breath and opened the car door. Nothing would make her buy this car now, no matter how cheap. Her dear mother had always said you got what you paid for, and Danielle wasn't about to use some of her precious savings just to drive her baby around in a bomb like this one. She'd rather catch the bus into the city center the way she did now, where she worked three days a week helping Angie in the boutique. Of course, once she had the baby she'd need to stop at the day-care center before and after work.

"I'm sorry, but this really isn't what I'm looking for." She pushed herself off the passenger seat, wanting to get out of the car and away from this man who was making her uneasy.

He hopped out of the driver's side and looked at her over the roof of the car as she got to her feet. "I could probably take a couple of hundred off the price," he said, desperation growing in his tone.

She didn't want to think what he needed the money for. There was something about him that didn't sit well now. Heavens, she'd been a fool to get in the car with him, no matter that Angie said he was a friend of a friend.

"It's really not what I'm after, Turbo," she said in a placating tone.

"But you said—"

"The lady said she's not interested." A hard male voice came out of nowhere, and Danielle's gaze flew to the man standing a few feet away on the footpath. She sucked in a sharp breath, her heart hammering foolishly for one brief second. Flynn Donovan stood there, looking as if he wanted to do someone harm.

And that someone was probably *her*.

Turbo spun around, his mouth closing when he saw Flynn. All at once the young man appeared even skinnier and shorter, especially up against Flynn's well-muscled body dressed in a gray business suit.

Funny, but she actually felt sorry for Turbo then. The tattoos, the pierced nose and the missing tooth were merely a front so that people wouldn't notice his acne and too-thin body.

Flynn took a step closer and any suspicions she had about Turbo being up to no good disappeared under Flynn's intimidating stance. She glowered at him. Couldn't he see the younger man was nothing more than skin and bones?

"Flynn, don't—"

"Forget it, lady," Turbo interjected, his eyes wide with fright as he jumped in his car, gunned the engine and sped off, leaving behind a trail of exhaust smoke that sickened her in the humid tropical air.

But Danielle ignored it and glared at Flynn. "There was no need for that."

Reciprocating anger flared in those dark eyes. "Of course there was."

She bristled, half-afraid he was right but not willing to admit she'd acted foolishly. Not when she'd been trying so hard to do this all by herself.

Her chin tilted. "I could have handled him."

He arched a brow. "Really? It may have escaped your notice but you're pregnant."

"I know a man's weak parts as well as the next woman."

"Obviously." His mocking gaze traveled down the length of her floral shirt and white capri pants to the white sandals on her feet. For all his anger, she felt as if he'd just whispered kisses all down her body, right down to the tips of her toes.

Her hands balled into fists. "Mr. Donovan, just because I'm pregnant doesn't mean I'm helpless."

"Glad to hear it," he taunted.

She squared her shoulders. "Oh, I get it. You're one of those men who can't help but interfere in a woman's business. Well, I'd appreciate it if you'd stay out of mine in the future."

"Oh, I intend to." He started walking toward her, a dark glitter in his eyes. "After this."

She watched him warily. "What are you doing?"

Another two strides and he had her by the arm. "Getting you off the road before you get run over," he muttered, then started leading her back toward the building. "Or is that considered interfering, too?"

She was about to reply with something equally sarcastic, but all at once a funny feeling washed over her. Her head began to swim and, just as she reached the footpath, she felt the blood drain from her face and her knees turn weak. She clutched at Flynn with her other hand. God, she felt strange. Very, very strange. It must be the heat.

Suddenly both fear and panic that she'd done something to hurt the baby came crushing down on top of her. She took deep, calming breaths. *No,* she and the baby would be all right. It'll pass in a moment or two. She only had to wait.

"Danielle?" he said sharply.

She moistened dry lips. "I'm okay. I feel a little faint, that's all."

He muffled something under his breath.

"I should be fine now," she said in a small voice, and pushed herself away from him, but was unsteady on her feet.

He swore again and slipped his arms around her waist. "Let's get you upstairs."

Swinging her up in his arms, he punched in the security code he'd memorized from his last visit to the luxurious penthouse and headed inside to the coolness of the building. The elevator was available and he strode over plush carpet and into it, the lump of fear in his throat almost strangling him.

It was *her* he should strangle, he decided, as she rested her cheek on his shoulder, the soft fragrance of her perfume surrounding his nostrils. She didn't make a murmur.

Once inside her air-conditioned apartment, he laid her down on the leather couch in the living room, noting the faint sheen of perspiration covering her soft, almost translucent skin.

"Stay there," he grated, and headed for the telephone.

She lifted her head off the cushion. "What are you doing?"

He began punching in the first digits of the phone number. "Calling my doctor."

"What? Don't you dare!" She started to sit up, and he slammed the phone down and strode back to her side.

"You need medical attention," he growled, helping her to sit up fully. She was so light, even with the baby growing inside her.

The baby! Alarm rocketed through him again until he saw some color had returned to her cheeks.

"It was the smell of the exhaust fumes, that's all," she said, brushing some blond strands out of her eyes.

Powerful relief filled him, followed by a burst of irritation. How could she take this so casually? He hated to think what may have happened if he hadn't decided to come here today. No one would have heard her screams if that thug had roughed her up a little.

Or a lot.

He straightened, then impaled her with a stare. "You were taking your life in your hands with that idiot back there."

The pink in her cheeks reddened defensively. "His name was given to me by a friend."

His lip curled. "Terrific. The police will know exactly where to go *after* they find your mutilated body in Darwin Harbor. That's if the crocodiles don't get you first."

"Ever thought about writing bedtime books for children?" she mocked, sounding almost back to normal, if there even *was* such a thing as normal for her. She was the most ambiguous woman he'd ever met.

And he was in no mood to appreciate a sense of humor right now. "People don't always go around with Murderer tattooed on their foreheads."

She stirred uneasily, her beautiful face clouding over. "I wouldn't have gone with him if I'd really felt threatened. I have my baby to protect."

Flynn's eyes were drawn to where her hand rested on her stomach. He swallowed tightly, his gaze moving up and resting back on her face as he squashed the urge to pull her into his arms.

"That guy wouldn't have taken no for an answer," he

reiterated, knowing that if he got her in his arms he would shake her first. Then kiss her.

Fear came and went in her eyes. "I know that now."

Some of the tension eased out of his shoulders but he still couldn't let go of the suspicion that she'd do something foolish.

"Why are you here, Flynn?"

Absorbed in his angry thoughts, it was the sound of his name on her lips that broke through to him.

But it was her words that reminded him of the paperwork inside his jacket… Reminded him that she'd do almost anything to get his attention. This was all about getting her own way. She was definitely high maintenance—in more ways than one.

He smiled unpleasantly. "I've come to give you something."

She blinked warily. "You have?"

He took the contract out of his jacket and tossed it onto the sofa next to her. "Consider the loan paid in full. You no longer owe me two hundred thousand dollars."

For one moment something flashed in her eyes, before she quickly looked confused. "I don't understand."

He watched her with cynicism. He'd seen her eyes lit up with what he suspected was satisfaction. "Of course you do. Your letter…the checks…the run-down car…were all a bid for sympathy to get my attention and win me over. Why not just admit it?"

Her eyes flared wide. "What?"

"I'm one step ahead of you." He glanced pointedly at the paperwork. "Go on, pick it up and take a look. It's the contract. You can rip it up or burn it. Do what you will for all I care, but let's just cut our losses and get on with our lives. Separately."

Her delicious mouth opened and closed. Then, as if pretending she couldn't believe it, she looked down at the paper next to her and slowly picked it up. Her hands shook slightly and Flynn pushed aside a stab of guilt. They shook because he knew what she was about. He was probably the first man to so quickly see through her beautiful exterior to the hard core of selfishness beneath. Pregnant or not, this beauty intended to have it all.

Suddenly her head lifted and a deep anger bounced around in her blue eyes, surprising him.

"My God! I'm doing everything in my power to pay back the loan, and not only do you throw my effort back in my face but you accuse me of *subterfuge*."

Oh, she was convincing, but her actions spoke louder than words. She was angry because he'd caught her out. Her wealthy appetite was never more apparent than now, here in her expensive apartment.

He gave her a sweeping glance. "I know women."

She made a choking sound. "What a colossal ego you have."

"Then tell me how wrong I am about you," he said bluntly. "Tell me how you can afford an apartment like this—" he jerked his head at their swish surroundings "—yet not a decent car?"

A look of discomfort crossed her beautiful face before she tossed him a look full of sarcasm. "What? You mean you don't already know everything about my finances?"

She was as guilty as hell and disgust flooded through

him. She cried poor yet could afford to move into this? Perhaps he needed to get a new report done on her, and not just her business affairs this time.

"No doubt you have a lover or ex-lover paying most of your bills. What's the matter? Did you overspend and now he won't buy you a new car? Too bad."

"Think what you like," she said coolly.

"Oh, I will."

She flung him a look of intense dislike. "By the way, you can take your offer and..." Without warning, her voice wobbled and she blinked rapidly.

"Yes?" he taunted.

She cleared her throat. "Mr. Donovan, no matter what you say, I intend to pay the loan back, even if it takes me a lifetime."

He felt a flash of admiration, until he remembered this was just another ploy to trick him into believing she had integrity. She'd fooled Robert Ford at first, too.

All at once he wondered how far she would go in her quest to live the good life. How mercenary could she be? Would she take a new car if he offered it? He rather liked the idea of proving himself right. And dammit, he wasn't a charity but he couldn't bear to think of her pregnant self in a vehicle like he'd just seen. There would be no smooth ride in that thing.

He smiled with derision. If there was one thing she was used to it was a smooth ride, he decided, watching her sit back on the sofa like the lady of leisure she was, the contract casually resting on her lap.

Pushing aside his fanciful thoughts, he briefly glanced at his watch, noting the time. He had a half hour to get back to his office to meet with a visiting dignitary from overseas. What he really felt like doing was getting on his yacht and going for a sail along the coastline, letting the majestic view and cool sea breeze ease the tension out of his body. A tension that one woman had put there.

And still did.

He strode toward the door, but as he reached for the handle he suddenly pictured Danielle fainting. And what if she couldn't get up? She'd have to crawl to the telephone. Perhaps she'd be unable to do even that.

He opened the door then turned to look at her over his shoulder. "Do yourself a favor and get a cell phone." His gaze slid down to her stomach then back up again. "You never know when you'll need it."

Apprehension wavered in her eyes, then one of her eyebrows rose mockingly. "Gee, I wonder what pregnant women did before cell phones."

The muscles at the back of his neck bunched together as he glared at her. "Good question," he rasped, and shut the door on the way out.

Four

Everything about Flynn Donovan was so intense that Danielle brushed off his comment about pregnant women and cell phones. She had no idea why he'd accused her of ripping him off for not paying back the money for the loan, then turned right around and canceled it. Not that she had any intention of accepting the offer, as much as she'd wanted to take him up on it for just a split second. Oh, no. There would be conditions attached no matter what he said. As it was, she'd rather eat dirt.

But when a new shiny green sedan arrived courtesy of Donovan Enterprises, she was both stunned and dismayed. Could he know it was her birthday? Even if he did, why on earth would he make such a gesture? He couldn't get her into bed now. He'd made it more than clear he didn't *want* to get her into bed now. Why spend even more money on her if he didn't want something in return? It just didn't make sense.

But during the drive to his office to give the car back, a horrible suspicion occurred to her. Was he like Robert and wanted to play nasty little games with her? Robert had been spiteful when he didn't get his own way and would have done something like this just to make her suffer.

Was this Flynn's way of being spiteful because he couldn't have her in his bed? Did it give him some sort of satisfaction pretending to terminate the loan, then committing her to a new car so that she was still tied to him?

It had to be. She could think of no other reason a man would throw away good money, especially when he'd already made it clear he didn't give a damn about her as a person.

Thankfully his assistant wasn't at her desk, giving Danielle the opportunity to walk into Flynn's office without knocking.

He looked up from some paperwork, his eyes showing mild surprise, but she didn't give him the chance to speak. "I don't understand you," she said, walking toward him. "You accuse me of taking your money yet you want to spend more on me?" She slapped the car keys down on some papers. "No thanks. You can keep your money and your car. I don't need your help. I can manage to buy a car all by myself."

"Really?" His lips twisted. "You're not doing a very good job of it from what I can see."

Her cheeks filled with angry warmth. "Thanks for the compliment."

"Oh, so it's compliments you want, not my concern over the safety of you and your child. Or do you really want to drive around in a death trap like the one you were in yesterday?"

A shudder went through her. "You really know how to play dirty, don't you?"

"It's come in handy over the years."

She just bet it had.

He leaned back in his leather chair. "Why are you being so difficult about this?"

She clenched her teeth. "Why not? Isn't that how I get your *attention?*" she said sarcastically.

He straightened, a sudden icy contempt flashing in his eyes. "Look, you wanted a car, you've got one."

She lifted her chin. "I didn't ask."

"I didn't say you did. But you'll accept it, anyway. Well?" he proceeded.

She'd like to throw it back in his face but couldn't afford to right now. Instead, trying to gather her thoughts, she put her purse down on the desk and took a few steps over to the tropical fish tank next to the wall. For a couple of moments she watched the colorful array of fish swimming around in the clear water and felt an affinity with them. No matter how you looked at it, they were trapped.

Like she was.

Dear God, could she swallow her pride and refuse the car? Worse, could she risk her baby's life by buying a cheaper one that was perhaps not as safe?

Suddenly she knew what she had to do and she gave an inner groan. It would be hard but somehow she'd manage.

She turned to look at him. "I'll accept it on one condition. I'll pay it off, along with the other loan."

"Of course you will," he mocked.

Her eyes widened. "You don't believe me?"

"What's to believe? I've already told you to forget the money."

"And I said I'll accept the car, but I *won't* agree to not paying back the loan," she pointed out.

"Don't make a song and dance about it," he said, but there was a tiny muscle jerking at the corner of his mouth. "You're not fooling anyone but yourself if you think I can't see what you're about."

She pushed aside a sense of hurt. Once again she was being accused of something unpleasant. He thought all this was just a pretense on her part…that her objection was just lip service and she was actually reveling in him giving her a valuable car. It was obvious he expected her to take what she could get out of him.

"You're a fine one to talk. You're obviously doing this for your own sick reasons that have nothing to do with *me* but everything to do with *you*."

"Is that right?" he drawled, but she saw an alert look in his eyes.

"You want to hold it over my head, don't you? It makes you feel important to know that it will take me a lifetime to pay the loan back."

"I don't need you to make me feel important."

"Not from where I'm standing."

His mouth tightened. "I don't play games."

"Unlike me, you mean?"

"You said it."

That did it. She'd had enough.

Of Flynn and his unfounded suspicions.

Of the whole darn world.

She straightened her shoulders. "Mr. Donovan, you owe me one hell of an apology," she said, determined to stand up to him and to keep on standing up to him for as long as it took.

One of his arrogant brows lifted. "For what?"

"You're wrong about me."

"I don't think so." His eyes were so cold that not even the hot Darwin sun could defrost them. "Now, stop wasting my time." He picked up the car keys and held them out to her. "Take it or leave it."

She looked at the keys, then back at his derisive face. "Thanks. I'll pass."

"Danielle…" he growled.

All at once she knew that if she didn't get out of there she was going to burst into tears. She twirled toward the door.

"Where are you going?" he demanded.

Moisture welled in her eyes and she tried to blink it away. "That's not your concern."

"Danielle, stop," he warned.

She kept on walking out the door and hurried toward the elevator.

"Danielle, I mean it," he said, coming up behind her.

"Big deal," she choked as she punched the button for the elevator and the doors slid open. Thankfully it was vacant and she rushed into it before she did something really stupid, like crying.

But she only managed to hold back the tears until she stepped inside, half-blindly pressing the ground floor button. Then they swelled up in her eyes so quickly she couldn't even see what she was doing.

All at once Flynn stormed in next to her, making her jump. She turned her back and blinked rapidly, determined not to let him see how upset she was. This would just be another thing for him to accuse her of faking.

She heard the elevator door close.

A moment passed.

"Danielle, look at me," he said softly.

"No." She didn't want him to see her like this. Not when she felt like a weepy female.

His hand touched her shoulder and he gently turned her around. At the oddly concerned gleam in his eyes, she moaned and did the exact opposite of what she'd told herself not to do. She burst into tears.

After a moment or two a snarling sound came from deep in his throat and he pulled her into his arms. "Shh. Don't cry."

"I can't help it," she mumbled into his shirt, hating him, wanting him. Oh, she didn't know what she felt for him.

He gave her his handkerchief and she cried even harder, until she thought she was never going to stop. Until the tears began to dry up and she could sniff for a few more moments. And then she began to notice how wonderful Flynn smelled, the tantalizing warmth of his male body mixing with the clean scent of his shirt.

"Danielle?"

She heard the deep rumble of her name, felt the rapid beat of his heart against her cheek and couldn't seem to pull away. She felt lethargic all of a sudden. Wonderfully lethargic. Heat was engulfing her. Male heat. And it was coming from Flynn. She had the sudden urge to take long, intimate breaths.

"Danielle?"

This time she did move back. And looked up into dark eyes that made her heart skip a beat. Up close like this, the look was much more than powerful. It was potent. And possessive. She dared not breath. Otherwise he would kiss her. Would lay his lips upon hers and ravish her mouth, and she didn't think she would be able to resist him.

He bent his head….

The elevator jolted to a stop, making her jump back, horrified by what she'd been about to let him do to her.

He reached out to steady her as she bumped against the wall. "Careful," he said roughly, his touch making her skin quiver, as if the thin material of her top beneath his hands didn't exist.

She took a shaky breath. It was time to put some distance between them. "I think I need eyes in the back of my head," she said, trying to sound glib but the huskiness in her voice gave her away.

"It would help," he muttered, a vein throbbing at his temple, telling her he was as affected as she was. "Maybe then I wouldn't want you."

She gave a soft gasp. "I—"

"Don't say a word, Danielle. Not a word or I'll carry you back up to my office and make love to you right now."

She'd known there was a sexual spark between them from the start, but hearing him say out loud that he still wanted her was shocking. "But…I'm pregnant."

"I know," he said, his mouth grim.

For a moment she stood there, stunned as the doors behind him slid open to an empty lobby. Flynn Donovan still wanted her. And dear God, she wanted him, too. But pregnant widows weren't supposed to want a man. It just wasn't done.

Yet how could she want a man who thought the worst of her? A man who had accused her of stealing his money? Of lying and cheating?

A moment crept by, then with a hint of regret in his eyes, he took her arm, gently pulled her past him and pushed her out into the lobby, but not before she felt his hard body brush against her own.

"The car's yours," he said roughly, not moving from the elevator. His eyes held hers for another instant, tiny flames firing in them, then anger flared and he reached out and shoved the car keys in her hand. "Take them." He turned and stabbed the elevator button.

The door closed shut between them and she took a steadying breath. Flynn Donovan stirred a need within her that was more than physical. Something deeper. More intimate. *Oh, God.* Hadn't she had enough heartache where men were concerned?

It was all his PA's fault that he had to return Danielle's purse after work, Flynn decided. If it were left to him, he would have sent it back by courier. As it was, if *he* didn't do it, she would. She'd said so when he'd returned from seeing Danielle off at the elevator and Connie had stood there with the purse in hand and a worried look in her eyes. He hadn't been about to let that happen. If Danielle got her clutches into Connie, then she would have won.

Of course, his PA was more than happy for him to return the purse. Delighted in fact. He was still in her good books after yesterday when he'd walked into the office and ordered her to go buy a new car.

"For you?" Connie had said with a frown.

"For Danielle Ford," he'd snapped.

Her eyes had widened. "What about the loan?"

"She refused to tear it up."

Connie had nodded, as if agreeing. "She has integrity, that one."

He'd shaken his head, still amazed his usually perceptive assistant couldn't see the truth. "She's just trying to pull the wool over your eyes."

"I don't know why."

He did, but he'd refused to mention his theory that Danielle was after a rich man to marry her. How else could she keep herself and her baby in the manner to which she was accustomed?

"No matter. Right now a car is her immediate concern. That's if it meets with your approval," he'd derided.

Her eyes had softened with understanding. "That isn't why you did it, but thank you, Flynn."

"Connie, don't turn me into a saint."

"Heaven forbid," she'd joked. Then her forehead had creased. "Hmm. Perhaps I should go and see—"

"No," he'd growled.

"But someone should keep an eye on her."

"Don't get involved, Connie."

"But—"

"Say one more thing about Danielle Ford and I'll fire you myself." And he'd meant it.

She'd given him a look that said it wasn't over, but she'd done what he'd ordered and bought a car.

So now he would return the purse, then go home and dress for his date and he'd make damn sure he enjoyed himself tonight, he decided, as he strode down the hallway toward Danielle's penthouse door. He had a date with an ex-lover and he fully intended to make the most of his night and the last thing he needed was a glimpse of Danielle Ford to remind him what he couldn't have with her.

His eyes narrowed when he saw her door standing open. Bloody hell, was she *expecting* him? Had she deliberately left the purse on his desk? Of course she must have.

Anger filled him as he strode forward, the sound of the television meeting his ears as he got closer to the open doorway. "Danielle?" he called out in a sharp tone.

No answer.

He stepped into the living room and called louder, "Danielle?"

Still no answer.

He looked around the room and over to the kitchen. Why didn't she answer?

A muffled sound came from the other direction and a frisson of fear rolled down his spine. Despite it, he strode forward, a knot growing in his gut with each step he took. If she'd hurt herself...

He pushed the door open. And there she was, wrapping her hair up in a towel, having just stepped out of the shower. She looked up at the doorway and screamed.

Then she let out a shaky breath. "Oh, Flynn. It's only you."

Only him.

His eyes dropped from her face to her breasts, over her still-flat stomach to the blond triangle of hair at the junction of her thighs. His body hardened in the hot, steamy room. This woman would turn up any man's blood pressure. She was a seductress. A sexy witch. And he wanted her more than he'd ever wanted a woman before.

"Flynn?"

The soft sound of his name on her lips made him want to take her in his arms. To press her breasts against his chest. To ease the ache between her thighs, *their* thighs, with the sweetest possession of all.

His gaze roved back up to her face, and her eyes told him what he already knew. Danielle Ford wanted him as much as he wanted her.

"You're beautiful," he rasped and saw her eyes deepen to a smoky blue.

"I'm—" Apprehension flicked across her face. Suddenly she made a grab for the short robe resting on the towel rack. "Pregnant," she said unsteadily, sliding her arms into the material and pulling it close. "I think you've forgotten that."

"You're still sexy, Danielle. Incredibly so."

"Don't," she whispered.

"Don't what?"

"Come in here and seduce me."

He noted the way the soft, sky-blue material of her robe clung to her damp breasts. "That's funny. I thought you were the one doing the seducing."

Color flooded her face. "How? By stepping out of my own shower?"

He straightened. "Your door was open," he reminded her, then held up the purse. "And you left this in my office today."

Recognition flickered in her eyes. "Oh. Yes, I know. I was going to come by and get it tomorrow."

He sent her a mocking look.

Her eyes widened. "You think I left it there deliberately?"

"You mean you didn't?"

She opened her mouth to speak, then closed it, her forehead crinkling. "Wait a minute. What do you mean my door was open? It was closed. I'm sure it was. I always close it."

"Perhaps the lock's faulty?" he said, sneering, knowing she'd set him up well and truly.

She stiffened. "Perhaps it is. The Realtor said they'd changed the locks." She jerkily pulled the towel from her head and combed her fingers through her hair, then stopped to look at him. "Anyway, I'd appreciate it if you'd leave."

He wasn't used to being dismissed, certainly not by the woman he wanted. "Found another willing male to help you out?" he said cynically.

She bristled with indignation. "I resent that remark. I've never once asked for your help. You forced the car on me. I didn't want to take it, remember?"

"You needed help for your baby."

"We would have survived without it."

"No doubt." This woman was a survivor of the worst kind. She survived on other people's money.

"You don't seem to understand that my independence is important to me," she said, the proud tilt of her head at odds with what he knew about her.

"Don't I?"

She drew herself up as she tightened her robe. "In the future I'll thank you to stay away from me. I accepted the car but that doesn't give you the right to walk into my apartment anytime you like."

His mouth pressed into a grim line. "That isn't why I'm here," he pointed out.

"Sure it isn't," she mocked, trying to turn the tables on him, looking so darn beautiful that she grabbed his breath away. If he didn't get out of here soon he was going to march up to her, pull her into his arms and kiss her until she surrendered to him completely.

Drawing a sharp breath, he twisted on his heels and headed toward the front door. The woman was a danger to herself and to every man she smiled at. Even the ones she didn't smile at would succumb to her beauty. All men were suckers for a beautiful lady with charisma.

"I'd better check that lock," he said roughly, not believing that it was faulty but needing to make sure.

"There's no need," she said quickly, coming up

behind him. "The landlord will fix it if there's a problem."

He stopped dead, and so did she. "I thought you'd want to fix it yourself," he scoffed. "Seeing you're so independent and all."

Her enticing lips tightened. "You're taking that out of context."

He didn't think so. "Anyway, if it *is* faulty—" and his tone said he very much doubted it "—you won't get the landlord to look at it before Monday. And I don't want to get up tomorrow morning and find your murder front-page news."

"Don't be silly," she scoffed, but all at once her voice sounded uncertain as she touched her stomach.

A shiver went down his spine again. "I'm checking the lock whether you like it or not." He strode to the door.

Unfortunately it didn't take him long to spot a problem with the catch. He swore, not liking the sudden feeling of guilt. And not liking that perhaps he had been wrong about her.

This time.

"What is it?" she said behind him.

"Looks like I owe you an apology."

She expelled a little sigh. "See. I told you I was telling the truth." She moved closer. "What's wrong with it?"

The exotic fragrance she'd rubbed all over her body was suddenly blinding him to all the reasons he should step back and leave this apartment before it was too late. "It isn't catching properly."

"Where?" she said, moving even closer.

And that was it.

All at once the air hummed with electricity. As if she felt it, she turned to face him. Their eyes met and she gave a soft gasp, and in that heartbeat, Flynn knew he had to kiss her or regret it for the rest of his life.

"Don't stop me, Danielle," he growled and didn't give her time to argue. He lowered his head, his eyes homing in on her mouth. For a moment she held out against him and he knew she was fighting herself rather than him. Then her lips quivered and opened on the smallest sigh of surrender.

Adrenaline pumped into him and his tongue slipped inside her to taste the moist, dark warmth of her. She tasted superb. Just as he'd expected. Just as he'd imagined since the first time he'd seen her.

Without warning, her arms inched up and slid around his neck, pulling him closer. He could feel her against him, arousing him, and suddenly everything was getting out of control. *His* control. She was pregnant, for God's sake. He had to stop.

He broke off the kiss and swore, "Hell."

"Flynn?" she whispered, her eyes darkened with that smoky hue again.

Heat engulfed him and he groaned. "Just one more kiss," he muttered, pulling her to him.

A goodbye kiss.

A farewell kiss.

A kiss to end all kisses.

Only, when their lips met for a second time, it suddenly didn't matter that she was pregnant. Nor that she was a woman out to get all that she could. Nothing mattered except the delicious taste of her, the glorious scent of her, the explosive feel of her in his arms, rubbing up against him, turning him on.

Shuddering, he let his mouth slide along her cheek to her ear, catching her delicate earlobe between his lips, then his teeth, laving it with his tongue.

"Flynn, we have to stop." She moaned with pleasure, inflaming him further.

He pushed some wet strands of her hair aside with his lips and trailed kisses down the column of her throat, pressing his mouth against her wildly beating pulse. "Must we?" He just needed to touch her some more. Maybe then he'd get enough of her.

"We...have to." Her husky tones told him she had her eyes closed, savoring each precious moment. He did the same as he inhaled against her collarbone. Her scent was driving him wild.

"Let me love you just a little," he murmured, deciding to damn the consequences just for a moment more and moved back to push the silky robe off her shoulders, exposing the tips of her nipples. He looked down at her full breasts and sucked in air. "Beautiful. They're made for a man's hands. *My* hands."

She lifted heavy eyelids. "Yes."

"And for my tongue."

"Oh, yes!"

He slid the material off her shoulders, fully exposing her in a way that highlighted each golden globe. An aching need hit him right in the gut, then lower to where his erection strained against his trousers.

He ran a finger from one nipple to the other, her silky soft skin puckering to his touch as she rested her head back against the wall, giving short little puffs of breath. He repeated the action.

Then he ran his thumbs across each brown peak, before squeezing those little pebbles between his fingers. She moaned and her eyes feathered shut, and something deep inside him abated, filling him with a sense of rightness. He was meant to be here, with her in his arms. Right now, in this moment of time.

Groaning, he bent his head and took a nipple in his mouth, flicking it with his tongue.

"Flynn," she sobbed in a guttural sound that seemed to come from deep within her.

He did it again, then began to suck, harder and harder, wanting to give her more and more. He could hear the pounding of his heart in his ears, telling him to give her everything she needed. That only *he* could give it to her.

She moved restlessly and a picture of those blond womanly curls came to mind, making his fingers itch to touch her there. Lord knew he wanted to find out what she felt like.

He kissed her again and slowly slid his palm over her stomach, then down to the essence of the woman. God, she was wet and warm against his fingers.

He kissed her deeply, moving his fingers against her soft nub, stroking once, stroking twice. He wanted to give her pleasure. No, he wanted to give her a pleasure like she'd never known before.

"Let yourself go," he murmured against the corner of her mouth and touched her some more.

At first there was a slight ripple through her body, then her legs began to quiver. She gripped his shoulders, panting heavily, head flung back, eyes closed.

"That's it, sweetheart." He relished the expressive emotions flittering across her face as she reached closer to fulfillment.

And then the tremors of arousal began and she cried out his name as she went up in flames. She shattered as his fingers slicked back and forth. If he'd been inside her, he would have felt her grip and release as she rode the waves of ecstasy. It was almost enough to send a man over the edge.

He held her until the turbulence inside her slowed to a halt. She leaned against him, resting her head on his shoulder while she caught her breath.

Finally she looked up at him and in her eyes was pure embarrassment. She looked more than beautiful. Stunning. Intense male possessiveness ripped through him, even as he wondered about her self-consciousness.

"Flynn, I—"

"Don't say anything." He gathered the sides of her robe together and tied it with the sash.

She licked her slightly swollen lips. "But you haven't... You didn't..."

"No, and I don't need to," he rasped.

"But—"

"No buts, Danielle." He gazed at her, forcing himself to concentrate on the moment. "I enjoyed watching you."

She gave a soft gasp and he bent his head, quickly taking advantage of her open mouth. He parted her lips with his tongue, then spent a long moment absorbing the heady taste of her. It was a taste flavored by a new sensuousness between them.

Then suddenly there was a knock on the door.

Danielle broke off the kiss, pushed at his chest. "Oh, God!" she gasped.

He frowned as the outside world intruded. "What's the matter?"

"It's Monica," she whispered, her eyes darting down the hallway as if looking for an escape.

"Monica?"

She glanced back at him. "Um...my mother-in-law," she said, then looked away nervously, giving him the impression she didn't want him to know too much about the other woman.

His jaw clenched at the reminder that Danielle had been married. That she'd belonged to another man. Robert would have touched her, loving her in many ways, making her his own. Flynn was suddenly jealous of the other man. Of every second Robert Ford had spent with her.

"Don't answer," he said roughly, keeping his voice low.

Her eyes clouded over. "I have to. She's coming for dinner. It's my birthday."

Something odd kicked inside him. "Your birthday?"

"Yes," she said almost absentmindedly, then bit her lip nervously. "If I don't answer the door, she'll think I'm still at work and..."

He jolted. So she *did* have a regular job and didn't just volunteer at the hospital as he'd imagined.

"Then if I don't come home, she's likely to call the police."

"Did you say she was your mother-in-law, or your mother?" he mocked, not liking the sound of this Monica.

"Mother-in-law," she mumbled, missing his sarcasm.

"Then just open the door and act as if nothing happened."

And that would be the biggest lie ever.

She moistened her lips, her eyes darting past his shoulder, looking everywhere but at him. "I can't. She wouldn't understand."

The muscles at the back of his neck tightened. "Are you scared of her?"

Her eyes swung back to him. "Of course not," she said, but there was a hollow ring to her words, and he knew she was definitely scared of something. "She's just..." She winced. "Well, she's Robert's mother. I don't want her to find us like this."

"Like what? I was only checking your lock," he drawled.

She blushed, her gaze dropping to his chest. "Flynn, I don't think—"

Another knock at the door cut across her words, making her jump. Flynn swore softly. This was a ridiculous situation.

She brushed back her damp hair, then tightened the collar of her robe. She swallowed. "I have to face her."

He suddenly felt proud of her, so he dropped a light kiss on her lips, tempted to linger. He wanted to say to hell with this Monica, but if he did that, then he'd have to sweep Danielle up in his arms and carry her to the bedroom for a night of hot pleasure.

And then what?

He shuddered. It was as well this Monica would call the police. It was the wake-up call he needed. From this point he would back off and leave Danielle to get on with her life. In about six months time she would become a mother, for God's sake. And he'd never seen anyone sexier.

"Flynn, I'm ready."

He gave a nod, then pulled the door open, making the well-dressed woman on the other side almost leap out of her skin.

"Monica," Danielle exclaimed, pretending surprise, though Flynn didn't think she did a good job of it, considering she was such an accomplished liar at times. "I didn't realize you were there."

The mother-in-law's gaze traveled from one to the other, then up and down, her obsidian eyes turning colder by degrees. "So I see."

"This is Flynn." Danielle gave a smile but he saw the uneasiness beneath. "He's been checking the lock on my door."

"Really?" Monica said haughtily, then dismissed him by smiling coolly. "You should have called, dear. I know a locksmith."

He'd bet a thousand dollars she didn't, Flynn thought, taking an instant dislike to Danielle's mother-in-law, noticing how her smile didn't reach her eyes. She was too cold. And calculating.

"Yes, well," Danielle said. "The landlord will have to fix it now. Flynn hasn't got the right equipment."

"Oh, I don't know about that," he drawled, and

was pleased when two spots of color appeared on Danielle's cheeks.

Monica looked at Flynn. "If only my Robbie were here. He was good at fixing things."

"I'm sure he *was*," Flynn said, emphasizing the last word. If Monica thought she was warning him off Danielle, then she could think again. He'd already made the decision to stay away and it had nothing to do with her mother-in-law.

Monica's narrowed eyes told him she got the message, and right at that moment, Flynn could see how much Robert Ford had been like his mother. From the moment he'd met the other man he'd disliked him intensely.

As if Danielle sensed something going on between the two of them, she turned toward him, her eyes agitated. "Well, thanks again, Flynn," she said, almost pushing him out the door. "I appreciate your help."

He was tempted to stay just to annoy this Monica. Instead he stepped through the doorway and into the hall. "Make sure you get the lock fixed as soon as possible."

"I will. And good night."

"Yes, *goodbye*," Monica said, moving past him into the apartment, almost elbowing him aside. "Nice meeting you."

"And you." He could play the game as well as she could, he mused, watching her continue on to the living room. Her rigid back gave him an immense sense of satisfaction.

Danielle glanced over her shoulder, again reminding him she was uneasy with this woman in her home, and a protective instinct rose in him, which he firmly squashed. He had no doubt Danielle would continue to hold firm against the other woman. After all, Danielle could take care of herself. He had to remember that.

"I'd better go in." Danielle started to close the door, then stopped briefly, awareness in her eyes shooting desire through every region of his body. "Thank you for returning my purse."

He held her gaze for one long moment, angry she was who she was, but wanting her with every fiber of his being. "It was my pleasure," he rasped, watching with satisfaction as a flush spread up her neck to her face just before she closed the door.

He stood there for a moment and inhaled her scent still clinging to him. Then he spun on his heels and headed toward the elevator. He was supposed to be going out tonight but the thought of talking to another woman, of being with another woman, of making love to a woman other than the woman he wanted, filled him with distaste.

Dammit, there was no way he could go on his date now. Not after what he'd just shared with Danielle. He only hoped that even this small sample of how pleasurable it could be with Danielle Ford hadn't ruined his love life.

Forever.

Danielle shut the door, then let out a shaky sigh. She had been so close to disaster just now. If Flynn had mentioned the loan to spite her... If Monica had decided to use it to get the baby...

No, she wouldn't let it happen to her.

Straightening her shoulders, she took a deep breath before turning into the living room to face Monica. Her mother-in-law was bound to say something about Flynn having been in the apartment.

"Here. Let me take those," she said when she saw Monica with a pile of her personal papers in the other woman's hands.

Monica spun around, a flash of guilt crossing her face. "Oh, you startled me. I was just moving them so I could sit down."

Danielle was sure she'd been reading them, not moving them, but she let it pass. They were only some bills and the lease to the apartment, which she'd been meaning to put away, anyway. Thankfully there was nothing about the loan in among that lot, she thought with intense relief as she took the papers and put them in the bureau drawer, out of sight.

Monica sat down on the couch and stabbed her with her eyes. "Tell me, Danielle. How do you know Flynn Donovan?"

Danielle had already prepared herself for the question. "He was visiting my neighbor in the other penthouse," she lied, hating it but knowing it had to be done. "My door was open and he came to tell me and we discovered the lock was faulty."

"So you don't know him personally?" she questioned further.

"No." Something occurred to Danielle. "But obviously you knew who he was."

Monica shrugged. "Only from what I've read in the newspapers."

Surprisingly, Monica appeared to accept the explanation. Then her assessing gaze raked down Danielle's bathrobe. "That's new, isn't it?"

Danielle suddenly felt exposed and vulnerable, even more than when she'd stood naked in front of Flynn, if that was possible.

"Yes, it is," she said, trying not to get defensive. She'd bought the silk robe a couple of weeks ago when she'd needed something to cheer herself up and the price had been so cheap it had almost jumped off the rack at her.

Another look at Monica, and Danielle decided she'd be too uncomfortable to stay dressed like this another minute. "I'll just go and change."

"Hmm." Monica weighed her with a critical squint. "I'm not sure Robbie would like it on you."

That old feeling of being smothered returned and Danielle stiffened. She had to be strong and continue to dodge being snared by her mother-in-law's need to control. "Really?"

"And, Danielle, dear, a bit of advice. You shouldn't wear something like that in front of another man. It may give him ideas, especially one as rich and successful as Flynn Donovan."

Danielle whirled around and started walking to her bedroom so Monica wouldn't see her face turning red. "Not in my condition it wouldn't."

"You'd be surprised. Some men find pregnancy rather attractive," Monica warned, her voice rising as Danielle continued walking.

"I'm sure you're wrong," Danielle said, then closed her bedroom door and leaned back against it.

Heat washed over her body and her legs trembled. From the moment Flynn had stepped into her bathroom, she'd been his for the taking. Oh, she'd fought herself all the way to the front door, but when she'd turned and seen the hot desire in his eyes, she had melted for him.

But it had been so long since she'd felt attraction for a man. So long since she'd made love to a man she desired. Flynn had made her come alive again, had recognized her needs and taken her beyond the edge of satisfaction. She'd never had such an experience before. He made her feel like a woman again. And he'd given back what had slowly diminished in her marriage to Robert. Her sense of feminine self.

For that she owed Flynn Donovan a lot.

Of course, that didn't make him any less arrogant, nor the right man for her, she reminded herself. She needed to keep that in mind and fend off her attraction for him.

Just then, there was a light knock on the door. "Are you coming out, Danielle? I want to give you your birthday present."

Danielle let out a slow breath and counted to ten. Monica always did this, stalking her until she felt smothered. Robert had been the same. And that was a timely reminder that the battle for independence had been too hard fought and won.

"I'll be there in a minute, Monica. Why don't you put the coffee on?"

A moment's silence, then she said, "Fine."

Danielle waited a moment more, then pushed herself

away from the door with trembling hands. She was never going to let herself be dictated to again.

Never.

And that applied to Flynn Donovan.

No matter how wonderful he made her feel.

Five

After the function, Flynn dropped his date off at her apartment, drove home to his mansion in Cullen Bay, then spent the early hours of the morning sitting on the balcony of his master bedroom. An electrical storm had raged during the evening while he'd been at the dinner, and now his lushly landscaped garden was beautifully moonlit.

He'd realized one thing tonight. He'd rather spend an evening being antagonized by Danielle than being sweet talked by a bevy of beautiful women.

God, what *was* it about Danielle Ford he couldn't shake? As much as a part of him didn't want to see this woman who was far from an angel, he knew his body still hungered after her. It was a hunger that he wasn't about to appease, so why was he putting himself through this? He couldn't have her...shouldn't have her...but he'd tormented himself anyway.

Yet every time he looked into her blue eyes it weakened his determination to stay away from her. And tonight...no, yesterday...he couldn't stop thinking about the way she'd melted for him back there in her apartment.

And that baffled him. For a woman who would have used her body many times to get what she wanted, according to her former husband, she hadn't been as experienced as he'd expected. Her slight hesitation and occasional lack of control...while thoroughly tantalizing...had told him otherwise.

Dammit, she just didn't add up. She seemed to be a mixture of truth and lies. Of innocence and guilt. Independent yet reliant. Look at the way she'd left her door open for him...or not. The lock *had* been faulty, he admitted.

And she'd mentioned her job in the stress of the moment. So it was a real job, after all, not a volunteer one as he'd suspected. It was time he actually got that report done on her. A personal one this time, not just a financial one. He wanted to know everything about her. Everything and more from the day she'd been born.

And dammit, yesterday had been her birthday and he hadn't known until too late. It turned out that the car he'd given her had been an inadvertently well-timed gift, but spending the evening with a cold, unfeeling mother-in-law who obviously didn't have an unselfish bone in her body wasn't exactly a great way to celebrate.

Danielle deserved better.

She also deserved an Oscar, he forced himself to remember as he hopped in his Mercedes just after breakfast, intending to drive to her apartment before she went to work. He was determined to make sure she had dinner with him tonight.

Him and no other man.

He was just leaving his driveway, about to turn out onto the main road when a figure stepped in front of the car. He swore as he slammed on the brakes, stopping just short of hitting the person.

Then he saw who it was.

Monica Ford.

His jaw clenched as he got out of his car and walked toward her. She'd obviously been waiting for him to leave his house, though how she'd known where he lived made him uneasy. He didn't like this woman.

And that hated look in her eyes said she was still remembering meeting him yesterday at Danielle's apartment.

"Monica," he said, inclining his head in greeting.

"It's Mrs. Ford to you, Mr. Donovan," she spat.

He paused for effect. "I see."

"Do you?"

She was obviously spoiling for a fight.

"Why are you here?"

She glared at him. "I want you to stay away from Danielle. Or you'll be sorry."

He felt his anger rise in response. "I don't take kindly to threats."

"Danielle and the baby belong to Robert. I won't let you have either of them."

Sudden apprehension rolled over in his chest. "Is this some kind of joke?"

She pulled herself up straighter. "My son is no joke. Danielle loves him and he loves her."

He mentally took a step back. "Your son is dead," he pointed out, trying to judge if this woman was as mad as she made out to be.

"How dare you say that!"

He scowled. Whether she was mad or not, she was definitely mentally unbalanced. "Listen, I think you need help."

She wagged a finger at him and hissed, "You just stay out of the picture. That's all the help we want."

We?

Giving him a hateful look, she said, "Whatever you think you're going to get from Danielle won't happen. *I* won't let it." Then she spun on her heels and hurried toward a car parked down the road.

Flynn waited until she'd driven off, a horrible feeling in his gut. She was definitely sick in the head, exactly how sick was the question. But he knew one thing. He preferred her coldness yesterday over the hate today.

He still felt uneasy on the way over to Danielle's place, but more for her sake than his own. He could handle the likes of Monica, but the woman was unstable and he wasn't sure Danielle knew that. He vowed to keep an eye on things though he suspected Monica wouldn't hurt Danielle and the baby. If anything, it was *him* Monica would want to hurt.

When Danielle opened her front door, he pushed all that to the back of his mind.

Adrenaline surged through him at the sight of her. He

hadn't seen her since last evening…since she'd come apart in his hands.

She was as sexy as hell. Her coral halter-necked top doing marvelous things for her skin tone and denim shorts showing off those gorgeous legs of hers, down to her bare feet.

She lifted her chin in the air. "Flynn, we need to talk," she said, not inviting him in, obviously ready to do battle. "I don't want you getting the wrong idea about last night. About it leading anywhere or anything. I mean…" All at once she faltered a little in her speech. "We're both adults and things got out of hand, that's all."

"In more ways than one," he drawled, her reluctance to have anything to do with him stirring his senses and urging him to take her in his arms and force her to change her mind.

"Last night was a mistake. I'm not ready for an affair. I'm having a baby."

His mouth flattened into a straight line as her words hit home. He may not be able to argue with the truth, but one thing was for certain. If she hadn't been pregnant, she'd be in his bed right now and they wouldn't be merely *talking* about making love. He'd be inside her warm body, knowing this woman intimately.

Just thinking about it aroused him more than he'd ever been before. And it had nothing to do with being celibate for a couple of months now. It was all to do with Danielle.

His jaw clenched. "Did you phone the landlord about getting your lock fixed?"

She blinked, took a moment to note the change of

subject, then gave a nod. "Someone will be here Monday."

Pleasure coursed through him that she had followed his instructions, in this at least. "Make sure you close your door properly until then," he said, partly thinking of Monica.

Danielle held herself stiffly, a rush of heat coming into her cheeks. "Why are you here, Flynn?"

He had to think past how gorgeous she looked with that soft color tingeing her high cheekbones. "I didn't get to say happy birthday to you last night."

Her eyes widened in surprise, then mellowed with something that hinted at gratitude. But in the blink of an eye, they suddenly hardened. "What's the catch?"

"No catch."

"You could have sent flowers."

"But then," he drawled, "I wouldn't have had the chance to blackmail you into having dinner with me tonight."

Her hand slipped from the doorknob. "Wh-what?"

"I'll pick you up at seven." He started to walk away.

"Wait!"

Something in her tone made him stop and turn back to face her. A vulnerable look in her eyes made his chest tighten.

"Flynn, I—" she hesitated "—I don't think we should."

An unusual feeling of tenderness rose up inside him but he firmly squashed it. "Danielle, you owe me."

Her chin angled higher. "I've told you. I'm paying back the money for the loan and the car."

"I'm talking about the lock."

She looked confused. "But you didn't fix it."

"No, but I came close," he said, pleased at the double entendre.

Her cheeks reddened. "I know you've been more than generous but I think I'll stay home tonight."

"Alone?" he said sharply as jealousy slithered through him. And that was happening far too often for his liking. No other woman had ever made him feel that particular emotion before. He wasn't going to let it get a stranglehold now.

"Yes."

"Seven," he ordered, turning toward the elevator so she couldn't see his intense relief. "Be ready."

He didn't wait for her to answer. As if on cue, the doors opened for him and he stepped inside.

Danielle then spent the day warring between feeling angry with Flynn for his "Me Tarzan, you Jane" attitude, but suspecting he had a kind heart beneath all that arrogance. Certainly Robert had only ever taken her out to dinner once on her birthday and that had been when they were courting. After their marriage, he and Monica had mostly preferred to dine at home on special occasions.

It was this very reminder of the past that made Danielle change her mind about going out with Flynn tonight. She was a free woman and she would do as she liked and go out with whomever she liked. Just because it happened to be Flynn Donovan…

When her doorbell rang at seven, she nervously patted some wisps of blond hair back into her chignon, then smoothed the front of her short black dress. The soft silky material was complemented by a loose-fitting jacket of the same material.

She swung open the door and her breath caught in her throat. Flynn looked incredibly handsome in a black suit that emphasized the width of his shoulders and the length of his legs. A white shirt beneath his jacket only added to his compelling sense of presence.

"You are more beautiful each time I see you," he murmured, his voice deep and husky, a light at the back of his eyes hinting that just looking at her switched on something inside him.

She wished she could have stayed angry with him. It would have given her the impetus to ignore the admiration he made no effort to hide. Instead, she dissolved like bubbles in a bath.

"Thank you," she whispered, then cleared her throat, finding her mental balance. "I didn't know how fancy this restaurant is, so I wasn't sure what to wear."

"You're perfect."

Her heart skipped a beat but didn't settle to a nice easy pace. "Um…I'll get my purse." She turned and walked over to the sofa, breathing easier as she put some distance between them. But when she turned back, Flynn had entered the apartment, closing the door behind him.

"This is for you," he said, holding a small gift-wrapped box in his hands she hadn't noticed before.

"It is?" Silly delight skipped along her spine before she brought herself back down to earth. He'd already helped her too much. Okay, so he was wealthy and could afford it, but taking her to dinner was more than enough.

"I'm sorry. I can't accept another present from you, Flynn. I hardly know you," she said, reminding him they were nothing to each other, when all was said and done.

"But you *do* know me, Danielle. I was the man who made you crumble in my hands yesterday." He jerked his hand behind him. "By that very door."

The breath hitched in her throat but she managed one word. "Flynn."

"Remember?"

How could she forget the way he'd made her feel? How his touch had scorched her body. How he'd taken her to the heights, then released her into a tide of passion.

"Yes, I remember." She wet her suddenly dry lips. "Nevertheless, I—"

"You haven't even seen it yet," he pointed out dryly, moving toward her.

"No, but—"

"It isn't jewelry, if that's what's bothering you."

They both knew that wasn't really what bothered her. It was the attraction between them. The sensual tension that threatened to spiral out of control every time they were together.

He stopped right in front of her. She could smell his aftershave, a distinct scent of sandalwood and cedar that endorsed his masculinity and threatened to overwhelm her.

Feeling it would be churlish to refuse now, she shakily held out her evening purse. "Hold this please," she said, accepting the small box from him. The quicker she got this over with the better. And, yes, she really was a little excited to be getting a present.

She ripped the paper slightly as she undid the package to reveal a bottle of an expensive perfume she'd wanted to buy herself for ages but hadn't. This particular scent was way out of her price range these days, and when she could have afforded it—when she'd been married—she hadn't wanted to wear it. Not for Robert.

"Oh, my."

"You don't like it?"

Her eyes shone. "Of course I do. I love it."

"*Allure,*" he murmured. "I think the name's appropriate, don't you?"

A quiver surged through her veins. "Thank you," she said, deciding to ignore the remark. "It's just what I wanted." About to place the box down on the sofa, she froze as he reached out and touched her arm. Without warning, a billow of awareness fell over the room.

"And this is what *I* want," he drawled, putting his hand under her chin, tilting her mouth up to him.

It happened so suddenly she didn't have time to react the way she knew she should. Instead, she trembled as his head lowered toward her. Trembled, but her lips parted even before their mouths touched.

It was a stunning kiss, one that swept her straight back to yesterday, to being in his arms, him doing delicious things to her, doing them with just his mouth this time, nothing else. Nothing but his tongue sliding over hers, his velvet touch so very sensitive against her own. So sensitive that her senses reeled.

She moaned but he continued to caress the moist cavern of her mouth, gentle yet demanding, coaxing her toward abandonment, toward the sensual heaven he offered.

And then, ever so slowly, he began to ease back. He teased her lower lip with his teeth for a long moment, letting the air move in where before there was only him.

Finally his head lifted. He stared into her eyes, his own dark and sensual. "Happy birthday for yesterday, Danielle," he murmured.

"I..." She swallowed, licked her lips, tasted him there. "Um...thank you."

Giving her a look that said he wasn't unaffected, either, he took the package out of her hands and replaced it with her purse. "Let's get out of here," he growled. "Before I kiss you again."

She let him lead her to the door, the touch of his hand searing through the material of her sleeve, the scent of him making her light-headed as they rode down the elevator.

Without speaking they walked out the building toward his parked car. She tried to clear her mind of him but it was impossible with his presence beside her.

It was no better in the confines of his Mercedes. He was so close, almost touching, he only had to lean toward her, pull her toward him.

She swallowed. If it didn't smack of cowardice, she would have hopped out right then and there, thanked him for the offer and gone home. An evening spent watching television was better than feeling so... Well, it was better than *feeling*. Period.

Flynn caught her sneaking a look at him and braked. "It was just a kiss," he rasped.

Her throat felt dry. "I know."

"Then don't look at me like that."

"Like what?" she said, despite herself, despite knowing what he'd say.

"Like you think I'm going to devour you at any moment."

Devour? Yes, he was like a tiger circling her, ready to leap and make love to her at the first hint of weakness. If she ever let him past her guard, she'd pay for it dearly.

His sensuous lips began to twitch. "I promise you I only pounce when there's a full moon. And there's no full moon tonight."

The absurdity of it made her smile to herself. "I'm glad to hear it."

"Relax, Danielle."

She arched an elegant brow. "Now that *is* asking too much," she mocked, and received a stunningly sexy smile in return.

Fortunately for her, he pulled out of the parking spot and they drove the few kilometers along the waterfront in a less tense atmosphere. The amazing orange of the sky as the sun started to sink below the horizon calmed her and made her feel as if she might just be able to get through this evening.

Situated on the esplanade, the restaurant was fashionably busy. The maître d' welcomed Flynn with reverence and immediately escorted them to an intimate table for two in the corner with a spectacular view of the now dark, turquoise ocean beaded by the last rays of the setting sun.

But she couldn't look out the window forever, and eventually turned back to the beauty of her immediate surroundings. Leafy ferns near their table provided a sense of privacy she could have done without as she glanced around the elegant decor, honing in on the small dance floor at one end of the room. Her skin quivered at the thought of dancing in Flynn's arms, but perhaps she was getting ahead of herself. Perhaps he didn't dance.

And perhaps the world had just stopped turning. There was no way he wouldn't take the opportunity to get her in his arms again. She knew that as surely as *sexual appetite* was his middle name.

"They seem to know you here," she said for something to say after the waiter took their order for drinks.

"I've been here once or twice."

With who? she almost asked, then decided it was none of her business whom he took to dinner.

Right then, a tall, extremely handsome and well-dressed man around Flynn's age spied them from across the room and came striding toward them.

"Flynn, I *thought* that was you," he said with a smile that said he was really pleased to see him.

"Damien," Flynn said, surprising Danielle when his face relaxed into a smile, surprising her even more when he stood up and the two men gave each other a brief hug.

Flynn pulled back. "What are you doing here? I thought you were in Rome this week."

"I was, but I had to come back for a series of meetings in Sydney." Damien glanced at Danielle and gave her the full impact of his shrewd, knowing eyes. "Hi, I'm Damien Trent," he said, holding out his hand. "And I'll be taking my last breath before my friend bothers to introduce us."

She put her hand in his and gave a polite smile. "I'm Danielle Ford."

"It's nice to meet you," he said, those eyes studying her in a fashion that reminded her of the man standing next to him.

Goodness, here was another ladykiller, she mused.

Damien looked back at his friend. "I've been meaning to arrange a poker night for when Brant gets back from his honeymoon."

Flynn gave a wry smile, though Danielle sensed he'd noted Damien's scrutiny of her. "I doubt he'll want to play poker for a while yet."

Damien grimaced in good humor. "Don't tell me that. I'll be shattered if Kia doesn't let him come out to play once in a while."

Flynn laughed. "Yeah, I'm sure he'd rather play poker with us than spend time with his new wife."

"You have a point. Kia's a beauty. A man would have to be crazy to leave her side for even a minute." He glanced over his shoulder at the woman at his table. "And speaking of leaving a beauty alone, my date's looking impatient."

"Anyone we know?" Flynn mocked with what was obviously an in-joke.

Damien gave a low chuckle. "No." He held out his

hand for Flynn to shake. "Look, I must run. We've got tickets for a show. I'll give you a call next week about the poker game." He inclined his head at Danielle. "Nice meeting you, Danielle," he said, then strode back over to the other side of the restaurant where the blonde sat at a table waiting for him.

Danielle watched the man walk away, then glanced at Flynn. "He seems like a good friend of yours."

Flynn sat back down, his smile disappearing as an invisible barrier came back up. "Yes, he is."

And that was all he said.

Just then the waiter brought their drinks over, a mineral water for her and a whiskey for Flynn.

Once they were alone again, Flynn picked up his glass, the material of his suit making a soft, sensual sound as he raised his hand in a toast. "Happy birthday for yesterday, Danielle."

She raised her glass and clinked it against his, the small action somehow more intimate than it should be. "Thank you," she said, avoiding his gaze as she took a sip then quickly set the glass down on the table, almost as if it burned her.

She thought of something to say. Something that didn't hint at touching each other. "I gather that was Brant Matthews you two were speaking about?"

He gave her a dry look. "What do I get for telling you the answer?"

"A pleasant evening," she quipped.

"And if I don't tell you?"

"A pleasant evening by yourself."

He gave a soft chuckle that rippled along her spine.

"Then I'd better answer. I don't want to give you any excuse to leave." He leaned back in his chair and took a mouthful of his drink before speaking. "Yes, it was. Brant, Damien and I grew up together."

She'd read about Brant Matthews in the newspapers, so she knew he and Flynn were millionaires. And Damien looked just as successful.

"Was that here in Darwin?"

"Yes. In the same street actually, though the area's a bit more upmarket now than when we were kids," he said with dry humor.

"Do you still have family here?" She found it odd thinking of him with parents and perhaps brothers and sisters. He seemed such a loner at times.

"My parents are dead."

"Oh. I'm sorry." Despite his toneless response, she knew the loss he must feel without them in his life.

He shrugged. "It was a long time ago. My mother died when I was young and my father eventually drank himself to death," he said with a grim twist of his lips.

Her heart cramped with sympathy for him. He wouldn't want her pity but she couldn't help herself. "That's so sad."

"I survived." His look said he was what he was today because of his past, and he'd make no apologies for that. "Now tell me your life story."

She let out a slow breath. He gave an inch but wanted a mile out of her. "My parents are dead, too. They both drowned at the beach when I was thirteen," she said quietly. "We used to live in this little town on the Sunshine Coast in Queensland, until my mother got swept out to sea by a rip and my father tried to save her."

His mouth flattened in a grim line. "Life stinks at times," he said tersely.

"Yes, it does," she said, feeling that same old tightening in her chest whenever she thought of them. "After it happened, I felt like I'd never laugh again. But life goes on. I moved in with an elderly aunt here in Darwin. She treated me like a daughter but she died a few years later. I decided to stay anyway. I had nothing to go back for."

He studied her. "You were young to be on your own."

"I survived," she said, mocking his own words.

Only, he didn't smile as intended. His gaze continued to search her face. She could feel him trying to look inside her mind, her heart, her soul. She tried to break away from that mesmerizing look but couldn't.

Thankfully the waiter returned with the menu and she was able to look away and take a breath. Flynn ordered swordfish steak without reading the menu but she spent the next few minutes deciding on a seafood cocktail entrée, followed by Tasmanian grilled salmon. Through it all, she could still feel him watching her, assessing her through her past.

"How long were you married?" he suddenly demanded, once the waiter departed.

She took a sip of her drink before answering. "Three years."

"Were you happy?"

Her hand gripped her glass tighter. "No." Those years

had almost choked the life out of her. Of course, he wouldn't understand that. As far as he was concerned, she and Robert deserved each other.

He frowned. "No?"

"I guess that's not entirely true. The first year Robert and I were quite happy."

A nerve pulsed near his temple. "So what happened?"

She expelled a shaky breath. "I just don't know. One minute we were in love and the next...it was gone." She grimaced. "Perhaps if Robert and I had lived alone it would've been different. But with Monica there, as well—"

"Monica *lived* with you?" he said, his eyebrows shooting upward.

"Yes. Robert didn't want to leave her on her own, and I could understand that. Her husband died years ago. Until I came along it was only her and Robert."

One corner of his mouth twisted. "Her husband's probably not dead. He's hiding."

She gave a delicate snort. "Don't I know how that feels."

He watched her with a measuring look. "You got out, that's the main thing. It would have taken courage standing up to someone like Monica."

She blinked rapidly even as a lump welled in her throat. He was admitting that he understood about Monica, at least, and that touched her deeply.

"Thank you," she murmured. "It did take courage."

He considered her across the table. "I gather this is the basis for your stand on independence?"

She inclined her head. "Yes. Having someone like Monica around really made me appreciate living alone."

And Robert had been his mother's son.

"Does she frighten you?"

She paused. "You asked me that last night, too, and I said no."

"Are you sure that's the truth?"

She tilted her head with a frown. "Why are you pushing?"

He shrugged. "No reason."

"Tell me about your job," he suddenly said.

She hesitated, confused by all the questions. "Er... what do you want to know?"

"You said yesterday Monica expected you to be home from work in time for her arrival. So I gather you work. I'm interested in what you do."

Her brow lifted. "You mean, you don't already know?"

"No."

She sent him a wry look at the one-word answer. "My friend Angie owns a boutique and I work there three days a week."

"Have you been there long?"

"Long enough," she quipped, giving him a taste of his own medicine.

Just then, a curtain rolled back at the end of the dance floor to reveal a woman sitting at a piano. At the sound of applause, she burst into a song. Danielle appreciated the interruption and sent Flynn a wry smile, receiving a knowing look in return.

The songs continued while they ate their way through their meal, talking only sporadically. The singer had a very good voice so it was pleasant listening to her. Besides, it gave Danielle the chance to gather her thoughts before the next onslaught from Flynn.

Then the singing finished to further applause, but the woman continued to play. One of the couples rose from their table and strolled out to dance on the parquet floor, slipping into each other's arms as if they knew exactly where they were supposed to be in this world.

Then another couple followed and another. She didn't want Flynn to think *she* wanted to dance, so she looked down at her plate and began pushing the remaining salmon around with her fork.

"You're not hungry?"

She glanced up and gave a polite smile. "It's delicious but I don't seem to have much of an appetite lately."

He placed his napkin beside his empty plate. "You'll have dessert."

She bristled slightly at the order. "None for me."

"But you've got to have something for your birthday. What about some of that chocolate concoction the woman over there is eating?"

Danielle glanced at the other table and felt sick at the thought of more chocolate. "No, I couldn't. Three o'clock this morning I was eating celery dipped in a jar of hazelnut chocolate. Lovely at the time but—"

"You should be doing other things at three in the morning," he suddenly growled, bringing sensuality back into focus. Without warning, he stood up. "Dance with me."

Her heart jumped in her throat as he helped her to her feet, then walked her out to the floor. She knew she went into his arms as if she were made to be there, just like those other couples had with each other.

He pulled her close and she quivered and gave a small sigh, giving herself up to the moment, unable to fight him this one time. He smelled so good, so wonderful, so Flynn. His hand was against her back, caressing her, holding her against him, as if he'd never let her go.

Long moments crept by as they danced slowly around the dance floor, a possessive gleam in his eyes that both thrilled and disturbed her.

"Did you know your eyes turn smoky-blue at certain times?" he murmured thickly.

Her throat went dry. "When I'm angry?"

"When something moves you. When you get passionate."

Her breath caught in her lungs. "You shouldn't talk like that."

A muscle pulsated in his cheek. "We're adults, Danielle. We're allowed to talk any way we want." His arms tightened around her. "And do anything we want to do."

Her heart rate accelerated as if someone had pressed a button inside her and forgot to stop. There was a whole other subliminal conversation going on beneath their words…had been going on from the moment they'd met.

"I…um…need some fresh air," she said, her heart thudding against her ribs.

His gaze rested on her heated face. "Let's go for a walk."

"Ye—" she swallowed "—yes."

She didn't look at him as she let him take control, while

he paid the bill and ushered her through the restaurant and across the road to Bicentennial Park. She needed to get outside, to inhale some night air fresh from the ocean.

"Is this better?" Flynn asked as he tucked her arm through his and they began to stroll along the pavement.

"Yes, thank you. It was so hot in there." She glanced away when he sent her another knowing look.

As they walked, she forced herself to concentrate on her surroundings. The world had grown a little quieter at this hour. Older couples passed by, others headed home for the night. Younger people were just beginning to gather for the bar scene. Out on the ocean, lights from a distant boat bobbed in the water. Just behind them, the city's low skyline silhouetted itself against a black velvet sky.

And none of it could make Danielle forget that this virile man was beside her, the touch of his arm beneath her own shooting ripples of delight through her every step of the way.

Suddenly she noticed a commotion a few yards ahead and she automatically stopped dead. An old man was sitting on the pavement, crying. A younger man was trying to get him to stand up.

"Come on, Dad. Let's go home," the younger man said. "My car's just over there."

The father gave a sob. "I don't wanna go home, boyo. I wanna stay here."

"Dad, listen. You've got to come home. Mum's had enough. She can't take much more."

Danielle's heart went out to the son. The man obviously had a drinking problem. She went to hurry over to them, wanting to help if she could.

Flynn put a hand on her arm, stopping her. "Leave them."

Her eyes widened and her heart dipped with disappointment in him. She'd never been one to ignore a cry for help and she wasn't going to start now. "But they may need my—"

His face tightened. "They don't."

"Flynn, don't be silly."

"The man's an alcoholic, Danielle," he said harshly. "There's nothing you can do for him."

"But—"

"Let's leave his son with some dignity," he said, his face hardening as a crowd began to gather around the other couple.

The younger man looked up and she saw the despair and shame in his eyes. Flynn was right. He didn't need an audience.

"You don't belong in that world, Danielle," he said, taking her arm and leading her back toward his Mercedes.

She went without a murmur, the closed look in his eyes touching her deep inside, making her heart clench with a compassion she wouldn't have said he deserved a week ago. Instinctively, she knew he had done this before himself, probably as a boy with his own father. It explained a lot about Flynn. He must have been so hurt and humiliated all those years ago. No child should have to grow up like that.

They rode back to her apartment in silence, not even talking as they came out of the elevator and walked along the hallway. Danielle surprised herself by wanting to slip her arms around his waist and hold him tight, ease his heartache, but she knew it wouldn't be appreciated. He was a man who stood alone, no matter what the circumstances.

Their steps slowed as they reached her door. She swallowed as she turned to face him. "Flynn, about that man back there…"

"Forget him. I have."

No, this was important. "I want you to know…that I understand."

"Good." But he was suddenly looking at her lips.

She moistened them, not deliberately, but it didn't matter. She saw his eyes darken. "Thank you for dinner. It was a lovely evening."

He moved closer. "Nowhere near as lovely as you."

The breath hitched in her throat. She knew what he wanted. Knew the whole evening had been inching toward this in a silent, sensual way that had been sneaking up on both of them. "Flynn, no."

"No?" he said huskily.

She tilted her chin, trying to fight his attraction, trying *not* to reach out and touch him. "I can't let you make love to me."

He stilled. "Because of your pregnancy?"

"No. It's just that—"

He lifted his hand, ran a finger along her lower lip. "I want you more than I've ever wanted a woman, Danielle. Being with you tonight, having you in my arms, is driving me crazy."

She gasped as his finger left her mouth and slid down

the column of her throat. "There's some things…you can't have," she murmured, loving the feel of his touch against her skin. "I'm one of them."

He picked up the gold chain at her neck that had been her mother's and held it loosely between his fingers. "Tell me you don't want me," he challenged. "Give me a reason to walk away from you right now."

Her legs began to tremble as her stomach curled with need. "I…can't."

He dropped the chain against her skin, his finger sliding back up her neck, along her jawline. "I want you in my arms tonight, Danielle. I want the scent of you on me. But I want no regrets." His finger stilled under her chin, waiting.

She shuddered but she knew what she would do. She couldn't refuse him, not when every pore in her body was calling out to be embraced by him. Dear God, the only thing she'd regret right now was *not* making love to him.

"No regrets, Flynn," she whispered, and his eyes flared with white-hot heat. "Not tonight."

Tomorrow could take care of itself.

Six

Danielle's knees shook as she stepped inside her bedroom, with Flynn right behind her. She had no doubt this was meant to be, no doubt at all this was where she *wanted* to be, yet she was afraid.

Of herself.

Of Flynn.

Of the sheer breadth of sexual attraction between them.

"Look at me," he murmured and put his hand on her arm, slowly turning her around to face him, making sure she could see the very masculine look in his eyes that said he was all male, all possessive. That he wanted her. That he would have her. She could not deny him. Or herself.

"Flynn, I think…" She paused, suddenly not sure what she wanted to say.

"Don't think. Just feel, Danielle. *Feel* me touch you." His fingers began to stroke her arm through the thin material, the light touch so powerful it made her *feel* him, all right. She felt boneless as those dark, smoldering eyes held her in place while his hand slid up and cupped the curve of her shoulder, savored it before sliding his palm around to the back of her neck.

"Now come to me." He gently pulled her to him.

She went willingly, more than ready for his kiss, yet unprepared for the sensual onslaught he made on her mouth. For long moments his tongue brushed hers like a paintbrush to canvas, each touch adding more layers of sensation, intensifying with each caress, bringing her to life. She moaned at the taste of him, a combination of fine whiskey and a flavor that could only be Flynn.

He broke off the kiss and leaned back. "You are so beautiful," he said huskily, his eyes appraising her features, making her skin quiver, making her heart race, making her wonder how she'd existed before she knew of his touch.

His gaze traveled down to the creamy swell of her breasts. "I want to see all of you," he murmured, pushing her thin silky jacket from her shoulders, stripping away the layers of consciousness between them as the material slithered to the floor. Her dress followed and her stockings, leaving her in a black lacy bra and panties.

Suddenly she felt a little self-conscious. "This is embarrassing," she managed to say, quickly putting her hands across the front of herself, knowing it was useless to try and cover herself, but doing it all the same.

He moved her hands aside. "There's no need to hide from me, Danielle." Then he stilled, his piercing eyes riveting on her face. "Now it's just you and me. No one else."

She knew what he was saying. That the rest of the world, including her baby, had to take a backseat for the moment.

"I understand," she murmured.

Tiny flames leaped in his eyes and he began to make love to her in earnest. He undid her bra, letting it drop on top of the other clothes, then enlaced her breasts with warm hands that made her throat close off. His head lowered and his mouth suckled first one nipple then the next, drawing a moan from deep within her, making her burn with need. She curled her fingers through his hair and held him to her.

"It's not enough," she murmured, wanting to touch more of him. No, she *needed* to touch more of him. *All* of him. Her hands slid beneath his jacket, her palms smoothing over the hot skin under the material of his white shirt, spreading even more heat from his body to hers.

But before she could touch him further, he groaned and stepped back to pull his jacket off, rapidly followed by his shirt. Then he reached for the zipper of his trousers. She gave a small gasp as he stripped down to nothing before her very eyes.

Yet "nothing" could be further from the truth. He was magnificent, with a dark smattering of hair arrowing down his chest, over the rigid muscles of his stomach, to the irrefutable proof that he wanted her.

Heart beating wildly, she hesitated for a split second.

"You're gorgeous," she said, reaching for him, her hand sliding around his tight, hard erection to hold him as a lover. She watched with satisfaction as his jaw clenched and unclenched while she got to know him, heard the harsh uneven sound of his breathing when her thumb traced the smooth head of his arousal.

A shudder rumbled through him. "Enough! I want to pleasure *you*," he growled, taking her hands away and placing them on his chest, pulling her into his rip-cord arms. His eyes darkened with something primitive as he nudged her intimately, her thin panties the last barrier between them.

His mouth covered hers hungrily, and she kissed him in return until she felt the room twirl around her, until she could feel herself being guided, until the bed touched the back of her knees and she was suddenly helped down onto the mattress.

And then his lips began to trek a downward journey to where she melted for him. He whispered words of passion as he slid her panties down her legs, then kissed his way up them, teasing nerve endings along the inside of her calves, up along her inner thighs, before settling in to kiss her intimately. She gasped in sweet delight as Flynn marked her with his mouth.

Then his tongue stroked her, and her stirring pulse jumped to attention and rushed through her veins. He quickened his pace, and so did her pulse. She'd never felt more alive.

She wanted more.

More of this.

More of him.

More of everything.

But before she could burst with pleasure, he came up over her and nestled full length between her thighs, his arms supporting himself so he wouldn't lean on her too heavily.

He looked down at her, his eyes glittering with desire. "Are you sure?" he rasped, waiting, watching.

Her heart turned over as she looked up at the forceful planes of his face, knowing he wasn't the type of man to hesitate taking what he wanted, yet he hesitated with her.

"Come into me, Flynn," she said, her voice catching with the intensity of the moment.

He gave a low groan and parted her legs farther with his thighs. He entered her slowly, carefully, his eyes locked on hers. Those eyes devoured her as he set a slow sensuous rhythm, moving inside her with leisurely thrusts that were far from casual and built the tension inside her.

As if he felt it, too, he suddenly lowered his head and took her mouth by storm, and she gave her lips up to him as she had offered her body. He took it all, kissing her erotically, his tongue dipping in and out, around her lips, making a flush spread throughout her as his thrusts increased momentum, each movement sucking her more and more into a vortex of sensation.

And then sheer magic took over as she was sucked down and down, drowning in a shock wave of the most exquisite pleasure. She'd never felt this way before. Never suspected.

Then all thought left her as she fell into the deepest climax she'd ever had, every fiber in her body quivering around this man, quivering for him, *with* him.

Dear God, she never wanted it to end.

For a few seconds more, Flynn remained inside Danielle, leaning on his arms, looking down at the radiant picture she made beneath him. She was so soft to touch, so beautiful to look at, he didn't want to move away.

And he certainly didn't want other men knowing her like this, came an unbidden thought, as an intense streak of possessiveness filled him. She was *his,* for as long as he wanted her, and right now that was going to be quite a while. A man couldn't make love to a woman like Danielle and not want to keep her as his own.

Except she was pregnant.

Pregnant with another man's child.

And she hadn't hesitated to use that to her advantage.

Just then she moved slightly and he pushed his thoughts aside, determined to ignore them. There were other things to think about when he had a sexy woman in his arms. "Are you okay?"

"Wonderful," she murmured, her eyes sensuously drowsy.

He was tempted to arouse her again, but he could see she was tired and needed a rest. Giving her a hard kiss, he rolled onto his back, pulling her close to his side, her head resting in the curve of his arm. She fit snugly against him.

"Flynn, I'm so…" her eyelids fluttered shut "…tired."

"Sleep," he said, and kissed the top of her head, then heard her breathing soften and deepen as she fell into a deep slumber.

He lay there for a long time, thinking about this woman in his arms and what it meant that she had given herself to him. If he hadn't known she was a con artist, he would have said she wasn't a woman who would give herself lightly. He would have said she'd have to care about him in some small way to be lying here like this with him. And he definitely would have said that for her it wouldn't just be about sexual attraction.

Not the way it was for him.

He swallowed hard and knew he was lying to himself. He found Danielle deeply attractive, but he had also begun to care about her in spite of himself. Yet it was a feeling he didn't appreciate or want, and with the same determination that had taken him from a pauper to a very rich man, he put his emotions aside to concentrate on what was important. And that was right here, right now.

During the night he reached for her and they made love again, and this time *he* was the one who fell heavily asleep as soon as it was over.

But he still knew when she slipped out of bed in the early hours of the morning. In the moonlight he watched her pad naked to the bathroom across the hall, his body stirring even before she'd closed the door behind her.

He waited for her return, the bed feeling big and empty.

Right at that moment the bathroom door opened and he caught a glimpse of her dressed in her bathrobe before she flicked the light off. Good heavens. Did she think a bit of material would stop him from wanting her? Stop him needing her in his arms?

But instead of coming back to bed, she quietly went and opened a drawer and took out some clothes. He knew then what she was up to. His mouth thinned. She was about to sneak out without waking him and go into another room to spend the rest of the night. Perhaps on the sofa.

And the next time he saw her she would have put up that wall of reserve again. He wouldn't allow it.

"Come back to bed, Danielle."

Startled, her gaze flew across to him. "Flynn! I thought you were asleep."

He leaned up on his elbow, letting her know he was wide-awake and not about to let her run away. "You thought wrong."

"I was just going to—"

"Take that robe off and come back to bed," he murmured, lifting the sheet, aching to make love to her, but prepared to let her sleep if need be.

She hesitated.

"Danielle," he said firmly, not prepared to wait any longer.

She placed her bundle of clothes on the dresser and quickly undid the robe, dropping it from her shoulders, exposing her glorious naked body to him, making him catch his breath.

Then she slid in next to him and he pulled her up close. His heart thumped when she curled her fingers through his chest hair in silent invitation, and soon she had him making love to her, until she begged him to take her again and he could no more deny her than deny himself. Afterward, they fell into a deep sleep in each other's arms.

He awoke to find her still in his arms, the side of her face pressed against his chest. He decided he liked waking up next to a beautiful woman like Danielle. In fact, he rather liked the idea of having her in his bed all the time.

She began to stir. The sheet covered her shoulders but didn't quite hide her bare breasts, a sight he enjoyed as she stretched, her leg sliding along his own, thigh rubbing against thigh, her fingers flexing out over his stomach, fanning lower.

She froze and her eyes flew open. For a moment he saw the confusion, then a flush began to rise up her throat and into her cheeks. Her reaction was just a simple thing, but it told him she was no longer used to being in a man's arms like this. The thought warmed him.

And then she pushed against him and tried to sit up. "Um…I think you'd better leave."

He scowled and held her still, making her look at him. "We said no regrets, Danielle."

She shook her head. "It's not that. It's Monica. If she comes by… If she sees you here…like this…" She winced.

All at once he realized Danielle was frightened of her mother-in-law. She may not admit it to herself, but it was there.

And after the little episode he'd had with Monica himself yesterday morning, he shouldn't have been surprised. The older woman definitely had a way of disturbing people.

Hell, the woman was *disturbed,* herself. And if she thought Danielle had gotten involved with him—worse, was sleeping with him—she'd be more than disturbed. Seeing Danielle's reaction now, it suddenly didn't seem so far-fetched for Monica to hurt her and the baby. And he knew he could only protect them so much. He swallowed hard. God, if Monica hurt either one of them, he'd never forgive himself.

A thought crystallized inside him.

"Marry me."

Her head had gone back, her eyes wide in astonishment. "Wh-what!"

"I want you to marry me." All at once he felt he was doing the right thing.

She pushed herself away from him. "I don't believe I'm hearing this," she whispered, disbelief ringing the irises of her blue eyes.

"Why not?" When she had time to think about it, he was sure she'd come around to the proposal.

"First you accuse me of trying to get you to marry me for the sake of my baby, now you *want* me to marry you?"

"Prerogative is not only the domain of the female." The more he thought about it, the more the idea was growing on him. Surprisingly, he didn't care that she wasn't quite the woman he wanted her to be. Being a gold digger was one hell of a fault in her, but he would cope with that. He'd make sure he kept her under control. But he had to protect her from Monica.

"But you think I'm a liar and cheat. You've accused me of trying to get all I can out of you." Her eyes held a sudden wary look. "What's changed your mind?"

He didn't miss a beat. "Nothing a prenuptial agreement couldn't solve." If she suspected it was because of Monica, she would refuse his offer. "Oh, and I'd want it in writing that you'll remain faithful to me, of course."

"Gee, thanks."

He ignored that. He had the money to keep her in the lifestyle she obviously enjoyed. And if he made her sign the prenuptial and watched her like a hawk so that she couldn't get herself into trouble, then they could have a good life together.

The alternative was suddenly unthinkable.

She shook her head. "This is about honor, isn't it? You feel you have to do the honorable thing."

He had to smile. "I've made love to many women but I didn't feel I had to marry any of them."

Her eyes narrowed with suspicion. "Then it's because I'm pregnant."

"I'd ask you to marry me whether you were pregnant or not." That was the truth. Pregnant or not, he needed to protect her at all costs.

Always.

She sat up against the pillows, pulling the sheet up under her chin, her eyes confused. "I don't understand."

He started to speak but then thought better of it. He may have feelings for this woman but he wasn't yet ready to lay them on the line. He'd always played his cards close to his chest and he would do the same here.

"Simple. It's time I got married."

"And the woman you consider a fortune hunter is the chosen one? How nice."

He ignored her sarcasm as he swung his legs over the side of the bed. "I'm getting older. And you're the first woman I can imagine waking up with for the next twenty years."

"So it's not a lifetime guarantee?" she quipped.

He acknowledged her wit with a thin smile as he looked back at her. "I was speaking figuratively."

She shot him a speculative glance. "You would want children?" she said, as if testing him.

His smile vanished into thin air as the memory of his mother dying in childbirth all those years ago came to mind. His jaw clenched and his heart slammed against his ribs. He'd sworn never to have children. Sworn never to risk a woman's life for the sake of procreation.

But now that pledge had been taken out of his hands. Danielle was going to have her baby whether he feared for her life or not. So he would make sure she got the best medical care. These days it would be highly unlikely for a woman to die in childbirth, he reassured himself.

"Of course I want more children," he said brusquely. "With you."

Her hand went to her stomach, as if in protection. "And what about *this* baby?"

That previous sense of protectiveness rose up inside him. "I would bring the child up as my own."

Her bare shoulders tensed. "But would you love my baby as your own?"

"Yes." And he would. Every child should be valued

and protected and, this child, being Danielle's child, would be more than special.

Her shoulders relaxed a little, but she continued to stare at him as if she couldn't quite believe this was happening.

Then a look of panic crossed her face and she threw back the covers, attempting to push herself off the bed. "No. I'm sorry. I can't marry you. I don't want to marry anyone."

Her previous marriage must have still reminded her of unpleasant things. And that reminded him of Monica. His stomach clenched tightly as he stood up and strode around the bed to help her.

He tried a change in tactic. "Think of it this way. If you married me, you would never have to worry about money again. I can give you everything you need."

She flinched, then ignoring his outstretched hand, she pushed to her feet and went to pick up her robe from the floor. Saving her the trouble, he scooped the robe up and held it open for her, taking pleasure in her naked figure as she quickly slid into it.

"Once I sign an agreement, right?" She didn't wait for him to answer. "You're as calculating as my husband."

Displeasure furrowed his brow. "Don't you mean your *late* husband?"

She began to speak then stopped.

For some reason, the culmination of her comments about Robert Ford hit him in the gut. "What did he do to you, Danielle?"

Her eyes flashed with remembered pain. Then she said, "Nothing."

"Tell me. I'd like to know."

She held his gaze for a moment, then as if believing his sincerity, she took a shaky breath. "He smothered me, Flynn. Smothered me until I couldn't make a move without him. Until I couldn't breathe. He was very much like his mother in that respect."

His jaw knotted, not liking the picture she painted. Now more than ever he was glad he'd proposed marriage. He had to get Danielle away from her mother-in-law. "Perhaps he wanted to spoil you?" he suggested, not for a moment believing that was true. Not after having met Robert Ford.

"Spoil me?" she scoffed. "By making sure I never got a moment to myself? By criticizing everything I did? By sucking the life out of me?" She shook her halo of blond hair. "No, the only one who was spoiled was Robert, only I didn't see that when I first married him."

Flynn began to burn for her. "*I* wouldn't do that to you."

She shuddered, the look in her eyes clutching at his heart. "You're doing it already. Flynn, I only went to bed with you. I didn't expect a proposal of marriage."

He forced himself to relax. He would show her that things would be different with him. He would prove it to her, if she let him. "I'm not asking you to cut off an arm, Danielle."

Her lips twisted. "At least that would be quicker than the slow torture of being smothered to death."

Dammit, her husband had made the mistakes, not *him*. He wasn't about to pay for the faults of another man, especially a dead one.

"You won't get a better offer," he pointed out.

She shot him a cold look. "I don't *want* a better offer. I don't want any offer at all." She headed for the bathroom door, then stopped and glanced over her shoulder. "And, Flynn, this isn't the beginning of an affair. This is the end of it."

He watched her go, heard the click of the lock behind her, but not for a minute did he agree that this was the end for them. He hadn't got where he was by giving up on something he wanted badly. And right now he not only wanted to protect Danielle and her baby, but all at once he wanted Danielle in his life, as crazy as it sounded.

And he always got what he wanted.

Seven

Danielle leaned her hands on the bathroom sink for support and swallowed away the lump in her throat. *Marriage!*

How could Flynn do this to her? How could he take something so beautiful like their lovemaking last night and spoil it with a proposal of marriage? He had to be the last person she'd expect to want to marry her. The last person who'd want to tie himself down. After all, he was a virile man who was sure to have a string of women more willing and able.

Yet he wanted *her*.

The supposed gold digger.

The supposed fortune hunter.

The supposed woman who would do anything to get his attention.

She just didn't understand it. But it didn't matter anyway. Dear God, she couldn't go through another marriage to a man who needed to possess her for the sake of possession. She wouldn't be able to breathe again. Just thinking about it made her throat tighten. All she wanted was her independence.

But she *had* to think about it, in case she found herself weakening toward Flynn. She had to remember and be strong. She must never forget what Robert had done to her in the name of love. Never forget Robert wanting to know where she was every minute of the day, even when she was at work. Never forget the "suggestions" of what to wear, not just by Robert but his mother. Nor the criticism whenever she'd given an opinion, until she'd given no opinion at all.

She'd been young when she'd married, too young, really. And she'd been looking to fall in love when she'd met Robert. She'd missed her parents and had wanted someone to love her back.

But she'd chosen the wrong man, the wrong family, and by the time she'd discovered that, it had been too late. She'd married Robert Ford.

And his mother.

And Flynn wanted her to walk back into the fire? There was no way she would make that mistake again. No amount of sex, no matter how fantastic, would be enough to get her to marry him.

Thankfully Flynn had gone by the time she came out of the bathroom, and Danielle escaped for a stroll through the botanical gardens, appreciating the cooler lushness of the tropical surrounds in the steady heat of the day. But it did nothing to ease her mind, though she kept looking over her shoulder as she walked. She had the feeling someone was watching her, but she soon dismissed the thought. If Flynn were anywhere near her, she'd know about it. And then she spent the rest of Sunday at home on edge that Flynn would come back and put pressure on her to accept his proposal of marriage.

What nerve he had.

Not that she doubted for a moment she would give in, but she wasn't really prepared to withstand him right now, not after their night of lovemaking. And she wouldn't put it past him to use their sexual attraction to try and get a promise of marriage out of her, either.

She'd fought too hard to get to this point in her life, pregnant or not, and the last thing she wanted was to trap a man into marriage. *She* would be the one who'd be trapped...trapped by a man who obviously thought of women as useful for one thing only.

Thank heavens she *was* pregnant. The very thing that Mr. Flynn Donovan feared was the one thing that would save her from his clutches.

Her baby.

In the end he never came by, neither did Monica, and she had an uneventful day preparing her clothes for work and cleaning the apartment. Afterward she rearranged the furniture in the baby's room, then sorted through the pile of baby clothes Angie's friend had given her.

Her hands trembled as she lifted the little vests and jumpsuits. So tiny and sweet. She found it hard to imagine something so small would even fit into them. Even harder to believe she was carrying that baby inside her and in six months she would be holding her child in her arms. She'd tried to prepare but there was no doubt a baby would make a huge difference in her life.

Unfortunately she *wasn't* prepared for a bombshell the next day at work. Ben Richmond, the Realtor who'd offered her the apartment, called her at the boutique midmorning while Angie was out doing some bank business.

"Danielle, do you think I could come and see you? It's important."

"What is it, Ben?" Something was wrong. She could tell by his tone.

"How about I come by in an hour? Does that suit you?"

"Yes," she agreed, but once she hung up the telephone she worried about what the problem could be. Ben had been so guarded on the phone.

He was even less cheerful when he pushed open the door to the store and saw her standing beside a row of clothes. His gaze behind the horn-rimmed glasses immediately dropped to her stomach, then back up to her face. "I'm sorry to ask you this, Danielle, but are you pregnant?"

Danielle frowned. "Yes, but—"

He winced then shook his graying head. "So you're having a baby?" he said, as if he still didn't want to believe it.

Frowning, she glanced down at her black trousers and sleeveless, body-hugging, cream-colored top that gave no hint of the baby beneath her stomach. "What's that got to do with anything?"

A momentary look of discomfort crossed his face. "I

hate to tell you this, but the lease you signed said no children." He held out his hands in a helpless gesture and shrugged. "I'm sorry, but there it is."

"Wh-what?" Her legs threatened to buckle and she made her way to one of the chairs.

Ben shot her a sympathetic glance. "If it were up to me, I'd let you stay. Unfortunately your landlord called us this morning after receiving a complaint from one of the other tenants and that leaves us no choice."

Danielle tried to take it all in. "Are you telling me I have to *leave* my apartment? My home?"

He gave an encouraging smile. "Don't worry. We're not going to kick you out tomorrow or anything." His smile faded. "But the landlord *is* insisting that you leave as soon as possible. He sincerely apologizes but he has no choice, either."

"But…but…I don't remember that clause in my lease." She'd been so grateful to be moving in she hadn't read it thoroughly.

"It's there, but I can't let you take all the blame. I should have pointed it out. I just didn't think about it because I knew you and Rob didn't have any children. I didn't realize you were already pregnant."

Her fingers fluttered to her neck. "It took so long to find something suitable that I jumped at it without thinking." Tears pricked her eyes. "Now I've got to find somewhere else to live."

Ben looked worried. "Don't upset yourself. I'll help you. I've got a couple of places in mind not far from where you are now. You'll like them, I promise."

The thought of moving again filled her with dread.

What if they couldn't find somewhere suitable? She'd have to return to Monica's.

"Are you all right?"

His words stopped her panic in its tracks. She took a deep breath and straightened her shoulders. One step at a time. She'd manage.

"I'll be okay."

Ben's face relaxed with relief. "Why don't I call you tomorrow? We'll go take a look at some other apartments."

She tried to smile. It wasn't his fault she'd been so careless. "Fine."

His eyes filled with regret. "I'm so sorry about this, Danielle."

"I know." She started to rise.

"No, you stay there. I'll see myself out." He walked to the door.

All at once, she just had to know. "Ben, I don't suppose you can tell me who complained?"

He stopped and turned. "I honestly don't know. The landlord called my boss about it. That's all he would tell me." Ben left just as a woman customer entered the shop. The woman looked at her oddly, but Danielle couldn't risk a smile so she stood up and went back behind the counter, leaving the woman to browse.

But as the numbness wore off she tried to think who was the culprit. The yuppie couple on the first floor? The businesswoman living next door to them?

Danielle automatically knew all of them would hate the thought of a baby living in the building, crying at all hours of the night. Why, even Flynn would object to…

She sucked in a sharp breath. Was it Flynn who had called her landlord? Would he stoop so low? She swallowed as something horrifying occurred to her. Had his intention been to force her into marrying him?

Suddenly it all made sense and she felt sick to her stomach. How could he do this to her? They'd shared a night together and now he thought he could manipulate her. She wouldn't put any dirty tricks past him. God, were all men swines?

Just then, Angie returned. Not wanting to worry her friend who had enough on her plate, somehow Danielle managed to act normal as she stood up and said she needed to go out for a short while. Angie gave her a searching glance, mentioned that Danielle looked pale and asked if she was okay, then said to take the rest of the day off if she wanted. Danielle politely refused, though she was grateful for the offer.

And then she left the store and walked to an office block in the city center. Flynn Donovan was in for a surprise today. And she could guarantee he wouldn't like it.

Only, when she reached his office, his secretary apologized and said he'd gone home to change before flying out to Paris later this afternoon.

Danielle swallowed hard, feeling the tears threaten. She was about to lose her home and the instigator was leaving town.

The older woman frowned. "Look, let me give you his address. I'm sure he'll be happy to see you."

Danielle knew that was one thing he *wouldn't* be, but she couldn't say that, in case the woman withdrew the offer. She just hoped the secretary didn't get into trouble on her behalf.

"That's very kind of you."

"I'm glad to help." The woman smiled encouragingly. "You'd better hurry. I'd hate for you to miss him."

So would she.

Ten minutes later she stopped her car in front of one of the houses along the waterfront, thankful she could see Flynn's Mercedes parked on the paved driveway. She glanced up at the luxurious, two-story residence with its expansive glass windows absorbing the view of the sea. Anyone who owned this placed never had to worry about having somewhere to live.

Not like her, she thought, pushing aside her despair as she got out of her car and stormed up to the house. She was just reaching the dozen or so steps when the front door swung open and there stood Flynn with an older couple behind him. For a moment she was disconcerted.

Then she remembered why she was here.

"There you are, you coward!"

To say Flynn was surprised by the woman on his doorstep was an understatement, but he didn't show it. What on earth was Danielle doing here? She hadn't just dropped by for a friendly visit, not with those lovely blue eyes blazing at him beneath pencil-slim brows, her glossy lips thin with anger, her chin tilted at an irate angle. She looked beautiful and feisty.

"Danielle," he growled, stepping through the doorway toward her as she reached the top step. "Perhaps you should come inside."

"Oh, that's right. Be polite. Let's not disillusion your

staff about the type of boss they have." Her furious gaze swept over the older couple. "I bet you think he's a decent human being. Well, so did I and look where it got me?" She slammed her hands on slim hips covered by a clingy top. "I'm pregnant and Flynn Donovan doesn't care if I have this baby out on the street."

He swore under his breath. "I don't know what your problem is but I suggest we talk about this in private." Taking her by the elbow, he marched her inside past Louise and Thomas, then closed his study door behind them and turned to face her.

His eyes narrowed. "Now. What the hell is wrong with you? And what's all this about you having the baby out on the street?"

She shot him a hostile glare. "Don't pretend you don't know."

His mouth set in a tight line. "I'm not pretending. I haven't the faintest idea what you're going on about."

"You told my landlord about me having a baby, didn't you? You must have found out children aren't allowed to live in the building." Her voice suddenly broke on an emotional note. "Now I—" she swallowed, her eyes glistening "—now I have to leave."

"You think I'd do that?" he rasped, striding toward her but she quickly stepped back, refusing to let him come any closer. He stopped a few feet away.

Her chin set in a stubborn line as she blinked back the tears. "Absolutely."

"Even after last night?" he said in a brusque tone, a growing heaviness centering in his chest.

"*Especially* after last night," she said without hesitation.

He drew himself up straighter, taut with anger. "I'm sorry but I don't see the connection."

"Then you're the only one. You made me homeless so I'd have to marry you."

He flinched inwardly. Was this the same woman he'd made love to last night? The same woman who had slid back into bed with him and begged him to make love to her?

"Danielle, you have my word that I had nothing to do with this."

But he knew who did.

Monica.

Thank heavens he'd put a guard on her yesterday as soon as he'd left her apartment…a woman who knew she'd better do a good job or else…until he could get back from Paris and protect Danielle himself.

Her eyes distrusted him but he saw a flicker of doubt. "How can I believe that?"

He drew himself up straighter. "In business, my word would be enough."

"This isn't business. This is personal." As soon as she said the words, she flushed, a becoming tint highlighting her cheekbones.

"Yes, very personal," he drawled, pleased by her reaction.

"You know I don't mean it like that," she said, her voice softer now, the look in her eyes more gentle.

His gut clenched. "I can't help what you think about me, but getting someone thrown out on the street is not my style."

She stared, her eyes assessing him as the seconds

ticked by. Then her mouth relaxed a fraction. "Why do I believe you?"

Fierce relief launched through his veins. "Because you know it's the truth," he said, pulling her toward him, the scent of Allure perfume filling his nostrils, stirring his senses. He hardened with desire and pressed himself against her, letting her feel what she did to him.

Her eyes darkened and she shuddered, her body emitting an aura that curled around him. "No," she mumbled, pushing out of his arms and spinning toward the study window, where she stood with her back to him.

"You're fighting a losing battle, Danielle."

She let out a slow breath and turned to face him. "There isn't going to be any battle," she said, deliberately misreading him. "They're the ones calling the shots. I have to leave the apartment. I have no choice."

He was about to ignore her comment when something occurred to him, making him angry just thinking about it. "Surely the person who got you the apartment in the first place should have told you about the no-children policy," he snapped.

She shot him a withering glance. "For your information Ben is a friend of Robert's and, no, he didn't know about the baby. And by the way, he's a Realtor, not an ex-lover." She winced. "I think he felt sorry for me living with Monica."

Strangely enough, he suspected she was telling the truth. Yet could she really believe this Ben didn't have other intentions? He was a man and any male would have carnal thoughts of Danielle and bed.

He forced his hands to unclench. "Do you know who told the landlord you were pregnant?"

"No."

God. She really had no idea, no suspicion that Monica would do this to her. Danielle didn't deserve a mother-in-law who tried to get her thrown out on the street.

Actually it was probably because of *him* that Monica was being so vindictive in the first place. He'd stirred the older woman up and now she was taking it out on Danielle.

All at once he stilled as another angle to this occurred to him, just the way it did in his business dealings. Any attempt by Monica to get her daughter-in-law back was bound to send Danielle running in the other direction.

Toward *him*.

Hmm. This may end up better than he'd thought.

"What does it matter now, anyway?" Danielle said, but her eyes flickered with uncertainty. "The damage is done. Ben said he would find me something else."

He gritted his teeth. This Ben sounded far too helpful for his liking. "You could fight it."

"What's the use? Others in the building obviously don't want me there." Full-blown pride angled her chin. "And I'd rather not stay where I'm not wanted."

He hated to see her hurting this way and once again he realized there was more depth to this woman than he'd previously believed. "I know a place where you're wanted," he said pointedly. "Very much."

She held his gaze, lifted her chin more. "Thank you for your concern but I'll be fine."

His jaw tautened. "Come on. I'll take you home."

"I have my car."

"I won't have you driving while you're upset. My car's out front."

"Don't you have a plane to Paris to catch?"

Connie must have told her, including giving Danielle his address. Not that he minded.

He glanced at the gold Rolex on his wrist. He could delay the meeting or send someone else, preferably the latter. "I won't be going now."

"Oh, but—"

"I'm taking you home."

Despair crossed her face. "Flynn, I don't need you to drive me home. I can manage."

"No." He reached for the door handle, then looked at her. An odd tenderness swelled inside him. "Sit down and relax for a minute. I'll be back shortly."

As soon as Danielle stepped inside the penthouse and looked around what had so quickly become her home, a sense of despair filled her. Tears sprang to her eyes. She would miss this spacious apartment, with its glorious view of the ocean, sweeping around to the city skyline and backdropped by the brightest of blue skies.

Yet it wasn't about the luxury. This was her new beginning. She felt safe here. Safe and secure.

And now it had come to an end.

Flynn tugged her toward him, and for once she knew she needed to lean on someone. On him. It would be the last time, she promised herself as she went willingly into his arms. They were surprisingly comforting and full of a strength that seemed to pour into her and helped her blink back the tears.

"Sorry," she mumbled against his shirt, hating to cry even a little. It was just those silly hormones again.

"No need to apologize," he said, his deep voice rumbling in her ears.

She sniffed and leaned back to look up at him. Right at that moment she realized it wasn't just this apartment that made her feel safe and secure. It was being in Flynn's arms, too. She felt protected, as she'd never been protected before. But in a good way, unlike with Robert.

Robert. A sensation tightened her throat as she pushed away bad memories and concentrated on now. She was about to lose her home.

"Oh, Flynn, I thought this place would be mine for a few years at least. It's going to be so hard to leave."

He reached out and tucked a strand of hair behind her ear. "Try not to worry about it."

She frowned. "How can I *not* worry? I signed a lease in good faith. I never, ever sign anything without reading it first. I wouldn't even sign that paperwork Robert insisted…" All at once she remembered.

He stilled, but his eyes had grown alert. "Are you talking about the paperwork for the loan?"

Her breath stopped. Dear God, if she told him the truth would he tell Monica? Could she beg him not to? Could she throw herself on his mercy for the sake of her child? Of course she could.

"Danielle?" he warned in a low voice that said this was very important.

She totally agreed.

"Yes, Flynn, I *am* talking about that loan," she admitted, stepping back, needing to separate herself from him while she talked. "I knew nothing about it. In fact, looking back I can see that Robert tried to get me to sign the paperwork but I felt uncomfortable so I threw it away. I never heard another thing until you sent me that letter and even then I didn't realize Robert had forged my signature. Not until I saw it on the contract you showed me." She took a ragged breath. "But why believe me now when you didn't believe me before?"

A muscle pulsated in his lean cheek. "I know you now and I believe you're telling me the truth."

She choked back a short laugh. "How magnanimous of you."

"I deserve that, but why didn't you insist on telling me the truth before?" His gaze narrowed on her. "What are you trying to hide, Danielle?"

She sent him a wary glance. "I thought you might go to Monica and ask her for the money," she admitted uneasily, praying she was doing the right thing. "That's why I kept sending you those checks. I couldn't risk her knowing. You see, if you didn't believe me about the forged signature then she might prefer not to, as well. I knew she would use any opportunity to take this baby away from me." She hugged her stomach protectively. "She still could. She'd drag me through the courts until my name was mud and she had my child in her custody."

"Over my dead body," he snarled.

Her throat seemed to close up but she managed to say, "Thank you."

"This is why you were agitated when Monica came

to your door, isn't it? You thought I might mention the money to her."

She nodded. "I was trying to get you out of there as fast as I could."

"Danielle, I wouldn't have mentioned the money then and you have no need to fear I will tell her now. That woman would be the last person in the world I'd want to raise a child. Any child. And definitely not *your* child."

She swallowed a lump in her throat, blinked back sudden tears, then straightened her shoulders. "Unfortunately none of this fixes my immediate problem."

He considered her. "Why not just wait and see what happens?"

That was easy to say when a person had plenty of money the way he did. He could afford to move into a hotel. She grimaced. He could afford to *buy* the hotel.

"No, I have to face reality now. It's no use burying my head in the sand."

"We'll figure something out. Trust me."

We? He planned on helping her? *Again.* That was why he wasn't too worried on her behalf.

She took a shuddering breath and faced him. "Flynn, in case I haven't made it clear, I do *not* need your help."

"If you married me at least you wouldn't have to worry about having nowhere to live."

She gasped, dismayed he was back on that subject again. "I *will* have somewhere to live. Ben said—"

"Forget Ben! He's going to stick you in a tiny apartment in some run-down part of Darwin somewhere."

She boldly met his gaze. "It doesn't appear to have done *you* any harm."

Anger flared then died in his eyes. "Not quite everyone from my street turned themselves into a millionaire," he drawled.

"Oh, you mean, no one but you and your friends have the brains to do what you've done?" she said sarcastically.

"Marry me."

She tensed. "No."

"You'll be very happy. I promise."

"Don't make a promise you might not keep."

A muscle knotted in his jaw. "Do you want your child to suffer without a father?" he asked harshly.

She gasped. "That's not fair. I plan on being the best parent a child can have."

"But you had parents. Plural. Are you going to deny your child something he should automatically have?"

Her chin lifted. "Maybe I'll marry one day, but to the right man. That's not you."

He swore low in his throat.

"This is harassment, Flynn."

"Wanting someone is *not* harassment."

"You used sex to get what you can't have. *Me*." She shot him a shrewd look. "And I find it oddly telling that you haven't mentioned anything about love."

He didn't move a muscle. "I'd prefer not to start off our marriage with high expectations."

"I…am…*not*…marrying…you," she said with gritted teeth.

"I'm sure we'll learn to love each other in our own way over time," he said, ignoring her protest. "For now, our desires will give us a few years grace. We'll make a good marriage together."

"No, we won't."

His mouth thinned with displeasure. "Danielle, I'm not arguing." He went to reach for her but she spun away.

Only, she spun too fast and without warning she felt dizzy. Too dizzy. Her knees felt weak and nausea was rising up her throat. She could hear the blood pounding in her ears.

"Flynn," she whispered, and suddenly he was there, his arms around her, holding her, his presence comforting.

"Danielle?"

She rested her head on his shoulder and heard him say her name in a worried tone, but she was too busy trying to stop the world from spinning.

His arms tightened a little. "I'm here, sweetheart."

A moment passed, then another and thankfully the dizziness started to ease, the nausea abating, the blood not pounding quite as loudly in her ears.

"Are you okay?" he murmured, his heart thudding against her cheek.

She pushed back a little and looked up at him. "Yes," she said on a shaky breath. "I felt a little faint, that's all."

"This is happening far too often." He swooped her up in his arms and headed for her bedroom. "I'm calling my doctor. And I don't want any argument from you."

This time Danielle didn't *want* to argue. For all her talk about independence, she knew he was right. She hadn't been feeling right lately, so another checkup by a doctor was in order. She didn't want to risk losing the baby. She couldn't. Her baby was the only thing worthwhile in her life. She would be heartbroken if anything happened.

"How do you feel now?" Flynn said after he'd made her comfortable on the bed, then called the doctor on his cell phone.

The concern in his eyes halted her inner panic. "Better."

He sat down next to her on the bed and squeezed her hand, as if trying to instill strength into her. "I won't let anything happen to you or the baby," he assured her.

She looked at his grim mouth and pale face and her heart softened. "Flynn, you can't stop it."

"Don't," he muttered, and she realized he was taking this much too personally. But she knew all about regrets and she wasn't about to let either of them take responsibility for this.

Her throat thickened. "You can't blame yourself for my feeling faint."

"I shouldn't have tried to grab you like that."

"You weren't being rough, Flynn. You never are."

He held her gaze. "Thank you for that."

The softened look in his eyes made her heart tumble over and she almost wanted to faint again, but for a different reason. "Um…how long do you think the doctor will be?"

Arrogance returned to his face. "Bloody quick, if he knows what's good for him."

She had to smile, glad to see the old Flynn back. And for the first time she actually noticed his marine-blue polo shirt and gray chinos that made him look both casual and sophisticated. There was something very distracting about the way the fine material of his shirt hugged his shoulders. Far too distracting.

All at once he kissed her hard on the mouth then jumped to his feet. "I'll get you a drink of water. Call out if you need me."

She watched him walk away, tempted to call out and say that she *did* need him, but that might be admitting too much, even in jest. He'd use it to his advantage at some time or other, no doubt.

When the middle-aged doctor came, he was introduced as Mike. She reddened when Flynn stood by watching her being examined.

Mike straightened. "The baby's fine."

Sheer relief washed over her. "Thank God," she said, seeing the same reflection on Flynn's face.

The doctor eyed her. "Have you had any stress lately? Getting enough sleep? Eating right?"

"She's had a lot of stress, Mike," Flynn said, and she shot him a look that said she could speak for herself.

Mike frowned. "Hmm, then I hope you don't live here alone."

"Yes, she does," Flynn said again before she could get a word in. She glared at him again.

"Not a good idea." The doctor put his stethoscope away and clicked the bag shut. "Don't you have a friend or relative you could move in with for a while? You need to rest. Otherwise I might have to put you in the hospital," he said, making her gasp. "It would only be a precautionary measure," he assured her.

"She'll be staying at my place," Flynn said with authority, sending her heart slamming against her ribs.

"Excellent," Mike approved. "But you must take it easy from now on, young lady. You need to eat properly and rest. No work for a week and be careful after that." He glanced at Flynn. "You can continue intimate relations. That shouldn't be a problem."

Flynn inclined his head. "Good."

Sharp anxiety was twisting inside Danielle, so she didn't pay much attention to the rest of the conversation. Then something occurred to her.

She waited until the doctor left before sending Flynn an accusing stare. "You two planned this, didn't you?"

Surprise, then annoyance crossed Flynn's face. "Perhaps I should call Mike back? I'm sure he'd love to hear his integrity being questioned like this." He paused. "Not to mention my own."

She grimaced. "Okay, so I got it wrong."

"You're moving in with me. You're sick and not well enough to look after yourself. And you need to move out of this penthouse permanently."

She could feel herself being swallowed up again by him and his tactics. "I won't be your mistress, Flynn. I have my child to think about. No. I'll find another place."

His eyes flashed at her. "And then what? I leave you alone so you could possibly die?"

The breath caught in her throat. "Don't exaggerate. I'm fine. Mike just said so."

All at once, the anger seemed to leave him. His eyes clouded over. "Allow me to do this for you and the baby, Danielle."

She realized he still felt guilty. She swallowed the lump

in her throat. Seeing this side to him softened her, made her admit to herself that he was in an awkward position.

But she was torn whichever way she went. If she stayed at her apartment it would only be temporary. And she would still have to look for a new apartment as well as go to work. She'd probably make herself sicker, perhaps even risk having a miscarriage.

But if she went to Flynn's place, would he see it as a sign that she was weakening toward marriage? Perhaps they could come to a temporary truce.

"Okay, I'll move in, Flynn, but only until I have the baby." Then she'd go back to work full-time and get her own place, away from Monica and definitely away from Flynn.

Deep satisfaction showed in his eyes, but it was the barely perceptible easing of his shoulders that somehow reassured her in her decision.

"You're doing the right thing," he said.

"For who, Flynn? You or me?"

"For your baby."

Eight

When Danielle stepped inside Flynn's mansion, she was introduced to Louise and Thomas, the older couple she'd seen there earlier in the day. They'd known Flynn a long time and looked after him and his house, and Danielle had no doubt *she* was included in the package now.

But when she found that Flynn had hired a nurse to keep an eye on her, she almost turned around and walked out the door. It was too much. Everything was happening too fast. Suddenly the enormity of the day overwhelmed her and she felt tears sting her eyes.

The middle-aged nurse took in the situation quickly. "Come on, pet. Let's get you to bed."

Thankfully Flynn didn't follow them up the sweeping staircase and into a superbly furnished bedroom, and once she was in bed Danielle began to relax under Jean's professional but sympathetic eyes. She fell asleep thinking how much the nurse reminded her of her mother. The two women had that same caring attitude.

She woke a few hours later thinking about Monica and what she would say about all this, and her stomach clenched with tension. Her mother-in-law had flown south to stay at her sister's place in Alice Springs for a few days, so at least she had a reprieve until the next day when Monica was due to call. Then there would be hell to pay.

She mentioned it to Flynn when he came into her bedroom later that evening. "I'll have to tell Monica where I am," she said, once he'd finished inquiring if she felt better.

"*I'll* deal with Monica," he said, his tone telling her the issue wasn't open to negotiation.

"No." She had to stand her ground with him. "I'll speak to her."

"I won't have you getting upset."

Not for the first time today, she saw past his arrogance to his concern. It warmed her. "She needs to know, Flynn. And she needs to hear it from me."

"Then I insist on being with you when you tell her."

"Fine," she agreed, but if she could help it, she had no intention of letting him be around when she broke the news to Monica. Her mother-in-law was going to be very upset as it was.

"You didn't eat much dinner," he said, cutting across her thoughts, obviously having spoken to Jean.

"I wasn't really hungry." A light soup had been all she could manage.

"You've got to eat."

That's when she realized *he* looked tired. It had been a long day for him, too. "Have *you* eaten?"

He appeared surprised by her question. "No. I thought I'd dine in here and keep you company."

She moistened her lips. "Er...in here?"

"This is *our* bedroom, Danielle."

She swallowed as her heart started to beat fast. "I don't remember saying I would share a bedroom with you."

"I don't remember asking."

"Flynn, I—"

His gaze locked with hers. "We start as we intend to go on."

"All of a sudden it's *we?*" She could feel herself being suffocated. Just as Robert had smothered her.

"Forget about him," he said harshly, reading her thoughts.

She took a shaky breath. "I can't."

"Face the facts, Danielle. He only wanted you physically because he couldn't have you emotionally. *That's* why he wouldn't let you go."

She knew he was right but it still hurt to know she'd been used in such a way by the man who'd been her husband. "And your reasons are different?"

"My reasons are my own, but I'll tell you one thing. They're a damn sight more noble than his ever were." With that he stormed off into the bathroom.

Danielle bit her lip, then lay back against the pillows, knowing Flynn was right. Despite his arrogance, he had an honor code about him that Robert would never have understood. It gave her a strange comfort and seemed to fill an empty void inside her that had never been filled.

Not by Robert.

Nor Monica.

As for the older woman, Danielle had the opportunity to talk to her sooner rather than later when Monica rang while Flynn was eating dinner.

There was a knock at the bedroom door and Jean opened it at Flynn's command. "Excuse me, Mr. Donovan, I know you don't want Dani... I mean, Mrs. Ford to be disturbed, but there's a very irate lady on the telephone demanding that she speak with her." The nurse glanced at Danielle. "She said she's your mother-in-law."

Trepidation filled Danielle as she looked across the room at Flynn sitting at the small table near the window. "How does she know I'm here?"

"I had your phone calls forwarded," he said, giving no excuse for not mentioning it previously. He glanced back at the nurse. "Danielle will call her back tomorrow."

"But—"

"No," Danielle refuted. "I can't do that to her, Flynn. She'll worry herself sick all night."

"Better than her making *you* sick."

"But I'll worry all night, too." Danielle looked at Jean's concerned face. "I'll take the call."

The older woman hesitated, then nodded at the phone on the bedside table. "Line one," she said, and closed the door behind herself, leaving her and Flynn alone again.

Danielle glanced at the phone, then at Flynn. "I'd like some privacy please."

"I'm not leaving," he said, leaning back in the chair and picking up his wineglass.

"Flynn—"

"Monica's waiting," he pointed out, and took a sip of wine as he watched her through narrowed eyes. Danielle gritted her teeth, then reached for the phone.

She took a deep breath and lifted the receiver. "Monica, it's Danielle."

"Danielle?" the other woman said anxiously. "What's going on? I come back from my sister's early and call you at home and now I'm being put through to you at someone's house."

"Monica, I have something to tell you. I'm er... staying at a friend's house for a while."

A gasp came down the line. "A friend? What friend?"

As briefly as she could, Danielle explained about being kicked out of her apartment. She deliberately didn't say anything about feeling faint.

"Why are you staying there instead of with me?" Monica demanded, her voice turning colder. "This has something to do with that Flynn Donovan. I knew he was up to something when I met him. His eyes were all over you."

As they are now, Danielle thought, suppressing a shiver. "You're being ridiculous."

"Ridiculous, am I? I bet he's had you kicked out of your apartment so you would move in with him."

"That's not true. Flynn had nothing to do with me having to move." She saw his glance sharpen, but Monica soon demanded the attention back on her.

"Aah! So you *have* gone to live with him. Oh, my God."

"It's only for a short while," Danielle tried to placate. "Just until I find another apartment."

"He's brainwashed you, hasn't he?" And then the tears started and once again Danielle was thrown back into the past. The other woman wouldn't let up, wouldn't even listen. Danielle was in the middle of trying to speak when the phone was suddenly taken out of her hands.

Flynn spoke into the receiver. "Monica, this is Flynn Donovan. Danielle is staying here with me. Get over it." He hung up the phone, then stood looking down at her, his eyes banked with displeasure. "Don't let her manipulate you, Danielle."

She gasped with hurt. He knew what she'd been through yet he made it sound so easy. "Are you calling me weak willed?"

He sat down beside her, his hard mouth visibly relaxing. "Not at all. You're very strong willed, in fact. But you're just too nice to people at your own detriment." He reached out and touched her ear, his finger lightly tracing the shell-like feature. "Of course, I notice you don't seem to have a problem standing up to *me*." His finger stopped moving, his eyes trapped her. "Why?"

Her heart skipped a beat. "I don't like arrogant men."

"As opposed to self-centered, manipulative women like your mother-in-law?" he mocked, his finger on the move again, sliding along her chin toward her mouth.

He had a point, but that point was being reduced by his smooth touch. "You don't know what you're up against, Flynn," she said huskily.

"The only person I care to be up against is you, sweetheart," he murmured, his finger sliding onto her lower lip, stroking it. She was sinking fast. She knew it as well as he did.

"Flynn…" The tip of her tongue escaped to lick her suddenly dry lips, but instead brushed against his finger. She froze at the same time he did. His eyes darkened. He was going to kiss her.

But in one swift movement he pushed himself to his feet and stood looking down at her, his tension a tangible thing. "I want you again so much my gut aches," he said, his voice simmering with barely checked passion.

She couldn't look away.

Couldn't breathe.

She couldn't think past wanting him.

"But I can wait," he rasped, and strode out of the room.

An hour later, Danielle was flicking nervously through a magazine waiting for Flynn to return, when she heard voices coming from downstairs. Then one voice rose above the rest and her heart slammed against her ribs. Monica!

Swallowing hard, she slipped into her blue silk robe and hurried from the room, rushing to look over the balcony to the front entrance below. She stiffened in shock.

"I don't believe you," her mother-in-law was saying wildly to Flynn. "You've kidnapped her."

Flynn's hard gaze sliced through Monica. "Danielle hasn't been kidnapped. She's here of her own free will, though I doubt you understand that particular concept, Monica."

Her face twisted in anger. "You're a fine one to talk," she spat. "Danielle doesn't even like you. She told me so. She *hates* you. That's why I *know* you've kidnapped her."

Danielle had heard enough. She couldn't let this go any further. "Flynn is right," she said, walking down the sweeping staircase as they turned to look up at her. "I *am* here of my own free will."

"Danielle!" Monica rushed forward. "You don't have to say that just because he's here. I'll protect you."

Danielle reached the bottom of the stairs but she kept her distance from the other woman. "From what, Monica? Flynn has been nothing but kind to me." And when it came down to it, it was the truth of late. Her eyes told him so as she glanced at him and saw the encouragement in those dark depths. She felt an odd flutter in the region of her chest.

Monica paled. "You should have come home to me. I would have looked after you. It's not too late. Go get dressed and we can leave right now."

Danielle stood her ground. "There's no need."

Monica clutched at Danielle's wrist, as if she wanted to grab her and run out the door with her. "But can't you see he only wants one thing."

Danielle knew she couldn't deny that charge, but it wasn't what Monica thought. Flynn wanted marriage, not just sex out of her. Yet if she let her mother-in-law see she had hit a nerve, she would be lost.

Before she could say anything, Flynn stepped forward and extricated Monica's hand from Danielle's wrist. Danielle instinctively rubbed the tender skin, only now realizing how painful the other woman's grip had been. Then she felt Flynn's arm snake around her waist and pull her against him, hip to hip, providing a united front.

"The only thing I want from Danielle is for her to marry me," he said, his hand tightening when she froze, silently telling her to remain quiet.

Somehow she held back a groan of despair.

Monica inhaled sharply. "Marry you! You can't marry her. She's carrying my son's child."

"The baby is a part of Danielle and as my wife, he will be part of my life, too."

"You could never love another man's child," Monica choked.

"On the contrary."

Something happened to Danielle when she heard those words. She didn't know why, nor attempt to understand, but for the first time since her parents' death she felt warm from the inside out.

Monica flashed him a look of disdain. "You don't care about Danielle or the baby."

"*I'm* not the one upsetting her like this." Flynn's voice held an undertone of contempt.

As if she knew she was defeated, tears began to well in Monica's eyes. "Danielle, how can you do this to me? You know that baby is Robbie's."

Danielle's throat turned dry as the feeling of being smothered washed over her. Monica was being manipulative again but how could she *not* feel sorry for the other woman?

"Bloody hell," Flynn growled. "Get out of my house. I will not have you pulling these tricks on Danielle."

Monica's tears stopped as quickly as they started. "I told you to stay away from Danielle but you wouldn't listen, would you?" She hissed, but before Danielle could register the words fully, Monica turned on her and flushed an ugly look. "This is all *your* fault!"

The unfairness of the accusation made Danielle flinch inwardly, but in that instant she knew she'd finally had enough. She'd taken a stand against this woman over moving out of her house, but she now knew that had only been a token step. She had to stand up to Monica as a person in her own right. It was time to show her mother-in-law she would no longer be an extension of her dead husband.

"No, Monica. If it's anyone's fault, it's yours. You spoiled Robert so much you turned him into a brat who took everything he could from me."

Monica gasped. "You were his wife."

"I was his wife, not his slave to do what he wanted with me. I had rights, too."

For a split second it looked as if Monica would argue. She opened her mouth…. She tried to speak…. Then before their very eyes she began to crumple to the ground.

"He was my son," she wailed, falling on her knees. "My son! And now he's dead. What am I going to do?" She wept aloud, her sobs increasing with intensity.

The sound of her grief brought Jean running. The nurse immediately went to her aid. Louise and Thomas appeared, looking worried, and went to help Jean.

Danielle swallowed past the lump in her throat. No matter what had gone on between them, she felt for the other woman's heartache. It was deep and genuine. Just as Monica's love for her son was deep and genuine.

She went to move forward, too, but Flynn stopped her. "No. Let them handle this."

"But—"

"Jean's a professional, Danielle. Allow her to do her job."

He was right, so she let him walk her up the stairs. But she could feel his suppressed anger in every movement of his body. An anger that she knew was directed at Monica but made her shiver all the same. He looked hard and dangerous and ready to do someone harm. He would be a formidable enemy, this man. But then, she'd always known that.

He closed the bedroom door behind them and she walked across the plush carpet to the bed and sank down on the luxurious cover. A heavy silence filled the room.

Then some things fell into place for Danielle.

"Monica was the one who had me kicked out of the apartment, wasn't she?"

He inclined his head. "I believe so."

"And she warned you away from me, didn't she? You wanted to protect me from her."

He held her gaze. "Yes."

She swallowed, glad she now knew the reason for his proposal of marriage, yet oddly disappointed.

"But that's not the only reason," he added.

She sucked in a sharp breath even as her heart thudded against her ribs. "Um...it isn't?"

"I'm deeply attracted to you, Danielle. I want you as my wife. For me, not because of Monica. But if after the baby's born you still want to leave, I won't stop you."

At one time she would have told him to go to hell for being so manipulative, but now...after knowing he had tried to protect her...after hearing the way he'd spoken to Monica...she realized he did care for her.

Perhaps more than he wanted to.

"And I owe you an apology for something else," he said without inflection, but the tautened skin of his cheekbones belied the deceptively quiet statement.

A crease formed between her brows. "You do?"

A muscle ticked in his cheek. "Seeing Monica in action just now and the way she used everything in the book to emotionally blackmail you, I finally understood why you so badly crave your independence."

Emotion welled in her throat as the tension eased inside her. Having Flynn fully appreciate what she'd gone through meant so much.

"And I suspect this is just the tip of the iceberg, right?"

For several more seconds he held her gaze. She wanted to look away but couldn't. "Yes," she admitted.

His eyes glittered with something so strong, so palpable, she felt a shiver roll down her spine. "Tell me about your marriage."

She drew a calming breath, glad to be able to talk about it. "It was a mistake almost from the start, but I tried to pretend it didn't matter. After a while I couldn't even do that anymore."

"Did you love him?"

"I thought I did, but I soon found out his idea of marriage was different than mine. He wanted unconditional love and I…well, I just wanted to be free."

"Yet you fell pregnant to him," he pointed out, his eyes detached but she knew he wasn't.

"Not on purpose, Flynn. I would never have wanted my child to be brought up in that sort of atmosphere." She took a shaky breath, trying to ignore the sick feeling in her stomach at the thought. "No, it just happened. I was finally ready to leave Robert, but he convinced me not to walk out on our marriage and to give it one more try. I knew I didn't love him anymore. I knew he was probably being manipulative but…" She swallowed hard. "He said things would be different from now on, only he never got the chance to prove it. He was killed in a car accident a week later."

Slowly Flynn's shoulders looked less tense. "I'm sorry for what he did to you. For what they *both* did to you. If I could take away your pain, I would."

Sudden tears sprang to her eyes. No matter what had passed between her and Flynn, no matter how angry he'd made her feel, or what accusations he'd thrown at her or how arrogant he'd become, he'd given her so much.

"You already have," she murmured, blinking back her tears. "Oh, Flynn, when we made love, you made me feel like a woman again, instead of a poor example of a wife."

His dark eyes deepened in color. "You would never be a poor example of anything. Never."

She swallowed hard. "Thank you."

Just then the wail of a siren could be heard coming closer, and the real world intruded. She saw a shutter come down over Flynn's face.

He reached for the door handle. "Rest now. I'll see to this." He opened the door then looked back at her, his eyes bleak. "I'll be moving into the bedroom next door. You need have no fear of being smothered by me any longer."

"Oh, but…" His words clutched at her heart, making her aware that she suddenly didn't like this wall he was putting between them. "Flynn, I don't want you to use another bedroom. I want you to share my bed. I—" it was hard for her to say this "—need you right now."

He froze, his dark eyes riveting on her face. "Are you sure?"

"Yes." She moistened her lips. "So…will you be coming back?"

His eyes searched hers, reading her thoughts. "You can count on it," he said brusquely, then left the room.

She sat there for long moments after he'd gone, exhausted but incredibly relieved by his words. No matter how apprehensive she was about their relationship, no matter that it had progressed to another deeper level, it was somehow important to have Flynn by her side, if only until the baby was born.

After the ambulance left, Flynn went into the study, reached for one of the unopened bottles on the bar and poured himself a large measure of whiskey. It should have burned going down but it didn't. He was already burning inside. Burning to take a certain dead man by the throat and rip his heart out.

And Monica. She was certainly a piece of work. She'd admitted having her daughter-in-law kicked out of the penthouse and then tried to dump everything on Danielle's slim shoulders. It was just as well the older woman was on her way to a psychiatric hospital. She needed help and he doubted she would be released for quite some time.

Danielle must have gone through a living hell with those two. The thought of it appalled him.

But what appalled him even more was that *he* had been doing the same thing to her, telling her what to do and smothering her independence just as surely as Robert and Monica had done, not to mention accusing her of all sorts of things she *hadn't* done.

He'd found that out after Connie had called a half hour ago with the report he'd ordered on Danielle and Robert Ford. She'd unearthed the personal information that had made him feel sick at heart.

He now knew *all* his accusations had been unfounded. Danielle wasn't a gold digger. And she hadn't spent the money from the loan. And the penthouse hadn't been offered to her by an ex-lover. Nor had she wasted her husband's inheritance and frittered away a fortune of his money. The looking to buy a secondhand car for her and the baby had been genuine.

She deserved a medal for what he'd put her through.

Yet she forgave him.

And she still wanted him in her life.

He swallowed another measure of whiskey. It had taken a blond-haired, blue-eyed temptress to remind him that the world did not exist for the sheer pleasure of Flynn Donovan. He felt humble and that was a feeling he hadn't felt in a long, long time.

Nine

The next morning Danielle woke to find herself in Flynn's arms, her back up against him. Last night he'd come to bed, pulled her into his arms and explored her mouth with his tongue, stamping her with his kiss. Then he'd growled, "Get some rest," rolled over and slept with his back to her.

She'd lain there, aching for him, knowing he was awake, knowing he was wanting her as much as she wanted him, but aware he was thinking of her health. Yet she'd merely have to reach out and touch him to change all that, only she couldn't quite bring herself to do it. It was as if she'd made the first move, she would have been truly lost.

But that didn't stop her from giving a little sigh and

moving her buttocks against him now, then freezing when she felt his arousal.

"It's no use pretending," he murmured, his face buried against her nape.

"Er...pretending?"

"That you're not awake."

She released a breath. "Who said I was pretending?"

He went up on one elbow and rolled her onto her back. "Awake or not, you won't stop me wanting you."

"What *will* stop you wanting me?" she said, her voice husky.

"Nothing," he muttered. "Not a bloody thing."

"Oh, Flynn," she whispered.

His eyes filled with a hot, sensual look that made the very air pulse with desire. "Say my name like that again and I'll just have to make love to you."

Her bones melted at those words, at that look, and all rational thought went with them. She moistened her lips. "And I have no say in the matter?"

"None at all." A predatory gleam entered his eyes, then his gaze slid downward, pausing a moment on the swell of her breasts under her cream nightgown before they returned to rest on her heated face. "Your body wants me to make love to you."

She tried to hold back a moan but somehow it escaped, making his eyes darken, making him look even more devastatingly attractive. And dangerous.

"If I don't have you soon, there'll be hell to pay," he growled, lowering his lips to her bare shoulder beneath the spaghetti straps, making her jump. He inhaled deeply. "You're wearing the perfume I gave you." And then he began grazing his way along her collarbone, up the column of her throat, along her chin. "I'm going to kiss you now."

Suddenly she had no will of her own and her lips parted ever so slightly. His mouth took possession of hers, and she shuddered with pleasure, her defenses downing as if they were bowing to a master craftsman. Everything inside her welcomed him as she responded to each plunge of his tongue across hers. She quivered and slid her hands up to his shoulders, holding on to him in case this turned into a dream and he suddenly disappeared.

He broke off the kiss, breathing heavily, his eyes smoldering for her, the intensity in them making her heart thud against her chest. Something had strengthened between them that went beyond sexual desire.

And then with great care he stripped the nightgown from her body, kissing every inch of bare skin as it was exposed to his view. Tears stung her eyes at the precious way he made love to her.

"Danielle?" he growled, lifting his head from the slope of her breast.

She blinked back the tears. "Yes?"

"Are you okay?"

"Please don't stop. This is so…wonderful."

He gave an almost feral groan. "I have no intention of stopping," he said, then kissed her hard on the mouth. "Enough talk. Let's enjoy each other."

She couldn't have spoken anyway because after that he set her blood on fire, scorching her with a passion that set her *world* on fire. And when he was inside her, she tried to ignore the possessive glitter in his eyes that said *this time* he'd made her his own.

Two weeks later, Flynn had to go to Brisbane on business for a couple of days and Danielle soon found she missed him. Nothing was the same without him. Yesterday had seemed duller and longer. The house seemed empty, the bed big and lonely.

She tried to tell herself it was just as well, that eventually she'd have to get used to not having him in her life again, only she couldn't summon the energy. It was as if she were running low on batteries and she needed Flynn to recharge her.

"You miss him, don't you?" Louise said as she served Danielle a late dinner on the patio, the dazzling sunset casting a golden hue over the landscaped swimming pool and cascading waterfall.

"He's only been gone one night," Danielle teased.

Louise sent her a wry look. "You're fooling yourself, you know."

Danielle's cheeks reddened. "Flynn—"

"Needs you. And the baby. I can see how happy you make him, Danielle, and that makes me happy. I remember him as a child and he was a very sad little boy."

Danielle's heart squeezed tight at the thought of Flynn's childhood. She could just picture him as a dark-haired boy picking up after his drunken father, making them something for dinner, from the meager scraps in the cupboard, his clothes threadbare.

"Why didn't anyone help him back then, Louise? He was so young."

"We all tried, but his father was a proud man and wouldn't accept help and somehow the authorities never seemed to take any action."

How could any parent make their own children suffer in such a fashion? In *any* fashion?

"How did his mother die?"

"In childbirth."

Danielle gasped. "Flynn's mother died having a baby?"

"Yes, but it won't happen to you," Louise quickly assured her. "She died a long time ago. They have much better medical treatments now."

Danielle sat there, stunned. And he hadn't told her? For a moment an incredible hurt clutched at her throat.

Then she realized that perhaps he *had* told her, but not in words. There had been his seeming anger when he'd found out she was pregnant and living alone. He'd stayed away from her, not because he'd thought she was trying to trap him as she'd suspected, but because the child she carried was a painful reminder of how his mother had died. An agony he didn't want to deal with every day.

Yet here they were now.

"You love him, Danielle," Louise said, interrupting her thoughts. "I know you do. I can see it in your eyes every time you say his name."

Danielle blinked. "That's ridiculous. You've got it all wrong."

"No, I haven't." With that, Louise picked up an empty dish from the table and went back in the house.

Danielle sat back in her chair and stared after her. Louise was wrong. So totally wrong. She didn't love Flynn. She wouldn't let herself fall in love again, no matter how attracted she was to the man. She was stronger than that. Stronger and...a fool.

A fool in love.

Something unfurled inside her, came full circle and completed what had begun the day she'd met Flynn. Louise was right. She loved him. The thought staggered her, sent her reeling. Thank goodness she was sitting down.

She loved Flynn Donovan.

Oh, my God! She'd been too blind to see it before. Or maybe she just hadn't wanted to know. Because loving Flynn meant making a commitment. And commitment meant something inside her had changed.

But had she changed enough to lay everything on the line and marry him? Certainly if he learned to love her, too, the rewards would be great. But if it all went wrong? The pain would be unbearable.

She swallowed hard. Could she marry a man who may only lust after her for the next twenty years...if that long? Dear God, she just didn't know.

Suddenly her skin prickled and her heart began thudding in her chest. Her gaze shot to the patio door. Flynn stood there, his look so captivating in the fading light it sent a tremor through her.

"Flynn!"

In one fluid movement, he came toward her, tilted up her head and kissed her with a thoroughness that made her heart roll over. She melted into him, letting him take her lips as an offering of her love.

"You're pleased to see me," he murmured, easing back, a purely masculine look of satisfaction in his eyes.

She tried to act nonchalant. She needed more time. "I was bored. You break the monotony."

The corner of his mouth quirked upward as he straightened. "I'm glad I'm useful for something."

She moistened her lips. "Have you fixed the problem at the Brisbane office already?"

"No. I fly back first thing in the morning."

She frowned. "So why are you here?"

His gaze held hers. "I wanted to see you."

For a heart-stopping moment she savored the words. Then she released a slow breath. "Thank you for your concern, but I'm fine."

His expression held a note of mockery but before she could catch her breath, his eyes turned probing. "Tell me. Do you still think I smother you?"

All at once she realized something. His concern wasn't about stifling her. It was about *caring* for her. And he wasn't someone who wanted to control her for his own purposes, but someone who wanted to protect her because he genuinely had her welfare at heart.

No wonder she had fallen in love with him.

Her throat closed up and it took a moment to speak. "No, I don't feel smothered by you. Not anymore."

His eyes darkened. "I'm glad." Then he turned to face the pool and, if she didn't know better, she'd have said his movements were somewhat jerky. Because of her? Or slight jetlag?

"I could do with a swim," he said, loosening his tie. "Want to join me?"

The thought was far too tempting, but she didn't

know if she'd be able to control her words if she was in his arms right now. She might blurt out she loved him.

"Er...no. I've already been for a dip today." She watched as he started stripping off his suit. "Um...what are you doing?"

He gave a half-smile, full of confidence again. "Taking off my clothes."

Heaven help her. "But Louise?"

"Is in the kitchen making me dinner. Don't worry. I'll leave my underpants on. I'd hate to shock her." But his eyes said he knew it wasn't just Louise he wanted to shock.

As if mesmerized, Danielle watched as he stripped, then walked over to the pool, the garden lights having turned on automatically as dusk descended, the palm trees and ferns almost hugging him as he stepped onto the edge.

He stood there for a moment, looking down at the crystal clear water, his tight black underpants leaving little to her imagination as the underwater lights reflected his superb physique, all sinew and muscle, giving him a commanding air of self-confidence.

He plunged into the water as he had plunged into her heart, surfaced, then began to swim up and down the pool with long, powerful strokes that sliced through the water as he sliced through life, determined to thrust through any obstacle in his way to get to where he wanted.

Or to *what* he wanted.

He wanted *her*.

He'd told her so with words, with his eyes, with his actions. The thought both thrilled and frightened her, because now she knew his wanting her made her stronger, not weaker. To belong to Flynn in the truest sense of the word would be wonderful.

She swallowed. Oh, God. She wasn't ready for all these feelings overwhelming her. She had to think.

Pushing herself to her feet, she ignored the ache in her back and went into the kitchen, hanging around while Louise prepared steak and salad for his dinner. She could feel Louise's knowing eyes on her while Thomas chatted on about their nephew's new job.

Ten minutes later Flynn strolled into the kitchen and fell into conversation with the older couple. He'd wrapped a white towel around his lean hips, his tanned skin beaded with water. Danielle wanted to lick every drop off him, smooth her palms over the dark springy hair on his chest, rip that towel away and touch lower.

Make love to him.

She gave a silent moan and made for the door, intent on going up to the bedroom, putting some space between them.

He stepped in front of her, stopping her from leaving. "Come talk to me while I eat dinner."

Her eyes darted down to his broad chest. Big mistake. They darted up again. "I think I'll call it an early night."

His lingering gaze sent warmth creeping up her neck. "Then I'll join you later," he murmured, and stepped aside for her to leave.

Swallowing, she said good-night to the older couple and forced her legs to walk out of that room. She doubted she would sleep. Not when she wanted Flynn with every breath in her body.

***

Flynn scowled as he watched Danielle leave the kitchen. She was very beautiful and very pregnant now, but there was something different about her tonight. She seemed more on edge.

About the baby? Perhaps.

About each other? Definitely.

He swallowed tightly. He'd missed her last night. Nothing had seemed the same without Danielle in bed with him. He'd become used to her soft skin against his own. Her scent. Her quiet breathing. And, yes, her frequent trips to the bathroom.

He hadn't felt right when they weren't even in the same city. Hell, make that the same room. Without her beside him it was as if something vital was missing. It was the reason he'd arranged for his jet to bring him home tonight. He couldn't spend another night without her next to him.

But despite a strong urge to go to her now, he had to attend to some urgent business calls first.

It ended up being late by the time Flynn got to bed, so he showered in one of the spare bathrooms so as not to wake Danielle, then made his way to their bedroom. He crossed in the moonlight to the other side of the bed, quietly sliding in next to her.

She lay sleeping on her side facing away from him and he closed in on her but didn't touch. He wanted to pull her around to face him, but she was sleeping heavily and didn't have the heart to wake her.

Instead, he lay there for ages, breathing in her special fragrance. His gut ached to make her his own, yet oddly it was enough just to lie next to her, knowing there was no place else on earth he'd rather be. Eventually he fell asleep from sheer exhaustion.

And was awoken in the early hours by her cheek rubbing against his chest. He froze as he lay on his back. She had burrowed up against him, her soft breath sighing over his skin.

"Flynn?" she murmured half-asleep.

"It had better be," he muttered, his arms tightening around her. Just having her ask if it was him beside her made him want to possess her until she never asked again. He wanted no other man in her mind. No other man belonged there but *him*.

When he knew she had fully woken, his blood heated, ready to flow over her, merge with her, storm her if necessary.

A moment crept by and from out of nowhere she placed her lips against his chest and kissed him there. He sucked in air, then growled, "Danielle?"

"It had better be," she mimicked huskily, the caress of her fingers on his chest putting him on full alert. Her satin-covered breasts pressed against his arm as her fingers trailed down the center of his chest. In the moonlight streaming across their bed, he saw her smile.

Then her fingers slid across his abdomen and curled around his straining erection. He gave a moan from deep in his throat. He'd wanted her to initiate their lovemaking for a while now…to touch him first and not the other way around. Yes, she'd always welcomed him and responded to his passion, but that initial touch…that initial wanting…had always been his.

Until now.

"Are you sure?" he rasped, barely able to say the words but managing it all the same.

"Yes." She kissed him briefly on the lips. "Now lie back and enjoy this. Let me pleasure *you*," she said, sliding her hand along him, arousing him even more.

With a rough moan of surrender, he gave in.

Surprisingly, for all her insistence, she wasn't quite as sure in her movements, telling him she hadn't done this particular aspect of lovemaking before. A triumphant heat ran through him before he took charge, his hand over hers, guiding her, showing her what he liked and how he liked it. Together they stroked him, first with long slow movements, then picking up speed.

She grew more confident, so he removed his hand and let her fly solo. Only, there was nothing solo about this experience. She watched him as she caressed him, her eyes turning darker, smokier, with each passing second.

Awareness shot through him. Other women had pleasured him this way, skillfully using their hands and mouth to give him satisfaction. But this woman, with hands not quite so skillful, her delicious mouth not nearly close enough to his, gave him the most erotic experience of his life. It was the look in her eyes that did it, her pleasure in watching him.

When he finally finished shuddering, he rolled away for a moment. Then he spun back and faced her, giving her a long kiss. "Thank you."

She offered him a slumberous smile. "No, thank *you*."

He traced her lower lip with his finger. "You'll pay

for this," he teased, intending to take his time in pleasuring her.

"Oh, I hope so," she whispered, then rested her cheek against his chest and lowered her lashes, but not before he saw a strange look in her eyes, making his heart stop beating for a second.

But before he could wonder about that look, she murmured, "I'm sleepy now, Flynn."

He watched her eyes close fully and he took a breath, tenderly kissing her silky hair, holding her close until her body relaxed fully in sleep against him.

Yet the look she'd given had him thinking. He rarely second-guessed himself, but there'd been something different about that look. And his insides screamed she was holding something back.

Ten

Over the next few weeks as her baby grew inside her, Danielle found their relationship had moved to another level. For some reason Flynn had changed. He didn't seem quite as hard or alone as he'd been before.

She knew she had changed, as well. How could she not? Thankfully her pregnancy was making her increasingly mellow and she was grateful, now, that Flynn had asked her to come here to live. Loving him would one day break her heart, but that was in the future. She felt more at peace with herself than she'd felt in a long time.

Of course, loving him also meant she found it harder to erect her usual barriers against him. Lord knows she tried to keep an emotional distance when he suggested she redecorate the dining room then encouraged her to do the rest of the house, or came to her birthing classes, or even when he asked her over dinner how her day had been.

Then she'd see him watching her with a glittering light in his eyes that said he wanted her...and would go on wanting her and when he'd take her in his arms later that night she'd melt for him. She'd forget for the moment that after the baby was born, she'd need to walk away from the man she loved.

Her dreams usually reflected her thoughts, and more so now because of her pregnancy. So it was no surprise when Danielle had a dream she was swimming in the warm ocean. She felt buoyant and alive as she lay on her back, looking up at the bright blue sky, Flynn beside her.

And then the dream changed. The water had turned cold and her stomach had begun to cramp. She was beginning to sink. She reached out for Flynn but he wasn't there.

She woke with a start and realized the pain in her stomach was real, and her heart jumped in her throat as she lifted the quilt, relieved when everything seemed fine.

Then another cramp hit, making her gasp. Dear God. *The baby.*

Panic filled her and suddenly she wanted Flynn by her side. Her first instinct was to call him at work. She reached for the phone, but her hand stopped midair. He'd said he had an important meeting today. Should she interrupt him?

Then something struck her. Could she really ask this

of him now that she knew of his past? Hadn't he suffered enough from the scars of his mother's death? Could she put him through a possible miscarriage?

She almost cried at that last thought, and her hand dropped to her side. If she lost the baby…if it was going to happen…and, dear God, she hoped it didn't…she couldn't do this to Flynn. Not to the man she loved.

She'd go to the hospital first and take it from there. Perhaps she was overreacting. If everything was okay, she'd even call him from the hospital and tell him about it then.

She would go to the hospital, she decided, pushing herself out of bed, her knees shaky. The pain was low in her abdomen but she could still walk okay. She dressed and phoned down to Thomas, asking him to bring the car around as she had suddenly remembered a doctor's appointment at the hospital.

Louise was a bit harder to convince, her sharp eyes watching as Danielle told the housekeeper she didn't want any breakfast.

"You should eat something," the older woman insisted.

"I don't have time, Louise," she said, and walked out to the car as carefully as she could.

Thomas helped her into the Mercedes and she schooled her features as she felt her stomach cramp again. Thank goodness the hospital was only ten minutes away.

"My God!" Flynn whispered, a white mist seeming to cover his eyes, blocking his vision. He couldn't believe what Louise was telling him on the telephone.

Danielle had started having pains and had gone to the hospital without telling him.

"She didn't look herself when she came downstairs this morning," Louise continued. "And then I got suspicious when she said she had a doctor's appointment and I knew she didn't. So after Thomas dropped her off, I told him to take me to her."

"Don't leave her side," he ordered.

"Flynn, the doctor said she was going to be okay," she assured him quickly.

"I'll be there soon," he managed to say, not daring to believe that. He dropped the telephone back in place, then strode out the office door, throwing out instructions to Connie to get his car *now*.

How could Danielle even think about *not* telling him? Did she think he cared so little about her and the baby? Didn't she know he loved her?

It hit him then. They belonged together. She was his, and he was hers.

He loved her.

He swallowed hard and tried not to think about losing her. Losing them both. *Dear God, please don't take them away from me.* He couldn't imagine a life without her now. Danielle filled every crevice, every pore, every beat of his heart.

By the time he arrived at the hospital, he'd been to hell and back. He didn't even see Louise get up and leave as he entered the room. He had eyes only for Danielle, whose face had lit up when she saw him, sending a jolt of love through his chest.

"Flynn, everything's fine," Danielle said hurriedly as

he strode toward her. "The doctor did some tests and they're all normal."

An avalanche of relief swept over him…through him… Danielle and the baby were going to be okay.

He kissed her hard, then pulled back with a rough groan. "You should have told me," he rasped. "I wanted to be with you."

Her eyes softened as she reached out and touched his face. "I know how your mother died, Flynn. Louise told me."

He swore. So that was what this was all about. "She's fired."

"Don't be mad at Louise. She *did* tell you I was here, didn't she?"

Okay, so maybe he wouldn't fire her. Louise loved Danielle anyway. How could she not?

He brought her hand to his lips. "I love you, Danielle. I love you with everything in me. With all my heart."

Her lips parted on a gasp. "You do?"

He took a breath, stared intently into her eyes and thanked God he had a second chance to say what he was feeling to the woman he loved. "I want you, my love. And I want to be inside you. Not just with my body but with my heart. You are part of me."

A whirlwind of emotions flickered over her face, then settled to just one. "I love you, Flynn Donovan. You're everything I want in a man. You're good and kind and decent and you've lifted the darkness from my heart. I want to spend the rest of my life with you."

Flynn's heart expanded, stunned by the sheer look of love shining from her eyes. It wrapped around him, flowed through him, became one with him. He had to have her in his life. It was that simple.

He kissed her again, lingered, then shaped her face with his hands. "You already knew you loved me, didn't you?"

Soft pink entered her cheeks. "Yes. It was the time you came back from Brisbane just to be with me."

He remembered that night well. It had been the first time she'd initiated their lovemaking, when he'd felt she'd kept something back. Now he knew what that something was.

"Will you marry me?"

Her eyes shone. "Oh, yes."

"That's what I like to hear." Then he realized what he'd said and he winced. "I'll try not to smother you. I'll let you have time to yourself. You'd be a wonderful interior designer and I think you should do some training. You'll do well and—"

"Thank you for that," she said, reaching out and stroking his chin. "As long as you love me I'll be happy, my darling."

He kissed her mouth again, believing her, believing *in* her. "If my love is all it takes, then you're going to be one very pleased lady.

Epilogue

Danielle sucked in a sharp breath. "Oh. Here comes another one."

"Do your breathing exercises, sweetheart," Flynn coaxed.

A few minutes later, she relaxed back against the pillows, perspiration moistening her top lip. "That one's over." She looked at Flynn and sympathy filled her eyes. "You really don't have to stay with me. I'm fine."

He muttered a swearword under his breath. "I'm staying."

A worried frown marred her forehead. "It might get stressful," she warned.

He swallowed hard. "Do you know how stressed I already am?"

A soft curve touched her lips. "No. Tell me."

He caught her hand, kissed the inside of her wrist. "Temptress."

She smiled with love. Ever since their marriage three months ago, every day had been more than wonderful. She couldn't have asked for a more loving husband, nor for a better family and friends in Louise and Thomas, and in Flynn's friends, Kia, Brant and Damien.

She gasped. "Flynn, I need to speak to the nurse," she said as another contraction took hold.

"Where's the bloody doctor?" he growled, and strode to the door, looking up and down the hallway. "He should be here by now. I'm paying him enough."

As the contraction subsided, Danielle began to focus on her surroundings again. She looked at him and saw he was white around the mouth. Poor Flynn. He wasn't used to not being in control.

Another contraction hit. "Ooh, here comes another one. I think it's time to have the baby. I've got the urge to push. And it's gett-ing stron-ger," she panted.

He wiped her brow with a damp cloth. "Is there anything I can do?"

She grasped his hand and squeezed. "Just be with me."

He pushed the hair out of her eyes. "I'll be here, my love."

His words helped on one level, but not on another when the next contraction was fast rolling into the last one. They were coming so close together. She couldn't stop a moan of pain.

The next minute the medical staff arrived. "I don't think your baby's going to wait any longer," the doctor said after examining her.

The birth of her child began in earnest and everything became a blur. Contraction after contraction, the urge to push so strong that nothing could stop her now.

Flynn was by her side, encouraging her as the baby's head emerged.

He was there as her child slipped into the world.

And he was there by her side as the doctor announced it was a girl and she heard her daughter cry for the first time.

She cried as she cuddled her baby with love and wonder and looked up at Flynn, who kissed her gently on the lips.

"Well done, sweetheart," he murmured, his eyes bathing her in admiration. He looked so proud as he tenderly kissed the top of the baby's head. "She's perfect. Just like her mother."

Danielle's breath hitched in her throat. If anyone was perfect, it was this man she loved.

"Here," one of the nurses said. "Let me take the baby for a minute so I can clean her up." Before Danielle knew it, the woman had whisked her daughter to the corner of the room. "What are you going to call her?" the nurse asked over her shoulder.

Danielle had thought about names of course, but until now hadn't picked one out. But as she looked at Flynn, she knew. He'd been there for her throughout her pregnancy. He'd been here for her today. He may not be the father of her child, but he came, oh, so close.

"Alexandra," she said softly, seeing him give a start at the mention of his mother's name. "Yes, our baby's name will be Alexandra. Just like her grandmother."

For a moment Flynn looked stunned, then he leaned down and kissed her on the corner of her mouth. "Thank you," he whispered, the moisture in his eyes making her eyes glisten, too. They looked at each other for the longest moment.

But soon they were interrupted by other more important things and before too long, Danielle had been moved to a bed in a private room. Then they brought the baby in and suddenly the three of them were alone.

She took a shuddering breath. It was time to face Flynn and their future, but she had one more thing to do first. It was time to let go of the past.

She looked down at the baby in her arms and a swell of motherly love filled her. She kissed her baby's cheek, ruffled her fingers through the soft fuzz on her head.

"Sweetheart?" Flynn murmured.

She glanced up at him with tears in her eyes. Tears of joy. "Oh, Flynn, I was so afraid about having her. I thought deep down I might resent her because I didn't love Robert when we conceived her. I thought I might not love my baby in the way she should be loved." She gave a shaky smile. "But the love's there. She's in my heart."

Flynn's eyes brimmed with tenderness. "Has anyone ever told you what a beautiful person you are?"

She blinked back the tears, wanting to see this man she loved without hindrance. "No, not recently."

"Then let me do the honors, my love." Careful of the baby in her arms, he leaned forward and kissed her on the mouth. Softly. Gently. Wondrously. "You're a beautiful person, Danielle Donovan."

"Oh, Flynn," she whispered. "You always make me *feel* beautiful."

He kissed her again briefly. "I love you, sweetheart. You and little Alexandra and the other babies we will have."

Her heart turned over with love. "Others?" she teased.

"Not too many." He gently took the baby out of her arms, kissed Alexandra's forehead and placed her in the crib next to the bed.

Then he returned to Danielle, as he always would. "I want you to myself sometimes. No, I want you to myself *all* the time, but I'm willing to compromise. We'll get a nanny."

"I rather think Louise and Thomas might want to take on that job." Her smiled faded, her face growing serious. "Thank you for not giving up on me, Flynn. And for loving me unconditionally. And my daughter."

"*Our* daughter."

"Our daughter," she repeated as he lowered his head.

It was a long time before either of them came up for air. And that was just fine with Flynn. He rather liked being held captive by this woman who held his heart in her hands.

* * * * *

THE EXECUTIVE'S VENGEFUL SEDUCTION

BY
MAXINE SULLIVAN

Dear Reader,

This is my third book in the AUSTRALIAN MILLIONAIRES series, and I can't begin to tell you how wonderful it's been to write stories where the hero is rich and compelling and the heroine gorgeous and feisty.

And like my first two books, this story is set in Darwin, in the torrid zone north of Australia, where I lived for many years. How fitting it seems, then, to have my heroine, Gabrielle, return home to Darwin after a long absence. Despite hiding a tragic secret, Gabrielle falls in love all over again with Damien, and it proves to be just what she needs. She realises she has come home in more ways than one.

I trust you will enjoy this story of a prodigal daughter and a powerful executive, who find each other as difficult to resist as this city in the heart of the tropics. I see it as a fitting end to the series and I hope you do, too.

Happy reading!

Maxine

To Kaz Delaney and Sandra Allan
Firm friends, wonderful writers.
Thanks for the laughs, ladies.

One

Damien Trent acknowledged two things when Gabrielle Kane stepped from the elevator and walked along the corridor toward her office.

She was even more gorgeous than he remembered.

And he'd been a fool to let her go.

"Hello, Gabrielle," he said, straightening away from the wall, his gaze sliding over the soft gray material of her pantsuit that hugged her breasts and clung to her hips, down to the matching strappy sandals. She'd never looked more elegant and feminine than she did right now.

Her blond head shot up from searching through her purse, and her steps faltered. She paled. "My God! Damien?"

"You remembered?" he drawled, then felt something shift inside his chest when those blue eyes met his full-on. For a split second time reversed itself to five years ago. She'd walked into that business function with her father, and their eyes had met across the room, jolting him, making him want her.

Just like they were doing now.

She moistened her mouth, then appeared to pull herself together. "How could I forget?"

"That's something we have in common, then." He moved closer, pleased to see two spots of color rush into her smooth cheeks. "You've grown very beautiful, Gabrielle."

Her delicate chin angled. "Is this a social visit, Damien? You're a long way from home."

He mentally pulled back from wanting her. He was here for a reason. "We need to talk."

"After five years?"

His mouth tightened. She'd been the one to leave *him*. "It's important, Gabrielle."

Alarm flashed in her eyes, then was banked. "It's my father, isn't it?" she said, her tone without inflection now, but he'd seen her immediate reaction. She still cared for the father who'd cut her off after she'd walked out.

He cupped her elbow. "Let's go into your office," he said, feeling the slenderness beneath his palm, conceding that he'd missed touching her.

She turned away and with a shaky hand that was a dead giveaway she unlocked the door to a suite of offices with a sign reading Events by Eileen—The Events Organizer.

He followed her through the main reception area

and into another office, taking in the plush carpet and quality furniture and fittings. "You seem to have done well for yourself."

She walked around the desk and stood with her back to the large glass window, a breathtaking view of the Sydney Harbor Bridge and Opera House behind her. "Let's not pretend you don't already know all about me, Damien. I'm sure whatever report you had done on me must have told you what I do and who I work for." She crossed her arms, her face closed. "Just say what you have to say."

So. She was going to play it cool now, was she? It didn't surprise him. She'd always been a mixture of fire and ice. It was one of the things he'd liked about her—all that passion beneath a cool exterior.

He inclined his head at the high-backed leather chair behind her desk. "You might want to sit."

"I'd rather stand," she said, but her shoulders went back, as if preparing for a blow.

There was no easy way to say this. "Your father's had a stroke, Gabrielle," he said, hearing her gasp, seeing the shock she couldn't hide now. "It caused a cerebral hemorrhage in his brain. It was touch-and-go so they had to operate."

She swallowed hard. "Is he…"

"No, he's not dead. They're hopeful he'll pull through and will recover fully in time."

"Oh God," she murmured, all pretence gone now as she finally sank onto her chair.

He watched her, seeing the whiteness of her skin and the way she bit her bottom lip, and he knew he'd done the right thing by coming to get her. "My private jet's ready when you are."

She blinked up at him. "What?"

"You'll be coming home to Darwin to see your father."

She shook her head. "No...I can't."

His mouth thinned. "He's your father, Gabrielle."

She made a choking sound. "Obviously that hasn't worried him too much these past five years."

It was one thing to ignore your father's existence when he was in good health, but Russell had come close to death. It was time they sorted things out between them. Damien had told Russell the same thing not long before his stroke, when the other man appeared to be fretting over the loss of his daughter. Perhaps Russell sensed something had been about to happen.

"*You* were the one who walked out on him," he pointed out. "Your father found that hard to forgive."

"Perhaps I find it hard to forgive a few things, too," she said, remaining firm.

He was instantly alert. "Such as?"

A wary look suddenly entered her eyes. "It doesn't matter."

"Obviously it does or you wouldn't have mentioned it."

She looked across the desk at him. "Nothing can change the past now. Let's just say that when I left home five years ago I never looked back."

He arched a brow. "*Never?* I find that hard to believe."

She shrugged her slim shoulders and leaned back in her chair. "That's your problem, Damien. Not mine."

Her comment irritated him. "You walked out on me, too," he reminded her silkily.

Her chin rose in the air. "And did *you* find that hard to forgive?"

His jaw clenched. "Your note was sufficient."

"I'm glad you think so," she said with a touch of sarcasm.

He scowled as her comment slammed into him. "You said you wanted to end our affair," he reminded her. "You also said not to try and change your mind."

"And it suited you to believe me, didn't it?"

"Are you saying you lied?" he demanded, his stomach knotting.

Her eyelids flickered, as if she knew she was in dangerous waters. She sighed. "No. It *was* the truth. It was over between us."

He stared hard for a moment as something centered inside his chest. Things were far from over between them. He'd subconsciously realized that when she'd stepped out of the elevator and walked toward him like a vision from heaven.

"No, I don't think it was over at all," he said quietly.

She stiffened. "Really? You obviously didn't think that at the time."

"True. But we had other priorities back then."

She inclined her head but couldn't hide a hint of relief in her eyes. "Yes, we both had a lot of things going on in our lives."

"And I let that get in the way of what was important." He paused. "Things have changed."

She looked startled. "Changed?"

Now that he'd seen her again, he would have to

work her out of his system. In the most pleasurable way, of course.

"It's time to come home, Gabrielle. Your father needs you." Hell, *he* suddenly needed her, too.

Her gaze dropped, and she began to smooth her palms over the front of her silky jacket. Then she looked up as if making a decision. "I'm sorry. Please tell my father I wish him well, but I won't be coming back."

That wasn't acceptable. "And if he dies?"

She winced, then whispered, "Don't."

He couldn't let himself soften toward her. Not right now. He had a job to do. "You have to face facts. Your father is seriously ill. He needs to see you."

"Damien, I can't…I…"

"Not even for your mother's sake?"

Her mouth dropped open, her eyes widened. "Wh-what? My mother? When did you talk to my mother?"

"Caroline came home a couple of days ago when she heard about your father's stroke."

Gabrielle clenched her hands together. "No, she would never forgive him." Her mother would *never* have gone back to her father. When Caroline left, she'd sworn the marriage was over forever.

"She did. And I think you should, too."

"You're lying. This is a trick."

"No tricks, I swear. Gabrielle, your mother asked that I come and get you. She needs you right now."

She flinched. "That's not fair."

"I didn't say it was," he said as he was jabbed by an old heartache. Despite everything that had gone on, at least Gabrielle had parents who cared about her. She wasn't totally nonexistent to them, unlike his own parents. She had a second chance with her family. He doubted his parents would have even *wanted* a second chance. They'd been too involved with themselves...too selfish to consider that their son might just need some of their attention.

Just the thought of it made the muscles at the back of his neck tense. "Look, if you can't come back for your father, then do it for your mother's sake."

She glared at him. "I just can't walk out of here and leave everything to the others. This is a thriving business. We've got some major events coming up."

"I'm sure they can cope without you."

"That's not the point."

"Then what is?" he challenged. She was only making excuses and they both knew it.

She held his gaze for a long moment, then her eyes clouded over and she sighed with surrender. "Okay, I'll come home. But I'm only staying until my father's out of danger."

"Deal." By then he would have her in his bed again and out of his system once and for all.

The thought was completely satisfying.

Long after they were airborne and heading toward Darwin in the Northern Territory of Australia, Gabrielle finished making numerous calls to explain the situation to her clients, then turned off her cell phone to take a break from it all. Before the plane had left Sydney, she'd spoken to Eileen, who'd been supportive of her situation and had made her promise to phone as soon as she was settled.

Dear Eileen. If it hadn't been for the older woman taking her in and treating her like one of her daughters, Gabrielle didn't think she would be as "together" as she was now. Eileen had helped her through so much.

And so had Lara and Kayla, Eileen's daughters. Not only had she been homeless on her arrival in Sydney, but if it wasn't for all three, she would've had to swallow her pride and call her father for help when she'd been in that car accident.

Her heart wrapped in pain, she looked over at Damien Trent, sitting opposite her reading some business papers he'd taken out of his briefcase. If he only knew… Oh God. No, she wouldn't think about that. She'd think about him instead. That would give her something to do.

In his early thirties, he looked as trim and taut as ever, with dark hair and moss-green eyes that always made her catch her breath. He was a lethal combination of manhood.

Her Damien.

The man she'd loved without question five years ago. The man she'd let glimpse her soul. The man she'd have died for. How *had* she found the courage to walk away from him, knowing she was carrying his child?

Yet how could she have stayed when she'd known he hadn't loved her? Their relationship had never been about emotional depth. Not on his part, anyway.

Oh, she'd had no doubt he would have married her once he'd known she was pregnant. But she hadn't wanted that. Not after her father's drunken rage that night telling her to go, when she'd decided then and there that she'd rather her child not have a father at all, than one who hadn't loved its mother. She just hadn't been able to bear the thought of Damien treating her with disdain in front of their child in the years to come. *She'd* been that child with her own parents, and it wasn't a nice feeling.

No, it had been better to cut the ties back then. And from that point on she'd decided she had to stand guard and protect herself from hurt. Love brought too much pain, and she'd wanted nothing more to do with letting anyone so deeply into her heart. And she hadn't.

Until today.

Until Damien had stepped back into her life.

All at once she realized Damien's eyes were upon her. "Everything okay?" he asked, watching her with a light in his eyes that went beyond the sexual, as if he were trying to decipher her thoughts. It made her uncomfortable.

She nodded and turned away, looking out the small window at the blue sky surrounding them, then down at the unimaginable vastness below. They'd left the red dust of the Outback behind some time ago, and now she could see greenery beneath them, growing increasingly greener with each mile, and the closer they got to the coast.

Then time passed and not far in the distance, she could just catch sight of the ocean at the "Top End" of Australia. She sat there for ages absorbing it all, letting it wash over her. This was where she'd been born... where she'd grown up...been happy and sad...passionate and heartbroken.

"You're home," Damien said as the plane swept around over the ocean then banked toward the runway.

Beneath them the city of Darwin glistened in the hot tropical sun.

A lump swelled in her throat and she had to blink rapidly. Damien was right, no matter how much she'd denied it to herself all these years. This was home. And home was where her heart was.

It always had been.

Two

Once Damien's plane landed they stepped straight through the invisible sheet of humidity and into a waiting BMW, before speeding through the Darwin suburbs toward the private hospital.

Gabrielle tried to hold her apprehension and worry at bay, but all she could think about now was her father. All these years she'd believed she'd prepared herself for news like this, but now she knew that wasn't possible. The emotional distance she'd worked so hard to maintain was going down the drain. No matter what had gone on between them, he was still her father and she loved him despite everything, and the thought of him dead brought a lump to her throat.

As for her mother, she was still amazed Caroline Kane had returned home to be a wife again. Her mother had been a well-paid doormat to her rich husband, but infidelity was the one thing she hadn't been able to accept. Caroline had been distraught when she'd left the house for good after discovering that Russell had been having an affair with his secretary. She was too upset even to take her teenage daughter with her, even though Gabrielle had begged her.

Repeatedly.

God, did she really have the courage to face them both again? She knew so little about them now. They were her flesh and blood, yet they'd hurt her a great deal. How was she to treat them? Like parents? Like strangers?

Dear God, did any of that matter right now anyway? she wondered as she rode the elevator in silence, her senses conscious of Damien's strong presence, the scent of aftershave a vivid reminder of being in his arms all those years ago.

But once they stepped out of the elevator and into the corridor on her father's floor, she shook off her reaction to Damien's closeness when an attractive woman stepped out of the room ahead of them. As if in slow motion, Gabrielle watched the woman turn toward them. And shock ran through her.

"Mum?" she murmured.

The woman froze. Her eyes widened and her mouth opened, only nothing came out.

Gabrielle stared back. Gone was the pretty but drab woman who'd always worn sedate clothes and her brunette hair in a bun. In her place stood a vibrant fifty-year-old woman with a stylishly cut blond bob and clothes to match.

Suddenly Caroline rushed forward. "Gabrielle!" she cried, and wrapped her arms around her daughter tightly.

Gabrielle couldn't breathe. She stood stiffly. One part of her wanted to sink into the embrace and acknowledge she'd missed this feeling of belonging that went bone deep. This was her mother after all. The woman who'd given birth to her.

It was also the woman who'd left her teenage daughter to cope alone with an increasingly volatile father, she reminded herself.

Caroline pulled back, tears in her eyes. "Oh, my goodness. I can't believe it's you, darling." She blinked rapidly, not seeming to notice Gabrielle's lack of response. "Let me look at you. You're beautiful." Caroline glanced at Damien with a watery look in her eyes. "She's beautiful, isn't she, Damien?"

Gabrielle forced herself to glance at Damien, seeing a hard but admiring look in his eyes before he gave her mother a slight smile.

"Yes, she is, Caroline. Very beautiful."

Despite the moment, his comment sent a tingle through her that she didn't appreciate. She'd always known he'd found her attractive. He'd totally swept her off her feet five years ago, but hearing him say it now after so long away from him made her cheeks grow warm.

"Oh, wait until your father knows you're here," Caroline said excitedly. "It'll be the best medicine."

At the mention of her father, anguish came rushing back. "How is he, Mum? What did the doctors say?"

Caroline squeezed her arm. "Darling, he's doing better than expected."

"Thank God."

"Yes, thank God," Caroline said in a shaky voice. Then she reached up to Damien and gave him a quick kiss on the cheek. "And thank you for bringing my daughter home, Damien. I can't tell you how much this means to me and Russell."

"She was happy to come." He turned toward Gabrielle with mocking eyes. "Weren't you, Gabrielle?"

Gabrielle held his gaze, but her face felt tight. "Yes," she lied.

For the first time her mother seemed to notice Gabrielle's lack of warmth. The light in her eyes dimmed. "Darling, I know we have a lot to say to each other," she said cautiously. "But perhaps that can wait until later? Let's just get through this first."

Gabrielle nodded, thankful for her mother's suggestion. The past didn't disappear just because her father was so ill, but neither was this the right time to air grievances.

Caroline put on a bright face. "Good. Now let's go take a peek at your father," she said, heading back to the room she'd just exited. "He's not supposed to have any visitors except me, but I'm sure it's okay for you to just see him for a moment." At the door she stopped to look at Gabrielle. "Prepare yourself, darling. He's not his best at the moment."

Her mother was right, Gabrielle decided, standing beside her father's hospital bed a little while later. Her eyes misted over as she looked down at his prone body, the white sheets and bandage around his head highlighting his ashen skin, his body thinner than she remembered.

Gently she reached out and touched his cheek. He

moved his head slightly but didn't waken, and she gave a soft cry. It was as if he knew she was there.

Just then the nurse came into the room, and in a compassionate tone advised that there should only be one visitor and perhaps Gabrielle and Damien could come back tomorrow.

Gabrielle nodded, then leaned over and kissed her father's cheek, whispering, "I love you, Dad."

Then she felt Damien's hand on her arm and she looked up at him, surprised by the sympathy in his eyes. She let him lead her from the room, her mother behind them.

Outside, Caroline said regretfully, "Darling, I wish I could come home with you but I need to stay by your father's side for a day or two, just until he's out of danger."

Gabrielle understood. "Mum, it's okay. I can stay at the house by myself."

Her mother's eyes filled with worry. "But that's the problem. They'd just started major renovations when this happened to your father, so I've let them continue while I'm sleeping here at the hospital. But a lot of strange men are working around the place and I don't want you alone there."

Gabrielle accepted that. She wasn't sure she'd even wanted to stay at the house anyway. There were too many bad memories. "Then I'll stay at a hotel."

Her mother clicked her tongue. "Oh, but I don't want you staying in some impersonal hotel room, either."

"Mum, I have to stay somewhere," she half joked, then felt a slither of apprehension when she saw Damien's dark brows jerk together.

He turned to her mother. "Don't worry, Caroline.

Gabrielle can stay at my apartment. I'll even rent her a car so she can get around town."

Gabrielle stiffened. "No, that's not necess—" she began until Damien shot her a dark look silencing her.

Her mother's face had already filled with relief. "That's wonderful, Damien. I'll feel so much better knowing you're close by."

He nodded. "You just concentrate on helping Russell get better."

"But—" Gabrielle began again, not wanting to stay within an inch of this man. They'd been lovers. She was still feeling the pull of his attraction. She couldn't live with him, not even for a day.

"It's no trouble, Gabrielle," Damien said in a tone that brooked no objection.

Caroline gave her daughter a heartfelt hug goodbye. "Darling, let Damien take care of you for a while. Ohh, I'm so glad you're here. And your father will be, too, once he wakes up." Gabrielle wanted to say she didn't need to be taken care of, but Caroline was already kissing Damien on the cheek again. "Look after my baby, Damien. She's precious to me."

"I will."

Just then another nurse went inside the room, and it was obvious her mother was anxious to follow. Gabrielle knew there was nothing for it but to put her own worries aside. "Mum, go back to Dad. I'll see you tomorrow."

"Thanks, darling," Caroline said warmly before she slipped back inside the room.

Then it was just her and Damien again.

Just as it would be at his apartment.

Sharp anxiety twisted inside her, making her testy. "You've got a nerve telling my mother I'll be staying at your place. I'd prefer a hotel."

Displeasure furrowed his brow as he took her arm and started toward the elevator. "You heard Caroline. She's worried about you and wants to know you're safe."

"With *you?*" she scoffed.

"You're always safe with me, Gabrielle." He captured her eyes with his. "It's yourself you're not sure about."

The breath caught in her lungs, but thankfully the elevator doors slid open and she quickly stepped inside, standing away from him, wishing it wasn't empty.

The doors slid shut, enclosing them alone together. "It would be easier if I stayed in a hotel," she insisted stubbornly, knowing she was fighting a losing battle but determined to fight all the same.

He glanced at his Rolex as if he didn't care one way or the other. "My apartment has a spare bedroom. You may as well use it." Yet when he looked up, his eyes had darkened to a jungle green, and just as untamed.

A quiver surged through her veins. "You didn't have a spare bedroom before," she said stupidly, saying the first thing that came to mind, trying not to let him see her reaction.

"That's because I didn't have this apartment before," he drawled.

She flushed. "Fine," she said, giving in to stop from blathering like an idiot again. "But it's only for a few days and that's all."

A satisfied looked crossed his face, making her even more tense. "That's settled then," he said, just as the elevator stopped and the doors opened so other people could get in with them.

She and Damien moved to the back of the compartment, but she was still very aware of him. She tried to resist the compulsion to look sideways but decided one quick look wouldn't hurt.

And that was her mistake.

His gaze lingered on her figure, making her nipples tighten beneath the light material of her pantsuit. She'd chosen the outfit because it flattered her moderate bustline and slight swell of her hips, and because she always felt good in it. The last thing she'd expected when she'd dressed this morning was an X-ray treatment from a man who'd been her lover and knew every inch of her body.

Oh God. Her staying at his apartment may have been settled, but she had the uneasy feeling nothing else had been settled at all.

Having Gabrielle in his apartment was more than Damien expected on her first day back in town, but he would take it one step at a time. He wanted her in his bed but he also wanted a willing partner and was prepared to wait until she was ready.

It won't be a long wait.

She could fight herself all she wanted, but it was obvious she was fighting a losing battle. She wanted him as much as he wanted her. He could *smell* that want in her...that need of desire. He felt the same. Her scent filled his nostrils...filled his apartment even now.

And all she had done was walk through to the spare

bedroom, he thought with a wry smile as he remembered her cool comment that she'd see him at dinner. But she hadn't been cool inside. He knew the two of them struck sparks off each other and that it was only a matter of time before they burst into flames.

In the meantime he didn't mind playing with matches, he mused as he showered and changed for dinner, then arranged for dinner to be delivered.

Then he sat on the sofa to do some paperwork, though his mind kept flicking to Gabrielle and her parents. He had to admit that Russell hadn't been the best father in the world after Caroline had left a few years earlier. And what had gone on before that, he didn't know. He hadn't known them then, having moved to Melbourne for a few years, building his fortune, only flying back to Darwin every so often to play poker with his best friends, Brant and Flynn.

Then one day he'd decided he missed the tropics and he'd come home for good. Fortuitously, Russell had been looking for a business partner at the time, and *he'd* been looking to make more money. He'd gone on to forge his own company and make his millions. It had worked out well.

Until now.

Until Gabrielle Kane had walked back into his life.

Just like she was doing this very minute as she made an appearance at the living room doorway. She was worth the wait, dressed in a sleeveless, teal-colored crocheted top and long white pants that clung to her gorgeous figure, making her look casual yet stylish.

"Hungry?" he said, putting the papers aside on the sofa and getting to his feet.

"A little."

He started across the open-plan apartment toward the dining table nestled over in the corner. "Everything's ready."

She slowly followed him, then frowned when she saw the table laden with food. "Are others coming?"

"No. Just us. I ordered from the restaurant across the street." The chef *had* gone a little overboard with the array of tropical salads, dishes teeming with prawns and lobster, Tasmanian salmon and barramundi fish. "I told them plenty of seafood," he said, deliberately reminding her that he remembered how partial she'd been to this type of food.

Her eyes brightened, then she flushed. "Thank you, but I doubt I'll do it all justice."

"No problem. My housekeeper will be delighted to take the leftovers off my hands." He held out the chair for her. "Sit here."

She moved forward and did as he suggested. Once she was comfortable, he took his own seat and poured wine into their glasses.

Her gaze darted around the room. "This is a really nice apartment."

"I know. Lucky for me one of my friends married a very talented lady who loves to decorate."

The place hadn't been half-bad before, but Danielle had suggested some ideas and he hadn't had the heart to dissuade her. He and Flynn had smiled at each other as she'd enthusiastically promised a stylishly furnished apartment with class and sophistication that was ideal for executive living. And she'd lived up to that promise.

The open plan of the living and dining area, abundant with natural light, soaked up the magnificent panoramic views of the harbor...her words, not his. She'd done a great job of it.

"It's lovely," Gabrielle agreed.

"Just like you are, Gabrielle," he said, holding her eyes with his. One day soon he would hold her in his arms. And he would show her how lovely he thought she was.

A pulse beat at the base of her throat. "You know, I'm suddenly really hungry," she said huskily, and began piling the food on her plate.

He was too, but it wasn't for food. Dammit, waiting was already harder than he'd expected.

It would be easier once he said what he needed to say. She wasn't going to be so placid then, he decided, as they ate in silence for a while, listening to the soft background music, but eventually he knew he couldn't put this off. She wasn't going to like it.

He raised his glass in a toast. "To you, Gabrielle."

Her eyes widened. "Me?"

"For having the courage to come home again."

She looked pleasantly surprised as she picked up her glass and clinked it against his. "Thank you," she said, a slight catch to her voice that unfurled something soft inside his chest.

He took a sip of wine, then said, "Your mother was pleased to see you today."

"Yes."

"I imagine Russell will be, too."

"Yes."

"Aren't you glad now that you came?"

Her forehead creased a little, her eyes growing puzzled. "Yes, I am."

He rested back against his chair. "And you're happy to be here in Darwin?"

She eyed him with sudden suspicion. "Okay, what's this about, Damien?"

Leaning forward, he placed his wine glass on the table, then dropped the bombshell. "Your cousin has taken control of the Kane Property and Finance Group."

Her cousin was an idiot.

A dangerous idiot.

She gaped at him. "Keiran? How on earth did he get involved in all this?"

Damien's mouth tightened. "Some years ago your father sold forty percent of the company shares to him, that's why."

She sat up straighter. "What! Why would he do that?"

"Russell wanted to keep it in the family if anything happened to him, and Keiran worked on him until he sold him the shares." Damien had advised Russell against it, but the older man seemed to have a blind spot where his nephew was concerned, and now his company that specialized in providing investment property finance here in Australia and the growing Asian market, was paying the price. "Your father also left written instructions with his attorney that if he became incapacitated, then *you* were to get forty percent of the shares as well."

"What!"

"You each now hold forty percent of the Kane Property and Finance Group."

She shook her head. "I don't believe I'm hearing this."

"Believe it."

"Oh my Lord." She sat there for a moment looking stunned.

"Keiran's been at Kane's for some years now and he knows the business. As soon as Russell had the stroke he stepped in and took over. Your cousin was always quick when there was something in it for him."

"I know."

He paused, then, "And that's exactly why you needed to be here."

"Me?"

"Yes."

Her eyes widened. "Good heavens, you don't expect me to step in and start running a multinational company, do you?"

"Why not? Keiran did. He's already made some decisions that would give your father another stroke if he knew, and we can't do a damn thing to stop him." The only person who could stop him was sitting right here. "If you assume control, Keiran will hopefully slink back into his own little office where he can do no more damage."

She stared at him in disbelief. "But Keiran owns as many shares as I do now. He's not going to give up the top job."

Damien could feel his jaw clench. "Let's try him first."

She shook her head, obviously trying to get it clear in her mind. "Hang on. Why didn't you tell me all this back in Sydney?"

"Would you have come home?"

"I don't know," she said, her forehead marred with a

crease. "And I don't understand why my father left *me* forty percent."

"Perhaps he expected you would come back if he needed you. And he *does* need you now, Gabrielle."

A cynical light came into her eyes. "You mean he thought it was a good way of blackmailing me into coming home if he ever needed me." She shook her head. "It's still all about *him*, isn't it?"

Damien ignored that. "Your father wouldn't expect you to take over if you weren't capable."

Her eyebrows shot up as realization dawned on her. "Oh, so he's been keeping tabs on me, too."

He had no idea, but it was highly likely. "Russell doesn't always take me into his confidence." The older man had been a friend and mentor but he'd never spoken about his daughter until recently. "Look, I'll help you. I've delegated some of my own business dealings to others. I've got the time."

A flicker of apprehension crossed her face. "To work with me every day, you mean?"

"Yes." And if he got to make love to her sooner, all the better.

Her beautiful blue eyes hardened and narrowed. "What's in it for you, Damien?"

He returned her look with a level one of his own. "I want to help Russell. I owe him a lot."

Seconds ticked by. "That's commendable of you," she said somewhat sourly.

His mouth tightened. "I admire Russell and what he's achieved."

"And look at the price he paid for it," she pointed out.

"He lost his wife and then his daughter, and now he's losing his company. Don't admire him, Damien. Pity him."

"So why aren't *you?*" he challenged, and saw her startled look. "Come on, Gabrielle. Tell me. Why aren't *you* showing your father some pity?"

She bridled. "I'm here, aren't I?"

"Under protest."

She dropped her gaze to the table. "That may be so, but I do love my father nonetheless." Her eyelashes lifted. "But even if I wanted to help more, there are limits to what I can do."

"How do you know? You haven't even tried."

Her lip curled with sarcasm. "Your understanding amazes me."

He took his time before saying what needed to be said. "You're the only one who can save the company from ruin, Gabrielle."

"What about my mother?" she said as sudden hope swept across her face. "Perhaps I can sign over the shares to her and she could stop Keiran from taking over the company. She only needs to put in an appearance and you could do the rest."

"You would ask that of your mother? When she's having a hard enough time as it is?"

"Yet it's okay to ask it of me?" She grimaced, and a slight flush tinged her cheeks. "That sounded selfish. I didn't mean it like that."

He inclined his head. "Caroline's got enough on her plate looking after your father right now."

She raised her chin. "And if I don't choose to be a part of this?"

"I don't think you'd forgive yourself if your parents lost everything."

She exhaled a long, ragged breath. "You really know how to tighten the thumb screws, don't you?"

"Sometimes we have to do things we don't want to do but we do them anyway."

"Okay, okay, I'll try," she snapped. "But once my father's on the mend, I'll be leaving and going back to Sydney. Don't forget that."

"You've already made that clear." But he was more than satisfied.

For the moment.

She placed her napkin on the table and pushed to her feet. "Somehow I've lost my appetite. I think I'll go to my room. Good night."

It was more than clear she wanted time alone. Time he could afford to give her.

He inclined his head. "Good night, Gabrielle," he said, watching her walk away with a sway to her hips that would draw any man's attention. Yet he wasn't just *any* man. He'd been her lover, if not her confidant.

And she'd walked out on him without a proper goodbye. It had left a loss he only recognized now that he'd seen her again. A loss that went deeper than he'd expected. And because of it, he could feel an odd sort of anger simmering beneath the surface. An anger he wasn't ready to face. Perhaps once he had enough of her body he'd *never* have to face it.

Three

Gabrielle retired to the spare bedroom and stood looking out the window at the harbor. Being around Damien wasn't conducive to being clear-minded. He always seemed to be watching her, waiting for her to lower her guard. And keeping up that guard was exhausting when she had other things to think about.

God, it was mind-boggling that her father had given her forty percent of the shares in the business. Of course, she thought cynically, he hadn't been able to bring himself to give her the remaining sixty percent of the shares—not that she wanted them.

No, he'd been hedging his bets. He'd given her limited control of the business, but had withheld twenty percent of the shares for himself just in case his incapacitation had proven temporary. And that was predictably her father. He could never let go of total control.

As for Keiran holding forty percent of the shares, well, that was a justified worry. Her cousin had always had his eye on the main chance, no matter what had been at stake, whether it be tripping her up as a kid so he could jump in the swimming pool first, or trying to suck up to her father during her parents' separation. She had no doubt Keiran was capable of anything. She disliked him intensely. He was the one person who should *not* be in charge of a multimillion-dollar business.

As for Damien, it was typical he hadn't told her about this before now. If she didn't know him better, she'd think he was just like Keiran, keeping secrets to himself and using them for his own benefit.

Only, she knew he *wasn't* like Keiran.

Not at all.

Damien wasn't underhanded, just arrogant. She couldn't see Damien tripping anyone to get in the pool first. He just wasn't that kind of person. Damien would manipulate to get what he wanted—oh, yes, and he was good at that—but there was a difference. Damien wasn't the type to lie or cheat if confronted over an issue. If Damien said something, he meant it. If he gave his word, he would stand by it.

Heavens, never in her wildest dreams had she imagined she'd ever be spending another night sleeping under Damien's roof. And in separate bedrooms, too. And that was just as well. He'd been a sensual man when she'd met him and she knew he hadn't changed. She could still feel the sensuality rolling off him in waves. Even now she remembered the force of his desire from the day she'd walked into that function with her father and she'd felt the pull of a man's eyes from across the room.

Damien.

It had been that strong.

But that's all it had ever been with him. She'd only ever known him in the physical sense, never the emotional one. For two glorious months over a tropical summer it had been all about sex and attraction on his part, while she'd fallen headlong in love with him.

And she'd wanted him to love her in return, only it was never going to happen. She'd realized that the day she'd left home for good. It had given her the strength not to look back. If she had, she would have weakened and gone running into his arms.

But not into his heart.

It had taken her years to get over him, but time and distance had put things into perspective. It had been lust, not love. Attraction, not affinity. It was important to remember that, she decided as the adrenaline pumped through her veins, taking her a long time to fall asleep. Once she did, exhaustion gave her some blessed relief from the relentless thoughts going through her head, and when she stepped into the kitchen the next morning, she felt more rested than she'd dared hope.

Until she saw Damien standing at the counter, contemplating the mug of coffee in his hands as if it held the secrets to life itself. He obviously hadn't heard her enter because he didn't move. Strange, but he looked sort of…lonely.

She must have made a sound because his head shot up,

and a seductive glint slid straight into his eyes. "Ah, the prodigal daughter has awoken," he drawled, his gaze going over her red sleeveless dress cinched at the waist with a belt of the same material, and matching leather pumps.

"And good morning to you, too," she said coolly, forcing herself to ignore the pull of his physical appearance. So what if he was dressed in dark trousers and a white shirt that looked like they'd been born on him?

A lazy moment passed by as Damien considered her, then he placed his mug on the counter behind him. "I phoned the hospital earlier. Russell's doing as well as expected."

Her heart fluttered with anxiety at the reminder of her father. "Thank you. I was going to call shortly myself." She moved toward the percolator on the counter, badly needing her morning cup of coffee. "I plan on going to see him soon."

"They said not to come until this afternoon. Apparently they've got a couple of doctors checking him over this morning." He must have seen her give a start. "Your mother said it was nothing to worry about."

Her panic subsided as she poured coffee into a cup. "Then I can go see Keiran instead. I planned on it, anyway."

"Aah, so that's why you're dressed like that."

Something in his voice made her look up, and she found his eyes sliding over her again, making her catch her breath. She put the coffeepot back with a shaky hand and tried to act casual. "I'm not about to go into my father's office in jeans and a tank top."

"Might get some favorable comments."

"More likely they'd direct me to the janitor's room," she quipped, looking at him over the top of her coffee cup.

All at once he smiled. A rare smile that knocked her off balance. For a moment she could only stare at him across the width of the room.

Then that smile faded and something in those eyes darkened and he moved forward, making her heart drop to her knees. He stopped right in front of her, took the cup out of her hand then placed it on the counter beside her.

"It's been a long time, Gabrielle," he said huskily, in a voice so Australian, so thick and delicious, it swirled around her heart like a long-lost friend. "Miss me?"

She swallowed. "Does a bear miss a toothache?" she managed to say, the breathlessness in her voice disturbing her.

He gave a soft laugh and slid his hands over her shoulders with an ease that only an ex-lover can have. "Hmm. I like your hair this length." Provocatively, one finger coiled around some blond strands that curled below her neck. "It suits you."

She shivered as his warm breath wafted over her and wrapped her in its minty scent. It seemed like only yesterday when she would have leaned into the hard wall of his chest and relished his strength. And only yesterday that they had made love with a passion that had stolen her breath away.

"You're even more beautiful than I remember," he murmured, his hands sliding down to her hips.

Up close, his green gaze was a caress, his male scent too enticing, the tension between them building, overwhelming her, restricting her breathing, making her forget that never again had she wanted to be close enough to see into the irises of his emerald eyes...or the grain of his skin as it weaved and dipped its way over a strong nose and lean cheekbones...nor had she ever wanted to touch the fullness of his lips, to know she'd once ached to have them on her body.

"Stop it," she whispered, hating herself for letting him affect her like this.

"Stop what?"

"Damien..."

"Gabi..."

Gabi. He'd only ever called her that once before. He'd been thrusting inside her and she'd been welcoming each plunge of his body. They'd reached their climax together. It had been the only time she'd felt his equal, and not some young woman who'd been the daughter of his business partner.

All at once she had to get out of the kitchen.

It was too small.

There wasn't enough air.

She pushed his hands off her and spun away, heading for the door, not even sure if Damien had hired a car yet for her, but willing to catch a cab if necessary. "I need to see Keiran...at the office...in case he goes out." She was babbling but couldn't seem to stop herself.

He came up behind her, putting his hand on her arm, stopping her but not in a forceful way. "I'm coming with you," he rasped, the huskiness still in his voice, the desire still glittering from the depths of those green eyes.

His touch sent a tingle along her spine. "There's no need."

His mouth tightened and he dropped his hand. "I said I'd help and I will. Don't underestimate Keiran. There's power in numbers, Gabrielle."

She sent him a wary glance. "I know my own cousin."

"Then you know you need me with you."

As much as she didn't want it to be, what he said was true. She abruptly nodded her head. "Okay, but I need to get that rental car later for my own use," she said, giving in but perhaps not as gracefully as she could, and that was more to do with needing to get away from Damien's presence than *not* needing him to help her deal with Keiran.

But in the confines of his car, her mind couldn't stop from going back to Damien. She realized that being a woman desired by him was more dangerous to her now than five years ago. Now he would want more than girlish enthusiasm in his bed. He'd want a woman's response, slow and deliberate, not a rushed and naive eagerness. And he'd expect her to be a mature partner, able to handle a sexual relationship without too much emotion. It was a world of difference to five years ago.

She pushed all her thoughts to the side as they walked into the building that housed the head office of her father's company. The first person she saw was one of her father's managers she remembered from years ago. He greeted her warmly then expressed sympathy over her father's condition.

"Thank you, James. I'm glad to see you're still here."

The older man's eyes flicked to Damien then back to her. "Not for long I'm afraid. I've accepted a position with another company. I finish up at the end of the week."

Dismay filled her. "Oh, I'm sorry to hear that."

"Gabrielle, I've got nothing to lose by saying this. I've always enjoyed working for your father, but it's going to be a while before he's back on his feet. I'm sorry but I can't work with *him* until that happens."

"You mean Keiran?" she said to clarify, but knowing all Damien had told her was true.

James nodded. "I don't mind saying I think that man's going to ruin the company with his ideas. And I'm not the only one leaving, either. There are two heads of departments who have put their resignation in and another planning on it." He clicked his tongue. "They're men who are going to be taking a whole lot of experience and knowledge with them when they go, I'm afraid."

She tried to look confident. "James, that's why I'm here. My father wanted me to take over if anything happened to him and that's what I'm going to do."

Relief flared then died in his eyes. "Keiran isn't going to step aside so easily," he warned.

She squeezed the older man's hand. "Keiran won't have a choice."

But when Damien opened the door to her father's office and Gabrielle saw her cousin sitting behind her father's desk like he owned the place, every instinct inside wanted to tell him to get the hell out of there.

Keiran glanced up at the interruption and for a moment looked like an animal caught in the headlights. Then he went rigid. "Well, well. If it isn't my long-lost cousin." He pasted on a false smile as he stood and came around the desk. "Gabrielle, how nice to see you again."

Her mouth tightened as he pecked at both her cheeks like a chicken. "Keiran, you haven't changed a bit." He was two years older than her, and he'd wielded his older stance often during their childhood.

"You're still the sweetest thing," he joked as he glanced at Damien. But his eyes were wary beneath his blond head and they held a heartless gleam that had been in them since the day he'd been born. Now, here was one person her father *should* have cut off, she thought, suppressing a moment of pain that it had been his own daughter her father had ignored instead.

She stepped away. "What are you doing in here, Keiran?"

His smile flattened. "What do you think I'm doing in here? Someone had to step in when your father had his stroke."

"Then thank you. I appreciate it but I'm here now."

His piercing eyes contrasted sharply with his relaxed stance. "Not so fast. You can't just walk in here and take over."

She arched a brow. "Why not?"

He strode back around the desk. "You've been gone five years. And before that you never worked here in any capacity anyway."

She refused to let him see his comment had hit its mark. "I spent a couple of school holidays working here, remember?"

"And that gives you the experience to run a multinational company dealing in property and finance, does it?"

"From what I hear, I could do better than what you've been doing," she said coolly.

As if a storm was brewing, the air seemed to sizzle with electricity. "I don't know what you mean."

"I mean that from all accounts you're running the company into the ground. All our managers are leaving."

He waved a dismissive hand. "They were old and stale. We need new blood."

She gave a soft gasp. "That's a callous statement."

His lips twisted. "Perhaps I'm a chip off the old block."

She held herself stiffly. "My father would never have dumped his employees."

"Sure? I think if Russell kept them on, it was for his own selfish reasons."

She didn't want him to see that he was probably right, so she ignored that. "Look, I'm here now and I have Damien to help me."

"No."

She blinked. "What do you mean no?"

Keiran's glare resented their presence. "I have every right to be in this office, Gabrielle. Just ask your friend, here. That's why he went to get you to bring you back. Don't fool yourself it was only about your father's stroke."

"I ought to hit you for saying that, Keiran," Damien said, his eyes as cold as dry ice.

"But you can't deny it."

"You're not worth refuting."

Keiran sat on the chair with a smirk. "May I suggest you go and rethink your position. I own forty percent of this company and I intend to take it places Russell never even dreamed about."

Gabrielle gasped, and Damien growled, "You've bitten off more than you can chew, Keiran."

Keiran shrugged. "I'm in charge, Trent, whether you like it or not." He picked up a pen. "Now. If you'll both excuse me I have work to do. Major changes are on my agenda."

Gabrielle stood there for a moment, stunned and shaken. "Don't make too many changes, Keiran. I'll only have to change them back."

He waved a hand at the door. "Don't let me keep you."

For a moment Gabrielle thought Damien might leap across the desk and throw the other man out, but with a pulse ticking in his jaw, he thrust open the door and let her precede him through it.

They didn't speak as they rode the elevator down with another couple to the parking lot beneath the building. But once they were in the BMW she sat while he came around to the driver's side, her mind ticking over. What the devil were they going to do? If indeed they could do anything at all to wrestle the company from Keiran's grip before he did too much damage.

Damien slid onto the driver's seat. "Are you okay?"

She blinked. "Yes, I'm fine," she said, but just as quickly realized she wasn't. Whether it was because Keiran had put such a bad taste in her mouth, she suddenly felt the need to go home to where she'd grown up. All at once she wanted to touch base with something familiar.

"No, I'm not. Damien, take me home please. To my parents' place." She took a shuddering breath. "Just for a little while."

He stared at her, watching her with some indefinable emotion in his eyes, then nodded. "I've got papers in my briefcase. I can work from there."

Sudden resentment grew. Couldn't he see she needed to be alone for a while? "Or you could just leave me there and I'll get a rental car sent around."

His mouth thinned. "I'm not leaving you alone with a group of strangers working around the place."

She glowered at him. "Why not? Frightened I might run off with one of them?"

He swore. "Don't be ridiculous, Gabrielle. You're upset over Keiran. Don't take it out on me."

She sighed. "I'm sorry, you're right. Just take me home, Damien."

He started the car and ten minutes later drove through the open gates of her parents' home that she hadn't seen in five long years. She gazed up at the two-level mansion of grand proportions dozing in the tropical Australian sunshine. She'd grown up playing dolls on that wide balcony around the house. And later she'd sought refuge looking through the large windows of her bedroom over treetop views to the Timor Sea and distant horizon. It had been a wonderful place to grow up. If only her parents hadn't fought all the time in those latter years. If only she'd had a brother or sister to share things with.

Thankfully Damien strode off toward the sound of hammering in the kitchen as soon as they stepped inside, saying he would tell the workmen to take a long break, and Gabrielle left him to it.

It was an odd feeling walking up the sweeping staircase to the second floor. Five years had passed, yet it only seemed like yesterday. But as she pushed the door open to her old bedroom, her mind reeled in confusion.

The room was like a time warp. Everything was the same. The bed she'd often cried her heart out on, despairing over her parents' troubled marriage, was still covered in the same quilt. Posters of some obscure pop star whose name she couldn't even recall still hung on the wall. And even the clothes she'd left behind were still hanging in the wardrobe...almost as if they were waiting for her return.

She swallowed a sob. A new and unexpected warmth surged through her that was a welcome relief after her tussle with her cousin today. If ever she needed proof of her parents' love for her, here it was. They had kept her memory alive.

Just like she did with her own child.
Damien's baby.

A baby she'd miscarried at six months because of the car accident. God, how she wanted to tell Damien about their unborn baby that she'd loved and lost. Only, she knew she couldn't tell him...could never tell him. He may not have cared for her, but she had no doubt he would have cared for their child. And she would never want any person knowing that brand of heartache.

Certainly not the baby's father.

Damien glanced up from his paperwork and saw Gabrielle stroll out onto the patio, then stand looking out beyond the swimming pool, over the manicured lawn and lushly landscaped gardens.

Adrenaline kicked in as he watched the sun beat down on her face, giving a glow to her smooth skin. The high humidity of the November build-up toward the wet season wisped strands of the blond shoulder-length hair at the base of her neck. God, he couldn't get over how beautiful she was. In the past five years he'd made love to other women, some more beautiful than Gabrielle, but none of them had...what was the word he was looking for?

Connected.

Yes, that was it. None of them had connected with something deep inside him the way Gabrielle did. Something fundamental. Something that was grabbing at him even now.

He thrust his papers aside and pushed off the sofa to go to her. "I'm impressed," he said as he stepped through the open patio doors to join her.

She spun around, her face quickly assuming a blank mask that made him want to strip aside all the layers and get to what was truly inside this woman. "You are? With what?"

He went to stand beside her at the balustrade. "You." He saw her start of surprise. "I like the way you stood up to Keiran."

Her mouth curved into an unexpected smile, fascinating him. "Well, now you know. You're not the only one I can stand up to."

He went still, caught by an invisible pull of attraction. "I can see that," he murmured, his gaze dropping to those kissable lips.

Awareness flared in her eyes, and she quickly turned and looked down at the garden instead. "Let's hope my father gets better soon."

"It's going to take some time for your father to recover enough to get back to work." If indeed he came back at all. "Many months at best."

She sighed. "Then there's nothing further I can do here. I may as well leave Keiran to it."

Damien's gut clenched. It wasn't just the thought of Keiran ruining everything for Russell that made his spirits sink. It was the thought of Gabrielle leaving. She would be on her way back to Sydney just as soon as Russell pulled out of danger. A week was probably all she'd stay, and that wasn't good enough. He wanted her in his arms and in his bed. He would settle for nothing less.

Just then an idea clicked inside him and his pulse began to race. It was the answer to the company's prayers. Surprisingly, he wasn't averse to the idea either. Lately, he had been watching Brant and Flynn with their wives and he'd felt like he was missing out on something special that came from being a couple. And Gabrielle was the only woman he could imagine being a couple with.

"Of course, we could always combine our shares and get Keiran out that way," he said quietly.

Her eyes were confused as she turned to face him fully. "I don't understand. How would we do that?"

He captured her eyes with his. "I'm a silent shareholder. I own the other twenty percent."

Her head snapped back. "What!"

"And I have the perfect solution."

She blinked and a wary look crossed her face. "You do?"

"Marry me, Gabrielle," he said smoothly. "Marry me and let's make sure Keiran never takes control of Kane's again."

Four

Gabrielle stared at Damien, unable to believe she was hearing right. "Marriage! To *you?*"

The line of his mouth tightened. "That's the idea."

Her heart constricted. Did he know what he was asking? "But why? I mean, I know you feel my father gave you a helping hand years ago but this is going too far, Damien."

"No. I'd say it's going just far enough." A look of implacable determination crossed his face. "It's the only way to stop Keiran."

She winced inwardly, trying to remember this was about Keiran, not about her and Damien. Yet she and Damien would pay the price. *Again.* Hadn't they already paid enough?

She tilted her head. "But even if we marry, my shares

belong to me and your shares belong to you. It doesn't give us controlling interest."

For a long moment he stared at her. Then, "It does if I sign over eleven percent of my shares to you as a wedding present."

"What!" she exclaimed, giving him a glance of utter disbelief.

He arched a brow. "Can you think of a better way to get Keiran out?"

She swallowed hard. "There must be another way," she said, trying not to let the desperation show in her voice.

"If there is I'd be glad to hear it."

She gathered her wits about her. "Let me talk to Keiran again. I'm sure I can make him see reason."

"Keiran will only see reason if there's something in it for him. And I don't think anything you offer will tempt him away from the top seat, do you?"

He was right. It would take much more than anything she had for Keiran to step aside.

"Of course," Damien drawled, wry amusement entering his eyes. "We could always kill him to get him out of the way."

She glared at him. "This is too serious to joke about."

"Who's joking?" he mocked, but there was a hardness to his tone that bode ill for the other man. "I'm just trying to make you see that marriage between us is the only alternative. It may not be what you want to hear but it's the best there is."

No, she couldn't believe that.
She wouldn't.

"Surely you don't want to get married, Damien? More to the point, surely you don't want to marry *me?*"

"I'm glad you know what I don't want," he snapped. "Actually, it's time I settled down. I'm getting older and I want a wife and…" a moment crept by "…you're the wife I want."

She swallowed hard. For a minute there she'd thought he was going to say he wanted a family with her. She wasn't sure if she were up to that.

But being Damien's wife…

"Would this be a temporary arrangement?" she asked, not considering it but asking all the same.

"No."

Her eyes widened. "You mean…"

"Once we marry, we stay married." A muscle ticked in his cheek. "It's forever, Gabrielle. Remember that."

"I don't think I could forget it," she muttered. Then a hopeful idea came to mind. "Of course, you could always just sign over the eleven percent to me anyway. That would be a good way to repay my father."

"No, the best way to repay your father is for us to marry. A united front will put confidence back in the company for our clients." He paused. "Oh, and Gabrielle. I will want your parents to think this is a real marriage between us."

Her heart thudded inside her chest. "You mean you want them to think we're in *love?*"

He nodded. "Yes. I'll tell your father about me giving you the shares, of course, but only after he's on the mend. I don't want him getting even a hint that we married to stop Keiran from ruining the company. It could set back his recovery."

Damien was right about her father not needing to hear bad news. "But surely my mother should be told the truth?" she questioned, even as she told herself the point was moot.

He shook his head. "No, if we're going to do it, we may as well do it properly. I don't want any slip-ups in front of your father, and with your mother being under a lot of stress, it wouldn't be fair to burden her."

He made it all sound so rational. Yet how could she pretend to be in love with this man? And why the heck was she considering this, anyway?

She lifted her chin. "I'm sorry but I won't marry you, Damien. My father wouldn't want me to go that far."

He arched a brow. "Really? I'm sure Russell would want you to do everything in your power to save all he's built over the years. And that includes marriage to me."

She straightened her shoulders. "Look, you can be a martyr about it, but I will *not* sacrifice myself like this for the sake of the company. Not for my father. And not for my mother, either," she added, preempting him.

His eyes narrowed. "Then what about for all those people who work for your father?"

Her hands clenched. "It's no use, Damien. Just give it up."

"No, you need to give *in*. There are people depending on your decision. People like James. People who have worked for your father for years, not just here in Darwin but all around Australasia. If Keiran destroys the company then there's going to be a hell of a lot of people out of work."

"I can't take responsibility for the whole damn world," she choked. If this was what it was like at the top, then they could have it.

His dark brows jerked together. "Don't swear, Gabrielle."

Her eyes widened. "How can you take this so calmly? This is our *lives* you're talking about ruining."

His face closed up more than usual. "I don't think marriage between us will ruin our lives. We may even enjoy it."

She gave a strangled laugh. "It may not ruin yours, but it will definitely ruin mine. I don't know what you've got planned for the rest of your life, but being married to you isn't on my list."

His green eyes darkened to near black as a hardness rippled through him like a chain reaction. His mouth opened. He went to speak.

And his cell phone rang.

He held her gaze a moment more, watching her. Then he took the phone out of his pocket and answered it. She was just beginning to take a breath when she noticed his gaze shoot to her. She tensed immediately, sensing it must be the hospital.

"We'll be there soon," he said into the phone, then hung up and returned it to his pocket.

"It's my father, isn't it?" she whispered, expecting a blow.

"He's fine. But they've finished some tests and now

he's awake. Your mother said it's a good time to come visit for a couple of minutes."

Intense relief washed over her. "We'd better hurry, then," she said, wishing she'd thought to give her cell phone number to her mother so that she'd always be available if anything happened. Not that she wanted to think about the worst happening, she decided, spinning on her heels to go back through the patio doors, glad to put an end to this discussion with Damien.

"We'll finish this later," he warned.

She had to stand her ground with him. "There's nothing to discuss."

Their eyes met and shock ran through her. There was a firm look on his face that said he wasn't giving up. The thought tore at her insides and made her heart plummet to the depths of her soul. Damien always got what he wanted. It was just a pity he wanted a marriage of convenience with *her*. Dear God, the last thing she wanted was to be a *convenience* to this man.

That thought kept her resolute on the way to the hospital. She had to make sure she kept up her guard against Damien. Always, just when she thought she could hold her own with him, he'd change tack and sweep the rug out from under her. He was a ruthless businessman.

A ruthless *man*.

Just like her father, she reminded herself.

Of course, her father didn't look too ruthless when she stood beside his hospital bed, his hand engulfing hers and a tear slipping down his cheek. Her eyes misted over and she leaned forward to kiss him, but ended up burying her face against his neck, careful not to cause him pain. For a split second all her hurt melted like candle wax. This was her father. And she was his little girl again.

"Gabrielle," his shaky voice rumbled in her ears, and she swallowed hard. It had been so long since she'd heard him say her name so lovingly. Too long.

"Oh, Russell, our baby girl's all grown-up now," Gabrielle heard her mother say. It startled her to hear her parents actually talking civilly to each other for a change.

"Yes," he said gruffly, and squeezed her hand again as if he never wanted to let her go.

Gabrielle took a deep breath and straightened, blinking back tears. Then her gaze fell on Damien and all at once her heart flipped over at the touch of tenderness in the back of those green eyes.

For her.

But Damien tender? Common sense told her that if he did feel any softening toward her, it was because he wanted something from her. She flinched inwardly. Oh, he wanted something all right.

Marriage.

"Sorry," her father mumbled, pulling her thoughts away from her problems with Damien.

"Dad, shh. We'll talk when you're better." Though what she'd say to him, she wasn't sure. Deep down there was still hurt and anger over all that had happened. She couldn't dismiss those feelings easily.

"Sleepy," her father murmured, shutting his eyes.

She kissed his cheek. "Go to sleep then, Dad. I'll be back tomorrow," she said softly, sure he was asleep before she'd even finished speaking.

Her mother's eyes filled with gratitude. "He'll recover well just knowing you're here."

"I'm glad," Gabrielle said, unable to prevent herself from still sounding wooden, then felt guilty for the tiny wince her mother tried to hide.

"Then we'll see you tomorrow," Caroline said, forcing a friendly tone. "The doctors don't want him overdoing things."

"Of course."

After that they said their goodbyes but once in the car, Damien turned toward her, his eyes piercing. "Your father's still got a long way to go."

Gabrielle grimaced. "You don't have to remind me."

"Yes, I do. You seem to think if you ignore everything, then it will just sort itself out."

"Maybe it will," she said coolly.

"And maybe it won't," he snapped. "When your father struggles through all this to get better and finally comes home to find out his company has been decimated, will you tell him why there's nothing left? Or will you be back in Sydney and won't give a damn?"

She drew herself up straighter in the passenger seat. "Have you finished?"

"No I bloody well haven't."

She sucked in a sharp breath. "God, you're so like my father it isn't funny. The two of you could be twins."

A pulse began to beat in his cheekbone. "What are you talking about?"

Her heart squeezed tight. "You like things your own way, Damien. I won't marry you. I would end up a doormat who occasionally got taken out on special occasions. Just like my mother."

"No," he growled.

"You desire me, but once you get bored with me you'll move on to some other woman, and a marriage license won't stop you." She lifted her head high. "I want something better for myself than what my mother had with my father, and if I can't have a warm, loving marriage, then I don't want a poor imitation of one."

He went very still. "You don't know what I feel for you," he rasped.

"Exactly." She'd always known when he wanted her, but that hadn't been about his *feelings*. He'd kept his real feelings from showing.

"We'll talk later." He turned away and started the engine. "Let's get something to eat. It's way past lunchtime," he said, confirming what she'd just said about ignoring any feelings. "Then I need to go to my office for an hour or two."

She hadn't eaten a thing all day and she wasn't sure she could. Her appetite seemed to have disappeared. "I'd prefer to go talk to Keiran again."

His mouth tightened. "Best leave Keiran to think over things for the rest of the day. Otherwise we're going to antagonize him more, and right now that's probably not a good thing. I'll give James a call after we eat. He can keep an eye on things until tomorrow."

"Fine." She knew what he said made sense. But tomorrow, whether Keiran liked it or not…whether *Damien* liked it or not…she was going to take charge and damn the consequences.

Back at the apartment, while she made ham sandwiches for a late lunch, Damien got on the phone and arranged for a rental car for her use. Then they sat on the balcony and ate lunch.

"By the way," Damien said after a few minutes silence. "I have a dinner to attend tonight. I want you to come with me."

She placed her half-eaten sandwich back on her plate, a little hurt by his insensitivity. "Thanks but I'll pass. I don't feel like seeing people when my father's sick in hospital."

"It'll do you good to get out."

Her lips twisted in a grimace. "The last thing I feel like doing is attending some business dinner with a bunch of strangers."

"This isn't a business dinner. It's with friends."

She gave a choked laugh. "I didn't know you *had* any friends. Except *women* friends, of course."

He arched a brow. "You sound jealous."

"Only of their ability to put up with your delightful company," she said sweetly, ignoring the fact that he looked so handsome sitting there with the sun's shadow on his lean face.

He tilted his dark head, a slight smile on his lips. "Our marriage is going to be very interesting."

She stabbed him with a glare. "I am *not* marrying you, Damien."

The smile left his mouth. His gaze became shuttered. "Tonight's a good time to introduce you to them."

She felt as if she was going round and round in circles. "Damien, I—"

"Be ready by seven," he said, pushing his chair back and getting to his feet.

She looked up at him, suddenly tired of fighting him, knowing he wasn't about to give up. He'd probably even try to dress her himself if she wasn't ready. "Okay, fine. I'll go. But they're all probably a bunch of boring suits, anyway."

His eyes narrowed. "You might be surprised."

"About you? Never. I know the sort of man you are and the sort of friends you'll have."

A muscle began jumping in his cheek. "I'm glad you think you know me," he snapped, then strode back inside the apartment.

A few moments later she heard the front door close in a quiet, controlled manner. In a way she wished he'd slammed it instead.

A couple of hours later they drove up to a luxurious mansion along the waterfront at Cullen Bay. Gabrielle, dressed in a silky blue dress that had received an approving look from Damien, was proven right about his friends.

Yet wrong.

The house obviously belonged to moneyed people, but when she stepped inside the front door it was to find one other couple besides their hosts and a warm greeting that softened the hardness around her heart and made her feel very welcome. They were all very different from what she'd expected. And that added an insight into the man beside her that she would never have seen otherwise.

Danielle and Flynn Donovan owned the house, and

Kia and Brant Matthews were obviously close friends and frequent visitors. The women were gorgeous and friendly, the two men handsome and suave, but with a slight reserve that told Gabrielle they were the same breed as Damien. They didn't let down their guard easily.

Dinner was quite a lighthearted affair in a magnificent dining room that really showed off the house to perfection.

"This is such a lovely room," Gabrielle said to Danielle once they'd finished the first course and there was a lull in the conversation.

Danielle flushed, looking pleased. "Thank you. That's really nice of you to say so."

Something occurred to Gabrielle and her eyes widened. "I've just realized. *You* were the one who did Damien's apartment, weren't you?"

Danielle nodded with pleasure, though Gabrielle mentally acknowledged the mention of her knowing Damien's apartment had been noted by all of them.

"My wife is quite the decorator," Flynn said, sending his wife a loving look. It was a look that Gabrielle herself had hoped to receive one day from the man she loved.

At the thought, her gaze slid to Damien opposite her, and saw him watching her through half-closed lids. She wondered if Damien would ever be as relaxed as the men around their wives. He'd always seemed so alone.

Appearing nonchalant, she reached for her wineglass and took a sip, but her thoughts were far from casual. Damien had never sent her a loving look like the one Flynn had given his wife. Lustful yes, but not a warm look filled with respect.

Not that it mattered. She didn't plan on falling in love

again. Nor did she plan on marrying for a long time to come, despite what Damien said. For the moment she was just going to be one of those women whose dreams of being swept off her feet were just that—dreams.

"Gabrielle Kane?" the other woman, Kia, said with a slight frown on her beautiful forehead. "Your name seems familiar. Are you from Darwin?"

Gabrielle darted a look at Damien, but Kia's husband, Brant, pulled her gaze to him instead. "You're Russell Kane's daughter, aren't you?" he said, a curious gleam in his eyes that made her wonder what he knew about her. "You've been living interstate for the last couple of years."

She moistened her suddenly dry lips. "Yes, I have."

"Oh, that's right. Your father recently had a stroke," Kia said sympathetically. "I remember reading it in the newspapers now. I'm so sorry, Gabrielle. How is he?"

Gabrielle inclined her head in gratitude. "Thank you." Her voice broke a little, so she cleared her throat. "He's heavily sedated at the moment."

"But we're hoping he'll soon be on the mend," Damien added, his voice losing that steely edge, surprising Gabrielle, making her feel less alone in her fears.

"I'm so glad," Kia said with sincerity. She paused, her eyes a little surprised. "You know, Gabrielle. You're not like we expected."

Gabrielle grew a little wary, but wasn't sure why. "I'm not?"

Kia's lips curved into a smile. "You're much nicer." The other woman sent Damien an approving look. "I'm really glad Damien brought you here tonight."

Gabrielle let out a silent sigh of relief even as she refused to look at Damien. "So am I." And she meant it. She just wished it hadn't been because of Damien that she was here.

Then she realized the others were looking at her as if they knew there was more to her and Damien's relationship, but thankfully talk turned to general things while they worked their way through the rest of the meal.

Just as they were finishing dessert, the housekeeper, Louise, came into the room to tell both women that their babies were growing restless. Kia and Danielle instantly jumped up and so did their husbands, jokingly saying that they wanted to see their daughters, too.

Danielle went to leave the room, then stopped and frowned. She opened her mouth to speak but Damien cut her off, "Don't worry about us, Danielle. We'll be fine until you come back."

"Are you sure?"

Damien gave a slow smile. "What man in his right mind would complain about being left alone with such a beautiful woman?"

Danielle laughed. "Oh, you're such a smooth talker." She winked at Gabrielle. "Watch out for him, Gabrielle."

Gabrielle tried to smile but it felt forced. Her heart was thumping, and not just because she would be alone with Damien. She was so thankful the housekeeper hadn't brought either of those babies into the dining room. She wasn't sure she could bear it.

She waited until the others left the room, then put her

napkin on the table and stood. "I need some fresh air," she choked, hurrying toward the patio doors. They were closed to keep the room air-conditioned and she prayed they weren't locked. They weren't.

But as she stepped outside onto the well-lit terrace, the humidity that swamped her was as heavy as her heart. She stood there for a moment, letting it overwhelm her, welcoming the pain...the ache of loss.

"You don't like children?" Damien said from behind her, making her jump.

She schooled her features into a blank mask before slowly turning around. "What makes you say that?"

"Gut instinct. Most women usually fuss over babies and all that motherly stuff." His eyes pierced the distance between them. "You didn't."

She held his gaze. "Perhaps I have other things on my mind."

"Like what?"

"My father."

He inclined his head, conceding the point as he came toward her. "For your information, Kia's baby, Emma, is only a few weeks old. Danielle's little girl, Alexandra, is about nine months."

"I'm sure they're gorgeous," she said, her heart breaking even as she was surprised he knew the ages of his friends' children.

"They are."

She wanted to ask if he liked children. And if he ever planned on having another one day. Only, she couldn't say that. Not to the man who'd unknowingly fathered one child already. A child who had died.

She swallowed hard and tried not to let him see her anguish. "Your friends are really nice," she said, pushing aside her heartache.

"Not boring suits at all, eh?"

She winced. "No." She felt bad now for being so judgmental about them.

"Apology accepted."

Her eyes widened. "I didn't apologize."

"I know," he said with a slight smile as he came toward her.

She was suddenly too aware of how close he was. Quickly she turned away to look out over the lush landscape. "Um, this is a beautiful house. And this garden is just lovely."

Desperately she tried to concentrate on the beauty of the well-lit setting. A light breeze dipped palm fronds in the swimming pool, and flowers from the frangipani trees spread a blanket of white over a patch of lawn. Hibiscus provided splashes of red-orange color.

He put his hand on her arm and turned her back to him. Something deep kindled in his eyes. "Not as beautiful as you," he murmured, pulling her toward him.

Oh God. Five years ago she'd lacked the know-how to control her crazy feelings for him. Now she could feel the same craving for him gnawing beneath the surface.

"What do you want, Damien?" she said huskily, unable to stop herself from savoring the warm, male scent of him rising up in the pocket of air between them. At a subconscious level, it tantalized her senses and turned her legs to jelly.

His gaze dropped to her mouth. "You."

His head began to lower, and she unwillingly swayed toward him. Dear Lord. Suddenly five years was too long between kisses.

In the space of a heartbeat, he molded her mouth to the fullness of his own. Unable to ignore the taste of warm memories, she groaned and kissed him back, as a wonderful sensation quivered through her. Heat licked at her veins and she needed no further coaxing to let him venture into the hollows of her mouth while she clutched at his shoulders and let him intoxicate her.

Long moments later he broke off the kiss. She watched a pulse beat wildly in his throat, her mind staggered with incredulous wonder. She hadn't known it until now, but she'd missed this feeling of sharing and being one.

With him.

And then reality hit at the sound of the others coming back into the living room.

He stepped back and gestured for her to precede him through the patio doors. "After you," he murmured, the huskiness still lingering in his voice, affecting her, making her legs feel shaky as she hurried inside.

After that, the rest of the evening was nerve-racking for Gabrielle. Damien appeared to enjoy his friends' company, but whenever he looked at her, the desire in his eyes made her heart thud against her ribs.

Yet knowing she'd tapped a raw nerve back there on the patio gave her strength. She was glad their kiss had affected him as much as it had her. It made her feel not so needy. The downside was that it made her vulnerable. How could a woman *not* feel stirred knowing she'd touched a chord inside a man like Damien?

She breathed easier when he left the room to take a call on his cell phone, but his return sent a flutter of panic through her. There was an odd look in his eyes.

It was hard.

And determined.

She tried to ignore an uneasy feeling, but her heart jumped in her throat when not long after he suggested they leave. He didn't mention to the others she was staying with him. Not that it was anyone's business, and certainly Damien would never find the need to explain such a thing to anyone. Not even to his friends.

He didn't speak on the way home, either, but the tension increased within the confines of the car. Would he try to get her in bed? It certainly wouldn't worry him if he did, of that she was certain.

As soon as they stepped inside his apartment, the door to the spare bedroom appeared to be far too close for her liking. She darted a look at him beneath her lashes and saw a muscle ticking in his jaw. Her stomach tied itself in knots.

"Don't worry. I'm not going to seduce you," he mocked, striding over to the bar.

Her brows rose. "You're not?"

"Not yet anyway." He poured himself a small amount of scotch.

She moistened her lips, all at once certain there was something else going on here. "How…generous of you."

There was a moment's pause, then, "I've decided to wait until our marriage."

Frustration clawed through her. "Damien, will you please stop—"

"Tomorrow."

The air whooshed out of her lungs. "Wh-what?"

He took a swallow of his drink. "We're getting married tomorrow, Gabrielle, like it or not."

She gasped. "Look, I told you—"

"Keiran just lost a three-million-dollar contract."

Her head reeled back. "Say that again."

"That phone call I took was from James. Keiran lost a deal your father had been working on for the past year." He paused as he slammed the glass down on top of the bar. "Now. Don't you think it's time we got married?"

Five

The next afternoon Gabrielle married Damien in a simple ceremony held in his apartment, and Damien signed over eleven percent of Kane Property and Finance Group shares to her.

The only "family" Damien wanted to invite were his two best friends and their wives, and his attorney. No one else knew. Everything had to be kept secret so that Keiran wouldn't get wind of the marriage and do something underhanded to prevent it, if indeed there was anything he *could* do about it.

As for her parents, Damien suggested it was best not to tell them about the wedding until afterward. The excitement might not be good for her father, and her mother might let something slip to Keiran, especially since Damien had said later that Caroline had no idea about the shares.

Still, it had been hard for Gabrielle to visit her parents earlier that morning and act as if nothing momentous was about to happen. Thankfully, her father had been sleeping and her mother had asked Gabrielle to sit with him while she went home to shower and change. It had been a blessed relief not to have to put on a brave face. Nor was Gabrielle sure she wouldn't have begged her mother to stop her from doing a crazy thing like getting married two days after returning home.

And it *was* a crazy thing to do, she kept thinking when Kia and Danielle arrived carrying a gorgeous white sheath of a dress with a miniveil, and a posy of glorious miniature yellow roses. Suitably horrified at the speed Damien had arranged everything, they gave him a scolding about rushing the bride off her feet, yet they all knew why.

Thank goodness she didn't have to play the blushing bride in front of everyone, Gabrielle told herself while she was dressing, with Kia and Danielle sympathizing over her predicament in the background. Brant and Flynn's attitude was that Damien was doing the right thing, which made all three women smile wryly at each other in a moment of bonding.

Of course, once the ceremony was over and she stood next to the ladies beside a table covered with scrumptious food, she was on autopilot as she sipped at her champagne. The men had gone out on the balcony on the pretext of admiring the panoramic ocean view, but were deep in discussion instead.

"You know something, Gabrielle," Kia said. "Damien reminds me so much of Brant and Flynn. Handsome. Gorgeous. And wonderful husbands once you get past the wall of detachment that's inherent in men like them."

Sudden despair wrapped around Gabrielle's heart. She was sure Damien would be just like her father. And she would turn out just like her mother.

"Good heavens, your hands are shaking," Kia exclaimed in a sympathetic tone. She squeezed Gabrielle's arm. "Honey, we understand. Danielle and I felt the same way about our guys when we first met them."

Danielle nodded in agreement. "That's right. And one day we'll tell you all about it, but not now. It would take too long to explain why Flynn thought I was after his money," she said with rueful smile. "But I do want to say one thing—trust that it will work out for the two of you."

Gabrielle appreciated their kindness, but there was so much that they didn't realize. For one thing these women didn't know about her and Damien's past affair. Nor about her miscarriage—the one Damien didn't know about, either.

Just then she looked up and saw the three men coming back inside the apartment through the sliding glass doors. Damien looked magnificent in a dark suit and white shirt and was grinning at something one of the others had said. It was a striking smile that curled her toes and sent her heart thudding against her ribs.

And then he saw her staring at him and he paused briefly, before his mouth tilted in a sardonic grin. "I hope you ladies aren't plying my new bride with alcohol," he said, walking toward them.

Kia gave a light laugh. "Of course we are."

"I have something much better." He nodded at the waiter, who proceeded to hand out fresh glasses of champagne.

Despite his relaxed air, those piercing eyes studied her thoughtfully for a moment, giving nothing away. And then she saw a hint of satisfaction lurking at the back of them, and fear rippled through her. Fear, not of Damien himself, but of where all this was leading. He may not have planned to marry her when he'd brought her back from Sydney, but he certainly intended to profit from all this…in more ways than one.

He held up his glass. "A toast. To my new wife."

From somewhere deep inside her, she managed to raise her own glass and smile right back at him. "And here's to my old husband."

That evening, alone with Damien on his luxury yacht, Gabrielle ignored the man beside her and purposely focused her gaze on Darwin Harbor. In the remaining light, she watched as other boats sailed past them over the deep, calm water, the sound of laughter and clinking glasses sometimes drifting through the air, early evening being all about relaxing and having fun.

Not for them, of course. She didn't want to be here. It was under duress and Damien knew it. So she wasn't feeling particularly friendly toward him right now.

Okay, so he'd looked handsome and virile as he'd motored the vessel out himself, then dropped anchor, the cream polo shirt enhancing his well-built body as he'd moved, the black trousers molding perfectly to his long legs.

She'd always loved looking at his profile, and he looked even more attractive this evening with the water reflecting on his face. There was something very potent about the picture he made, and she felt a tremor inside knowing she was now married to him.

Her husband.

All at once he turned his head toward her. His moss-green eyes stared across the table and into her own with a burning intensity. "You were a beautiful bride."

She realized she was gripping her wineglass so tight she might break it. She forced her fingers to relax. "Thank you."

"You won my friends over well and truly," he added.

She grimaced. They both knew Brant and Flynn approved because they thought she was doing the right thing for the business. "I'm sure Kia and Danielle feel a certain…empathy for me."

His slight smile noted her comment. "The girls might be able to relate, but you can't discount the fact they are very happily married."

She met his gaze levelly. "They're in love, Damien. We're not."

He didn't miss a beat. "You're right. Here's to *not* being in love," he drawled, lifting his glass of white wine.

Five years ago she would have been devastated by his words, but she knew she was beyond that now.

She raised her glass and clinked it against his. "That's a toast I can relate to."

"And to us," he added.

She pulled the glass back. "There's no such thing as 'us,' Damien. There's you. And there's me. Two separate entities."

"Not after tonight."

The pit of her stomach began to churn. "I could scream, you know."

"So could I."

The comment was so unexpected that her lips twitched.

"Is that a smile I see?" he teased, sounding as if he was truly amused. It was a glimpse of how it could have been if only…

She remembered what their marriage was about. "No," she said, not looking at him, instead looking everywhere *but* at him. "I have nothing to smile about."

A moment passed by. "You're my wife now," he said with quiet emphasis. "Accept it."

She lifted her chin as she looked at him. "I guess I should be honored to be Mrs. Damien Trent?" she said sarcastically, even as she suppressed a tingle at her new name.

"Naturally."

She made a choking sound. "Your arrogance astounds me," she said, and caught a look of surprise on his face that in turn surprised *her*. He really had no idea his words had come across as arrogant. He really did believe she should be honored to marry him.

As if!

No way would she be grateful to a man who forced her into… She winced inwardly. He hadn't forced her into anything. Yes, he'd married her for his own purposes. And yes, he'd married her for her father's sake—but for an honorable reason.

She hadn't quite thought about it in this light before, but by marrying her today he was showing what kind of man he was—an honorable one. He must have had a good upbringing.

Suddenly she realized, Damien hadn't mentioned his parents today, not once. And she'd been too preoccupied and busy to ask the question.

Now she had the time. "Why didn't you invite your parents to the wedding, Damien?"

He tensed. "It would be a bit hard. They're dead," he said in a clipped tone that didn't ask for sympathy and would accept none.

A wave of compassion swept over her. And as strange as it seemed, she felt a little sad that she'd never get to meet the parents of this man. Five years ago they'd been on a round-the-world cruise, though she suspected he wouldn't have introduced her, anyway. About the only other thing she knew about him was that he didn't have any brothers or sisters, and even getting that out of him had been like asking for state secrets.

"What happened?" she asked sympathetically.

The line of his mouth flattened. "My father picked up some sort of bug during their cruise. It killed him before he could get proper medical attention."

Her eyes widened. "Oh my God. That's dreadful. Your poor mother. Did she—"

"She died two years ago."

She listened in dismay. "I'm so sorry, Damien."

"Thanks," he said, looking out to sea, making her

think he had hidden depths she was only now beginning to notice.

"So you're all alone in the world?" she said, trying to find what made this man tick.

He looked at her with eyes turned hooded and dark, a sure sign she'd touched a nerve. "If you want to think of it that way, yes." Then as if he'd had enough talking, he rose up from his chair like some god ready to sacrifice a virgin. If she'd had time she would have laughed at the thought, but her heart was jumping inside her chest as he came around the table toward her.

"Wh-what are you doing?"

He stopped in front of her, took the glass out of her hand, and pulled her to her feet, his hands circling her waist. "What do you think I'm doing?"

"No, Damien."

Something lazily seductive seeped into his eyes. "Yes, Gabrielle."

"Damien, I'm not ready—"

"I'm five years ready."

She blinked. "Are you saying…you've been celibate for five years?"

He snorted. "I'm a man, not a saint."

Of course. How silly of her. "Then what did—"

"Shhhhhh." He lowered his head and kissed her. She inhaled sharply and his tongue swept into her mouth, sweeping aside her objections like he did with everything else.

The sheer passion behind it…the possessiveness in it…took her breath away. She melted into him with a low moan, a part of her dismayed at how easily she weakened, another part gloriously alive, reveling in the feel of his lips against hers.

And with each passing moment those firm, manly lips hardened with increasing hunger, growing more urgent and demanding. She returned his kiss, her heartbeat throbbing in her ears, his scent hugging her lungs until all she knew was him.

He lifted his mouth and sent her a heated look, and a private message passed between them. He, too, remembered how it had been. A delicious shudder swept over her. She could almost taste the saltiness of his skin and feel the heat of his body as they lay entwined in bed together.

"It's time, Gabrielle."

"Time?" she asked breathlessly, delaying the inevitable, though she wasn't sure why now.

"For our bodies to do the talking."

Before she could say anything…or *do* anything except admit to herself she had a need for him…he put her hand in his and drew her along behind him, down the stairs to the cabin below.

She allowed him to lead her, all at once feeling this was meant to be. She could no more stop this from happening than stop the tide from turning. She didn't *want* to stop it now. Deep down she'd known that all along.

And then they were beside the bed and Damien stood looking at her, the lights from the deck filtering in through the windows, giving their world a pearly glow.

A sense of intimacy swirled around them as his fingers feathered up her arm, igniting little sparks where they touched her skin…up over the curve of her shoulder…along her collarbone…under her hair at her nape, admiring the blond strands cascading over his fingers.

"My blond beauty," he murmured, and brought her mouth to his once more, this time capturing it in a slow and sensuous possession.

She dissolved against him, loving the way his sinewy body embraced hers, his needing her as much as she needed him. And she was lost. As lost as any woman had a right to be when in the arms of a man she'd once loved.

Moments crept by before he eased away from mouth. "It's been a long time for us," he said, placing his lips against the column of her throat.

Ahh! She tingled at his touch, every pore in her body recognizing him, acknowledging him. It was five years since he'd made love to her like this. In her dreams it had sometimes seemed like yesterday. In her nightmares it had been forever.

"Say it, Gabrielle. Say you missed this, too."

She stretched her neck back allowing him access to the base of her throat. "Yes," she whispered. "I missed this."

His grunt of approval made her head spin as his hands slipped around to her back and slowly lowered the zip of her dress. The material fell to her waist and she stood in her lacy black bra, her nipples swelling in anticipation, her pulse rioting with need. She wanted to feel his mouth against her breasts.

"Mine," he said, his voice rough with need, arching her up for his indulgence, his eyes darkening as he took what was so willingly offered.

"Yes," she murmured, then gasped at the touch of his lips closing around a nipple.

He sucked hard, the lace emphasizing the abrasive action of his tongue, and she clutched at his shoulders as he moved to the other breast and repeated the rhythm, creating wonderful little bursts of ecstasy within the very core of her.

Then he undid her bra and it fell to the floor. Her breasts spilled into his hands and she moaned aloud with sheer pleasure when he began to fondle them. Oh my, did he know what he was doing to her?

Then those hands…those superb male hands…slipped over her rib cage, his firm fingers kneading her skin. Her dress began to slip downward, over her hips, her stomach…and all at once she was conscious of what he would find, and she stiffened, preparing herself for the moment he felt her scar. It didn't take long.

His fingers stopped on the flat skin of her stomach. "What the hell!" He put her away from him, twisting her toward the light shining in through the window to get a better look.

A flush seared her cheeks. "I'm sorry, I—"

"What happened?" he demanded, holding her hips firm, a muscle jerking in his cheek, an angry look exploding in his eyes. Angry and…pained.

She tried to pull away but he wouldn't let her. "A car accident. I know it looks horrible but—"

"No," he growled. "It doesn't." And he fell on one knee to place his lips against the two-inch jagged scar radiating downward from her belly button.

She shuddered helplessly. Of all the things she expected, it wasn't that he would touch her with such sensitivity. In a strange way it made her proud of him. Proud to be his woman, if only in a physical way.

"Thank you," she said softly.

"No need," he muttered, and placed his lips against her scar one more time. Then his hands left her hips and cupped her bottom, pulling her forward and pressing his face against the very intimate part of her.

Her heart stopped for a long moment as he held her like that, as if discovering her scent again and reveling in it. She grasped his shoulders before her legs buckled beneath her.

He took a deep breath and moved back to slowly peel her panties down her legs. Leaning on him, she stepped out of them, but he stayed where he was, just looking at her.

Suddenly she felt self-conscious. Damien had been her only lover. And it had been five years since he'd seen her naked body like this. She went to cover herself, but he made a sound low in his throat and pushed her hands away, then began kissing his way upward, his lips like silk along her thighs, over the blond curls hiding her femininity, skimming up over the sensitized skin of her breasts before anointing each nipple again, then moving up further and settling on her mouth.

His tongue danced with hers as he pulled her against him, his hardened body straining the material of his pants, sending a flash of heat through her. She was ready for him. More than ready.

"I want to feel you against me," he rasped, and stepped back, stripping the clothes from his body so fast he made her head spin. She wanted to say "take your time, let me look," but a more-eager part of her had a need low in her stomach at the sight of his obvious arousal.

He sank down on the bed behind him, drawing her close, positioning her so she stood between his legs. His mouth began to tease her nipples and she closed her eyes, welcoming his touch, winding her fingers through his hair, holding his head tight between her hands.

Just when she thought she could no longer stand, when a cry of pleasure was about to burst from her lips, he lay back on the bed and slowly stretched her out alongside him, so they were facing each other.

She moaned, and buried her face against his throat, savoring the touch of every inch of masculine skin lining hers. Dear heaven, she only had to guide him inside her and they would be one.

For several long seconds they lay there, as if he too, were soaking up the feel of skin against skin, the rocking of the boat giving a lulling sensation to their lovemaking.

Then he leaned up on his elbow and slowly began to trace a fingertip over the top of her breasts, his finger scorching everywhere he touched, down her cleavage pressed tight by the angle of her body.

"Look," he ordered thickly, his gaze descending between them. Her limbs quivered as she looked down to where their bodies touched. All the way down.

Man against woman.

"A perfect fit," he said, his eyes now locked on hers.

She swallowed tremulously. "Yes," she said, growing warm and welcoming, a wantonness forming in her lower limbs.

All at once he rose up over her toward the bedside table and took a condom out of the top drawer. "Here," he said, handing it to her, a pulse beating in his neck.

The breath stalled in her throat. "Oh but—"

"You want me to wear it, don't you?" he challenged in a raw mutter.

She moistened her lips. She couldn't think. Yes. No. "Um…yes."

"Then put it on me," he rasped with his usual arrogance, only she couldn't seem to respond in kind. Perhaps because she could see her effect on him. He couldn't hide how he was feeling right now; it was an empowering thought.

She tried to open the small foil package but her fingers shook and she dropped it. Giving her a look that said he was pleased she *wasn't* an expert in this, he took it and ripped it open with his teeth, then held it out to her.

But she didn't take it just yet. Swallowing hard, she looked down at him and felt a sizzle run through her. She had wanted to touch him before, and now she would.

She reached out and slid her hand around his erection, hearing a groan rise up from his throat, making the breath hitch in her throat. His skin felt warm under her palms. Warm and vital and so very Damien.

Without warning he muttered, "No more," then put his hand over hers and released her fingers from around him. In the blink of an eye, he rolled the condom on himself, moved her back against the bed, then nudged her thighs until she opened herself to him.

Only, he didn't enter her just then. He waited, looking

down at her with darkened eyes, the cords in his neck straining as he held his body above her…waiting…

"Come into me, Damien," she said, sliding her palm over his chest.

And that was enough. On a groan, he pushed himself into her wet warmth.

Slowly.

Exquisitely.

Filling her with a sense of completeness.

Even five years ago their lovemaking hadn't been as rich as this. It was much richer now in intensity, in depth, in experience.

And then he kissed her deeply as he moved erotically in and out. She loved the way he explored her inner womanhood with a thoroughness and pleasure that stamped her as his own, leaving no part of her untouched.

She moaned and inched toward the peak of desire. Unable to hold out against such an onslaught, she shut her eyes giddily. And she told herself to wait. That she wanted it to last forever. But her body wasn't about to stop from rejoicing in their mating.

She escalated higher and higher, with nothing to hold on to except this man within her. "Damien, please… Damien, I need you…Damien…"

"Gabi," he rasped, and she felt him pulsing into her, her own femininity cupping him tight in her climax, welcoming his sheathed essence.

A long moment later she was left with one thought and one thought only. The last time they'd made love he'd called her Gabi. And he'd been inside her back then, too.

* * *

The next morning Damien kept his eyes closed as he enjoyed the slight rocking of the boat and inhaled the scent of Gabrielle in the tropical air. It woke his body, arousing him with the pleasure of the night.

Many pleasures of the night.

He rolled on his side and reached for her, but his hand found a cool cotton sheet instead of a warm body. His eyes opened. She was probably in the bathroom. Or making coffee in the galley.

He listened for any sound of her. All was quiet. He sniffed the air and waited. Any minute now the aromatic smell of coffee would tantalize his nostrils. When nothing happened, he eased into a sitting position and looked around the cabin. Unless she'd jumped overboard, she'd still have to be on the yacht.

His heart started to thump. Or perhaps she'd taken the dingy. If she had, he'd kill her, he decided, throwing back the sheet, his gut knotting as he pulled on his trousers. He didn't bother about a shirt as he took the stairs two at a time.

When he found her on the top deck, it took a moment to steady his heartbeat. Then he strode toward her and hauled her into his arms.

"Damien, what the—"

He dropped a fierce kiss on her lips. It was supposed to be an angry kiss for being foolish enough to leave him. Only, after a moment or two, with her palms flattened on his bare chest, he found he was more hungry for her than angry, more searching than punishing. He wanted her to know how waking up this morning without her had felt. It had been the same feeling he'd experienced five years ago.

He broke off the kiss and muttered, "There's no escape."

She looked confused. "I wasn't trying to escape."

Okay, he'd panicked. He wouldn't do it again. "Tell me about the car accident."

Her face closed up and she stepped out of his arms and went to sit down on a seat. "Why? Am I imperfect now, Damien?"

"No." She was too damn perfect to look at. That was the problem. He winced inwardly. No, he didn't quite mean that. Gabrielle wasn't just about her looks.

She leaned back and stared up at him, gorgeous in white pants and a lime-green top. "What do you want to know?"

"How it happened. *When* did it happen. Everything."

Her lips, still slightly swollen from his kiss, curved in a wry smile. "You don't ask for much, do you?"

He didn't find it remotely funny. "I'm telling, not asking."

Her eyes clouded over. "Yes, that's more your style."

"Gabrielle, you're procrastinating." His eyes narrowed. "What are you hiding?"

She looked startled. "Nothing," she said, much too fast for his liking. She moistened her delicious mouth. "Er...it happened a few months after I went to Sydney. I was a passenger in a car with one of Eileen's daughters, Lara. This drunken idiot came out of nowhere and his car hit the front passenger side and some metal buckled and cut me."

"Sweet Jesus!" The thought of it made him taste bile.

All at once she was looking at him as if realizing his shock. "Damien, I'm fine," she said gently.

Her tone didn't soothe him. He felt savage. Like he wanted to commit murder. "What happened to this idiot? He'd better be in jail."

"I don't know. I was in hospital for a few days, then I was too busy getting back on my feet."

"If I'd known…" he growled, a burning sensation in his throat. "If Russell had known…"

An uneasy look entered her eyes. "Thankfully neither of you did." As quickly, she drew herself up, a certain coolness taking over. "And thankfully neither of you had a say in my life after that." She paused for effect. "I just wish you didn't have a say now."

The muscles at the back of his neck tensed. "You're married to me, Gabrielle. From here on in, whatever happens, I want to know about it."

Her eyes flashed with cynicism. "It didn't take long for you to start trying to control me."

He stared hard at her. She'd taken that the wrong way. He was concerned for her, not controlling. He wanted to make sure she'd didn't get hurt again. God, he hated thinking about her trapped in a car. About her lying in hospital.

His jaw clenched. But if she preferred to think the worst of his motives, then let her. He wasn't explaining himself to anyone.

He made a move toward the stairs. "Get your things together. We're going back to shore."

Six

When they arrived back at the apartment, Gabrielle half expected Damien to carry her off to bed, and firmly squashed a sense of disappointment when he strode straight over to the dining table and started sorting through his briefcase.

"You're working *now?*" she asked, then realized how that sounded. "I mean, aren't we going to see my parents?"

He glanced at his Rolex, his attitude telling her he was a busy man. "I've got a couple of calls to make, then we'll go break the news of our marriage to your mother. We'll leave it up to Caroline to decide whether to tell Russell yet or not."

Gabrielle swallowed, feeling guilty. In a way she didn't really feel she *should* feel too guilty about it. Not after everything her parents had put her through. Yet she did.

"And by the way," he added. "I've ordered a Porsche to replace the rental car."

Gabrielle groaned, feeling swallowed up by him. "You did?"

"And I've told your ex-boss, Eileen, we were getting married."

Her eyes widened in dismay. "You didn't!" Now *this* she did feel guilty over.

"I had to give her some reason why I was having your things sent up here."

She couldn't believe he'd done all this without asking her. "You really are a piece of work, aren't you?" she snapped, then spun toward the spare bedroom, intending to use the phone in there. "I'd better phone her on the other extension and explain." Eileen had been so good to her and would be disappointed not to have been invited to the wedding.

"Gabrielle?"

She stopped at the bedroom door. "What?"

"You're in the master bedroom now," he drawled, nodding his head at the other bedroom door. "With me."

A tremor of desire quaked through her body. "*Master bedroom?*" she scoffed. "Oh, goodie. I can sit at your feet and feed you grapes all day."

His expression relaxed into a smile, and it was devastating. "I can't see you being part of a harem."

"I'm amazed you appreciate that."

His eyes dropped to her breasts. "Oh, I appreciate you just fine, Gabrielle."

She moved slightly to cover her tingling nipples beneath her lime-green top. "Don't you have some calls to make?" she pointed out sourly, intending to shower and change out of her white slacks and into something more suitable for the office, just as soon as she spoke to Eileen.

His lips curled faintly upward. "They'll be brief."

"Well, *I* could be a while," she said, letting him know he'd caused problems and now she had to clean up his mess.

He ignored that. "I'll come get you when you're ready."

"So you have X-ray vision and can see through walls now?" she derided. "I think you've been eating too many carrots."

"No, grapes," he mocked, then strode out onto the balcony, already pressing the numbers on his cell phone, already forgetting her.

She didn't smile, though she secretly appreciated the smart comment. And she was still appreciating it after talking to Eileen, and then an hour later when they took her mother aside and told her the news. Gabrielle had already insisted that she wanted to be the one to tell her mother, though how on earth did she explain without telling her the true reason?

She didn't expect Caroline to burst into tears. "Mum, I'm sorry but it was a spur-of-the-moment thing."

Caroline dabbed at her eyes with a tissue. "But I'm your mother, Gabrielle. I would have liked to be at my only child's wedding."

Damien put his arm around Gabrielle's shoulders and pulled her close. "Caroline, we knew you'd be torn about leaving Russell's side, so we decided it was best we didn't tell you until it was over."

She still looked hurt. "But couldn't you both have waited until Russell was better?"

"I'm sorry, no," Damien said quietly but firmly. "I wanted Gabrielle to marry me and I couldn't wait a moment longer for her." He looked down at Gabrielle with a warm look in his eyes that totally shook her, then he squeezed her shoulder, urging her to back him up, making her realize it was all a front.

"Yes, that's right," Gabrielle confirmed. "We just couldn't wait. I'm sorry," she said, feeling really bad now. She knew her parents loved her. She didn't like causing them pain, despite how much they'd caused her.

Caroline sniffed. "You must love each other very much," she said, relenting.

"We do," Damien said without hesitation, and for a split second Gabrielle actually thought he meant it. Her heart gave a thud, then settled down to reality.

"Russell will be pleased," Caroline said. A frown marred her forehead. "But perhaps we shouldn't tell him until I speak to his doctor?"

"Good idea," Damien said. "And look, I know Russell's been too sick to have visitors, but don't let Keiran in to see him just yet. He might slip up and give it away about our marriage, and I'd hate to set Russell back because he received a shock."

She nodded even as she looked startled. "Keiran knows about your marriage?"

"Not yet. We're on our way to the office soon to tell him."

"Oh, good. He'll be so surprised. And delighted, too, no doubt. He's taken on a big responsibility trying to fill

Russell's shoes, always phoning me and checking to see how your father is doing. He's been such a comfort." She smiled warmly. "As you both have."

"Don't worry, Caroline," Damien said. "We intend to help him as much as we can."

Her mother's brow rose. "We?"

Gabrielle knew she had to tell her mother their plans. "Mum, Damien's going to help me run the company until Dad gets better."

Her mother's face lit up. "Really?"

"Yes." Deliberately she didn't mention Keiran. If her mother asked, she would say he intended to help out in another capacity at the office.

"That's wonderful, darling. I'm so proud of you." She glanced at Damien. "Russell always thought of you as a son, Damien. I'm sure he'll be thrilled about this."

Damien cleared his throat. "He's been like a father to me, too, Caroline," he said, sounding gruff.

Caroline gave a light laugh. "Good heavens, I now have a son-in-law. Who would've believed it?" She winked at Gabrielle. "And maybe one day I'll be a grandma?" she teased, a sudden speculative light in her eyes.

Gabrielle stiffened, but she was sure only Damien felt it. "Not yet, Mum. I have too much to do to help Dad first."

Caroline looked only slightly disappointed. "That's okay, darling. But I look forward to the day when you're ready to give me a little grandbaby."

Gabrielle swallowed hard. She wasn't sure that day would ever come again.

As if Damien knew she was uneasy, he changed the subject. "How about when Russell's better we have another ceremony? A big event with lots of family and friends. What do you think, Caroline? Would you and Russell like that?"

Caroline's eyes lit up. "Oh yes, that would be wonderful." Then the light in her eyes dimmed. "Of course, I'm not sure where I'll be once Russell gets better…"

Gabrielle's heart thudded to a halt. "Mum?"

Caroline patted her hand. "Darling, I came back because I love your father and he's sick, but I don't know whether he still loves me."

Gabrielle was horrified. She'd thought her parents were back together. "Mum, of course he does."

Caroline frowned. "To be honest, I'm not sure." Then her mother fluttered a dismissive hand. "But this is about you and Damien, not me and Russell. And I promise that no matter where I am I'll come back for another ceremony."

Gabrielle was having trouble trying to come to terms with her mother's admission that she hadn't resumed her marriage, so she was thankful when Damien stepped in and suggested they leave.

"Don't let the comment about grandchildren worry you," he said on the way out of the hospital. "Your mother's just doing some wishful thinking. It's only natural."

Somehow she found the strength to pretend she didn't care that her parents should have already been grandparents. If only…

No!

Instead, she shot Damien a glare. "Did you know they weren't actually back together?"

"Yes," he said, opening the car door for her.

"What! You told me—"

"That your mother had come home because of your father's stroke. She did."

"But—"

"Let them work it out themselves. We have other things to worry about right now." He took her elbow and guided her onto the passenger seat. "Keiran being one of them. He's bound to be difficult."

The thought of facing Keiran kept her quiet as Damien closed the door and came around the other side of the BMW. A short while later they entered her father's office to find her cousin again behind the desk, looking so self-satisfied she wanted to wipe that look right off his face. Thank goodness she'd dressed in a short black skirt and cream silk blouse that looked very businesslike.

"Keiran," she said, walking over to the chair in front of the desk and taking a seat as Damien went to stand by the window. "Do you realize you lost the company a three-million-dollar contract?"

Keiran suddenly looked wary. "They wanted more than we could give. We don't have the resources for what they wanted."

"No," she snapped. "My father would have bent over backward to find a way to keep that contract."

Keiran glared at her defiantly. "I did all I could."

"I'm sure you did. But this company isn't only about you and what *you* can and can't do, Keiran. It's about being a business. About keeping people in jobs."

Keiran stiffened. "Don't come in here and start

preaching to me on how to run things, Gabrielle. I'm in charge now and there's nothing you can do about it."

"Correction. You *were* in charge."

He rolled his eyes. "Don't start that again. You and Damien are—"

"Married."

He flinched, then quickly recovered. "So?"

She leaned forward and slapped a copy of the marriage certificate and the document transferring the shares on the desk. "We're married. We were married yesterday. And Damien's given me eleven percent of his shares as a wedding present," she said, enjoying dropping that bombshell. She made a point of standing up. "So thank you for holding the fort, but I'll take over now."

"Like hell you will," Keiran snapped, his face turning an ugly red.

"Gabrielle has every right to be here," Damien pointed out curtly.

The other man swore. "You won't get me out that easily."

Damien's brow rose. "Really?"

Keiran jumped to his feet. "Oh, you both think you're clever, don't you?" He snatched the copied certificates and shoved them in his jacket pocket as he strode around the desk. "I'm going to see my lawyer."

"Feel free," Damien said in a cool tone. "And Keiran?"

Keiran stopped on his way to the door. "What?" he snarled.

"Make sure you go back to your own office next time."

The door slammed shut behind him.

Gabrielle's heart tried to settle. "That went well," she half joked.

"Better than expected," Damien returned with a small smile that made her heart beat faster despite the tenseness of the situation with Keiran.

Ignoring the effect he had on her, she got to her feet and walked around the large desk. For a moment she stood, looking over the spacious office, suddenly feeling overwhelmed.

She was in charge.
She had business decisions to make.
Employees to look after.

"Oh God. What was I thinking, Damien? Keiran was right. I don't know how to run a business, let alone a big company like—"

"But *I* do. And I'll help you all the way," he reminded her.

She nodded and sat in her father's chair. She should have felt intimidated even further, but all at once just sitting where her father had sat every day for years, knowing he was in hospital and needed her help, gave her strength.

She took a deep breath. "Thanks. Now where do we start?"

A hint of admiration entered his eyes, warming her. "First order of the day, I need to go see a few people and try to win back that lost contract."

She frowned. "Do you think you can?"

He gave her a wry look. "Do you doubt it?"

She had to smile. "No."

He gave a slight smile in return, and something sizzled in the air between them.

Then he stepped toward the door. "I'd better go see these people and repair the damage."

She watched him walk away, the huskiness in his voice making her pulse race through her veins.

Then all at once he stopped to look back at her. "Don't forget that we need to act like a loving couple, otherwise it could undermine confidence in the company."

His words put everything back into perspective. Her lips twisted. "I'm not likely to forget it," she said with a touch of sarcasm, and received a sharp look in reply. He had no idea how much he sounded like her father.

It was seven-thirty before Damien walked into his apartment that evening, his body impatient as he waited to see Gabrielle again. They'd had a productive day, first with a promise from their previous clients to revisit the contract, and next with the meeting of department heads, who'd shown them total support. Then he'd dropped Gabrielle off here before going back to his own office to tidy up a few loose ends.

And now soft music greeted him. He dropped his briefcase on the sofa just as he heard a noise from the kitchen. He strode toward the sound, the blood beginning to pound through his veins. He and Gabrielle had acted like a newly married couple today at the office, though neither of them had gone overboard. Just a slight touch of their hands. A soft look at each other. A smiling agreement to a work decision.

Tonight he wanted more of her attention.

She was a sight for sore eyes, he mused, as he stood in the doorway watching her sprinkle chocolate pieces over some sort of dessert topped with cream. She was concentrating so hard, the tip of her tongue appeared, as if in temptation. A tip that had ran itself around his mouth last night while making love.

He groaned to himself as his gaze slid over her. She'd changed into a long, summery, floral dress that flared around her slim calves. Below it she was barefoot, her sandals having been kicked to the side as if she'd flung them off in a moment of passion.

"Damien!" Gabrielle said, as she'd turned and saw him in the doorway. "I didn't see you there."

"I know," he muttered, having trouble dragging his eyes away from those pink toenails and slender arches.

She seemed to realize he was mesmerized by her bare feet. A blush stole into her cheeks and she quickly stopped what she was doing and went to step into her shoes. "My feet were hot and the floor was cool and—"

"Leave them off."

She blinked. "Wh-what?"

"I like seeing you barefoot."

For the space of a heartbeat he thought she was going to comply. Then she continued putting her sandals on. "No, that's okay. My feet are cold now anyway."

"Then you must be the only person in Darwin with cold feet," he teased.

She ignored that. "It's the air-conditioning. I turned it up," she said, hurrying to the refrigerator with the bowl of dessert, looking delightfully flustered.

Then he watched her go over to the wall oven and turn on the inside light to check the casserole. His brows drew together. "I don't expect you to come home from the office and make dinner, you know. That's why I have a housekeeper."

"I know, but I can put a casserole in the oven. And it didn't take much to whip up dessert." She gave a tiny pause. "As a thank-you for all you did today."

Something inside his chest tilted and suddenly he wanted to kiss her. "You made dessert for me?"

"Yes." She spun away and went to the sink, but her voice held a husky tone. "Perhaps you'd better go shower?"

He loosened his tie. "Want to join me?"

She looked over her shoulder at him. "And ruin dinner?" she said dryly, but her cheeks turned rosy.

"We wouldn't want that," he mocked, deciding he would make her pay for that remark later. He turned and walked away.

In the bedroom, a strange comfort swelled inside his chest when he saw that she'd hung her clothes in the walk-in wardrobe next to his. Then he entered the bathroom and saw her makeup and hairbrush on the counter. It was such a feminine sight that he smiled to himself as he showered. It was an odd feeling sharing his private space with a woman.

Permanently.

Fifteen minutes later they sat at the dining table. "Did you phone the hospital?" he asked as he spooned beef casserole onto his plate.

She swallowed her mouthful of food then nodded. "Dad was asleep, but they're pleased with his progress. Mum said that if she hires a nurse, they might let him go home next week"

"Good." He placed the spoon back in the dish and reached for the scalloped potatoes. "Tell me. Did you ever finish your degree?"

Her fork suspended in midair, wariness filled her eyes. "Er...no."

"So you've given up your dream?"

Her expression clouded. "What dream?"

"I remember how you wanted to become a dietician. You said you wanted to help children learn to eat healthily so they'd grow to be healthy adults."

She shrugged. "Maybe one day I'll return to it."

He frowned with the feeling that she wasn't being as offhand as she pretended, but left it at that. He hated to see anyone give up on their dreams but now was not the time to sort this out. They had too many other things to settle first.

After that, they ate without talking. The casserole was delicious, and so was the chocolate mousse topped with whipped cream she'd made for dessert.

"Leave it," he said when she went to tidy up.

She grimaced. "I can't leave all these dirty dishes for your housekeeper."

One eyebrow slanted. "That's why I employ her. If you do her job, she won't have one." He must remember to tell Lila about his new change in circumstances, though she'd probably guessed something was going on, with Gabrielle's things in his bedroom, he mused.

Gabrielle's lips quirked. "That's true. But let me just put the leftovers away and the dirty dishes in the dishwasher. We can't leave this sitting here all night."

"Fine. I'll help you." He reached for the empty dishes.

She blinked in surprise. "You will?"

"Of course. I don't usually leave a mess, either."

She relaxed into a smile. "So you're domesticated?" she joked as she started carrying some of the plates back to the kitchen.

He looked at those lips and wanted to kiss the smile right off them. "Sometimes," he drawled, following her. Then he helped her tidy up, but as soon as they'd finished, he strode over to the entertainment unit in the living room. "Come watch a movie with me."

"Um...sure." She followed him more slowly. "Any movie in particular?"

"You choose." He opened the door of a cabinet to reveal racks of DVDs.

Her eyes widened. "That's quite a collection."

"My housekeeper buys a selection for me every couple of months." He took a seat on the black leather sofa.

Her finely arched brows drew together. "I wouldn't have taken you for a man who watched movies."

He shrugged. "I have to unwind sometimes."

For a few seconds she was silent as if weighing his words, though he wasn't sure he liked her deciphering him. She'd probably get some idiotic idea that sometimes he felt a sense of aloneness inside this apartment. That sometimes at the end of the day he would like to share a peaceful moment or two with a woman who understood him. He grimaced inwardly. Of course, Gabrielle understood him a bit too much at times for his liking.

She walked over to the collection and began rifling through the DVDs. "What about this one?" she said, holding up a fairly tame thriller that had been a huge success a couple of years ago.

"As long as it doesn't give you ideas," he joked, and saw her mouth twitch with amusement before she popped the DVD in and went to sit on the chair opposite.

He patted the space beside him. "Sit next to me."

She hesitated. Then, "Is that an order?"

He gave a wry smile. She was a challenge, this one. Every step of the way. "No, a request."

She inclined her head and did as he asked, but still sat a foot away from where he wanted her to be. "Closer," he murmured.

"I'm fine right here."

He leaned over and half lifted her next to him. "Closer," he insisted. "And *that's* an order."

"Damien, I—"

"Shh. The movie's starting."

She remained tense for another ten seconds or so, then he could feel her begin to relax slightly, which was just as well because if she didn't stop arguing he would have to kiss her into submission.

As it was, he would wait to make love to her until after the movie. Oh, he knew he could have her right now, just as he'd done last night on the yacht. Her body was emitting a million little signals that told him she wanted him again.

But like the most delicate tidbit, he would savor her. Call him a masochist, but for five years the memory of this woman had left a burning imprint inside him. Now, to have the very scent of her filling his nostrils, the curve of her bare shoulder beneath his palm, the warmth of her body next to him, was driving him mad again with appreciation and anticipation.

For this woman, he would linger.

Halfway through the movie she kicked off her shoes...and the lingering was over.

"You know," he murmured, his eyes resting on those beautiful toes. "I find your feet very sexy."

Her head snapped away from watching the television. Red rushed into her cheeks. "Um...they're only feet."

"Not to me. Here. Put them up here on my lap. Let me look at them."

A humorous gleam showed in her eyes. "You don't have a foot fetish, do you?"

His mouth tilted in a sardonic grin. "No." Her feet were just a starting point, gorgeous though they were. He would make love to every inch of her.

Starting with those feet.

"Lean back," he said, lifting them onto his lap, forcing her into reclining back against the cushions. He began to slowly trace the pads of his fingers over her delicate toes. "These are very feminine."

She expelled a surprisingly sultry laugh that rippled along his spine. "I would hope so."

He held up one slender foot. "See this arch? It tells me you're a sensual person."

She moistened her lips. "Um...it does?"

"Now if I were to kiss the top of your foot—" he did as he said "—like this."

"Damien..."

Her breathlessness turned him on, not to mention

her dress had crept back along a length of slender thigh. "You don't like that?"

"Yes," she whispered. "I do."

He kissed her ankle. "Too much?"

There was a tiny pause. "Perhaps."

"Not enough?"

All at once she tried to sit up. "The movie. We're supposed to be—"

He grabbed the remote and flicked it off, bathing them in muted light from the dining area across the room. "I'd rather watch *you*," he said, sliding to his knees on the plush carpet and helping her to stretch out before him on the sofa, just like that delectable meal she had prepared for him. "Lie there and enjoy it, Gabrielle."

She licked her lower lip. "What are you going to do?"

"Make love to you with my mouth," he said thickly, watching as her blue eyes caught instant fire. "Would you like that?"

"Er, maybe," she whispered, making him smile at her slight rebellion. Even now, with her body crying out for his touch, she was determined to hold something of herself back.

And he would make sure she gave in.

Totally.

He took possession of those luscious lips, and a few heartbeats later he heard her sigh of sweet surrender that told him she'd only been fighting herself, not him.

And then he explored the smooth, velvet warmth inside her mouth that drew his tongue back time and time again over her moistness, marking her as his own, sending a vibration of arousal through him that made him suddenly wonder who was the one being possessed here.

He broke off the kiss and inhaled a deep shuddering breath. He wanted to consume her, to let his tongue glide her to a climax, over the hills and valleys of her body…the peaked nipples, her flat stomach, the slight rise to her femininity. He only had to lift her in his arms, and he'd be able to place his lips anywhere he liked.

But first, he did what he promised to do and went back to her feet and lingered there, touching and stroking. Then he worked his way up one leg, inching up her dress, placing a kiss on the lacy blue triangle of material at the apex of her thighs before starting down the other leg.

Her floral dress had tiny buttons along the front of it, and he enjoyed undoing them and exposing her smooth skin by degrees. Until he got to the scar on the smooth skin of her stomach, and full-blown pain went right through him. He couldn't stand to think of her hurt like this, her soft skin having been ripped apart by the metal of a machine driven by some nitwit who deserved to be ripped apart himself.

With my bare hands.

"Damien?" she said softly, but there was understanding in her tone.

Her voice pulled him back from the brink and he made a sound wrenched from deep inside and forced himself to move on. Otherwise she might think he was hesitating out of distaste. And he wasn't. Nothing could be further from the truth.

"It's okay," he said in a brusque voice, then placed

his lips against the scar, hearing her gasp as he kissed the puckered skin.

And then he continued up her silken belly to her round, firm breasts that fit seamlessly in his hands. His heartbeat throbbed in his ears as he took first one swollen caramel nipple into his mouth, then the other, and sucked until she arched her back, raising her desire and in turn thickening the blood in his own veins.

"Damien," she moaned, his name slipping through her lips, her hands gripping his shoulders, her fingers kneading him.

He lifted his head and looked down at Gabrielle's glowing face. She was absolutely beautiful. Absolutely desirable. He knew it was time to taste the rest of her.

Inch by inch he moved back along the way he'd come, retracing his kisses, trailing his lips along to find the exotic scent of her that laced his blood with heat and something so primitive it belonged to just the two of them. Never had he wanted another woman as he wanted Gabrielle. Never would he take from another woman what he knew Gabrielle could give him...had always given him.

Herself.

He stripped the blue panties from her and lowered his mouth, loving the soft cry she gave as he began melting her with strokes of his tongue, eliciting a long moan from her. Small tremors started to ripple through her body, then strengthen. He kept on loving her, could feel her coming, shuddering beneath his mouth, her muscles tensing until she cried out with sheer release. He lapped her up in a flood of pleasure, urging her to even greater heights, to an even greater glory.

She held there.

Held longer than he expected.

He could wait no longer to be inside her. He needed to feel her muscles tightening around him. He needed to make her climax again but this time with him inside her.

He took a condom out of his pocket, ripped off his clothes and joined her on the sofa, entering her with one thrust, groaning into her mouth with the sheer enjoyment of having her slick flesh surround him.

And then a flame licked along his skin and he began to move, felt the tight clenching of her body that intensified with each plunge inside her. She pervaded his senses, clouded his mind and suddenly the world shimmied and he lost the ability to think. His body lost control.

And he lost his mind.

Seven

Gabrielle opened her eyes the next morning and found Damien asleep next to her in bed. He lay on his stomach with his face half turned into the pillow. It made him look so sexy, so rawly masculine.

He murmured something and she stilled. She didn't want to wake him. Not yet. Not when she could study him so freely. Not when she could take pleasure in every detail, noting the way his firm lips were relaxed, seeing the way his chin, too, seemed less arrogant.

Or maybe that was because he needed a shave, she mused as her gaze slowly lowered over the wide shoulders and trim waist, down to where the sheet hugged his hips and flanks, the urge to run her fingers along his spine so very tempting.

He made a sound that for anyone else would be a soft

snore, but not for Damien Trent, and she bit her lip to stop herself from laughing. If only she could tease him about this. But he was not the sort of man you could tease and get away with it.

But did she want to get away with it?

Perhaps not.

At the thought her pleasure faded. A feeling suddenly consolidated in her chest, everything becoming crystal-clear. Damien touched the deepest part of her and it frightened her, causing a wave of panic to riot through her veins. She turned away and buried her face against her pillow, wanting to hide from herself but unable to do so.

Dear God, she had fallen in love with the man who'd stolen her heart five years ago.

She had fallen in love with Damien Trent.

For the second time.

Just then the man she now knew she loved...the man beside her...started to move and wake up. She was tempted to jump up and run from the room, but she'd only be drawing attention to herself. If he came after her and started making love to her again, how would she react now she knew she loved him again? How would she manage to keep everything inside her until she had time to think this all over? Because suddenly the goal-posts had changed. And how that would affect her she wasn't sure.

So she lay there with her back to him and kept her eyes shut, pretending to be asleep, feeling him go up on one elbow and kiss her bare shoulder. She held back a moan, unable to turn toward him and end up in his arms again. She just prayed her didn't draw her over to face him.

And then the mattress dipped slightly as he rolled out of bed, and she expelled a silent sigh of relief. She heard him walk into the bathroom and the shower came on and a few moments later she could hear the sound of water hitting naked flesh. She could almost see the water spraying off his wide shoulders, over his chest, down the arrow of hair. She shut her mind off. She had to or she might just be tempted to join him, and right now she dare not.

Instead of getting up for her own shower, she forced herself to stay in a sort of mental limbo until he'd finished dressing. Then, just when she thought he was about to leave the room and go get some breakfast, his lips touched hers in a brief kiss.

Her lashes flew open in alarm, but all he said was, "Sleep in. Come to the office when you're ready." He started for the door.

It took her a few seconds to register what he'd said. "What?" She sat up. "Where are you going?"

He stopped at the door and turned. "To the office."

"Yours or—"

"Ours?" he joked.

She threw back the covers. "I'm not playing at this, Damien. I don't want to be just a figurehead and leave you to do all the work."

He looked surprised. "I don't think that, but it wouldn't hurt you to have a lie-in."

She got out of bed. "I'm used to getting up early and going to work," she reminded him, in case he'd forgotten she'd been a working woman down in Sydney.

His gaze slid over her short, silky cream nightgown

and his eyes darkened, but he made no move toward her. "Okay, if you're determined, then. I have an important meeting this morning so I have to go to my office first. I'll meet you at Kane's about eleven-thirty."

"Fine," she said, already heading for the shower.

An hour later Gabrielle asked her father's personal assistant, Cheryl, to organize a meeting in the boardroom for eleven-thirty. She and Damien still had things to discuss from yesterday with the managers.

"It doesn't take you long to start throwing your weight around," Keiran sneered as he came into the office just as she was gathering her papers for the meeting.

Gabrielle hid her surprise. This was the first she'd seen Keiran since he'd stormed out yesterday, but he was obviously back to cause trouble and that made her uneasy. Keiran always picked his target. He must have known that Damien wasn't with her.

"Keiran, don't you have work to do? In your *own* office?"

His mouth twisted. "Cheryl tells me you're having another meeting with the middle managers. It isn't going to help the company, you know. They would be more productive just getting on with their jobs."

"Perhaps you should take your own advice," she said coolly.

He sent her a withering glance. "You know, coz, I can't wait to see you fall flat on your face."

"Then you'll be waiting a long time."

"You think so?"

"I know so."

Just then Cheryl buzzed her on the intercom. Giving

Keiran a hard look, Gabrielle pressed the button and listened as the other woman said that Damien was now in the boardroom with the others.

"I'll be right there, Cheryl." Gabrielle stood. "You're welcome to come to the meeting," she told him as she came around the desk and walked toward the open doorway.

"How generous of you."

She'd had just about enough of him. Her mouth tightened as she went to step past him, but suddenly she somehow missed her step because she felt herself trip on the carpet then fall forward, giving a little squeal. Thankfully the door frame stopped her fall but it still shook her.

It was a couple of seconds before Keiran spoke, and then only after Cheryl came rushing over. "Are you okay?" the PA asked with concern.

"She tripped on the carpet," Keiran was quick to say, but Gabrielle was sure his voice held fake concern.

"I'm fine," Gabrielle said, looking down at the plush carpet, but there were no rips or snags. Then she darted a look at Keiran. For some reason he had enjoyed her being hurt. And that was typical Keiran. He was the type to pull the wings off butterflies.

Keiran's smile was sickly. "You always were one to trip over nothing," he said, but that just wasn't true. She'd never been especially clumsy, so she wasn't sure why he was using that excuse now.

Unless…

She frowned. He wouldn't have tried to hurt her, would he? He was certainly capable of it but could he really be that nasty?

No. She'd tripped by herself that's all. It was just one of those things.

"As long as you're okay." Cheryl said with a frown.

Gabrielle tried to smile warmly. "Thanks for your concern, Cheryl. I'm fine."

The other woman nodded as Keiran bent and picked up the papers Gabrielle had dropped. "Here we go," he said, handing them back to her. "We'll be late for the meeting if we don't hurry."

Gabrielle's brow rose in surprise as she took them. "You're coming?"

He smiled tightly. "Wild horses couldn't keep me away."

Gabrielle turned to head out the door. She'd been very much afraid that was the case.

Later that afternoon the phone rang in the office. Gabrielle had just spent the past hour with Damien poring over some of the paperwork Keiran had worked on, and she was now glad to put it aside for a while. Working so close to Damien was playing havoc on her senses. He smelled gorgeous, and he looked gorgeous, and she kept remembering how he'd seduced her on the sofa last night.

Thankfully they'd had a couple of other interruptions, so at least she was getting Damien in small doses, she mused as she picked up the phone. Damien in large doses was definitely an overdose.

It was her mother, telling her that Keiran had dropped by to see Russell but that she hadn't let him into the room. "Darling, we don't want him to let it slip about your marriage before I've had a chance to tell your father, so I told him to come back tomorrow," Caroline said, making Gabrielle want to kiss her. "But the doctor's just said I can tell Russell when he wakes up, and I know your father will want to see you and Damien once I tell him."

"Should we come to the hospital now, then?" Gabrielle said, seeing Damien's gaze sharpen.

"Yes, Russell's due to wake soon."

Gabrielle said goodbye, then hung up the phone and told Damien what had happened. She scowled. "Do you think Keiran's going to cause trouble?"

Damien's jaw clenched. "What else?"

She thought of something. "I'm surprised he didn't try and tell my mother we'd only married for the sake of the company."

"How do you know he didn't?"

"I'm sure if he'd said something she'd be upset. No, he's kept quiet about it, and that worries me. He's up to something," she muttered.

"It doesn't matter. He can't do anything about it anyway," he said with confidence. "Come on. Let's go. I want to make sure Russell is okay about everything."

Gabrielle hesitated briefly, and only because she was trying to come to terms with something. Damien was genuinely concerned for her parents, and it had nothing to do with money. How hadn't she seen such kindness in him before? Why was she only seeing it now when she was in love with him?

A warm glow stayed with her until she walked into the room at the hospital, and even then her father's joy did her heart good. Russell was actually sitting against the pillows, still weak but growing stronger.

After she kissed him on the cheek, he wagged a finger at Damien beside her, his face smiling like he'd won the lottery. "I always knew you had a thing for my daughter," he said, making Gabrielle start.

Damien grinned ruefully. "I didn't think I'd fooled you back then, Russell. Of course, as soon as I saw her again I knew I couldn't let her get away another time." He kissed her tenderly on the mouth. "Isn't that right, sweetheart?"

For a moment Gabrielle stood looking up at him, trying to find her voice. Oh, how she wished this moment were true.

Her mother made a soft sound from the other side of the bed. "Look at the two of them, Russell. Anyone can see they're in love."

Gabrielle drew her gaze away from Damien, realizing she must look like a lovesick fool. It hadn't been intentional.

"Yes, Caroline, you're right," her father agreed, but Gabrielle noticed he was looking at her mother with an odd longing in his eyes, only her mother didn't appear to notice because she was smiling at Damien. Quickly Gabrielle glanced up at Damien and knew he hadn't missed that look in her father's eyes, either.

Her father reached out for Gabrielle's hand, his eyes filling with deep regret. "Gabrielle, we never meant to hurt you," he said gruffly.

Perhaps loving Damien made her soft…or wiser… but suddenly she realized she was more than ready to forgive this man. "I know that now, Dad." Feeling emotive, she leaned forward and buried her face in his neck, choked up by what this meant. She hated that her father almost had to die before they could all come to their senses. Hated it, yet was oh so grateful for it.

All at once she heard her mother say, "We love you, honey. We're so sorry about what happened."

Gabrielle blinked rapidly to hold back silly tears filled with joy. She loved these two people. She wouldn't cut these ties. She wouldn't even try. Not ever again.

"It's okay. Really," she said, pulling back and putting her hand in her father's. And when her mother reached across the bed, Gabrielle put her hand in her mother's too. They stayed like that for a moment.

Suddenly the door opened and in walked one of the nurses. "What's this?" she teased. "A prayer meeting?"

Gabrielle looked at her parents and smiled as they let go of each other, but she noticed the soft look her father surreptitiously gave her mother. "Sort of," she muttered.

"Nothing wrong with that," the nurse said, walking over to the bed and checking her father's chart as Damien put his arm around Gabrielle's shoulder and pulled her close to him. She leaned into him for once, feeling weak with the emotion of the moment.

The nurse didn't stay long and when the door closed behind her, Caroline smiled at Gabrielle. "I'll have to take you to see your old room, darling. We've left everything as it was."

"I've already seen it, Mum." She stepped forward and kissed her mother's cheek. "Thank you," she murmured, then kissed her father's cheek, too.

Caroline looked as pleased as Russell. "Well, now

you're a married woman with a home of your own," her mother said. "You might want to come and take some of your old things as keepsakes."

Gabrielle arched a brow. "You don't mind?"

"Darling, they're *your* things." Caroline smiled briefly at her husband. "Besides, we already have our daughter. We don't need things to remind us of you."

"Oh, Mum," Gabrielle said, touched beyond measure as she blinked back tears, which then started her mother getting teary-eyed and had her father sniffing slightly, making Damien give a quiet chuckle.

Half an hour later Gabrielle walked into the apartment and dropped her handbag on the sofa. She went to turn toward the kitchen to get a drink of water, but Damien had entered the apartment and was standing behind her. His hands slid around her hips and pulled her up against him.

"What are you doing?" she said, feeling his instant arousal against her. She gave a delicious shudder.

"Reaping the benefits of marriage," he murmured, turning her around to face him. His eyes had a strange seriousness in them that captured her attention.

She moistened her lips. "We didn't have to get married for that."

"I know, but we may as well enjoy it." He started running his lips along her chin.

"But dinner—"

"Can wait," he said, and closed over her mouth with a kiss. A long drugging kiss that sparked an ache inside her and soon had her aflame for him, making everything so much more poignant for her now she knew she loved him. Poignant and incredibly beautiful.

They made love.

Afterward Damien held Gabrielle in his arms. Their lovemaking had been richly satisfying, but he couldn't seem to shake a slight melancholy that seemed to be sitting inside his chest. He didn't lack for anything in his life, yet somehow it felt as though he did. He had the most beautiful woman in the world in his arms, yet absurdly he wanted more from her. Hell, what was the matter with him?

Just then Gabrielle arched her neck to gaze up at him from the crook of his arm. "Did you see the look my father gave my mother? I'm sure he still loves her."

Her words surprised him. Usually she didn't talk after making love. She either fell asleep in his arms, or they both got up and did other things. Their relationship was not usually about sharing the moment after they'd sated their bodies on each other.

"I'm sure he does, too," he agreed, remembering the way Russell had looked at Caroline. "In any case, your mother's already told us she loves your father. It's just a matter of time before they get back together."

Gabrielle sighed. "They've wasted such a lot of years."

So did we, came the unbidden thought. It all fell into place then. The reason he felt unsettled was because of what had happened in the hospital room this afternoon. It must have subconsciously stirred up memories of five years ago.

"Why did you leave, Gabrielle?"

She looked startled. "Um, when?" she asked, lowering her gaze to his chest.

"You know when."

She shrugged, but still kept her eyes downward. "It wasn't easy living with my father after my mother left. And before that it had never been much good, either."

He paused. "No, why did you leave *me?*"

Her eyes lifted and he could see she'd known what he'd meant all along. "I explained it in the note."

And he'd brushed that aside at the time, allowing work commitments to prevail. Nothing and no one had been going to stop him from making his millions. Not even this beautiful woman in his arms.

"Ahh, the note," he murmured, half to himself. "You didn't want me coming after you, if I remember rightly."

She looked uneasy. "That's right."

And that made him wonder. "Why?"

She blinked, then gave a bland smile. "This is beginning to sound like an inquisition," she joked, but her strained look told him she didn't actually find it amusing.

He scowled. "What are you hiding, Gabrielle?"

Something flickered in her eyes, before she glanced downward at their naked bodies entwined on the bed. "Nothing, apparently," she mused.

She wasn't fooling him. She was using sex to get him to change the subject. And that meant she was definitely hiding something.

Or someone.

God, he felt like someone had punched him in the stomach. That thought had never occurred to him before. He'd always assumed *he* was enough for her.

He squared his shoulders, prepared for a blow. "Was there another man involved?"

Her eyes widened in total surprise. "What! No, of course not."

Fierce relief washed over him. He began to breathe again. "Just as well," he growled. "You're my wife now and if another man comes looking for you, I'll kill him."

She stared for a moment, clearly surprised. Then her eyes softened. "Damien, you have no need to worry. I won't be leaving you again."

He expelled a breath. For once she didn't sound as if their marriage was a fate worse than death, and suddenly he felt more than pleased about that. He'd never realized before how much he'd missed by *not* being married. He was enjoying being able to work alongside Gabrielle, coming home with her, sharing dinner, sleeping together. They were a couple.

And one day they might even have a family.

He swallowed hard. The thought of Gabrielle carrying his child made him feel kind of strange. Like he was standing on shifting sand.

"Damien?" she said in a low voice, querying his silence, sending him into action.

He eased her off him and rolled out of bed. "Let's get something to eat," he muttered, standing, glad to be back on solid ground.

The sound of water running in the shower roused Gabrielle at four the next morning. For a moment she lay there half-awake, remembering the feel of Damien's lips on hers after they'd gone to bed. He'd taken her with his body, conquering her, dividing her, seeming to know what she wanted before she did. It had made for an incredible union.

She must have fallen asleep again because she woke to the sound of water still running in the shower. This time her eyelids flew open. What on earth was Damien *doing* in there?

She threw back the covers and hurried into the bathroom. And stopped dead when she saw him naked in the shower, his forehead pressed against the tiled wall as if he didn't have the energy to hold himself up.

"Oh my God," she said, racing across the room. She slid the glass door back, thankful to find the water cold. "Damien? Are you all right? What's the matter?"

He looked up at her groggily. "I was hot," he mumbled, his eyes not really focusing on her, his cheeks flushed.

She felt his forehead. His skin was warm despite the cold water running over him. "You've got a fever," she said, turning the taps off.

He seemed to become aware of her. "Allergy."

A slice of panic raced through her. Allergies could be life threatening. "You need an ambulance."

"No!" He tried to straighten up. "My doctor. He knows. Call him."

Her panic receded as common sense took hold. If it had been life threatening, Damien would be dead by now. Oh God, she couldn't think that.

She took him by the arm. "Let me help you back to bed."

He made a feeble attempt to step out of the cubicle. "I can make it," he said, then swayed as he tried to stand by himself.

"I'm sure," she said wryly, grabbing a towel to throw over his shoulders and dry him, but he pulled it away and wrapped it around his trim hips, looking thoroughly sexy and masculine. "Here. Lean on me."

"I'm too heavy."

"Just lean a little, then. I can manage." She slowly led him back to the bedroom and helped him down on the bed. He groaned when his head touched the pillow, and she frowned as she looked down at him. "I'll go call your doctor."

"Good," he rasped.

She hurried away and made the call after finding his doctor's private number in the address book by the telephone. Thankfully the doctor seemed to take it in his stride that he was being called out before dawn.

When she came back, Damien had fallen asleep. His cheeks were flushed and he started mumbling. It was obvious he was a little delirious and that worried her. The doctor said he knew the problem and would come straight around, so she hoped he kept to his word. She didn't like seeing Damien like this.

All at once he started to move restlessly. "Mum?"

Oh, heavens. "Damien?"

"I'm sorry, Mum. Sorry I couldn't be..." He trailed off to sleep again, making Gabrielle wondered what he'd been about to say.

Just then the doctor arrived. "It's a food allergy," the older man said after she let him into the apartment and they went into the bedroom. "Some sort of preservative. It makes him dizzy and gives him a fever. He must have eaten some of it last night." He put his bag down on the bed and gave Damien a cursory glance. "Do you know what he had for dinner?"

"Our housekeeper cooked lasagna, but I'm sure she must know about the allergy." Gabrielle couldn't imagine Damien risking this too often.

The doctor opened his bag and started to prepare an injection. "It's hard to tell what's in some foods. He might've got a good dose of it by accident."

Deep concern filled her. "Isn't there anything you can do about it?"

"There's some allergy tests, but he won't have them done. He says he can handle it." His eyes held a rueful glint.

She found herself smiling back at him, relieved more than anything that he was here. "That sounds like Damien."

He gave the injection, then looked up at her again. "By the way, I'm Ken. I've been Damien's doctor for a few years now. I believe you're the new Mrs. Trent."

Her cheeks warmed. "So word's out?"

"Definitely. And there are a few very disappointed ladies around the place, let me tell you."

She pushed aside a sense of jealousy and let her mouth quirk with humor. "I'm sure they'll get over it." Not like her. She loved him too much to lose him again.

He gave her a speculative look, then nodded in approval. "You'll be good for him."

"I know," she said, serious now.

Ken left not long after, saying he'd be back before lunch to check on his patient. Reassured that Damien was okay, she made herself a cup of coffee then curled up on the luxurious leather club chair by the window and watched him as he slept. It was a rare opportunity to look at the man she loved, without fear of him catching her.

At that thought she blinked. Good Lord. This is what it had come down to. Her sneaking peeks at Damien to satisfy the longing in her heart. Yet she couldn't seem to stop herself. Everything about him... every feeling for him...was a precious thing to be cherished and savored.

It was just the way it was.

A few hours later he woke her, trying to get out of bed. "Damien?"

Sitting on the edge of the mattress, he turned his head slowly, his gaze sliding across the room at her. "What are you doing over there?"

"I fell asleep in the chair," she said, getting to her feet.

He paused while he swallowed. "You should have gone to the spare room."

"You might have needed me."

Another pause. "I'm fine," he said, but he didn't move.

She walked over to him. "Where are you going, anyway?"

"To the bathroom...then the office."

She raised an eyebrow. "Really? You can't even stand up. Besides, it's Saturday. There's no need to go anywhere."

"I work every day." But he still sat there, like he was trying to get his balance. "Is Ken coming back?"

"Later this morning." She touched his forehead and frowned at his damp skin. "Perhaps you should see about getting something done about this allergy?"

His mouth set. "No."

She let that go. "Come on. I'll take you to the bathroom."

"I can do it myself." He pushed himself up, then rocked on his feet.

"You're one stubborn man," she declared, pulling his arm around her shoulder. "Come on."

A few minutes later she had him back in bed. "You were delirious earlier on, you know," she said, trying to get through his thick skull this was serious and she had been very worried about him.

"I don't remember," he said, closing his eyes.

"You were talking to your mother."

His eyelids shot open, and a hint of the old Damien was back. "Is that so?"

"You were talking about being sorry." She considered him. "You really shouldn't keep things inside you, Damien. It's not good for you."

"Perhaps I'll hire a publicist," he mocked, but it was weak at best.

She hid a smile. "I can see you're starting to get better."

"Yes. So stop mothering me."

She winced inwardly even as she angled her chin. "I'm so glad my services are appreciated." She turned on her heels and headed for the door. Of all the ungrateful…

"Gabrielle?"

Hurt, she wanted to tell him to drop dead, but the memories of finding him in the shower were still fresh in her mind. She stopped at the door and turned to look at him. "Yes?"

"I'm sorry." His eyes softened with gratitude. "Thank you for looking after me."

Oh, she was such a weak woman where he was concerned, she decided, as tender warmth entered her heart. "You're welcome."

Eight

After that, life went into a holding pattern for a few days. Kia and Danielle took turns phoning, breezily chatting about Gabrielle's new Porsche that they'd heard Damien had bought for her, but really to see how she was coping with married life. Gabrielle tried to sound upbeat and positive. She thought she did a pretty good job of convincing them she was okay, but there was still a hint of worry in their voices that made her realize she wasn't really fooling them at all.

Somehow they knew she loved Damien.

Really loved him.

But they never mentioned it to her. She was pretty sure they didn't mention it to their husbands, either, for which she was eternally grateful.

As for Damien, he gave nothing away, but every

night he made love to her with a passion that made her love for him deepen. Beyond that she was afraid to think. She couldn't let herself. There was just too much of a heartache standing between them. A heartache he had no idea existed. One she prayed he *never* knew existed, not just for her sake but for his own. The more she loved him, the more she didn't want to see him hurt.

And then one evening after dinner, Damien had gone downstairs to get some paperwork he'd left in his BMW when his cell phone rang. Gabrielle wasn't sure whether to answer it at first, but thoughts of her father taking a turn for the worse had her hurrying over to the coffee table to snatch it up.

A woman gave a little gasp, then hesitated. "Er…is Damien there?" the husky voice said on the other end of the phone.

Gabrielle's heart sank as she wondered if this was one of the women Ken had said was "disappointed" about Damien's marriage. "He's stepped out for a moment."

"Oh."

She did sound disappointed, but Gabrielle wasn't sure it was because she knew he had a wife now. "He'll be back soon."

There was a tiny pause. "To whom am I speaking?" the woman asked, but not in a nasty way. She actually sounded rather well-bred and polite.

"Gabrielle." She almost said "his wife," but just didn't have the heart. "Can I tell him who called?"

"Um, yes. Please tell him Cynthia called. Perhaps he could call me back? It's important."

"I'll pass the message on," Gabrielle said as an unexpected feeling of jealousy hit her. Cynthia sounded like a nice person, and that was more dangerous than a hundred women who only wanted Damien for what they could get from him.

Just as she hung up, Damien walked into the apartment, looking so handsome he made her heart skip a beat.

"Who was that?" he said, lightly tossing his car keys on the table.

"Someone called Cynthia."

He looked at her sharply. "Did she say what she wanted?"

"You."

His eyes narrowed, telling her he got her point. "Does she want me to call her back?"

"Yes." She paused. "An old girlfriend?"

A shadow of annoyance crossed his face. "She's a...woman friend."

"Your mistress?" His words stabbed at her heart. She'd suspected, but hearing him say it out loud made her feel sick. "I expect you to be faithful, Damien."

His gaze held hers. "Who said I wouldn't be?"

"Then you'd better let all your...*women* friends know you're married now."

He held himself stiffly. "I'll be faithful, Gabrielle. You have no need to worry on that score."

Yes, but would he feel the same way in a few years' time? Men often played around, and rich successful men were no different. Most of them thought it was their right. Her father certainly had.

He walked over to her, captured her chin with his fingertips and tilted her face up to him. "Listen to me, Gabrielle. And I mean this." His eyes turned even more intense than usual. "You're all the woman I want."

"Am I?" she croaked, unable to stop the sinking feeling in her stomach at his words.

Want, he'd said.

Not *need*.

"Yes."

"Lucky me," she managed to say.

He stared at her, baffled. Then, "Perhaps I should show you just how lucky you are," he said, arrogance taking over as he scooped her up in his arms and strode toward the bedroom.

By the time she came up for air, he'd made love to her as if he'd wanted to imprint himself on her forever. And yes, she felt very lucky indeed. For a moment she reveled in that feeling. But then she realized he was only stamping what he considered to be *his*.

Yet despite fighting her feelings for a man who would try to control her if he knew she loved him, Gabrielle was happy to work alongside Damien at the office, helping him make changes that would benefit the company. She was impressed, not only by his business acumen, but by his consideration in teaching her things about the business that would take her a lifetime to learn elsewhere. Yet they both knew who was really in charge.

Him.

Not that she minded. She needed him to put the company back on the right track. Perhaps if Keiran hadn't messed things up so badly she might have stood half a chance of straightening things out herself. As it was, she was grateful for Damien's help.

And everyone was grateful that Keiran had taken a break from work the past few days. The office was a much nicer place without him around, putting her on edge, constantly sending her daggers with his eyes. She could easily see why all the department heads had been leaving for greener pastures. Thankfully the ones who hadn't left were now happy to stay, and Damien had even managed to get two of their top staff to return to their old positions.

Unfortunately, Keiran came back to work the morning Damien was absent at an important meeting. It didn't take her cousin long to walk into her office with a smug look on his face that somehow sent shivers down her spine and gave her a sense of déjà vu. She hoped she was wrong but she had the feeling he was up to something.

She gave him a cool look. "Do you think you could make an appointment with Cheryl? I'm a busy lady these days."

He came toward her. "Cheryl isn't at her desk."

"Then perhaps you could wait until she is."

He flopped down on the chair opposite her. "But I wanted to tell you something really important. I'm sure you'll find it fascinating."

She looked into his gloating eyes and knew he had trouble in mind.

"Guess where I've been?" he taunted, as was his way.

She picked up her pen, ready to ignore him. "Keiran, I don't have time for—"

"Sydney," he cut across her.

A wave of apprehension replaced that shiver down her spine. "What's so important about that?"

His mouth spread in a thin-lipped smile. "Ahh, but it's not what I did in Sydney. It's what I found out."

The breath seemed to have solidified in her throat. "Found out?"

"About you."

She blinked, hoping she sounded suitably surprised, but inside she was shaking. "Me?"

"Yes. And it was something very, very interesting."

Dear Lord, could Keiran know?

"Really?" she said, leaning back in her chair. She wouldn't...couldn't...let him see how fast her heart was thumping in her chest.

"I took one of your friends out to dinner."

Oh God.

She arched a brow. "One of *my* friends?"

"Simone."

As casually as she could, she managed to shrug. "Simone isn't really a friend of mine. I worked with her, that's all."

"Well, give the woman a bit of attention and she was happy to tell me *all* about you."

All?

Ignoring him, Gabrielle sat straighter in her chair and looked down at her paperwork, poised to write. Anything but let him see how afraid she was. "There's nothing to tell."

"Come on, Gabrielle," he scoffed. "You sit there looking all innocent, but underneath you have a dirty little secret."

Her head snapped up. "I don't know what you mean."

"You were in a car accident."

He knew.

Dear God, he knew.

"Tell me something I don't know," she scoffed back.

"You were pregnant." He paused for effect. "You lost the baby."

She swallowed hard. "I still don't know what you're talking about, Keiran," she said, but her voice wobbled and gave her away.

Keiran's eyes lit with a sick sort of triumph. "I wonder if that new husband of yours would be interested in all this? He thinks he's got a saint for a wife."

She squared her shoulders. "I never claimed to be a saint, Keiran."

"So you don't think he'd be interested in knowing you had an affair and carried another man's child?"

Her head reeled back. So he didn't know it was Damien's child. She wasn't sure right now if that was a good or a bad thing. And what did it matter, anyway? He was determined to destroy her.

"I see *that* got your attention," he drawled.

Needing to do something, she got to her feet and walked over to the window. "What do you want?" she said, keeping her back to him, looking out through the glass but seeing nothing.

"So you're admitting you were pregnant?"

She stiffened but didn't turn around. "I can't very well deny it, can I?"

"No, you can't."

All at once she'd had enough. This was her *cousin* doing this to her, for heaven's sake. How dare he threaten her in this way!

She spun around and glared at him. "Blackmail really is an ugly word, Keiran. It suits you."

"Sticks and stones," he mocked. Then his face turned deadly serious. "I tell you what I want. I'll give you one week. One week until your father gets home and is on the mend properly, then I want you to pack up and leave. For good this time."

She felt the blood drain from her face. "Wh-what?"

"You'll tell Damien you made a mistake, and you'll tell your folks you really couldn't put their past behind you. And you'll sign over twenty percent of your shares to me and tell everyone you think I'm the best man for the job. Then you get the hell out of our lives for good. I intend to take over again and I will. By the time Russell is better, this company will be well and truly under my control."

Despair cut the air from her lungs. "You're crazy."

"Yes, but I'll be *rich* and crazy."

"You have money now."

"Not like dear ol' Uncle Russell," he derided. "See, I want it all. Every single cent. Every bit of power." He puffed up his chest. "People will respect me from now on."

She realized that was the one thing no one had ever given him. *Respect.* But then, respect had to be earned. And this man didn't ever have a chance of that happening.

She tried to remain calm. Call his bluff. "I wonder what your parents will say if I tell them what you're doing?"

His eyes flared with anger. "Don't even try it, Gabrielle," he warned through gritted teeth.

"Why not? I could go see them and tell them everything. I'm sure they'd be very interested." Her father's brother, Evan, and his wife, Karen, had always supported their son in all his endeavors, yet Gabrielle had sensed a deep disappointment in them. She didn't think what she had to say would surprise them at all.

Keiran's anger disappeared, replaced by a coldness that chilled her to the bone. "Oh, but then I'd have to tell yours all about you and your sordid past, wouldn't I? How do you think your father will take the news that his precious daughter isn't as precious as he thinks? Do you think it'll upset him? Perhaps even bring on another stroke?" His lips twisted at her gasp. "You have a lot more to lose than I do, *coz*."

She expelled a defeated breath. He was right. No matter what, Keiran would bounce back even if it meant sacrificing his relationship with his parents.

She and her parents, on the other hand...

"Please leave," she said, walking to the door and opening it.

Insolently he stood up and walked toward her. "One week, Gabrielle," he whispered when he reached her. Then he saw Cheryl at her desk in the other office, and he smiled at Gabrielle as he picked up her hand and kissed the back of it. "And then it's bye-bye," he murmured.

Gabrielle winced with pain, not just in her heart but physical pain. He was squeezing the inside of her wrist with his other hand, hurting her. She tried to tug away but he held on a moment more, digging his fingers in while looking at her with eyes that blazed a shocking hatred.

"Don't forget what's at stake here," he reminded her.

She angled her chin at him, determined not to let him see her cower. "I won't forget," she said pointedly. She'd never forget, nor forgive him, for this.

His smirk acknowledged her comment, and finally he dropped her hand and said nothing more. She had to stop herself from rubbing her tenderized skin. She wouldn't give him that satisfaction.

Then he strode toward his own office, throwing Cheryl a satisfied smile on the way. For the life of her, Gabrielle couldn't manage a smile for her PA. Instead she shut the door and sank back against it, her legs barely holding her up. A tear rolled down her cheek as raw grief threatened to overwhelm her.

Oh God, how could she keep the secret of her miscarriage from the man she loved? Even if she threw caution to the wind and told Damien about their child… and she'd sworn never to do that…she still couldn't stay now. Once he discovered her deception, he would never forgive her.

Yet how could she *not* tell him something so important? What if years from now he found out about the baby and how the accident had caused her to lose their child? Their marriage would have been based on even more deception all that time.

A deceptive lie.

As it was now.

But there wasn't only Damien to think about. For her father's sake, she couldn't tell Damien the truth and risk him destroying everything her father had worked so hard to achieve. And he *would* destroy Russell Kane if he knew her father had told her to leave all those years ago, despite her father not knowing she was pregnant. She had no doubt about that.

Neither could she risk Keiran getting to her father

and doing his worst. And she couldn't tell her father herself. Keiran was right. The shock of her accident, let alone her losing her unborn baby, could bring on another stroke. And this time he may not recover.

Of course, when she left in a week's time it could very well bring on another stroke then, too. But what was worse? Telling her parents she wanted to go back to Sydney, letting them think she was unhappy here in Darwin but allowing herself to keep in touch with them? Or telling them about the loss of their unborn grandchild…and the anguish she had gone through alone five years ago…both sure to cause them grief.

No, somehow she had to find the strength to walk away from her parents a second time.

And from Damien.

From love entirely.

Nine

Gabrielle wasn't sure whether to be thankful or not when Damien left a message to say he'd be tied up for the rest of the day. At least she wouldn't have to put on an act for him, though how she was going to hide a breaking heart she wasn't sure. But somehow she would do it. She had to. This last week with him would be so very special. The memory of it had to last her for the rest of her life.

Just as she walked in the apartment after work, her mother phoned to say they'd sent her father home from hospital earlier in the afternoon. Wanting to share the good news, and wondering when Damien would be home for dinner, Gabrielle phoned him on his cell phone, expecting to leave a message. And was surprised when he answered.

"Are you going to see him?" he asked, after she'd finished telling him the news.

"I thought I might go over after dinner once he's had a chance to rest."

"If you can wait half an hour, I'll be able to come with you."

She blinked. "Um…okay."

An infinitesimal pause came down the line. "Better yet. Let's grab a pizza, go down to the beach and eat it, then we'll drop by the house and see Russell."

Her stomach did a flip-flop.

"Gabrielle?"

"Yes?"

"Is there a problem with that?"

Her problem was in loving him.

And having to leave him.

"No. That would be lovely," she said huskily.

"Fine. See you soon."

Gabrielle hung up the phone with a moan of inner pain. Before Keiran's ultimatum today she would have been secretly thrilled to share a pizza with Damien on a tropical beach. Perhaps she could have even let her guard down enough to enjoy herself. But now her heart was turning over as though it wanted to lie down and die.

Not that she let Damien see her thoughts when he arrived home just as she was walking out of the bedroom after showering and changing into something more casual. He looked so gorgeous that her heart started to pitter-patter like the sound of a rain shower.

Putting his briefcase down beside the sofa, he discarded his jacket before turning to look at her, his gaze sliding over her cream linen shorts and white tank top. "You look really nice."

The breath stalled in her throat at that look. "Thank you."

He started walking toward her, his eyes never leaving her face as he loosened his tie. "I'm hungry."

All at once she felt strangely excited. "Then we'd better—"

He gently captured her by the arm, his gaze burning a fire for her. "For you, Gabrielle."

Anticipation sent a feeling of exhilaration through her. "Oh."

His other hand slipped around her neck and pulled her closer. "I've been thinking about doing this all day," he drawled huskily, looking down at her open lips as if he wanted to kiss them right off her.

She moistened them anyway. "Really?"

He hovered just above her mouth. "Why are you surprised?"

His warm breath wafted over her. "Er, we only made love this morning."

A muscle ticked in his cheek. "I could have you ten times a day and still want more."

She suddenly felt boneless.

"Go on, Gabrielle. Say it."

Her heart pounded. "What?"

"That you feel the same." He ran a fingertip over her lower lip. "Be honest."

Of all the things that she *couldn't* be honest about with this man, this wasn't one of them. And what would it hurt to tell him the truth this once? This time next week she'd be remembering this moment and wishing she was back here in his arms.

"Yes," she admitted into the hushed stillness. "I feel the same."

Satisfaction crossed his face as he placed her hands on his chest, her palms against his shirt, letting her feel his body warmth. "Then make love to me."

Her heart skipped a beat. "You mean—"

"Take the initiative this time. Take the clothes off me. Then take me inside you," he said, his voice growing hoarse. "That's where I need to be right now."

For the space of a heartbeat they stared at each other. "Damien, I—" She wasn't even sure what she was going to say. She was just playing for time. She wanted him inside her, too, but was very much afraid that if she touched him like he wanted, she'd give herself away.

His green eyes glinted. "Do it, Gabrielle. You know you want to."

Yes, she did. Very much, but since her return she'd never really been game enough. Always it had been Damien making the first move. Damien who drew her close in bed, held her tight. Damien who caught her to him when she walked by him and pulled her on his lap.

Yet she did want to make love to him. And suddenly his very need for her gave her the courage to be bold. She would show him what she couldn't say.

"Yes, I want to," she said softly. She wouldn't think about tomorrow. This moment is what mattered.

He expelled a breath. "Go for it," he muttered hoarsely.

She paused only briefly before looking down at his half undone tie. He looked so casually sexy, so half-undone himself, that the breath hitched in her throat. She didn't want to spoil this picture of him. She could stand here and stare at him for hours.

But she needed to move on, so with shaky hands she began to finish the job of undoing the tie for him. She tossed the silky material on the plush carpet, then continued, slowly undoing the buttons on his shirt, one by one, feeling his heartbeat thudding beneath her hands, his personal male scent embracing her senses.

She gave a soft little sigh as her palms slipped inside his open shirt and skimmed over the wall of his powerful chest. She loved the feel of hard muscle softened by taut skin.

"You're gorgeous," she murmured, saying what she thought, seeing surprised pleasure flicker in his eyes. It made love rise up inside her, urged her on. She leaned forward and traced the tip of her tongue in the light mat of hair on his chest. "Mmm, you taste salty."

He released a guttural sound that reminded her of the feminine power she'd wielded years ago. Back then she'd had no such inhibitions once Damien had initiated her into the ways of making love. Now it was all coming back.

She inhaled him in. "In fact, you smell like a man who's ready for some loving."

A pulse leaped along his throat. "Then love me," he rasped, making her heart turn over, knowing he only meant physical love but willing to give him more.

She didn't need any further encouragement. She pushed his shirt the rest of the way off and dropped it on the floor. Then she let herself wander, teasing him with her hands and with her lips over the smooth golden skin, circling his nipple with the tip of her tongue, hearing another groan rise up from inside him before she transferred to the other side of his chest.

And then she trailed feather-soft kisses down through the dark hair in the center of his chest, arrowing down further to his belt buckle at his trim waist. She could see the effect she had on him even before she straightened and undid the buckle, lowering the zipper on his trousers, freeing him from his underpants.

He was gloriously aroused. All male and rigid muscle encased in warm satin. She slipped her hand around him and caressed him, loving the sound of the ragged groan he gave.

"Witch."

"You want me to stop?" she said, arching a provocative eyebrow.

"What do you think?" he growled.

She smiled. "What I *think* is that I'm going to have my way with you."

"Yes."

She looked down to where her hand held him. And her head lowered. And then for long minutes she made love to him with her hands and her mouth, tasting him with her lips and tongue, breathing him in, *loving* him, until he put her from him with a sharp hiss as he pulled her upward.

He caught her face between his hands and gave her a brief hard kiss. "I need you naked against me."

Her pulse was already racing through her veins, and his words sent it skyrocketing. "Then let me do the honors," she whispered, stepping back and undressing for him, quick not slow, wanting him now, too much tension between them.

She gasped in delight when he pulled her to him and his erection pressed up against her, hard and demanding. She savored the feel of his hot skin next to hers, the touch of his hands sliding up and down her bare back, the way the hair of his chest brushed against her aching nipples.

And then he swung her up in his arms and headed into the bedroom, tumbling her down on the comforter. "I thought I was supposed to be in charge here," she reminded him huskily.

He ignored that as he quickly protected himself with a condom before joining her on the bed.

Then he lifted her on top of him. "There." Adjusting them both, he eased her down on his thick shaft. "Take charge," he muttered as she took him into her.

An hour and a half later they were sitting on a blanket under the coconut palms on Mindil Beach, eating pizza and watching the glorious sunset. She was famished after another round of lovemaking in the shower before they'd dressed again and left the apartment.

But she still felt as if she was on sensation overload by just having him next to her, watching her with a speculative look in his eyes that belied his casual appearance.

"So, how did it go at the office today?" he said in a conversational tone, just like they were the usual married couple.

She winced inwardly. The usual married couple were in love. Neither did the usual married couple have a cousin blackmailing the wife, threatening to destroy every thing she held dear.

"Um...it was a challenge."

He nodded, and there was a pause as he took a bite of the pizza and looked out to sea. He would have no idea just how much of a "challenge" Keiran had been today.

All at once he turned his head to look at her, studying her thoughtfully for a moment. Then, "I want you to go back to university and finish your degree."

She almost dropped her food. "What!"

Amusement briefly twinkled in his eyes, before he grew serious again. "When I first met you, you were at university studying for your Bachelor of Nutrition and Dietetics. Your eyes used to light up whenever you talked about it, so I'm assuming you regret not finishing it. Am I right?"

"I guess so but—"

"Finish it, Gabrielle."

She dropped her gaze to the pizza in her hand. "I...I can't."

"Why not?"

How could she tell him that soon she had to go back to making a living? Eileen would have her back, but there wouldn't be time leftover for study.

She shrugged. "It's not something I ever think about."

"Then promise me you *will* think about it."

She looked over at him. "I promise," she said truthfully. She'd already thought about it, but that's all she could do.

"Good."

She tilted her head and watched the soft breeze ruffle his dark hair. Suddenly she was greedy. She wanted to know everything she could about this man before she set him free.

"What are *your* dreams, Damien? You never told me."

He took a sip from his can of cola and swallowed the liquid, then his lips curved in a wry smile. "What every man wants. To be rich, successful and have any woman he desires."

She grimaced. It was typical of him not to share his dreams with her, yet he expected her to tell him everything. "I'm serious."

His smile disappeared. "Seriously, then. I'm rich. I'm successful. And I've got the woman I desire."

Her heart turned all aquiver. "Oh."

His eyes assessed hers. "Is that all you've got to say?"

"Three out of three ain't bad," she joked, but felt far from laughing. A man like Damien would never truly admit to actually feeling something for a woman, other than lust. And that was just as well. She wanted no complications. He would survive without her as he always had done, and that would make it easier for her to walk away when the time came.

At the reminder of her departure, she dropped her remaining pizza in the box and jumped to her feet. "We'd better be going. I want to see my father before he falls asleep."

"Whoa!" Damien stood up and moved in close, frowning. "You still don't believe you're enough for me, do you?"

Her gaze darted away, then back. "Of course I do," she said, but even to her own ears she sounded less than convincing. Not that it mattered. Actually, it worked out better. If Damien thought she was upset over this, he wouldn't suspect she was upset over her upcoming departure.

A dark shadow crossed his features, but just as he opened his mouth to speak, some squealing children and a dog ran past them, kicking up the sand.

Thankful for the interruption, Gabrielle broke away from him and began collecting their things. After a moment he helped, too, but she was grateful he said nothing further on the way to her parents' house. For once, his running true to form like this…keeping his thoughts to himself…was working in her favor.

Yet just how she was going to achieve leaving him she wasn't sure. If she left without warning like last time, she'd have to leave all her belongings here. She wouldn't be able to pick up the threads of her old life. She'd been fooling herself to think that. Damien would be on her doorstep this time for sure. Pride would insist his wife come back to him.

But how could she start afresh somewhere and not tell her parents if she were to cut all ties? Could she really do that to them? If she only had herself to worry about, perhaps. But it was all so complicated. God, why had she ever agreed to come back here in the first place? She should have refused. It would have saved a great deal of heartache in the long run.

Fifteen minutes later she had to put her thoughts aside as she and Damien entered her old home. The front door had been left unlocked for them, and now they found her father lying in bed in the main bedroom, her mother reading one of the latest novels to him.

"What's this, Russell?" Damien said in a joking tone. "You getting soft in your old age?"

Russell chuckled. "It seems so."

Caroline closed the book and put it on the bedside table. "He tells me his days of reading the *Financial Review* are over."

Damien's glance sharpened. "So you're retiring?"

"Yes, son, I am. I want to enjoy the more important things in my life." His eyes encompassed Caroline and Gabrielle. "That's all that matters to me now."

Gabrielle's heart thudded. So many times she'd longed to hear such words, but now they only caused her more anguish and despair.

All at once her mother smiled a nice bright smile that went nowhere. "So, darling. When are you two going to have that proper ceremony? I'll need to put it in my calendar. I'm not sure where I'll be then but—"

Russell's eyes sharpened. "What on earth are you talking about?"

Caroline glanced at him, then away. "Um, I said I'm not sure where—"

"I heard what you said," he growled. "I'm just not sure *why* you said it. You're not going anywhere. At least not without me."

She flushed but held herself stiffly. "Russell, I came back because you had a stroke. Now that you're getting better you don't need me anymore."

"Wrong. I need you more than ever, Caroline," he said brusquely.

A tremor touched her mother's lips. "Russell, I—"

"Do you love me?"

Caroline's chin lifted as she met his gaze head on. "Why do you ask?"

"Because I love you," he said, the rough edge of emotion in her father's voice. "More than ever."

Her mother looked hesitant. "You do?"

"Of course I do." His gaze swept over them all, an arrogant tilt to his head that reminded her of Damien. "And I don't care who knows it."

Caroline bit her lip. "But...I didn't think you cared anymore. You've been acting so...polite at times."

"Only because I wanted to recover fully before convincing you to stay with me. As it is—" he looked down at himself on the bed, then up again "—I'm still not well enough, but I want you to stay with me anyway."

Caroline's eyes lit with hope. "You do?"

"Yes," he said on a broken whisper, holding out his hand toward her.

"Oh, Russell." She went into his arms.

Gabrielle's despair lessened at their avowal of love. Her parents would be okay without her. They loved each other after all. Love would get them through it.

As it would her.

Something pulled her tear-filled gaze away from her parents to the window. Damien stood, looking at her, his gaze penetrating and oddly watchful.

"Well, well, Russell," a male voice interrupted from the doorway behind them. "This is quite a development."

Gabrielle spun around and found Keiran standing there with a smile that oozed false charm. The torment of his presence sent sudden desolation sweeping over her.

"Keiran," Russell said, sounding pleased. "Come in.

Come in. I've got some news. I intend to renew my vows to Caroline just as soon as it can be arranged."

Keiran stepped forward into the room. "That's fantastic news. I always knew you two belonged together." He stopped beside Gabrielle and smiled across the room at Damien. "Just like I knew these two belonged together."

"Oh, so you saw it, too," Russell said, leaning back on the pillow with the air of a man who had everything now.

"I sure did. And it makes my heart glad for them both." He smiled at her, but his eyes were cold. "I'm sure nothing can come between them now. Don't you agree, Gabrielle?"

Her nerves tensed. "I—"

"You got that right," Damien cut across her from his position at the window.

Keiran inclined his head, but the smug smile stayed on his lips. He was in control of her and Damien's future, and he knew it.

Then Keiran looked down at Gabrielle beside him, making her jump when he lifted her wrist and turned it over. "Oh my, coz. How on earth did you get this nasty bruise?"

She'd been too upset to notice the bruise herself until now. It wasn't large but it was dark purple where Keiran had dug his thumb into her. Thankfully, it was on the underside of her wrist and hard to see.

Gabrielle snatched her hand back. "Um…I'm not sure," she said, darting a look at Damien and seeing his eyes sharpen.

"You'll have to be more careful in the future," Keiran said with fake concern.

Her mother moved closer and picked up Gabrielle's hand to check the inside of her wrist. "Keiran's right. That's a nasty bruise, darling."

Gabrielle could feel heat creeping into her cheeks. Her mother would be shocked to know that her nephew had put the bruise there. They would *all* be shocked. She found it hard to believe herself.

Keiran gave a light chuckle. "She tripped the other day and would have fallen if I hadn't saved her," he lied. "She always was a bit of a klutz."

Caroline frowned. "I don't remember that, Keiran."

"Me, neither," Russell said with a scowl, and Gabrielle's heart jumped in her throat. Her father was looking at Keiran with slightly narrowed eyes. Did he suspect the truth? Oh God, she hoped not. It would lead to dangerous secrets being exposed.

Her mother's face cleared. "How about I make us some iced tea?"

Gabrielle quickly forced a smile. "That would be lovely, Mum," she said, all at once knowing that Keiran *had* tripped her up the other day. It hadn't been an accident.

Keiran smiled at her mother, but Gabrielle thought he looked a little nervous now, as well he should. "Yes, that would be perfect, Caroline."

Gabrielle swallowed hard as her mother left the room with a spring in her step. Her father was still frowning slightly, but it was Damien whom Gabrielle was worried about now. His eyes were on Keiran with a lethal calmness that seriously worried her. She had the feeling he had caught onto what Keiran was doing.

* * *

Damien didn't know how he managed to get through the next half hour. He hoped to God he was wrong, but his gut was telling him differently. Tension coiled inside him.

"Okay, Gabrielle," he said once they were home. She'd been sending him wary glances on the way, and he'd done nothing to put her mind at ease. He wanted her to spill all, and he wanted no procrastination. "Tell me. How did you get that bruise?"

Seconds crawled by. She shot him an anxious glance. "Um…bruise?" she said, not fooling him for an instant.

He jerked his head at her hand. "The one on your wrist there. Or should I say the one *under* your wrist?"

"Oh, *that* one." She shrugged as she placed her handbag on the sofa. "I can't remember."

"Keiran knew it was there," he pointed out.

One delicate eyebrow rose. "What are you implying, Damien?"

They both knew she was hiding something. "Keiran was being a smart-arse about it. He doesn't do that for no good reason."

"That's just Keiran being Keiran."

He held back his irritation at her delaying tactics. "The thing is *why* did he feel he had to point it out?"

"How do I know?" she challenged, but there was something in her blue eyes telling him she wasn't nearly as defiant underneath. There was a hint of fear in her eyes.

His gut knotted more. "I think you do," he said silkily.

She squared her shoulders. "Are you calling me a liar?"

"Yes." He stared hard, letting her know he wasn't

about to give up. He would find out what all this was about if it was the last thing he did.

Suddenly her shoulders slumped just a little. "Damien, please let things be."

He expelled a harsh breath. "Jesus, did Keiran really put that bruise on you?" Even though he'd suspected, it was a different thing knowing for sure.

She wrapped her arms around herself in a defensive gesture. "Yes, Damien. He did."

A knifing pain sliced through his chest. "I'll kill him," he rasped, taking a step toward the door.

"No!" She stepped in front of him. "What's the use now, Damien? Let it be."

He stopped, looked down at her face. "Why didn't you tell me?"

"Because it didn't seem much at the time."

He swore. No one should put up with physical abuse, and certainly not from a weak-willed coward like—

"I wouldn't listen to him this morning, you see," she said, cutting across his thoughts. "He grabbed my wrist too tight, that's all."

He gave her a glance of disbelief. "All? He was gloating. He did it deliberately." Something occurred to him. "Hell, he was gloating over you tripping up, too. Did he trip you, Gabrielle? The truth please."

She winced. "I...I think so."

Damien's jaw clenched. There was more to this than she was saying. "Why wouldn't you listen to him? What was he saying?"

"Nothing. It was just about work," she said, but her eyes darted away again, making him increasingly uneasy.

"You should have told me. If he did it once he would do it again."

"I kept thinking he wouldn't."

"Not bloody likely," he rasped.

She sighed. "I know."

All at once he realized something else. Gabrielle had no trouble standing up to Keiran before. So why *wasn't* she standing up to her cousin over this? What did Keiran have over her? There was only one way to find out.

"Right." He sidestepped her and strode to the door. It was getting late but he couldn't stay here a moment longer without wanting to carry her off to bed and dull the thought of Keiran from her mind. And from his own. But tonight it wouldn't be enough.

"Damien, please," she implored behind him. "This is madness."

He continued walking. He was a man on a mission now.

"Damien, where are you going?"

He continued walking. "Guess."

"Damien, don't. Please let things be."

He stopped briefly and looked back at her. "No chance in hell." Then he walked out the door. He had things to sort out. And Keiran Kane was one of them.

Ten

Gabrielle watched Damien leave, sick with anguish. How could she have told him about Keiran's blackmail? He would have had to ask why.

And now he was on his way to find her cousin. What would he do when he got there? Would he actually hit Keiran? He'd certainly looked angry enough. Or would he be cool and calm and even more dangerous? Knowing Damien, it would be the latter.

Of course, Keiran wouldn't hesitate to tell him about the miscarriage. He'd even tell him it was another man's baby, though she could soon straighten that out.

What she couldn't explain was *not* telling Damien about his child. How could she look him in the eye and tell him she'd lost the marvelous little creation he hadn't known they'd made together?

She closed her eyes, her heart aching with pain. Damien was about to be blindsided, and she was about to lose the man she loved sooner than she'd expected. Dear God, she hadn't wanted to stir up anymore heartache, but heartache was definitely on the agenda.

Somehow she dragged herself into the shower before changing into her nightgown and slipping into bed. And her anguish turned to a different kind of pain when midnight came and went and there was still no sign of Damien returning. She could have called him on his cell phone, but a sickening thought brought tears to her eyes.

Had he gone to find comfort in the arms of another woman? Cynthia perhaps? He'd never explained who exactly that "woman friend" was and what she wanted.

Her father certainly had turned to other women years ago. It's what men did, wasn't it? When things got tough they went elsewhere. Would Damien come home smelling of Cynthia's perfume and with her lipstick on his collar? The thought ripped at her insides as she hugged Damien's pillow to her.

When first light came her heart was heavy. Damien must know about the miscarriage by now. He hadn't come home and his continued silence reflected that he didn't want her to stay.

It was time to leave.

Oh God.

And how did she tell her parents she was leaving? She wasn't prepared. *They* weren't prepared. Perhaps she could say she had to go back to Sydney to help Eileen? Just temporarily, she'd say. That would give her father more time to recover from the stroke so that in a few weeks when she didn't return, it may not be so hard on them. Not when they had each other now.

Okay, so it was a coward's way out, but she really *was* thinking of her father's health. She would do it this way and hope for the best for all of them. She couldn't see Damien telling them about her miscarriage. He just wouldn't do that to them.

But Keiran would.

She swallowed hard. Damn her cousin for putting her in this position. Well, if he wanted her out, then he would have to make a deal with her. If she left quietly, he had to keep quiet about everything to do with her losing the baby.

But her brief taste of victory soon disappeared when she remembered that she had to get through today first. She had to face her parents. She wouldn't think about Damien right now. She couldn't. One step at a time.

It was fortuitous, then, that she'd told her mother last week that she would come over and get some of her old things sometime. No time like the present. She'd go right now. She needed to keep busy, and if everything was about to cave in on her, she wanted some mementoes from her room.

Lord, this was going to be so hard, she decided, getting her empty suitcase out of the wardrobe, intending to fill it with all the things she hadn't been able to take with her before.

Her mother's eyes widened when she opened the door and saw the lone suitcase in her daughter's hand. Caroline looked beyond Gabrielle to the Porsche parked in the drive behind her, then back at her daughter, her eyes confused.

Gabrielle pasted on a smile and wondered how she could keep on functioning. "I'm here."

Caroline blinked as she tightened the belt around her silk bathrobe. "Darling, here for what?"

Gabrielle stepped into the house. "I thought I might get some of those things from my room."

Her mother looked taken aback. "What? Now?"

Gabrielle hesitated. "Is it a bad time?"

"No, of course not. I just didn't expect you here this early."

"I'm sorry. I rise early." She knew she should probably leave and come back later, but she wasn't sure she would have the strength to do this again. "How's Dad?"

"Feeling much better."

"Terrific." That was one good thing in all this mess. "I'll just go up to my old room, then."

Her mother closed the front door. "Stop in and see your father first. He's awake," she said, but her eyes were confused.

"Okay." Gabrielle went to turn away, then spun back and gave her mother a hug. "Mum, I'm so happy that you and Dad are back together again."

"Thank you, darling," Caroline said, drawing back after returning the hug, a worried look in her eyes now. Gabrielle couldn't bear it, so she spun away and took the staircase two steps at a time.

Her father looked surprised to see her there and immediately asked, "Where's Damien?"

She swallowed hard. *That's what I'd like to know.*

She pretended to appear nonchalant. "He went to the office early."

Russell scowled. "Does this have something to do with your cousin?"

Gabrielle tried not to show her surprise, but she suspected she didn't fool her father. "I'm not sure," she lied, before changing the subject to his health, then made her escape to her old room and started going through some of her things.

And that's where she almost fell apart. To give up all this just when she'd found it again was unfair. To give up her parents was tear-jerking. To give up Damien filled her with despair and desolation.

In the end she only took a few keepsakes. The rest could be thrown out. They weren't of importance to anyone but her, she told herself as she went downstairs to the kitchen to get a cup of coffee to fortify herself.

Soon she would go and tell her parents the news that she'd had an urgent call for help from a friend who'd helped her many years ago. They'd understand surely.

Her mother walked in as she was pouring the hot liquid into a mug. "I'd love some of that," Caroline said, brushing a piece of lint off the light-blue pantsuit she'd changed into and wore with confidence.

Gabrielle forced a brittle smile. "Sure," she said, and handed the mug to her mother, then got another one for herself. She loved that her mother looked so good these days. If only…

Caroline leaned against the marble bench and took a sip of her coffee before speaking. "You like our new kitchen?"

"Yes." Gabrielle's gaze swept the room. She noted the changes but they didn't really sink in. It was people that mattered, not things. People you cared for. People who—

"Is everything okay, darling?"

Gabrielle's eyes darted to her mother's worried face. "Um…I'm not sure what you mean."

"Why are you here so early this morning? Why aren't you with Damien? There's something wrong. I can feel it."

Gabrielle wanted to tell her she was imagining things, but that would only delay the inevitable. She put her mug down on the counter and took a deep breath. "Mum, I have to tell you something. I—"

"Perhaps you'd like to tell me too," Damien said from the doorway.

Gabrielle spun toward the sound. Panic flittered inside her chest, even as her heart swelled with love for this man. If she didn't know better she'd say there was relief in the back of those green eyes.

Then she noted how weary he looked. And unshaven, and he was wearing the same clothes he'd had on yesterday.

He stepped inside the kitchen. "Caroline, can I speak to my wife alone please?"

Caroline looked at her daughter. "Darling?"

Gabrielle gave a small nod. "I'm fine, Mum."

"Okay, but just call if you need me." She gave Damien a slight smile as she left the room.

Gabrielle squared her shoulders and met his gaze as soon as they were alone. "How did you know where I was?"

"A good guess." His eyes considered her. "Why did you take your suitcase and come here, Gabrielle?" he asked silkily.

She frowned. He'd been there in the hospital room

when she and her mother had discussed this last week. "I wanted to get some things from my old room. To keep as mementoes." No need to say why.

"You're not leaving me, Gabrielle."

That took her aback, even as she partly registered his words. "So you know, then?"

He started to walk toward her. "If you think I'm letting you go a second time, then think again."

She began to frown. "But Damien—"

He stopped right in front of her and put his hands on her shoulders. "No, you listen to me. You're my wife and you'll stay my wife. Is that clear?"

She wasn't sure what was going on here. Keiran must have told him about the blackmail, so if he knew about the miscarriage why did he want her to stay?

She frowned. "I don't understand. A baby—"

He went very still. "Is that what all this is about? Do you want a baby?"

She tilted her head at him in confusion. "Damien, did you go and see Keiran last night?"

His expression instantly clouded in anger as he dropped his hands from her shoulders. "I tried but I couldn't find him. I think he's gone into hiding. And so he should. I'll bloody strangle him when I catch up with him."

Her knees wobbled with a flash of silly relief. Thank God he didn't know the full story. There was still a chance he never would…still a chance that… No, she was being silly. She still had to leave.

Then she remembered something else. How she'd waited for him last night. "Where have you been all night, Damien?"

He frowned. "What do you mean? I stayed at the office and did some work."

"Really?" If only she could believe that.

"Didn't you get my message? I left one on the answering machine to say where I was."

She blinked. "But I was there all night and didn't hear the..." She paused. "Um, what time did you call?"

"Around eleven."

She winced. "Oh."

He frowned. "What does that mean?"

"I took a shower about eleven."

"And you didn't think to check the phone for any messages after that?"

"No. I was too upset."

The look in his eyes softened briefly, but just as quickly hardened. "Okay, I get it. You thought I was out all night with another woman, didn't you?"

She lifted her chin. "I considered that, yes."

He put his hand under her chin, making her look into his eyes, not allowing her to look away. "Gabrielle, I've told you before. I don't *want* any other woman."

It was weird but right then she couldn't *not* believe him. It was as if something had opened up inside her heart and made her see him as he truly was. He'd been kindness itself to her parents. And he'd married her out of honor for her father. He wouldn't be the man she loved if he was the type to be married and have a mistress.

"I know," she said softly. She loved him, but now that love had deepened and strengthened.

His shoulders relaxed. "Good. And perhaps we need to discuss this baby business."

Fear lurched inside her chest, even as she noted an oddly watchful look in his eyes. "Not yet."

He gave a jerky nod of his head that was touching. "Look, I have to go home and change, then get back to my office. Negotiations are taking longer than expected. The guy has to head back to England later this afternoon and there's still some things to be settled."

She was tempted to go home with him but they would only end up making love. As much as she wanted to spend every last remaining moment with him, his job was important, too, and she didn't want to mess that up further by delaying him. He'd already given so much to her father's business.

She nodded. "I'll stay here for a while yet. I want to visit with my parents."

A gleam of disappointment crossed his face as his arm snaked around her waist and pulled her closer. "I *need* to make love to you. Soon."

She swallowed hard. "There'll be time for us later."

"Yes." He kissed her hard on the lips, then turned and left the room.

Gabrielle's heart thumped loudly at the odd flare of something she'd seen in those green eyes. There'd been satisfaction there, and relief, too. But there'd been something else. Something that had looked like *need*, not *want*. He'd even said it himself.

Need.

A few minutes later her mother came into the kitchen. "Everything okay, darling?" Caroline asked cautiously, obviously having heard none of the conversation between her daughter and Damien.

Gabrielle took a steadying breath and pasted on a smile. "Of course it is. We just had a little tiff."

"I thought that was the case." Caroline's face brightened. "I'm so pleased you made up. Damien's a wonderful man."

"Yes, he is."

"And I'm so glad his upbringing didn't affect him at all."

Gabrielle's heart jolted. "His upbringing?"

Her mother's eyebrow rose. "He hasn't told you about his childhood?"

"No. Please tell me," she murmured, almost afraid to ask.

"Oh, darling, it was nothing horrific or anything," she said quickly. "So put that out of your mind. But I know someone who knew his parents. They were devoted to each other, pretty much to the exclusion of their son. Apparently they barely knew he existed." She drew her lips in thoughtfully. "I'm sure they loved him, but it was as if they'd used up all their love and had nothing left for Damien. I think that's why he strived so hard to become a millionaire and why he's so aloof at times. He's in control that way."

"Oh my God." Ignoring a child and pretending he doesn't exist was a form of emotional abuse. Was that why he'd said sorry to his mother during his delirium? Was he apologizing for just *being?*

Caroline clicked her tongue. "I shouldn't be surprised he hasn't told you any of this. Not yet anyway. He loves you but it'll take time to break down the barriers."

Gabrielle dismissed the comment about him loving

her. She couldn't ever think that. As for his aloofness at times, if only he'd hinted... No, she could see he couldn't do that. Otherwise he'd be letting go some of that control he'd fought so hard to maintain.

She expelled a slow breath as she finally knew what made Damien tick. It turned her insides soft, made her vulnerable yet strong in a way she'd never imagined. She savored the feeling, drew on it. It gave her the strength to get through whatever the future held for her without Damien by her side.

And then out of the blue, her world shifted focus and she found she was looking beyond herself. Hearing about Damien's background made her realize she would be doing the worst possible thing if she left him. After all, his parents hadn't needed him and had ignored him all his life. And now *she* was about to do the same thing by leaving. *Again.* She'd walk out and never come back, as if she didn't need him, just like his parents hadn't needed him.

And all because of Keiran and his greed.

Suddenly she saw everything with abrupt clarity, and she knew she'd had enough of Keiran's demands. She couldn't let her cousin throw his weight around and destroy their lives any longer. Damien needed her. She couldn't walk out on him, at least not until after she told him the truth. Then if he wanted her to go, as painful as it would be for her, she would.

But on *her* terms, not her cousin's.

Dear God, Damien deserved to know about the death of his unborn son and the circumstances surrounding it. *She* would want to know if the positions had been reversed, no matter how much it hurt or made her angry. She now knew it wasn't fair of her to keep that from him, whether he decided to destroy her father or not.

And if Damien did his worst—and please God he wouldn't—she had to believe her father and mother would still be okay. They had each other, after all.

Damien had no one.

Fifteen minutes later Gabrielle quietly closed the door to her Porsche and walked up to the front door of a small house nestled amongst the palm trees and ferns. It was midmorning and, as suspected, she could see Keiran sitting inside the living room. He was lounging on the sofa, watching television, as if he didn't have a care in the world.

Her mouth tightened as she pressed the doorbell. How dare he try and wreck her life and those of the people she loved. He deserved no less than what he got in future, she decided, waiting for him to open the door. The look of shock on his face was going to be priceless.

It was.

But he soon recovered. "How did you know I was here?" he demanded curtly.

She stepped past him and into the house. "You use people, Keiran. So I figured you'd still use an old girlfriend." She stopped in the middle of the living room and arched a brow at him. "How *is* Teresa, by the way?"

His eyes narrowed. "Get on with it, Gabrielle."

"I've come to tell you one thing. You're fired."

For an instant he didn't move. Then he gave a short laugh. "You can't fire me. I hold forty percent of the shares."

"You're fired," she reiterated firmly. She didn't care how many shares he held in the company.

He crossed his arms. "I don't think so, coz. Or have you forgotten that I'll tell Damien all about you? And your parents."

Her chin angled. "Do your worst, Keiran," she challenged.

Surprise flickered in his eyes before they turned cool and calculating. "Perhaps I already have," he said, sending shock running through her. "You see, I knew I'd blown it last night when I pointed out the bruise in front of everybody." All at once he glared at her as if it were *her* fault, then shrugged. "But no matter. I won't be coming back to Kane's anyway. I'll be selling my shares, and Teresa and I are going overseas to live on the money. It should last us a few years, don't you think?"

At that moment, an attractive woman came out of one of the rooms, then stopped dead, surprise flashing across her face. "Oh, hello, Gabrielle. I haven't seen you for ages."

Gabrielle nodded her head, but she wasn't in the mood to chitchat. Not that Teresa wasn't nice enough. Older than Keiran by about five years, she was always the one he came to when he needed help.

Teresa frowned as she glanced from one to the other. "Is something wrong?"

"Very," Gabrielle said.

"Don't listen to her," Keiran snapped. "She's only here to—"

"Fire him," Gabrielle said, feeling a little sorry for

Teresa, yet the other woman must know the type of man Keiran was.

Teresa gasped. "*Fire* him?"

"Ask Keiran about it."

"Shut up, Gabrielle," he growled.

"Ask him, but I doubt he'll tell you the truth."

"I said *shut up*," Keiran said through gritted teeth as he stormed toward her. And then he grabbed her arm and shook her.

Gabrielle shrugged him off. She was too angry now herself. "Ask him how he's been blackmailing me to leave my husband and my family and all that I hold dear."

"That's enough!" Keiran suddenly yelled, lifting his hand and slapping her across the face. The sound of it ripped through the air, and Gabrielle's head snapped sideways.

It took a moment or two for the stinging to set in. And the shock.

Teresa was the first to move. "Keiran!" she exclaimed, pushing him away from Gabrielle. "What are you doing?"

Gabrielle's hand went to her cheek as Keiran recovered his balance then just stood there, staring at her. He looked as taken aback as Teresa did, but Gabrielle didn't have time to feel even the littlest bit sorry for him. He'd really crossed the line this time.

She took her hand away from her face and drew herself up straighter. "Don't ever show your face at Kane's again, Keiran," she said, and on that note she sent Teresa an apologetic look and left them standing in the middle of the room. She walked out the door and quietly closed it behind her with cool, calm control.

And that's how she felt right now. Despite the slap, despite knowing what was ahead of her with Damien, she felt liberated from the clutches of her cousin. It gave her the tenacity to keep on going. If she and Damien were to have a chance at a life together, everything had to be out in the open. They couldn't move forward until they put the past behind them.

She decided to go home first and put a cool cloth on her face to stop the stinging and redness. By the time she'd finished, Keiran's imprint was nowhere near as bad as she'd expected, though she suspected she might end up with a bit of a bruise.

Then she drove to Damien's office, intending to wait until he'd finished his meeting. If Keiran had done his worst like he said he had, she just hoped Damien gave her the chance to explain.

But by the time she walked into the reception area of his office, anxiety had taken hold. She wouldn't be human if she didn't feel worried now.

His PA was nowhere to be seen, but a slight noise emitted from his office, so she walked over to the door that was standing open. Perhaps his PA was in his office tidying up.

She gasped when she saw Damien sitting at his desk with a bottle of scotch open and a half-empty glass. He'd had his head in his hands but he'd lifted it when she spoke.

He looked at her then, and her heart faltered at the pain in his eyes and the paleness of his cheeks. As if propelled, she slowly entered the room and stopped dead in the middle of it, the fine hairs on the back of her neck standing to attention.

"Why didn't you tell me?" he rasped, the words sounding as if they were ground out of him.

Her heart squeezed tight. "So Keiran *did* tell you."

"There was a report on my desk this morning when I came back from seeing you." He swallowed hard. "It said about this idiot who ran into you with his car. About the accident. About you...your unborn baby."

It was slowly sinking in that he finally knew. Her legs went from under her as she found her way onto one of the chairs. It felt like all the oxygen had been sucked from the room. "I'm so sorry, Damien."

His eyes pinned her to the spot. "You had another man's child," he said harshly.

She blinked, trying to clear her mind. She'd forgotten he would think that. "No!" She took a deep breath. "It was *your* baby, Damien."

His head reeled back. "Mine!"

"The baby was yours, Damien. And before you ask, the condom broke that one time, remember?"

He sat there, barely moving, but his face said an awful lot about the pain he was feeling. She felt it, too.

All at once he pushed himself back from his desk and stood, turning around to look out the huge windows behind him, but as if he couldn't bear the pain, he spun back to face her. "Why the bloody hell did you run five years ago if you knew you were carrying my child?"

Her throat tightened. "I just had to."

"I wasn't good enough to be the father of your child, was I?" he said in a low voice, like it was something he should have expected.

"No!" She was shocked he'd say such a thing. Not

Damien Trent. He was born secure. He'd never had an insecure moment in his life.

But then she remembered his childhood. And she knew differently. She took a deep breath and uttered the words that could destroy all their lives. "My father told me to leave."

His eyes sharpened. "*Told* you?"

"He was drunk one night and bitter over my mother. He told me to take my things and get out and never come back."

He scowled. "But he would have sobered up the next day. Surely you must have known he wouldn't mean it?"

"I was scared, Damien," she said, seeing the anger burst into his eyes before she'd even finished saying the words. "I was scared that eventually he'd lose control and hit me," she said, blinking back tears at the mere thought of it. "I couldn't risk that happening." Not like it just happened with Keiran.

He went quiet. A muscle ticked in his jaw. "And yet you couldn't come to me?"

A flash of guilt stabbed at her. "No. You would have made me stay."

"You don't have a high opinion of me, do you?"

"I do now. I'm sorry but back then I could only think you were like my father."

His green eyes remained steadily on her face. "I would never, ever physically frighten a woman, sober or drunk."

"I know, but I was young and I was hurting and I was confused by what I felt for you. And I had no idea what you felt for me." She bit her lip. "I guess I didn't really need much of an excuse to leave."

There was a lengthy pause as he seemed to assimilate that. Then, "Why didn't you tell me about the baby when you came back? You've had plenty of opportunity."

Cold fear returned full throttle, but she had to continue on the path of truth she'd chosen. "I was scared for my father's sake. I'm still scared that you'll blame him for everything. You see, if I hadn't left home I wouldn't have been in that car accident and I wouldn't have lost our child." She took a ragged breath. "But as far as I can see he doesn't remember a thing. And he's changed, Damien. We can both see that. So please, please don't say anything to him. And please don't tear down everything that he's built. He's my father. I love him. I don't want to see him hurt."

He stayed silent for a couple of interminable seconds, his face giving nothing away. "And that was our child he helped to kill."

Tears gushed into her eyes. Despite her plea, he was going to take revenge on her father after all. "Damien," she choked. "Anger won't bring our baby back. Please, you have to let it go. If you don't, it will destroy you in the end."

He held himself stiffly while some moments passed. "I admit I'd like to do Russell harm right now." Then something seemed to ease inside him. "But I won't."

She gave a sob. "Oh, thank you." The relief was intense and it washed over her like a wave. Her father and her mother could live their lives in peace now. *She* could live her life in peace now. She swallowed. Except there was the small question of what was to happen between her and Damien now.

"So, you'd rather I think badly of you than your

father?" Damien said, bringing her back to the present as he finally moved and sat again on the leather chair.

"Yes." But she wasn't going to be a martyr about it. When you loved someone you protected them from harm. That's all she'd been doing. "There's something else I have to tell you," she said, wanting it all out in the open.

He stiffened. "What?"

"Keiran tried to blackmail me. He said I had to leave and not come back." She went on to tell him about it, knowing she had to be completely honest. "And this morning I went to see him at his girlfriend's house. He slapped me, Damien," she said, putting her hand to her cheek.

Damien sucked in a sharp breath as he came around the desk toward her. "The bastard," he growled, tenderly cupping her chin so that he could see her cheek, his eyes so dark she thought they might never return to their true green color. "Did he hurt you? Are you okay?"

Her heart softened even more at his concern. "I'm okay. But it didn't get him anywhere in the end. I fired him."

"You did what!"

"I fired him. I couldn't let him get away with it."

A flash of admiration crossed his face. "I'm not sure Russell deserves you." He dropped his hand but watched her in silence for a moment. "Neither do I."

Suddenly she felt like she was losing him. "Damien—"

He twisted around and walked back to his desk. "You're free to go."

She blinked. "Go?"

"Leave," he said in a brusque tone, looking up at her. "I won't stop you from taking your things and going back to Sydney. I won't contest a divorce."

Her heart squeezed tight. "Damien, I—"

"Mr. Trent," a male voice cut across her as a young man walked into the office. "They're ready to resume the—" He stopped short when he saw Gabrielle.

Damien inclined his head. "Thank you, Liam. I'll be along shortly."

The young man nodded, his eyes darting back to Damien. "Um, Mr. Marsden said he doesn't have much time."

"Too bad," Damien snapped.

"Yes, sir," Liam said, flushing, then left the room in a hurry.

Gabrielle looked at Damien. Time was running out, in more ways than one. "Damien, I—"

"You don't have to worry about your father," he cut across her. "I'll continue to work at Kane's and help out until Russell gets back on his feet. James can take on more responsibility, too." He picked up some papers and got to his feet. "As for me personally…no doubt I'll survive."

She went to speak, to tell him she loved him. It was on the tip of her tongue, but suddenly she could hear voices out in the corridor and the moment was lost. You didn't tell a man you loved him when he had people waiting and a major deal to close.

Damien strode past her, leaving behind a whiff of sandalwood aftershave. "Goodbye, Gabrielle."

His words ripped through her but she let him go, his

back ramrod straight, his mind already blanking her out. She understood him now. She knew he was hurting, and that the only way to ease the pain was to stop feeling at all. He must have done that many a time when his parents ignored him.

Only, didn't he know by now that the pain didn't go away just because you blocked it out? It was there and would always be there. Unless you came to terms with it.

Well, she wasn't about to let him block *her* out. She wasn't going to do what his parents did and leave him to cope alone. She would make things right between them. How, she wasn't sure, except that she loved him and she would find a way to show him how much.

The first step was not to let him push her out of his life, she decided, taking the elevator down to the underground car park where she'd left her Porsche. Maybe by the time she got home she'd have figured out how to go about things.

Damien didn't know how he was stopping himself from going out and finding Keiran and giving the other man a taste of his own medicine. God, how could Keiran have hit a woman, and his own cousin, too? How could he have hit Gabrielle! It was the sign of a coward and a bully, and Keiran had well and truly burned his bridges with the Kane family now. The new Russell wouldn't stand for his daughter being abused...not that Russell ever would have, despite his drinking problem causing Gabrielle to leave five years ago.

And if Keiran knew what was good for him, he'd better

sell back those shares to Russell and get the hell out of town. *He'd* see that it would happen. Gabrielle wouldn't have to put up with—Oh God, Gabrielle wouldn't be around.

She was leaving.

And, dammit, he was sitting here at this interminable meeting when all he wanted to do was go back to the apartment to see if she had truly left. Of course, there'd been no reason why she *wouldn't* have left. He certainly hadn't given her a reason to stay. It wasn't as if he loved her or anything.

Like an onrushing wind, all at once he realized he *did* love her. No second-guessing. No thoughts of denial. Just sheer certainty that she filled his heart and made him complete. She's the one he'd been secretly waiting for deep within his heart.

Love surged inside his chest as he jumped to his feet. He couldn't wait a moment more. He had to talk to her before she left. This morning he'd almost had a heart attack when he'd come home and found her suitcase gone. He'd gone to her parents' house, praying she was there, determined to make her stay. This time he would *ask* her not to go.

Striding around the conference table, he apologized to John Madsen citing an urgent family situation, handed over to his second in command, then left the room.

But as he rode down the elevator to the car park below the building, his gut twisted with panic. Five years ago she'd left without telling anyone. Would she do that again? She could even catch a plane to somewhere else and not Sydney. He might never see her again. God, he hoped he hadn't left it too late.

His heart in his mouth, he stormed into the apartment ten minutes later. If she'd gone…

"Damien!" she exclaimed, coming out of the kitchen with a surprised look on her face.

He strode forward and drew her close. "Thank God," he uttered, holding her as tight as he could, terrified of her leaving, never wanting to let her go again.

She pulled back and looked at him, a question in her eyes, asking what this was all about. "You didn't have to come home yet."

"Yes, I did."

Delight flashed across her face then banked. "But I would have still been here tonight."

"Gabrielle, you can't leave. I—" He realized what she'd said. His brow rose, as did his hopes. "You would?"

Her eyes softened. "Yes, Damien, I would."

He held his breath. "For how long?"

"For as long as you want me," she said gently.

A lump welled in his throat. His hands tightened around her waist. "Darling, I'm never letting you out of my sight again. Never."

A soft gasp escaped her. "Damien, what are you saying?"

His chest filled with love. "The first time I set eyes on you, you stole my heart. The second time, you stole my soul."

"Are you saying…" She moistened her mouth, then started again. "Are you saying that you *love* me?"

"More than life itself," he said in a grated whisper.

Tears swamped her blue eyes. "I never thought… Oh God, I love you, too. I wanted to tell you, but there was too much between us."

A tear spilled down her cheek and he wiped it away with his finger. She looked vulnerable, and he wanted to make it better. There was only one way he knew how to do that. His mouth slowly descended to meet her lips.

He kissed her tenderly, fascinated by how soft her mouth felt. Soft and warm and all woman. Yet something was different. Something that made his throat convulse with sheer wonder. *Love* made the difference. It was right there, in the open. Neither of them could hide behind their fears any longer, not even if they had wanted to.

He broke off the kiss and stroked her hair. "Darling, I'm so sorry about our baby. You went through hell and I'll understand if you don't want more children."

She shook her head ever so slightly. "I *want* to have your children, Damien. And with you by my side I'll have the strength to look forward, not backward." Her eyes filled with regret. "Can you forgive me for not telling you about the miscarriage?"

He put his finger against her lips. "Shh. There's nothing to forgive. We'll both always be sad at what we lost, but if we have each other, the pain can be shared." He kissed her gently. "This is the way our lives are meant to be. We had to be apart so that we could find out we belonged together."

Her eyes shimmered with tears. "I think you're right."

"I *know* I am."

Her lips curved even as she blinked to clear her eyes

of moisture. "Oh, I forgot who I was talking to for a minute, there."

She was the sexiest woman he knew. And she deserved to be teased right back. "Don't worry. I won't let you forget ever again." He swooped her up in his arms.

"Where are we going?"

He stopped to look down at the woman who had taken his empty heart and filled it to overflowing with love. "To our bedroom. I need to show you how much I love you."

Her eyes sparkled so brightly they took his breath away. "What a good idea."

He smiled at her. "I'm full of good ideas."

She ran her fingers along his chin. "You know, this all sounds like a takeover, Mr. Trent."

He kissed her. "No, a merger, Mrs. Trent." Then with everything he ever wanted right there in his arms, he strode toward their bedroom.

Toward their future.

Epilogue

Six weeks later, Gabrielle and Damien renewed their wedding vows in a moving ceremony in the back garden of her parents' mansion. As she walked down the makeshift aisle, her father looked so proud, her mother smiling through her tears. Eileen Phillips had come up from Sydney, along with her daughters, Kayla and Lara.

Damien's "family" was represented by Brant and Kia, and Flynn and Danielle. Gabrielle had grown to love the other two women over the past few weeks, pleased they had welcomed her into their own private circle of friendship. But more than that she was thankful Brant and Flynn had been there for Damien all these years when he had needed someone to love him unconditionally.

As for the man himself…she looked ahead…and there he was in front of her.

Damien.

He was so handsome. So *right* for her. He made her feel beautiful and special and needed, and she knew he would make her feel like that for the rest of her life. Love did that to a person.

Her heart accelerated as her father let go of her arm and handed her over to her husband, not as a symbol of possession like she once would have thought, but of love. She went toward Damien willingly.

Later, at the reception, after they'd danced around the wooden floor under the marquee, he drew her away from the crowd to a secluded area amongst the ferns. The tropical moon shone down on them through the palm trees as Damien pulled her into his arms. "I need a kiss from my newish bride," he murmured.

She wound her arms around his neck and offered her lips up to him. "And I need *you*."

Damien groaned and kissed her deeply, his breath becoming one with hers.

As were their hearts.

Long moments later he lifted his head. "Are you ready for our honeymoon?" he asked, his hands slipping down to her waist.

She nodded. "A château in France sounds wonderful." Yet she knew she didn't care where she was as long as she was with Damien.

His eyes wandered over her face. "You are so beautiful, my love."

"And you're so handsome."

He grinned. "I think we'd better leave so we can do further admiring on our private jet."

"Oh, but—" She could no longer keep something a secret from him. "Darling, I have something to tell you. I wasn't sure if I should. I mean, I don't know if it's too soon—"

His eyes flared. "Tell me."

"I think I'm pregnant," she said, hearing the excitement in her own voice.

He shuddered, then tenderly cupped her face with his hands. "Thank you, my darling. That's the perfect gift for a man who has everything."

Her heart was full as his head lowered for another kiss. She knew exactly what he meant.

*****

So you think you can write?

Mills & Boon® and Harlequin® have joined forces in a global search for new authors.

It's our biggest contest yet—with the prize of being published by the world's leader in romance fiction.

Look for more information on our website:
www.soyouthinkyoucanwrite.com

So you think you can write? Show us!

HARLEQUIN
entertain, enrich, inspire™

MILLS & BOON

SYTYCW

A sneaky peek at next month...

By Request

RELIVE THE ROMANCE WITH THE BEST OF THE BEST

My wish list for next month's titles...

3 stories in each book - only £5.99!

In stores from 17th August 2012:

- Three Blind-Date Brides – Jennie Adams, Fiona Harper & Melissa McClone
- Top-Notch Men! – Melanie Milburne, Margaret McDonagh & Anne Fraser

In stores from 7th September 2012:

- The Million-Dollar Catch – Susan Mallery

Available at WHSmith, Tesco, Asda, Eason, Amazon and Apple

Just can't wait?

Visit us Online

You can buy our books online a month before they hit the shops! **www.millsandboon.co.uk**

Book of the Month

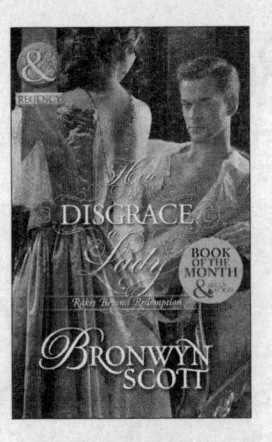

We love this book because...

Introducing RAKES BEYOND REDEMPTION, a deliciously sinful and witty new trilogy from Bronwyn Scott. Notorious Merrick St. Magnus is the kind of man Society mammas warn their daughters about... and that innocent debutantes find scandalously irresistible... He knows just *How to Disgrace a Lady*!

On sale 7th September

Visit us Online

Find out more at
www.millsandboon.co.uk/BOTM

0812/BOTM

Special Offers

Every month we put together collections and longer reads written by your favourite authors.

Here are some of next month's highlights— and don't miss our fabulous discount online!

On sale 17th August

On sale 7th September

On sale 7th September

Save 20% on all Special Releases

Find out more at
www.millsandboon.co.uk/specialreleases

Visit us Online

The World of Mills & Boon®

There's a Mills & Boon® series that's perfect for you. We publish ten series and, with new titles every month, you never have to wait long for your favourite to come along.

Blaze®
Scorching hot, sexy reads
4 new stories every month

By Request
Relive the romance with the best of the best
9 new stories every month

Cherish™
Romance to melt the heart every time
12 new stories every month

Desire™
Passionate and dramatic love stories
8 new stories every month

Visit us Online
Try something new with our Book Club offer
www.millsandboon.co.uk/freebookoffer

M&B/WORLD2

What will you treat yourself to next?

HISTORICAL
Ignite your imagination, step into the past...
6 new stories every month

INTRIGUE...
Breathtaking romantic suspense
Up to 8 new stories every month

Medical Romance
Captivating medical drama – with heart
6 new stories every month

MODERN™
International affairs, seduction & passion guaranteed
9 new stories every month

nocturne™
Deliciously wicked paranormal romance
Up to 4 new stories every month

RIVA™
Live life to the full – give in to temptation
3 new stories every month available exclusively via our Book Club

You can also buy Mills & Boon eBooks at
www.millsandboon.co.uk

Visit us Online

M&B/WORLD2

Mills & Boon® Online

Discover more romance at
www.millsandboon.co.uk

- **FREE** online reads
- **Books** up to one month before shops
- **Browse our books** before you buy

...and much more!

For exclusive competitions and instant updates:

Like us on **facebook.com/romancehq**

Follow us on **twitter.com/millsandboonuk**

Join us on **community.millsandboon.co.uk**

Visit us Online
Sign up for our FREE eNewsletter at
www.millsandboon.co.uk

WEB/M&B/RTL4